CW00550246

# Cry for the Bad Man

# Cry for the Bad Man

*Ted Darling crime series*

*'where does a wise man hide a pebble?'*

**L M Krier**

Cover design DMR Creative
Cover photo Neil Smith

CRY FOR THE BAD MAN

Fisherman's Friend is a registered trademark of the Lofthouse
of Fleetwood Ltd Company of Lancashire

ISBN 978-2-901773-10-8

# Contents

# About the Author

L M Krier is the pen name of former journalist (court reporter) and freelance copywriter, Lesley Tither, who also writes travel memoirs under the name Tottie Limejuice. Lesley also worked as a case tracker for the Crown Prosecution Service.

The Ted Darling series of crime novels comprises: *The First Time Ever, Baby's Got Blue Eyes, Two Little Boys, When I'm Old and Grey, Shut Up and Drive, Only the Lonely, Wild Thing, Walk on By, Preacher Man, Cry for the Bad Man.*

All books in the series are available in Kindle and paperback format and are also available to read free with Kindle Unlimited.

# Contact Details

If you would like to get in touch, please do so at:

tottielimejuice@gmail.com

facebook.com/LMKrier

facebook.com/groups/1450797141836111/

https://twitter.com/tottielimejuice

For a light-hearted look at Ted and the other characters, please consider joining the We Love Ted Darling group on Facebook.

# Discover the DI Ted Darling series

If you've enjoyed meeting Ted Darling, you may like to discover the other books in the series:

# Acknowledgements

I would just like to thank the people who have helped me bring Ted Darling to life: Beta readers: Jill Pennington, Kate Pill, Karen Corcoran, Jill Evans, Alison Sabedoria, Emma Heath, Police consultants – The Three Karens, The members of the Stockport Memories Facebook Group, who always help with questions about my former home town. In particular to Steve, Lou, Phillip, Ian and Don.

And a very special mention for all Ted's loyal friends in the We Love Ted Darling Facebook group. Always so supportive and full of great ideas to be incorporated into the next Ted book.

Thanks to all those who helped with this book in the DI Ted Darling series., beta readers Jill Pennington (Alpha) Emma Heath, Kate Pill, Alison Sabedoria, Christopher Nolan, Jill Evans.

Thanks, as ever, to the people of the Stockport Memories group on Facebook for reminders about the town in which I grew up.

*To Rosie and Fleur*

*my two little helpers*

# Chapter One

'Ted? You got time for a pint after work? Only if I don't talk to someone who understands, I'm not going to be fit company to go home to the missus tonight. It's not your judo or anything is it? And will your Trev let you come out to play?'

Detective Chief Inspector Ted Darling didn't drink pints any more. His days of sinking a few snakebites at the end of his shift were long behind him. But he understood immediately where Inspector Kevin Turner was coming from. There were parts of police work which officers could never share with wives, husbands, partners, family or friends. Sometimes only another copper could understand the difficulties of the job.

'Trev's at karate tonight, as it goes. He's on the team and there's a competition coming up so they're training hard. I was planning to work on a bit, try to clear some paperwork. Give me an hour to make some headway and you're on. I imagine you're hoping for a lift home afterwards?'

Kevin Turner gave a rueful chuckle.

'I can see why you're a high-flying detective and I'm merely a humble Woodentop. You saw through me straight away. I wouldn't say no, if it's not too much bother. I probably won't be fit to drive and it might not look good, travelling on public transport slightly pissed and smelling of booze.'

Ted fired off a quick text to his own partner, Trevor. He wouldn't pick the text up yet if he'd already gone to his karate session, but at least he'd get it later on and know not to expect Ted back early. Best of all, he would understand completely. Both Ted and Kevin were lucky to have understanding long-term partners. It was not always the case in police marriages.

Ted guessed what was on Kevin's mind and he was right. As soon as they were installed in The Grapes, Kevin with his pint, Ted with his non-alcoholic Gunner, Kev started to talk about what was currently troubling him.

'It's these kids, Ted. Killing themselves. What the hell's that all about? I don't remember it happening when we were kids. Not like now, I mean. Society must be completely broken if the only way out youngsters can see is to top themselves.'

Ted took a pull at his drink and opened the packets of crisps he'd bought for them. He'd guessed that Kev was feeling down. Knowing how much he liked to sink the ale when he was like that, he thought he'd better get something, at least, to mop some of it up, before he delivered him home to his wife, Sheila. It wouldn't be the first time he'd had to do it and it probably wouldn't be the last.

'Look at that little nipper last month. The jumper. Not yet fourteen and he had online gambling debts up to his eyes. How the hell is that even possible? Kids that age shouldn't have worries like that, for god's sake. How does it get that bad without parents noticing? What were you and I up to at that age, eh? I'm damn sure it wasn't stuff like that.'

He took a long swallow of his beer. Ted pushed the crisps towards him pointedly. Kev took a couple but he was well into his stride by now, not wanting to be hampered by crunching.

'I was out and about with my mates, on my bike, playing a bit of footy. Stuff like that. I know we didn't have computers and stuff back then but don't the parents monitor what they're getting up to? My dad knew everything I did and if I'd got into any kind of gambling or anything out of order, I'd have got a right clip round the ear.'

The rest of his pint all but disappeared with the next few swallows. Ted understood. The whole station had been affected by the recent spate of suicides of teenagers on their patch. Especially the first officers responding who had seen the ruins of young lives at first hand.

Wordlessly, Ted got up and went to the bar to get Kev another pint. He needed to talk and he needed to drink. And he needed to do both in the company of someone who understood and wouldn't judge. Ted asked Dave the landlord to make them a few sandwiches and bring them over. Crisps were clearly not going to be enough to soak up what Kev was likely to get through. He needed to at least try to take him home to Sheila in a decent state.

Ted couldn't relate to Kev's tales of childhood. His hadn't been the same thing at all. He'd known from quite early on that he was different to other lads his age. He'd had few close friends. It was difficult, partly because of Ted's dad. He didn't like taking people to the house. Not so much his dad's disability but that he drank heavily and it was sometimes obvious.

He'd had one good friend, through his junior karate club. A quiet lad called Martin. Learning martial arts for the same reason as Ted; getting bullied at his school. With the benefit of hindsight, Ted thought that Martin had probably been gay, too. He certainly didn't fit in with any crowd. He and Ted had hung round together for a while. Martin had gone fishing once up at Roman Lakes with Ted, his dad and his dad's friend Meurig who drove him everywhere. Martin had recoiled at the idea of putting live bait onto the hooks and had just stood by, watching.

They went their separate ways when they moved on to different secondary schools and lost touch. Ted made himself a mental note to see if he could find out what had become of him.

'Take this one the other day,' Kev reached gratefully for the second pint when Ted returned to the table. He'd finished the first one already. He carried on with his rant as if there'd been no interruption.

'What was he? Nineteen? His whole future ahead of him

and by the sound of it, a bright and rosy one. Good exam results, his first choice of university, just back from a great gap year. Then he goes and strings himself up. And did it out in those woods, all alone, to boot.

'Just how low does a young lad like that have to get to do that kind of thing?'

Ted knew he wasn't supposed to have any answers, let alone to voice them. His role was just to listen, agree and fetch the drinks.

Partly to slow down Kev's drinking speed, and in an attempt to stop him from getting too morose so soon, he asked, 'How's that little granddaughter of yours?'

It had the desired effect. Kevin's face and tone softened as he reached for his phone and started scrolling through photos. Ted had seen most of them before but was happy to indulge a doting new granddad.

'Our Mia? God, Ted, I swear, she gets more gorgeous every time I see her. Have I shown you these latest? Look at her, smiling at the camera.'

Ted kept him distracted for a time and managed to push him to eat a couple of sandwiches while they talked about his granddaughter. Out of politeness, Kev asked after Ted and Trev's cats, who made up their family, but it was only for show. Ted certainly didn't get his phone out with all the photos of their newest and youngest addition, Adam, and his amusing antics.

Then Kev started to get maudlin again.

'I think it's because of our Mia these suicides are getting to me so much. I keep thinking about her future. Why is it so different now to how I remember it? Are kids under too much pressure these days? What will her life be like?'

It was a mellow but reasonably presentable Kev whom Ted finally delivered home to his wife later on. He was at least in a better humour, having reached the stage of loving everybody. Ted had had to prise him away from repeatedly shaking Dave's hand in the pub and telling him what a good bloke he was.

'Will you stay for a cup of tea, Ted, or do you have to get back?'

'I won't, Sheila, thanks all the same. I think he's not too bad. I made him eat some sandwiches, at least, to mop up the beer.'

Kev was still standing, grinning broadly, a bit wobbly on his feet.

'You're a good friend, Ted, d'you know that? A really good friend. We could do a man hug or something. Just to show you I really appreciate you.'

'You're fine, Kev, there's no need. I'll see you at work tomorrow.'

Ted deftly avoided his outstretched arms and smiled at Sheila who sighed patiently, shaking her head. He wished her luck and said he'd see himself out.

Finally, he was free to head back to the sanctuary of his home, the warm, purring welcome of seven cats, the smell of supper in the oven. There was just enough time to shower and change before Trev got back from his karate club.


'Afternoon, Edwin, are you free?'

Ted hadn't been expecting a call from the senior Home Office pathologist. She would normally contact him regarding any murders on his patch. As far as he was aware, they didn't currently have any. Yet he knew Professor Elizabeth Nelson would not be calling him for anything minor.

'Hello, Bizzie, have you got something of interest to us?'

When it was just the two of them, they were on first name terms, although she was the only person who always insisted on calling him by his full name, which was not known to many people.

'I might very well have and it's not one we were expecting, so you probably weren't either. Could you pop round? Then I can show you as I explain.'

Meetings in the mortuary were not Ted's favourites. But then the pile of paperwork on his desk was possibly slightly less appealing. Somehow, he always managed to keep on top of it, but it was never easy. He decided he could award himself a quick break, especially if it was for a case his team might have to take on.

He grabbed his jacket and headed out into the main office. Most of the team were out working but Mike Hallam, the more senior of his two Detective Sergeants, was standing by the desk of their youngest team member, DC Steve Ellis, going over something with him.

'Hold the fort, can you, Mike, please. I've just had a summons from the Professor. Being a bit mysterious. She wants me down there to show me something.'

'Has she got something for us, then, boss?' Mike asked him, looking surprised. 'I didn't think we had any recent murders.'

'She's perhaps picked up on something the first responders missed. You know what she's like. Eagle-eyed. I'd be surprised if she was wrong. It would be a first since we've known her if she is. I'll ring you once I know what's what.'

He found Bizzie Nelson in her office, having a crafty cup of coffee from her flask. She offered to share it but Ted declined, anxious to know what she had for him. She stood up and led the way to where she'd been working.

'We've done all we can here for now but you'll still need to cover up. If I'm right, there could well be a call for a second post-mortem on this one,' she told Ted, handing him gloves and coveralls.

'This is the teenager from the suspected hanging the other day. It was thought to be routine so James was working on it; no need for my involvement at that stage. Then he spotted something.'

She led the way to where the body of a young man, barely more than a boy, lay on one of the steel tables. The familiar Yshaped incision, through which his internal organs had been removed for analysis, had already been stitched back up. His face was surprisingly peaceful, despite all that had happened to him both in death and whatever had gone before. Ted was struck by the disturbing thought that, at nineteen, the youth was the same age as Trevor had been when they'd started going out together.

'Do you read any G K Chesterton? Father Brown?' Bizzie asked him.

Ted was used to her abrupt changes of direction. He shook his head.

'I haven't done, no.'

'Then let me ask you this. Where does a wise man hide a pebble?'

Ted thought for only an instant before he replied, 'Somewhere there are a lot of other pebbles. A driveway, perhaps. Or on a beach.'

She smiled benevolently at him, like a teacher pleased with a pupil's progress. She was not all that much older than Ted was but her outmoded ways made her seem of a different generation entirely.

'An excellent deduction. So let me put it another way. What's the perfect way to hide a murder?'

Ted was instantly on the same wavelength.

'By dressing it up to look like a suicide. Especially if you know there's been a spate of them so it could well be overlooked.'

'Exactly so. Fortunately for us, young James has eyes like a hawk. Look closely at our victim's neck,' she ordered. 'What do you see?'

Ted had put a mask on as well as coveralls and gloves, to reduce the risk of him leaving his own DNA on the body, especially with the possibility of a second post-mortem being needed. He could have done with his reading glasses for close-up work but didn't want to rummage for them.

'Obvious signs of a ligature of some sort. A rope, possibly. The mark is rougher than I would expect from something smoother, like a tie.'

'Yes, yes,' Bizzie's tone now was slightly impatient. 'I doubt many teenage boys wear ties these days. Certainly not if they're planning to go out and hang themselves. But look more closely.'

She swung an illuminated magnifying glass overhead, so the light fell directly onto the damaged throat of the young man.

Ted bent closer and peered hard.

'There's a distinct pressure mark there. Not uniform across the whole throat, like the rest of the bruising. Not from the knot, surely? Would it not be usual for the knot to be at the side, or even at the back? Is the neck broken? Would it be more likely to break with a frontal knot?'

Bizzie was beaming her pleasure now. Ted guessed from her expression that he was along the right lines. He looked at her questioningly.

'Excellent, Edwin. No, the neck wasn't broken. From my initial findings, I would say that this young man was first manually throttled and then strung up, with the rope very carefully knotted in place so that it would look as if he had killed himself.

'Now this is a fit young boy. Muscular. Sporty, I would say. It is surprisingly difficult to choke the life out of anyone, especially someone like this. Unless it was some extreme, deviant erotic practice of which I'm not aware, a person would not just lie passively and allow it to happen. Even if it started out as consensual, once the body started to feel starved of oxygen, it would be flooded with adrenalin, triggering fight or flight mode.

'In light of this, I've ordered a full blood toxicology screen. You know it's not in my nature to guess, Edwin, as a scientific type. But if pressed, I would have to say it was more likely than not that he was first drugged, then manually strangled and then hung up. And if that is the case, you are very definitely looking at a murder. Rather a cold-blooded one, too.'

'So does that mean there's a chance the killer may have left traces of himself on the body?' Ted asked hopefully.

'Let's not get ahead of ourselves. We're a long way from such things at the moment. But from what I've seen so far I would be prepared to stake my reputation, such as it is, on this being a murder in disguise. The pressure mark you can see if almost certainly a thumbprint.'

She was being modest. Ted knew she was highly regarded in her profession and he had a high opinion of her himself from having worked with her on several murder cases.

'So with that in mind, whilst not wishing to tell you your job, I imagine you will want to get a full Crime Scene Investigation team out to where this young man's body was found hanging. I and my team will give you whatever information the body offers up, but if my theory is correct, there will be signs of a second person's involvement at the scene itself.'

'Thank you, Bizzie. I'll go back to the station now and set up a murder enquiry.'

Before he drove back, he fired off a quick text to Trev.

'Likely to be late home. Again. Sorry. Will make it up to you. X'

Trev's reply was rapid.

'I'll hold you to that. Xxx'


Ted called the whole team together for a briefing as soon as he got back to the nick. They were all back in now. His DI, Jo Rodriguez, both sergeants, Mike Hallam and Rob O'Connell and the DCs, Maurice Brown, Virgil Tibbs, Jezza Vine and young Steve Ellis. DC Sal Ahmed had recently left them to go back to Fraud, his speciality. Now they had a major crime to investigate, with the suspected suicide reclassified as a murder, he'd need to talk to his boss, Superintendent Debra Caldwell, the Ice Queen, about some extra officers.

'Right, everyone, I'm just back from talking to Professor Nelson. The hanging from last week now turns out to be not a suicide but a murder that's been disguised to look like one. Luckily, nothing much gets past the Professor. So we have a murdered nineteen-year-old on our hands and we want to find out who did this to him.

'Let's start with the basics. Thoroughly done, please. Liaise with Uniform, see what they have so far. Then get on to all his known associates. Girlfriend, boyfriend, close friends, everyone. He was recently back from his gap year travels, apparently. Did something happen to him while he was away? Any theories?'

'Drug mule who wouldn't cough up? Or coughed up then ran off with the gear?'

Jezza was always the one for lateral thinking.

'Possible,' Ted conceded. 'Let's make a start now and see what we can turn up. Jo, can you send a crime scene team out to where he was found and get them to do a thorough search. It won't be easy, with the lapse of time, but see what they can turn up. We're looking for the presence of someone else at the site. This is now a murder enquiry.'

# Chapter Two

Ted was in early the next morning to talk to his immediate boss, Superintendent Caldwell. He wanted to ask for at least one more officer for the team, now the case was a murder. He had a feeling he knew in advance what the answer was likely to be. But at least he'd get a decent cup of coffee to start the day.

The Ice Queen was always in early, as was Ted. He'd not yet had an opportunity to update her about the developments in the case. She'd been away for meetings at Headquarters when he'd got back from the mortuary. He'd decided not to interrupt her with the news. It would keep until the morning.

He knocked lightly on her door and put his head round it cautiously. She could be stiff and formal at times, but she greeted him brightly enough, told him to come in and sit down and asked if he'd smelled the coffee brewing. Encouraging signs.

'I didn't want to disturb your meetings yesterday but the suspected suicide from last week is now almost certain to be a murder enquiry. Professor Nelson called me to the hospital yesterday afternoon. The post-mortem showed what looks like a thumbprint underneath the ligature marks. It's looking probable that the lad was manually strangled before he was strung up.'

She frowned at the news.

'This is the teenager found hanging up near Roman Lakes? Callum Mitchell? Was that his name? I can't begin to imagine which news is going to be worse for the parents – that he took his own life or that he was murdered.'

Ted was always impressed by how much she had her finger on the pulse of everything that was happening on her patch, which was a big one.

'I'll organise an FLO for them as soon as possible.'

A Family Liaison Officer could help the parents in dealing with press intrusions and anything else the new developments in the case of their son's death brought their way.

'It's going to be even worse for them once the press get wind of this. And to that end, I'll also sort out a Press Release to go out. Who's going to go and see them to break the news?'

'I thought I'd better do that myself, as SIO on the case. I'll take someone like PC Heap with me.'

'Yes, I think that would be a good move. Assure them from the outset that we will do everything we can to catch Callum's killer. Is there anything else you need from me?'

'Extra officers, ma'am.'

Ted knew he was pushing his luck, with all the budgetary constraints, so he opted for the formality as he asked.

'We're a team member down, now DC Ahmed has left us. I'm going to need more to run a case like this.'

'Talk to Superintendent Baker,' she told him brusquely. 'He may have more in his budget than I have in mine. I can certainly look at drafting in more officers from other stations, but that's likely to be all I can do for you for now. Was there anything else?'

Ted drained his coffee and stood up. He considered himself dismissed. It was time to start his team briefing anyway. He'd made it a full meeting, too big for their own office, so they would be downstairs in the conference room.

Jo Rodriguez was already in there, setting up. A photo of the victim, Callum Mitchell, was now up on the white board, with all the details known about him to date. A copy of both had been circulated to everyone present.

The rest of the team members were filing in, joined by Kevin Turner and some of his officers from Uniform. Doug, from the Crime Scene Investigation team was also in attendance, complaining bitterly about the lack of early access to the site. He would be Crime Scene Manager on the case. He'd already sent his team out to start securing the area.

In his current role, Ted was answerable to two bosses, Superintendent Caldwell and Detective Superintendent Jim Baker. Jim and Ted were good friends outside the job but managed to keep it professional at work.

Jim Baker had been tied up in the same meetings as the Ice Queen had the previous day. Now it was reclassified as a murder enquiry, the case would come under his remit. It was to him that Ted would need to direct his request for reinforcements. He knew that, but he'd thought it was worth trying his luck with the Super to get a replacement for Sal.

Once all of the officers attending the briefing had taken their places, Ted called them to order.

'As you all now know, I spoke to Professor Nelson yesterday and what she told me has led to the reclassification of what we thought was a suicide,' he gestured to the white board as he spoke, 'as a suspicious death. So we're now treating this as a murder enquiry.

'The victim's name is Callum Mitchell. Nineteen. From Heaton Chapel. He was found hanging in woods up beyond Roman Lakes last week. Initially, the death was treated as a suicide, although no note was found and it appears to have been completely unexpected.

'From what the Professor told me yesterday, it seems likely that he was killed where he was found, possibly after being drugged, then hung up to simulate suicide. Who were the first responding officers?

He looked round the room. Two younger uniformed constables shifted slightly in their seats, looking uncomfortable. One of them spoke.

'Us, sir. There was a call about a body found hanging. Found by a dog walker.'

Doug, the Crime Scene Manager, gave an audible tut and muttered, 'More contamination, no doubt, with Fido snuffling and peeing everywhere.'

'The body wasn't fresh, sir. Looked like it had probably been there since the night before. We didn't see anything to suggest it wasn't a suicide.'

'How did he get there? Was there a vehicle?' DC Jezza Vine asked.

'We, er, we weren't really looking for anything like that. He had trainers on, looked like he could have been out for a run, perhaps. He had ID on him but there was no note, no mobile phone nor anything else.'

'Who notified the next of kin?' Ted asked.

'Me, sir,' PC Susan Heap told him. 'Once we had the ID, I went round to see the family and tell them Callum had been found dead. They were beyond devastated, I would say. They had no clue as to why he would have killed himself and again, no note at the house.'

'What did he use for a noose?' Jezza asked.

'Just a length of rope, the stuff you can get in any DIY shop,' the first constable told her.

'Did he have a backpack or something?' Jezza asked him.

The PC shook his head.

'No, nothing. There was nothing at the site except the body and the rope.'

Jezza made a gesture with her hands which Ted knew all too well. It was her 'well, dur' expression, when she thought something obvious was staring them all in the face.

'What's your point, DC Vine?' Ted asked her. His choice of the formal was a reminder to her to keep it civil.

'This was an intelligent lad, right? University material? Going to do law? None of this sounds very organised to me. He lives in Heaton Chapel. He goes all the way out to Roman Lakes to hang himself, apparently on foot. He carefully buys himself a length of rope from B&Q or wherever, to take with him. Where's the bag? Wouldn't he realise if he met anyone on his way they may think it a bit strange to see someone jogging carrying a coil of rope?'

She turned again to the PC.

'What did he stand on?'

He looked taken aback for a moment.

Jezza was trying to curb her impatience.

'How high up the tree was the rope? The PM showed the neck wasn't broken, according to what the boss told us yesterday. So he didn't climb up high and jump. There's something iffy about the whole scene, from what you've said.'

Ted had, as usual, been perching on a desk. He stood up now to make a point.

'All right, everyone, listen, please. A quick reminder that there is no blame culture here. If any mistakes have been made, procedures will be put in place to ensure they're not repeated. This wasn't initially considered to be a suspicious death. A suicide, and unexpected, but no more than that. It's only because of the PM that we now know differently.

'The first pathologist very nearly missed the signs. I needed a strong magnifying device to see the thumbprint on the throat. But we now know it was murder, and we need to start by looking for anyone who might have had a motive to kill this young man.

'PC Heap, tell us everything you learned about him from the parents, please.'

'He was just back from his gap year. He went to France, worked with a voluntary organisation helping immigrants around Calais. Especially young people, with family in Britain, trying to do the necessary paperwork to be able to join them. He was going to study law with a view to specialising in helping asylum seekers.'

'Far Right extremists wouldn't love him then, boss. They want to keep immigrants out, not help more of them to gain entry,' Jezza responded. 'We may need to start rooting around in some of their groups, perhaps. There's bound to be some active groups here; they're all over everywhere now, it seems. D'you want me to start looking into it?'

Ted shook his head.

'We'll need to think very carefully about who takes that on. Virgil, I think we can safely say it's not a job for you.'

Virgil Tibbs chuckled as he trotted out his standard response.

'Is it because I is black, boss?'

Rob O'Connell spoke up next.

'Boss, I imagine it must take a lot of strength to haul someone up like that. A dead body, so a dead weight. And strangling someone with bare hands can't be all that easy. So does that mean we're more likely to be looking for a man than a woman?'

'I've never had to do it with a dead body but I have hauled some immobile simulated casualties doing abseiling and rope training. It's more about technique than brute force but yes, on balance, it's more likely to be a man than a woman, I would say. Although let's not rule anything out so early on.

'PC Heap, the Professor pointed out that Callum was a fit young man. Muscular, was the word she used. Did you find out anything about him to account for that?'

'Yes, sir. I spent quite a lot of time with the parents. They were completely bewildered by the whole thing, as you can imagine, so they wanted to talk about him. I didn't have to ask them anything, just listen to them. He played football. He'd been on a local youth team which did quite well, when he was at school. Same for lacrosse. He did that too. That's why he specifically wanted to go to Durham University as they have lacrosse teams and not many places do.

'His parents said he loved his lacrosse. He'd stopped the football at seventeen but carried on with lacrosse. He was so thrilled to get his first choice of Uni so he could carry on playing as well as studying. He was full of talk about how much fun he was going to have. That's why they couldn't believe he would have taken his own life.'

'And we now know he didn't. Susan, after we're done here, I'd like you to come with me. I thought it would be best if I went in person to update them with the latest news.

'So, his ideals may have made him enemies. What other likely motives are we looking at?'

'Jealousy? Sporting rivalry?' Mike Hallam suggested. 'It sounds like he had a lot going for him. Promising career, choice of university, picked for teams. Any siblings, Susan?'

'There's a twin, Sean. I didn't meet him. But from what the parents say, they were chalk and cheese. Sean's not academically bright and not remotely athletic.'

'Sibling rivalry then?' Mike suggested. 'Although it does seem a bit extreme.'

'And is there any special significance to where he was found?' Ted asked. 'Did the parents say anything about that? Did they seem surprised at where he was?'

'To be honest, sir, they were just gobsmacked by the whole thing. But they had to ask me where Roman Lakes was, so it's clearly not somewhere that had any significance for them.'

'It's something we'll need to ask about when we go to see them, although of course he may have been taken there against his will. They'll also presumably be able to give us details of his friends and anyone he might have had contact with. And we'll need to start by checking his last known movements.

'There's just an outside chance our killer will have left clear traces of himself on either the body or the crime scene, which will make our job that much easier. The Professor is running tests on samples she's taken. Doug, we're hoping for the usual miracles from you and your team.'

The Crime Scene Manager was still looking disgruntled.

'I'd have been a lot more optimistic if we'd had access much earlier than this, boss. But we'll do the best we can, as usual.'

Doug always called him boss, like Ted's team did, although he wasn't obliged to. He approved of Ted because he liked cats and Doug bred and showed them. He was the one who'd persuaded Ted to take the kitten, now called Adam. Despite a flawless pedigree, Adam had turned out looking not remotely suitable for life as either a show or a stud cat so had joined Ted and Trev's menagerie.

'Nothing we can do about that now, Doug. Just give us what you can. The rest of you, let's start digging into Callum's background while we wait for whatever forensics can provide. Mike, can you assign tasks, please, but by morning briefing tomorrow, I want to know everything it's possible to know about our victim. Who were his friends? From school, from his sports teams. What was he doing up at Roman Lakes? Who might he have gone there with? How did he get there? If it was in a car with someone, are there any cameras anywhere near which might give us a lead?

'Steve, when Susan and I go to see the parents we'll ask for his laptop and phone. Your job will be to find out anything you can from them. Who was he in contact with? Did he mention to anyone that he was meeting someone the night he was killed?

'Inspector Turner, I'm sure you can lend us a few officers to help. We could usefully start with some house-to-house out near where he was found, although I appreciate there aren't many properties close to. In the meantime I'll talk to Superintendent Baker about some more officers.'

Ted liked to keep it formal in his briefings. He knew he was old-fashioned in that respect. As he was in his habit of saying please and thank you to everyone. It was how his dad had brought him up.

'Thank you everyone.'

Ted took time to phone Jim Baker before he and Susan left to speak to the parents. He filled him in on developments and asked about extra officers.

'You know the score, Ted. Cuts I can do. Extra officers I

can't. Not at the moment, anyway. The best I can do for now is second some for you from elsewhere. What about a couple from South Manchester? Any of those any use to you, since you know them?'

'Well, since we house-trained him a bit, Charlie Eccles could be quite useful if we could have DS Rakale as well to keep an eye on him. Leona's a first-rate officer, she'd be an asset to us. Young Graham Winters showed he had something about him, at least. He could easily hold the fort up there by himself if we borrow the other two for now.'

'Right, consider that done. I'll find out what they've got on and ship those two over to you as soon as they've cleared their desks. Who's going to tell the parents of this lad that their worst nightmares aren't over yet?'

'I'm on my way there next, with Susan Heap. I thought I'd better go in person. I don't think mistakes were made in the early handling of this. It's just such an unusual case and, from having seen the body at very close quarters, I can confirm how hard it was to spot that it wasn't a suicide. I want the parents to understand that and to know we're doing all we can. The last thing we need now on this case is for them to want to make complaints.'

He said much the same thing to Susan Heap as she drove them to the parents' house in Ted's service vehicle.

'I'm sorry if I contributed in any way to getting it wrong, sir,' she told him contritely.

'Not at all, Susan. It might have gone through as a suicide if the pathologists hadn't spotted the unusual marks, and they were hard to see.'

It was the boy's father who opened the door to them. He looked haggard, dark circles under his eyes, unshaven. He had the appearance of someone who hadn't slept in days.

Susan Heap greeted him, reminding him of her name, then introduced Ted.

'I wondered if we might come in and have a word with you

and your wife, please, Mr Mitchell?'

'Yes, of course,' he stepped back, opening the front door wider to allow them access. 'Have you got some news, then? Come through to the kitchen. We were just having a cup of tea. That's all we seem to do these days. Drink tea. It doesn't help much, but it's a comfort, of sorts. Would you like some?'

They both politely declined. This was going to be a delicate situation. Not something which was going to be easy, even without juggling with teacups.

Mrs Mitchell was sitting at the table, gazing blankly at a half-full mug. She looked even worse than her husband and wasn't dressed. She was wearing a fluffy dressing gown, pulled round her and tied tightly at the waist. Her look towards them when the three of them trooped in was vacant. Ted suspected she was on strong medication of some sort.

'Please, sit down,' Mitchell pulled out chairs and gestured to them. 'Do you have any more news for us? Do you know yet when we can bury our son?'

'I do have news, Mr and Mrs Mitchell,' Ted told them, 'and I should warn you it's not good. I'm so sorry to have to tell you but further tests have revealed that Callum didn't, in fact, take his own life. I'm afraid he was murdered.'

# Chapter Three

The young man's parents stared at Ted as if neither understanding nor believing the enormity of what he'd just told them. Ted had had to break bad news to many people in his police career. He thought this might possibly be the worst set of circumstances he could recall.

'I'm so sorry to have to press you at a time like this. I understand how you must be feeling ...'

Mr Mitchell spoke, his tone bitter.

'Oh, you do, do you? Do you have children, Inspector?'

'No, Mr Mitchell, I don't.'

'Then you can't possibly know. How can you begin to understand what we've gone through? My wife and I have been to hell and back, wondering what we can possibly have done wrong to make our beautiful boy kill himself. Then you come calmly along saying it wasn't that at all. Somebody murdered him. Is that supposed to make us feel better?'

Ted could see that the father was getting angry, while the mother looked as if the numbness was rapidly leaving her and she was on the verge of hysterics. He shot an appealing look towards Susan Heap.

'Mrs Mitchell,' she said quietly and calmly, 'we're going to need to look at Callum's computer, if he has one, to see if we can trace his friends and anyone he might have been in contact with. Is it up in his bedroom? Perhaps you and I could go and get it? Would that be all right with you?'

Wordlessly, Mrs Mitchell got to her feet and allowed herself to be guided from the room. Ted turned back to the father.

'Please excuse me, Mr Mitchell. It was clumsy of me ...'

The man rose to his feet, his anger evaporating. He went to put the kettle on yet again. The comfort of familiarity.

'No, I'm sorry. It's not your fault. This must be hard for you, too. I'm sure you've done this sort of thing endless times. But when it's not your own flesh and blood, your own lovely boy ...'

His voice broke and he needed a moment before he could continue.

'Have that cup of tea now, eh? And call me Eddie. Then we can sit down and talk. I can pretend we're just having a chat. That you're not telling me that the worst news of my life is even worse than I thought it was. And you can ask me anything. Anything you need to. I'll do whatever I can to help find who did this to our Callum.

'So, how do you take your tea? Or d'you want coffee?'

'White tea, milk, two sugars, not too strong, please.'

'Really? I thought coppers would be strong coffee, the stronger the better.'

He was making small-talk to avoid the issue. Anything to put off having to deal with what had happened to his son.

He made the tea in mugs and put one in front of Ted, sitting down with his own, from which he took a swallow before he spoke further.

'Tell me honestly. Did somebody make a balls-up? Coming to tell us Callum had killed himself when he'd really been murdered?'

'No, Eddie. There was nothing initially to indicate that it was anything other than a tragic suicide. It was only during the post-mortem that the pathologist noticed something and asked for a second opinion from a Home Office pathologist. Someone who specialises in murder cases.'

'And will you tell me how he died? Did he die by hanging? I need to know.'

'He was strangled before he was hung up,' Ted told him frankly.

Eddie Mitchell nodded his head a few times, trying to make sense of what he'd just been told. Then his face crumpled, he leaned forward to bury it in his hands and started to sob. Quietly, Ted got to his feet and went to stand next to him, a hand on his shoulder, awkwardly patting. He had no words to offer, but sensed that simply being there would help.

Eventually the man regained control. He lifted a hand, damp with his tears, and patted Ted's with it, apologetically.

'Sorry. Sorry about that. I've just been trying to be strong. For the missus. For my other lad. I hadn't done any grieving of my own yet.'

Ted went back to his seat and took a drink of his tea. Mitchell had made it just as he'd asked.

'So, what can I do to help? Ask me anything you need to. I want to know who did this to my son, so just ask your questions.'

'Tell me about Callum's mood since he got back from France. How did he seem? Did he appear to have anything on his mind? Was he worried about anything?'

Mitchell frowned.

'But why is that important? If he was murdered, and he didn't commit suicide ...'

Then his expression cleared and he continued, 'Oh, I see, you're wondering if he had enemies. If something had gone wrong while he was away. If someone was after him for something.'

'Would he have told you if he had any kind of problem?'

'Yes, I think he would. I've always got on well with my lads. Both of them. Never any trouble between us. Not really. They're both good lads.'

'And Callum's brother, Sean. Were they close? Did they get on?'

'Chalk and cheese,' Mitchell said immediately. It was

clearly a stock phrase he was used to trotting out about the twins. 'They're not remotely alike.' Then he corrected himself. 'They weren't. They weren't identical twins and they didn't look all that alike. Not really.

'Callum was the brainy one, but sporty as well. Outgoing, popular, always lots of friends. Our Sean is much quieter. More of a home-lover. Not so many mates. He works for me. I've got a garage. He's been keeping it ticking over for me, for the time being. I can't face going in to work. I haven't even been out since …

'And now it's going to be even harder, I suppose. Having to tell people what really happened, I mean. I suppose the press will get hold of it now?'

'We're arranging a Family Liaison Officer, to help you and your wife. It will be their job to deal with the press for you, to make sure your privacy is respected. I should warn you that the press can become quite intrusive.'

Ted didn't like to insist with his questions, but he noticed that Mitchell had only answered a part of his earlier ones. He may simply have been distracted but he wanted to be sure.

'So how did they get on together, Callum and Sean?'

Mitchell turned now bloodshot eyes towards him and regarded him shrewdly.

'You've just told me my son was murdered. Now you're asking me if I think my other son could have been the killer. Is that it?'

'Eddie, I'm sorry, I have to ask. It's my job. I want to find out who did this as much as you do.'

'I understand. No, they weren't close really. They had so little in common. Our Sean wouldn't have done anything to him, though. He's too bone idle, for one thing. They sort of rubbed along well enough, but no more than that. No hate or jealousy or anything like that. You'll need to talk to Sean, I suppose?'

'We will. It's a matter of routine in any murder enquiry. If you give me details of your garage, I could send someone round to talk to him there, if that would be all right.'

Ted noted the address the man gave him, assuring him again it was normal routine.

'What can you tell me about the last time you saw Callum? Did he say where he was going? Who he would be with?'

Eddie Mitchell was studying Ted's face closely. He clearly needed more answers and appeared to be weighing up his chances of getting honest ones from the police officer sitting opposite him.

'Would he have suffered, my boy? Would he have known what was happening to him?'

Ted looked him directly in the eyes as he replied.

'I'm waiting on the results of blood tests, Eddie. But the pathologist thinks there's a strong possibility that drugs were involved.'

Mitchell shook his head emphatically.

'Our Callum never did drugs. He didn't smoke and he hardly ever drank, either. He took his sports seriously.'

Then light dawned on his face and he went on, 'You mean someone gave him something? Spiked his drink, or something? So that would mean he knew his killer, or at least trusted someone enough to have a drink with them. And he was no fool.'

'Eddie, statistically it's more likely than not that he was killed by someone he knew. Family and close friends are more often involved than total strangers. It's why we always have to start close to home with any such enquiry. It really is just routine.

'So what can you tell me about that last day? Were you expecting him to be out all night? You and your wife weren't worried that he didn't come home?'

'Can I call you something? Other than Inspector?'

He was trying to make a connection. It was not uncommon in such circumstances. Ted had no problem with it. He could still maintain a professional detachment, even on first name terms. He never corrected anyone on his actual rank, which was Detective Chief Inspector.

'My name's Ted,' he told him.

'Another Edward, like me?'

Ted smiled as he shook his head. Few people knew his full name was Edwin. He never used it. It didn't even appear on his police warrant card or his office door.

'Just Ted. Ted Darling. So, Eddie, about that last day.'

Mitchell drank some of his tea while he thought back to the last time he'd seen his son.

'We all had our tea together, not long after me and Sean got back from work. So about six, half past. Somewhere round there.'

'Does your wife go out to work?'

'She's a registered child-minder. Special needs kids. She has a couple of regulars who come every day while their parents are at work. They get picked up just before we eat, usually.'

'What did Callum tell you about his plans for the evening?'

'He wasn't long back from his time in France and he was still catching up with all his old mates. He said he was going to see some of the football lads, from the team he was on when he was at school. He said he might stay over with one of his pals so not to worry if he wasn't back until the next day. He often did that.'

'Would he usually let you know? Send a text, or call you?'

'Usually, yes, but he'd been having trouble with his phone and hadn't had time to get it fixed, so he told us not to worry if he didn't get in touch. He didn't even bother taking the phone with him.'

His eyes were moist again. He wiped at them hastily with the back of one hand as he said, his voice thick with emotion, 'That was the last time I saw him. Apart from having to identify his body.'

'Can I just ask you why Callum was so interested in asylum seekers and immigrants, Eddie? Was there a particular reason for that? Just in case it turns out to be relevant to the enquiry.'

'He had a good friend, when he first went to secondary school. Yasir. From Africa. His parents had come here to settle. They were both doctors. They thought all their paperwork was in order and there'd be no trouble. Yasir started school and was doing really well. A clever lad; he wanted to go into medicine like his parents. He came here a lot with Callum. But there was something wrong with the paperwork. They were sent back. Callum never heard from Yasir again. That's when he decided he wanted to be a lawyer, to help people like them.'

'Thank you. Now if you could just give me details of all of Callum's friends, please. Anyone you can think of who he might have gone to spend time with that evening.'

Ted carefully took notes while Mitchell recited a long list of names and what contact details he knew. He hadn't been exaggerating when he said his son had had a lot of friends. He said that Callum wasn't seeing anyone in particular, in any kind of relationship. Not dating, as he put it. When he'd finished speaking, he once more looked directly at Ted.

'So when can we bury our son, Ted?'

Ted hesitated, trying to think how to phrase his answer as best he could. He knew it wasn't going to go down well. He explained carefully that with a murder enquiry, there could well be a call for a second post-mortem examination. Once they had a suspect and had charged them, the defence team would almost certainly ask for a repeat PM, especially with a case where any evidence might be contentious.

'So you mean our lad's got to stay there, in that morgue place? Stuffed away in a drawer for god knows how long?'

'We will do everything we can to find Callum's killer as soon as possible. If we haven't made an arrest within twenty-eight days, there'll usually be a second, independent post-mortem and it should be possible for Callum's body to be released for burial after that.'

'Twenty-eight days? Dear god, how's the wife going to start rebuilding her life if we can't bury him for another month or more?'

Almost on cue, they heard footsteps on the stairs and Mrs Mitchell came back into the kitchen, followed by Susan Heap. Susan was holding a laptop and a mobile phone, each inside an evidence bag.

Mitchell stood up and went to his wife, helping her to sit back down, fussing over her, doing the same inept shoulder patting Ted had done to him earlier. He went to put the kettle back on. She must have been awash with tea by now but it gave him something to do.

Ted and Susan took their leave, saying they'd show themselves out and promising to be in touch as soon as there was any further news. Ted left his card so the parents could contact him directly and he encouraged them to feel free to do so whenever they felt the need.

As he settled himself into the passenger seat, he let out a sigh.

'It's never easy, but that has to be one of the tougher ones. How did you get on with Mrs Mitchell?'

'I think she welcomed the opportunity to talk about him again, sir. To someone outside the family.'

'What was your gut feeling about Callum? Genuine, do you think? Or too good to be true? He must have had faults. Everybody does. I murder waste-paper baskets when I get angry,' he grinned at her guiltily as he said it.

'You're also hard to do first aid on, sir, when you keep insisting you're fine while you're busily bleeding out.'

Ted laughed. Susan had probably kept him alive until an ambulance arrived when he'd been injured facing a dangerous knife attacker.

When they got back to the station, Ted handed the laptop

over to Steve for his attention, then gave the list of friends to Jo Rodriguez to allocate people to interview them all. He sent Rob O'Connell round to the garage to speak to the brother, Sean Mitchell. He hoped that by the following morning's briefing there might possibly be some developments to report back.

He actually got home at a reasonable time. There was nothing much he could do to advance the case until he got more details. Once he'd got the various analysis results back, the enquiry would shift up a gear or two so he decided to take the opportunity to abandon his desk while he could.

Trev was home, putting something in the oven for their supper later on. He paused to deliver a hug, scanning Ted's face, gauging how his day had gone.

'You look tired.'

'It's not been an easy one today. I had to tell some parents their son hadn't committed suicide as they were told last week but that he'd been murdered.'

Trev repeated the hug, holding him longer this time.

'Shit, that's awful. I can't imagine how they must be feeling. And not easy for you, either.'

He let go of Ted and looked at him.

'Sorry if this sounds like me being a selfish sod, but I suppose with a murder like this on your plate, can I take it you won't be free to come and watch me in the karate tournament this weekend?'

Ted made an apologetic face. As they were talking, Adam the kitten was solemnly trying to climb up Ted's trouser leg. Queen, matriarch of the cat pack, was showing her disapproval by thrashing her tail and swiping at the miscreant with a paw, although she kept her claws sheathed. Which was more than Adam was doing. Ted gently unlatched him and set him on the floor, where he immediately started again.

'Unless we can make an incredible breakthrough between now and then, which isn't looking likely, probably not. Sorry.'

Trev shrugged.

'My fault for marrying a policeman. How tired are you? Could you help me train a bit? Even just half an hour or so. Then we could have a shower before supper. Economise. Share the water. Please, Ted, it would mean a lot.'

'You're better than I am these days. And you know it. I just don't have the training time I need.'

'But you're a brilliant *sensei*, Ted. You know I work better for you than anyone else. Please?'

Ted never could refuse his partner anything. And the prospect of a vigorous physical workout was doubly appealing after a tough day.

Besides, the shared shower sounded inviting.

# Chapter Four

There was a woman waiting for Ted in the reception area of the station when he arrived for work the following day. Not someone he recognised. Youngish, mid-twenties, perhaps, small and slim, neatly dressed and wearing a hijab. She approached him as soon as she saw him.

'Chief Inspector Darling? I'm PC Farrah Khan, sir, your new FLO.'

It was not unusual for an FLO from Uniform to be wearing civilian clothes for their role when working with families.

'Good to meet you, PC Khan. If you come with me, I'll show you the way. You're nice and early. Morning briefing doesn't start for another half hour.'

She fell into step beside him as he headed for the stairs.

'I heard you liked punctuality, and I also wanted the chance to talk to you quickly first, sir. I just wanted to check that me being a British Pakistani Muslim wasn't going to pose any problems with the family. I am who I am, but the last thing I ever want to do is to upset anyone when they're grieving. And it has happened, believe me.'

'You can never tell but I don't think it'll pose a problem with the Mitchells,' Ted told her, holding the main office door open and standing aside to let her go in first. 'I'll check if PC Heap – Susan – is free to go with you to introduce you to them. She's already met them and it might help all of you. I'm just about to make myself some green tea, before briefing. Can I offer you anything?'

'No thank you, sir, I'm fine. If I could just have a look at any case notes to bring myself up to speed before everyone gets here?'

Ted found them for her. He liked what he saw of her so far.

Once all the team members had filed in, ahead of time, and had met PC Khan, Ted began by asking for progress.

'First off, there are a lot of friends to track down and interview, boss, and we've only just made a start on them,' Mike Hallam said. 'Callum was on a junior football team when he was young, which is eleven players, plus reserves, and a lacrosse team, ten players plus reserves, and that's just for starters. Added to that there will be people like coaches, trainers, that sort of thing. And he seems to have stayed in touch with a lot of them even after he left the teams.'

'His mobile phone was recovered from the house by Susan Heap, as you know, and Steve has been working on that,' Jo Rodriguez put in. 'It's like you told us yesterday, boss. There seems to be an intermittent fault on it, but Steve's doing his best to find out who he's recently been in contact with using it.'

'Get Océane onto it if you get stuck, Steve,' Ted instructed him, knowing Steve would be pleased of the chance to contact his girlfriend for any reason, including work.

'We have got a glimmer of a possible lead though,' Jo continued. 'The first responders got photos of the body *in situ* as the victim was clearly beyond help so there was no hurry to cut him down. When he was taken down, the rope was cut so the knots, both round his neck and on the tree branch, were kept intact.

'The one on the body went immediately for forensic testing just in case there was anything relevant. It's lucky for us that the rest of the rope was removed without undoing the knot and was also sent off. Doug phoned to say that the knot might be significant. It's a round turn and two half hitches, which is possibly not something everyone knows how to tie. It's used in sailing, and it's still taught to Guides and Scouts. I have one of each amongst my brood so I know about such things, but not everyone would, not these days.'

Jo was the father of six children, three boys and three girls.

'It doesn't narrow it down all that much, but it may suggest someone who does sailing or is involved in youth movements of some kind, perhaps.'

'So was Callum in the Scouts or anything do we know yet?' Jezza asked. 'Or perhaps someone involved with the sports teams was also involved with other youth movements? Do you want me to check that out?'

'Make a discreet start, please. Find out if any names from the sporting side crop up anywhere else and keep us posted on what you find.

'Rob, how did you get on with Sean Mitchell? What did you make of him?'

'Seems like a nice enough lad, boss, but you can tell why he wasn't the one going off to university. A bit of a plodder, I would say. Not particularly ambitious. He admits he grew up a bit in his brother's shadow – he called Callum the Golden Boy – but he didn't seem to mind. Genuinely not to care.'

'His dad said he couldn't imagine him killing his brother simply because he'd be too bone idle, as he put it,' Ted confirmed. 'Let's not dismiss him yet as a possible suspect, though. Does he know where Callum went that last evening? And does he have an alibi for the time in question?'

'They don't seem to have had much in common at all. Never went out together, didn't do stuff together. He doesn't seem to know many of Callum's friends, except one of the footballing lot, a lad called Antoine, who often came to the house.

'Callum went out before him that evening. He didn't say where he was going or who with, just that he was going to meet mates and might not be back until the next day. Sean went to a nearby pub with a friend of his. I've got all the details and I'll check that out as soon as I can.'

'Are we doing a press conference on this one, boss?' Jo asked. 'It might speed things up a bit if we ask the public for sightings of him. We can check out all his known associates, now we have some names, but might it not be quicker to put out an appeal?'

Ted wasn't keen on press conferences. He hated having to parade in front of cameras. On this occasion, he thought Jo was probably right. It could save them a lot of time, some of it potentially wasted, chasing down what leads they had.

'I'll talk to the Super about it as soon as we've finished here. PC Khan, can you broach the subject with the parents, please? See if they would be willing to appear, to make an appeal to the public. I have a feeling the father would be keen, but I'm not sure if the mother would be up to it. You'll probably need to be there to support them.'

'Yes, sir,' she nodded.

'Back to motives, then. Any other thoughts? And while we're on that topic, Maurice, I want you to start checking out if we have any extreme right-wing groups who might be against the type of organisation Callum was involved with in France. So, any rabidly anti-immigration types. Get Steve to help with the search stuff if you need him to.

'Jezza, can you find a contact within the organisation Callum was with, the one behind his time in France. Find someone you can talk to about their work in general, plus anything they can tell you about Callum's time with them. Be a bit sensitive, please, because of course they might not know yet that he's dead. I imagine it's inevitable that a group like that will have its detractors, so see if you can find out from them if they get anything like hate mail. Who it's from, what sort of thing it says. With copies, if possible, if they do get any and if they don't simply junk it.'

'So why am I mixing with the Fascists, boss?' Maurice asked, although his tone was good-natured. 'Not all Geordies are racists. It was the Hartlepool lot who hung the monkey.

We're quite civilised in Newcastle.'

He was referring to local folklore which claimed the people of Hartlepool had once hung a monkey during the Napoleonic wars, having taken it for a Frenchman as it was in French uniform.

'It should be Rob. He's the skinhead,' he continued, having a jibe at Rob's buzz cut to hide his receding hairline.

His words raised a small ripple of amusement. Ted smiled.

'That would be DS Skinhead to you, Maurice,' Rob laughed.

'And Jo,' Ted went on, ignoring the banter, 'let's get someone round to Callum's school. Was he at Priestnall?'

When Jo nodded, he went on, 'I know it's more than a year since he left but let's see if there were any issues there which might be relevant. And I know there's a long list of potential witnesses but let's make a start. We need to know where he was going and who he was meeting. We desperately need a kicking-off point.

'Right, thank you, everyone. Let's have a catch-up at the end of the day if there's anything new. You too, PC Khan, please. Now let me introduce you to Susan Heap then you can get over to meet the family. Keep me posted of anything which might help us.'

Once the new FLO was on her way to the Mitchells' house, Ted went to find the Super to ask about a press conference. The victim's name had not yet been released. There'd been an initial press release confirming that a body had been found. Then a second one by way of an update stating that the death was now being treated as suspicious, but so far nothing more. Ted knew it was only a matter of time before they got calls from journalists wanting more detail.

'It could save us a lot of valuable time if we launch an appeal for information. At the moment, we've no idea where he was going or who he intended to meet and we're facing an awful lot of legwork to find out.'

'Would the parents do the appeal, do you think?' she asked him. 'You know that there's always a much better response if the parents appear.'

'PC Khan is going to talk to them about it. She seems very competent and professional. I'll let you know what they say to her.'

It was late afternoon when there was a timid knock on Ted's door. It could only be Steve. No matter how much Ted tried to be approachable, the young DC almost always seemed wary of him. He called out a 'Come in' in his most welcoming voice.

He was right. It was Steve.

'Yes, Steve, what have you got for me? Pull up a chair.'

Steve even sat nervously, perched on the edge of the seat as if poised for flight. He had paperwork with him, notes of his findings.

'Sir, I've started going through the phone and the laptop. But there's something not right. Something which doesn't ring true.'

'Go on,' Ted said encouragingly.

He knew that if he could just get the DC started on anything techie, all his inhibitions would melt away and he would speak with confidence on a subject he knew well. Far better than Ted did, most of the time.

'Well, sir, we can discount the telephone for now. The fault is genuine so that fits with what we were told. I think I need to pass that on to be looked into more thoroughly than I can do. But I'm into his laptop. His passwords weren't very inspired for someone so bright. Now, the interesting thing there is, while he was away he was in almost constant email contact with a group of lads who, I assume from their conversations, were the football team lot.'

Now Steve was into his stride, he was much more at ease, talking animatedly, not even adding a 'sir' into every sentence as he usually did.

'They all met up not long after he got back, which was less than two weeks before he died. They met at a lad called Antoine's house. He's on the list the father gave us, but he's not been spoken to yet, I don't think.

'But here's the strange thing. Since that date, there's been no email contact between them at all.'

He was looking at Ted so expectantly that he didn't want to sound if he was pouring cold water on his theory.

'Is that all that unusual, though? Now he's back in the country, might they not just be meeting up more often so they don't need to email as much? And perhaps once we get into the phone, we'll find that they were setting up meetings that way?'

Steve pulled a sheet of paper from the bundle he had with him and thrust it across the desk to Ted.

'Here's the last email between them all, which I found on Callum's laptop. Look how he ends it.'

Ted put his reading glasses on before looking at it.

'*We'll all meet up when it's done and the drinks are on me.*'

He looked at Steve over the top of his glasses as he asked, 'Is there anything in any of the other exchanges to give us a clue what this refers to? What the 'it' is that means a celebration?'

'Nothing at all. Whatever the 'it' is, there's nothing in writing to explain it and I'm guessing there'll be nothing on the phone either.'

'So they were planning something together, and they were going to celebrate the outcome. But what? This is good work, Steve. Well done. We can raise this once everyone is back in at the end of the day, including PC Khan. Then we can see if we can shed light on whatever this is about between us. It may well be important.'

Farrah Khan reported back at the end of the day to say that Mr Mitchell was keen to do a public appeal. His wife seemed less so but had agreed to give it a go. The Super was arranging everything to try to get something set up for the following afternoon. The sooner the appeal was out there, the sooner they might start getting some useful leads.

Jo had been to Callum's former school and was back with interesting news.

'The football team Callum played in wasn't directly connected to the school. But quite a few of the pupils from the school were on the team. I talked to a sports teacher who wasn't involved with the team but he did mention to me, when I told him about Callum, that the club must be an unlucky one. Apparently a younger lad than Callum and his mates, although one who would probably have been at training sessions and trials at the same time, committed suicide.

'It was nearly a year ago. He took an overdose. That's all he knew about it, so now we have that information, I'll start looking into that. It could be nothing but coincidence, but I know you don't like coincidences, boss, so I'll get it checked out.'

'So this team is part of a club of some sort? Can we have a dig into that in detail, see if there's anything else we need to be aware of, please. Right everyone, get your notes written up before we all clock off then we can start out fresh in the morning.'

Trev was on his mobile when Ted got home. He mouthed to him 'it's your mother' then carried on chatting away. The two of them got on like a house on fire and spoke either on the phone or by Skype most days since she'd moved back to Wales.

With lots of protestations of love and blown kisses, Trev handed his phone over to Ted.

'Hello, mam, how're you doing?'

There was always that slight awkwardness there, on Ted's part. His mother sounded happy, her Welsh accent more pronounced again now she was back home and speaking Welsh most of the time.

'You're sure it's still all right for me to come and stay with you next week, Teddy *bach*? I don't want to put you out.'

'Of course it's all right. You're always welcome here, mam, you know that. And Trev loves fussing over you. But are you absolutely positive you want to sell the house? You've not had second thoughts?'

'None at all, *bach*. I miss seeing you and Trev as often as I used to be able to, of course. But I feel much safer here.'

Ted's mother had put her house on the market to move back to her native South Wales after she was assaulted in the street by a racist who, hearing her speak Welsh, had thought it was Polish.

An early sale had fallen through because of a broken link in the buying chain, but the latest deal seemed set to go ahead with no problems. His mother was coming up by train from Ammanford and they'd invited her to spend a few days with them. Ted just hoped he would have some spare time to see something of her.

He said a hasty farewell and handed the phone back to Trev as his own phone rang. It was an unknown number so he went back out into the hall to take it.

A voice he knew well said, without preamble, 'I need a place to crash, Gayboy. Have you still got that house standing empty?'

# Chapter Five

Mr Green. Ted's special skills trainer. Who had faked his own death by drowning off the coast of South Africa so he could drop off the radar. A man who was probably incapable of forming friendships, but Ted was as close as he ever got to a friend.

'It's sold, but the contract isn't finalised until next Wednesday, if that's any good to you? It's completely empty now though, although the mains services are still on.'

Green made an impatient noise. He often treated Ted with a degree of contempt as if disappointed by how slow he was to catch on at times. Ted took it all with good grace. Green was the best there was in his field. If you wanted to learn from a master, you had to be prepared to put up with the little idiosyncrasies.

'I need a roof somewhere I'm not known, not an Ideal Home exhibit. And I need to meet up with you first. Somewhere we're not likely to be seen together.'

'Of course. You'll need the keys.'

Again the sound of irritation.

'I don't need keys. I just wanted to make sure the place was still empty. How soon can you meet me there?'

'You're already here?'

This time Green snapped.

'Get a grip for god's sake, Gayboy. I haven't time to wait for your brain to catch up. I'll be waiting.'

'Ten minutes,' Ted told him, though he wasn't sure Green had heard him before he ended the call.

He went back into the sitting room and made an apologetic face at Trev.

'Something's come up, sorry. I'm going to have to nip out for a bit, but I'll try not to be long. I'll just get changed quickly.'

Trev turned his head away from the television where he was watching the news. His expression was shrewd. Ted was always honest with him, just sometimes economical with the truth. If he was changing out of his work suit, he was probably not going back to the station.

'No chance of another training session before supper tonight, then?'

For one crazy moment, Ted considered bringing Green back to the house for Trev to train with. They'd never met. Ted always tried to keep the two sides of his life separate. It would have been interesting to see how Trev shaped up, fighting the most highly-qualified Krav Maga teacher in Britain. Then he brushed the idea to one side, promised to try to find the time, then sprinted upstairs to tear off his work clothes and jump into something more casual. For once, it was him leaving his clothing scattered about without hanging it up, which was usually Trev's trick.

He grabbed the keys to his mother's house as quietly as he could, not wanting Trev to hear and ask questions, then he got his car back out of the garage and drove off to meet Green.

He let himself into the house warily, never sure if he was going to be walking into the barrel of a gun pointing at him. Green could be classified as permanently armed and dangerous. Ted knew he walked a fine line which wavered from one side of the law to the other. He also knew he was often employed by mysterious forces to deal with dirty doings which no one else would touch. He preferred not to know too much.

He found Green sitting, apparently comfortably, on the kitchen floor, his legs stretched out in front of him, back leaning against a full bergen backpack. He looked remarkably relaxed and at ease. He'd already made himself a brew with equipment from the rucksack. He had none of the tension about him of Ted's last encounter with him. He also looked completely different from the last time Ted had seen him.

Gone was the bristling moustache and his thick head of hair had been given a severe No 1 cut. His sleeves were partly pushed back and Ted saw to his surprise that his regimental tattoos, for the Paras and the SAS, had been skilfully lasered away. He looked lean, fit, mission-ready. He was also tanned like old leather which just highlighted the cold greyness of his eyes.

'You're late, Gayboy,' was his only form of greeting.

'I couldn't just drop everything. I got here as soon as I could,' Ted said, aware that he always sounded defensive in Green's presence. He squatted down near to him as he replied.

'You said we had unfinished business, the last time I heard from you. Is that what's brought you back? Only remember I'm a policeman, so don't tell me anything that's likely to compromise me.'

Green scoffed.

'Or what are you going to do? Arrest me? Good luck with that. Between us we mopped up a few big fish in your paedo ring last time. But there are still a few more pond-life specimens swimming around out there that need dealing with. I've been engaged to do something about some of them. You don't need to know any details. It's better if you don't.

'But I do need some contact details from you. There's a former Met officer who was looking into the same sort of thing. You had contact with him. I need his number. I may be able to put an important witness his way but he's proving elusive.'

Ted knew he shouldn't be surprised that Green knew all about his contact with the man he knew as Harry. He seemed to have a handle on everything. But he shook his head.

'In the same way I wouldn't give him your contact details,

I'm not giving you his without his permission. I never know who you're working for.'

'I'm working for whoever offers me the best deal,' Green told him candidly. 'Sometimes it coincidentally happens to work for the greater good. It will in this case. You'll need my number. It was masked when I called you. I'll give you that, you get in touch with him and tell him it's in his interests to contact me as soon as possible.'

Ted noted the number then stood up.

'I'll get in touch with him then let you know. Don't forget you need to be gone by Wednesday.'

Green sighed and raised his eyes to the ceiling.

'Are you being deliberately stupid, Gayboy? Contact him now and give me his answer. I've got a narrow window on this. Tell him it's a key witness. One they're trying to discredit. One I can deliver, subject to assurances.'

Ted went back out into the hallway to make the call. It was some time since he'd spoken to 'Harry', when he'd been working to break up a paedophile ring. He wasn't even sure if he was still on the same number. He was someone who had to keep a low profile because of what he had uncovered.

Ted's call was answered on the second ring.

'Hello, Ted, what can I do for you this time? I hope you've not got more of the same on your patch?'

'It might be what I can do for you this time, Harry. I'm with someone now who wants to contact you but I wanted to check it was all right to put him in touch. I can vouch for him. He's a … well, I'm not sure how best to sum it up. A Special Operative? Anyway, he says he can deliver a key witness to you, one they're trying to discredit. If that makes any sense to you and if it's of interest to you?'

Harry gave a low whistle.

'This might just be all my birthdays come around at once. Is said operative with you in Stockport? Stockport which used to be Cheshire, now Greater Manchester?'

'Still Cheshire, according to many. Is there some geographical significance I'm missing?'

'There could well be. And if there is, I am very interested indeed in speaking to your contact, especially if you can vouch for him. Give him my number. Tell him to get in touch whenever he likes. If he's talking about who I think he is, this could be very interesting and significant.'

Ted was glad it meant something to Harry. It was all Double Dutch to him. He was too wrapped up in his own case to have time to join up the dots. He reported back to Green, gave him the contact number, then took his leave, reminding Green again of the completion date for the house sale. He'd keep the keys in his possession until then, just in case Trev decided to visit to give the place the once-over before the new owners took possession. Or worse, that he would decide to take Ted's mother there for a last look round. It could turn nasty if either of them innocently walked in on Green when he wasn't expecting company.

As he drove back, he decided the best idea would be to distract Trev as much as possible by agreeing to frequent training sessions, with all that they entailed. It would help him, too, as a good way to unwind after work, especially as they were on an enforced break from both their judo sessions and the junior self-defence club they ran, because of refurbishment works at the gym which was used as a dojo for both.

'Sorry about that,' he said apologetically as he walked back into the house. 'All sorted now, there should be no more distractions. Right, so, training, showers, a bit more training of a different kind, then some supper. How does that sound?'

Trev grinned at him suggestively as he unfolded his long, lithe figure from the sofa.

'That sounds like the perfect way to spend an evening, to me.'

Ted had only just got through the door of his office the

following morning when his mobile rang.

'Inspector Darling? It's Fred, from the Evening News. We've spoken before, a time or two.'

Ted remembered him, but had no idea why he was calling.

'What can I do for you? Although you know I'm probably going to have to pass the buck to our Press Office, whatever it is.'

'I just wondered if you could give me the heads-up on what the press conference this afternoon is all about. I suppose it's this latest murder on your patch. The young lad strangled then hung up to make it look like suicide. He was some sort of local sporting bod, I gather. Is there anything at all you can give me before this afternoon? Just so we can crack on a bit, beat off the competition.'

Ted was shocked with how much he knew, his anger rising at the thought that once again there was clearly a leak of information from within the station. He knew that both the Super and Jim Baker were going to go ballistic at the news of a further, significant breach. They'd been trying for some time now to uncover a mole, still without success.

'I'm sorry, there's nothing more I can tell you at this stage. You'll just have to wait for the press conference. You could try calling the Press Office, but I expect they'll say the same thing.'

'He was found up at Roman Lakes, wasn't he? If you could at least tell me exactly whereabouts, I could get a photographer out there to get some shots, ahead of anyone else. We've not really been able to get near. Then at least we'd have something exclusive to run with.'

'That's as much as I can tell you for now. Please call the Press Office.'

Ted rang off, furious. The only location which had been officially released to date was 'near Marple'. He sent his waste-paper flying with a precise kick which hurled it into the wall. He retrieved it guiltily, concerned to notice that it was slightly bent out of shape. It would no doubt earn him another telling off from the cleaning lady who had done his office ever since he'd been at Stockport.

He went in search of the Ice Queen to tell her there had been another confidentiality lapse. He knew she was going to be as angry as he was. The leaks had to be coming from within their own station. Nobody else would have the amount of information that was filtering out. And neither of them liked the idea that an officer there was acting as an informant, no doubt to pick up a few bob on the side.

She listened to his news, tight-lipped, busying herself with the coffee.

'We need to get on top of these leaks once and for all,' she said sternly. 'Remind your team, in the strongest possible terms, and perhaps you can ask Inspector Turner to do the same to his. I'll send round a memo, too, to make it official. I really don't like to think of anyone in this station behaving like this. I want it stopped.'

Her tone made Ted switch into formal mode as he said brusquely, 'Ma'am.'

They were both in early, as ever. Ted had time for his coffee and to bring her up to speed before he went back upstairs to talk to the team. He'd told PC Khan to go straight to the Mitchells' house to prepare them for the early-afternoon press conference, but to call him with any updates if necessary.

Ted's briefings were usually low key, with him perching on a desk or a table. He started this one standing in front of the team with his most serious face on. He didn't for a moment want to think that one of his own officers was leaking confidential information to the press. No more than Kevin Turner did about any of his. But he needed to deliver the message, loud and clear, that whoever was doing it would be found out, sooner rather than later.

'I'm only going to say this once. Someone inside this nick is once again passing on confidential information to the press.

I'm hoping that it's none of you. I hope we all understand one another well enough by now for that to be taken as a given. I would just stress that, should I be wrong on that, being kicked off the team by me would be the least of your worries.'

Steve had gone pink to the tips of his ears. Ted was completely sure that he was not the mole. He just had an unfortunate habit of looking uncomfortable and guilty even when he wasn't.

'It's not school and I'm not asking you to tell tales but if anyone does have any idea, even the slightest suspicion, of who might be behind the leaks, please come and talk to me in confidence.

'Right, that's all I'm going to say on that subject for now. So where are we up to with the Callum Mitchell case?'

'Boss, we now have the names of all the football lads Callum was in contact with and we're gradually working through them. There are eleven of them still, because a lad called Nigel Denby, who was always on the subs' bench, used to hang around with them too. So twelve of them including Callum. I've got a print-out of full names and contact details but just a quick run-through, we have Antoine, Jerome, Jordan, Wayne, Will, Sammy, Terry, Marvin, Alan, Gary and Nigel.

'The one we can't get hold of at the moment is Antoine. He's away on a course of some sort, back tomorrow. We've spoken to about half of them so far. They're all saying the same thing. They all met up with Callum soon after he got back from France, but they've not seen him since, nor been in touch.'

'And did any of them shed any light on what the 'it' was that meant Callum was going to buy them all a drink when it was done?'

'They all say the same thing. They were all going to help him in some way when he moved up to Durham to start his university course. He was going to be living in at college for his first year so they were going to help him move in. Then after that they were all going to meet up again and he'd buy them all a drink by way of a thank you.'

Ted considered thoughtfully.

'And they all said exactly the same thing?'

Jo nodded, knowing the boss was thinking the same thing as he was.

'Well, clearly Callum would have had his sports kit for lacrosse and possibly football to shift up there, plus all his law books, his clothes and personal possessions. But how the heck much other stuff was he planning on taking with him that it was going to take all twelve of them to pitch in?'

'Which is precisely what I was thinking, boss. As cover stories go, it stinks to high heaven.'

# Chapter Six

'Carry on with interviewing all of them, including this Antoine, when he's back. Jo, let me have all the notes of what's been said so far then I can go over them with fresh eyes to see if anything else jumps out at me.

'You say so far they're all sticking to the same story. Are they all solid or is there anyone who strikes any of you as being someone who might waver, with the right sort of careful questioning?'

'Boss, I spoke to Nigel Denby, the reserve. A semi-permanent feature on the subs' bench, it seems. Talking to him, I could see why,' Mike Hallam told them. 'Bear in mind I'm the first to admit I know next to nothing about sport, but if I was a team manager, I'd be worried about having to put him on in an important match. He lacks self-assurance and he's got that look of always wanting to please. Like a dog who knows it needs to do a trick to get a biscuit.

'I felt like he was watching me intently the whole time we were talking and was feeding off my body language, if you know what I mean. He stuck to the script, but if I made any gesture of approval, like nodding, he'd say a bit more. It didn't add anything, but he was wanting to get it right. I haven't talked to any of the others yet but my immediate impression of Nigel was that he could be a weak link and that was probably why he was always on the sidelines.'

'Thanks Mike, that's worth noting. I'll give you your biscuit after the briefing,' Ted told him with a smile, then he switched back to serious mode. 'How are we doing with the rabid Right angle? Maurice?'

'Can we do some of this lot for inciting racial hatred or something, boss? The stuff I'm finding is sickening. The edited highlights are stuff like "I can't get a doctor's appointment and when I do go the waiting room is full of brown faces. We don't need any more." So far it's mostly about wanting a total block on immigration, but there is some muttering about getting rid of the ones already here. No real specifics yet, but I'll keep wading through the filth. And yes, there are some local groups but they don't advertise themselves too openly, probably because of the kind of stuff they're posting.'

Jezza cut in at that point.

'And I want to know if I can put in for mind bleach on expenses, boss. I got in touch with the charity Callum had been working with. I spoke to someone really helpful. She didn't know Callum herself but she found out some information for me and they had nothing but praise for him. No trouble at all, as far as she was aware.

'They do get abuse, and lots of it. They've also had much more serious stuff. They have depots in various places in Britain for collecting supplies to go to Calais. Stuff like sleeping bags, tents, clothing. One of their places in Bristol had an arson attack. Luckily no one was hurt but all the stuff they'd been collecting for weeks was destroyed, along with two of the vehicles which were going to be used to transport it all.

'They forwarded me some of the hate mail they get and there was a flurry of it after the fire. Warnings that if they continued, the next time would be worse. So I think there's a distinct possibility that not everyone would be in favour of the type of voluntary work Callum had been doing. And especially not the sort of future career he had in mind.'

'As far as the local lot go, much as it goes against the grain, I think we may have to wait it out on them. For the time being, our top priority is the Callum Mitchell murder enquiry. Once we have that sewn up, if it's not led us directly to any of this lot, then we can go after them,' Ted told them.

Jo was shaking his head.

'I'm not buying the method of killing in this case as fitting in with that sort of person. I'm no expert on Far Right extremism, but I could more easily see them perhaps stringing someone up alive. Or a mob of them setting about him with baseball bats and boots, for instance.

'I'm probably not making it very clear, but what I'm trying to say is they strike me as a group who would be proud of their actions, even if they wanted to avoid the consequences. This killing was clever and it could so easily have slipped through as another suicide.'

'Speaking of suicides, Jo, what else do we know about the young lad from the same football team, the one who killed himself? Have we had chance to chase that up yet?'

'A young boy of fifteen, Páraic Shaugnessy, died of a self-inflicted overdose just under a year ago, so he was a bit younger than Callum and the others. Something of a rising star on the team. Seemed to have a lot going for him. His family had absolutely no clue why he would want to kill himself. Nothing came out in the enquiry or at the inquest to throw any light on his motive.'

'We definitely need to dig deeper into this football club. We'll need a list of everyone involved in the running of it and we need to interview them all. Was Callum or any of his friends still involved with the club in any way, even though they didn't play for them any more?'

There was an awkward pause.

'Come on, everyone, we need to be on top of this. We should have thought of that angle by now.'

With Ted it was always 'we'. If his team slipped up, he accepted full responsibility. It was why he was so popular. It was a reminder rather than a reprimand. It would have more effect like that.

'If the killing is related to the club then there's another

aspect we certainly need to look into and that's parents of other players,' Jezza put in. 'I used to do a bit of competitive junior kickboxing ...'

Virgil broke in with a chuckle.

'That must have been scary – for your opponents, I mean.'

Jezza totally blanked him apart from flipping him a discreet middle finger she hoped the boss wouldn't notice. When she'd first joined the team she would have exploded at the remark. She now realised the constant teasing was a part of belonging.

'Seriously, though, some of those parents would go to any lengths to get their kids on the team. We've mentioned sibling rivalry and team rivalry, but we really should look at parents as well.'

'Boss, stating the obvious, that's a heck of a lot of people to be seen and not all that many of us to go round,' Jo told Ted. 'Any signs of some reinforcements?'

'We should be getting DS Rakale and DC Eccles from South Manchester. I'm just waiting to hear when from Superintendent Baker.

'How have the other team members taken the news about Callum? Did they know already it was him, as the name hasn't been officially released yet? If not, how did they react?'

'His brother Sean phoned Antoine,' Rob O'Connell replied. 'Antoine was the team captain when they all played together and he seems to be something of a leader figure still, when they hang round together. He and Callum were close. They often went round to each others houses. Sean told him and he did a ring-round of all the others.'

'And we can't talk to this Antoine before tomorrow?'

'Boss, because I is black,' Virgil began, with his usual ironic humour, 'I'm talking to the black players from the old team. That's Jerome, Sammy and Antoine. I've spoken to the first two. Exactly the same story as the others. Antoine is next on the list. He's the poor little rich kid of the group. Father has money; a property developer of some sort. They have a big, posh house in Marple. He's set Antoine up in some sort of online trading in currencies and he's off doing more training for that. Means nothing to me, and it might not be relevant to the enquiry. He's definitely the one who was closest to Callum so I'll see what I can prise out of him.'

'And they're all claiming they didn't see Callum or have any contact with him in the intervening time since he got back, after that first meet-up? Does that ring true to anyone?'

A few heads shook at Ted's words, then he went on, 'It seems improbable to me. Virgil, you need to press Antoine on that. If he was close, then surely he would have been in contact with Callum at some point. So if he wasn't seeing any of his football mates, we need to know who he was seeing and where he was going. What about the lacrosse lot? We've got too many unfilled blanks at the moment to even start drawing up any real sort of a time-line.

'We know from what the parents have said that he had joint use of a car, with his brother, and we also know that neither of them took the car that evening. Sean because he was going out drinking, Callum because he was possibly going to be out all night and Sean might need it the next day.

'So wherever Callum went, it was possibly on foot or on public transport. We need to know which. If he caught a bus somewhere, there may be some CCTV.'

Rob O'Connell cut in at this point.

'Boss, I know the dad told you the lads weren't alike. But when I was talking to Sean, I could see a resemblance. I'd probably not have guessed at twins, but I might well have taken them for brothers so other people might have, too. So if we don't get anything from this appeal today, could we consider a reconstruction of his last known movements, using Sean?'

'It's certainly worth thinking about, but we don't know if he was picked up by someone close to his home or if he left on foot or walked to a bus stop. So if we got it wrong in a reconstruction, we could mislead potential witnesses,' Ted told him.

'With any luck, we might get some response from the press conference. Some of you might need to work on a bit this evening if it goes out on the early evening news and we do start getting calls. Let's have a catch-up end of play to see if there's anything else.'

Ted had just got back to his office and put his kettle on when his mobile rang.

'Morning, Darling.'

'Morning, Super.'

Ted and Jim Baker seldom passed up the chance to share the old joke.

'I'll be coming over for the press conference, Ted. I thought it might be a good idea to show the public we're taking this one seriously, no holds barred. You and I need a catch-up, too, about resources and budgets. But the good news is you can have DS Rakale and DC Winters as from Monday morning, hopefully for as long as you need them.

'How's it going so far? Are you making any headway?'

'We've got a lot of potential witnesses to get through, and we're still waiting on forensic results. Doug's complaining bitterly, of course, because of the delay in working the crime scene. He's not optimistic of them finding much for us.

'Oh, and we've had another leak. I had the press on, asking me things they could only have found out from someone in this nick, I would say.'

Jim Baker swore expressively.

'That's all we bloody need. It's time we got to the bottom of this mole business once and for all, Ted. Doesn't Bill know who it is? He usually knows everything that's going on in the nick.'

Bill Baxter was a retired sergeant working on the front desk. He was just back at work after sick leave. Ted had asked him several times over the years if he had any idea who the informant might be, but even he was in the dark. It had been going on for some considerable time but the mole's identity remained as much a mystery as it had ever been.

As soon as Jim Baker ended his call, Ted's mobile rang again. The display showed it was the local reporter this time. Ted didn't mind her quite so much. She wasn't as pushy as either her predecessor or the evening paper reporter. She was usually so timid Ted couldn't imagine how she got any decent stories.

'Yes, Penny, what can I do for you?'

'Erm, hello Chief Inspector.'

'Hello, Penny,' Ted replied patiently, wondering how long this call was going to take when he had plenty to be getting on with. When there was a pause, he thought he'd better take the initiative.

'If it's about the press conference later today, I'm afraid there really isn't much I can tell you beforehand. I'm sorry, but everything you need to know you'll get from that.'

He could almost sense her disappointment in the next silence so in a rare moment of feeling kindly disposed towards the press, he said, 'Come and find me before it starts and if there is anything fresh I can tell you, I will. Just don't count on it, though.'

Ted was opening the press conference. The Ice Queen had been insistent. Much as he hated the role, he was ideal for it as he always looked sincere. When he asked the public for their help, they instinctively wanted to give it. The Press Office had monitored success rates in terms of public response and there was an undeniable pattern. When Ted opened the appeal, there was a bigger response from the public.

'This is Callum Mitchell,' he began, knowing that cameras would instantly cut, at that point, to the enlarged photo of Callum on the board behind him. 'A young man, just nineteen, accepted by his chosen university, with his whole life, and a promising career, ahead of him.'

He spoke frankly, openly, about their lack of information for the time leading up to Callum's body being found and asked for anyone who could fill in the blanks to contact them.

PC Khan was with the parents. Mrs Mitchell was sitting between her and Callum's father, clinging desperately to both of them. She was clearly not in a position to say anything, but her husband spoke up firmly when it was his turn, only occasionally having to pause to regain control of his voice.

The Ice Queen was in the hot seat to answer questions when the floor was thrown open to the press. There was a decent turnout and Ted couldn't help but think that it was one small thing for which to be thankful to the mole. He doubted so many would have put in an appearance without a tip-off that there was more to this case than met the eye. The downside to the leak was obvious from the moment the questions began.

The tone was accusatory.

How had no one picked up earlier that a supposed suicide was nothing of the sort?

Why was there such a long delay before the enquiry started in the correct direction?

Was there any realistic chance of recovering valuable evidence from the crime scene after such a delay, especially with bad weather in the intervening time?

How did Mr and Mrs Mitchell feel about the delay?

Did they blame the police for poor handling of the case from the outset?

Ted sat back in his chair, happy to leave dealing with the flak to both his senior officers, as Jim Baker growled a word or two from time to time. But there was no doubt that Superintendent Caldwell was in her element. She was clearly born to command. Ted often wondered what she was like with her two teenage sons because she showed herself more than capable of quelling even the most determined reporter.

Afterwards she spent some time with the Mitchells, assuring them the team were doing everything possible, then seeing them safely on their way, accompanied by PC Khan.

When it was all finished, she headed back to her office, instructing Ted and Jim to join her for a debrief. Even Big Jim, her equal in rank and with more years of service under his belt, followed meekly in her wake, Ted bringing up the rear.

Once she'd set her coffee machine going for a fresh brew, she turned to smile at them.

'Well, all things considered, I think that went off quite well. So now we wait patiently for the phone calls to start, with any luck. We might finally be on the brink of a breakthrough.'

# Chapter Seven

When they'd finished their meeting with the Ice Queen, Ted and Jim Baker started to make their way to Ted's office. In the corridor they encountered Sergeant Wheeler, shepherding two young probationers on a guided tour. He stopped and stood to the side with a polite, 'After you, sirs.'

Outside the station, he was on first name terms with both. He'd been a close friend of Jim for years. They often went out together socially. But at work it was always formal, especially when he had the probationers in tow.

The two young officers knew who Ted was but not Jim Baker. To be on the safe side, they both stood almost to attention and said nothing.

As they continued on their way, Jim shook his head as he said, 'Is it me getting older or do they look more like kids every day? I can't see those two doing much to intimidate the local criminal population. At least not until they look old enough to shave.'

'I'm pretty sure I looked like that when I started out. Especially with my size,' Ted smiled.

'You never look your age though, you lucky bugger. You'd still pass for thirty in a good light,' Jim replied with a note of envy. 'I sometimes think I look older than I am. Bella's always on at me to lose weight, for one thing. But I've always been big. You're lucky, with your build. There's more meat on a budgie's lips.'

Ted couldn't resist teasing his old friend. He knew Jim was never entirely comfortable with his relationship with Trev. It was one reason he'd still not told him that the two of them had got married on the quiet. Very few people knew that.

'It's living with a toy boy that does it, Jim. That keeps me fit.'

'Put the kettle on,' Jim ordered him, brusquely changing the subject. 'That stuff Debs makes is nice enough but it's nearly as weak as the gnat's piss you drink.'

Ted did as instructed, tempted to suggest he should just pour the hot water straight into the jar of coffee granules. Then both men switched back into serious work mode while they sat down and discussed the case.

'What are your early thoughts?' Jim asked, as Ted put a mug in front of him. It looked like hot treacle to him but no doubt the Big Boss would still complain it was too weak.

'That we could end up with a lot of potential suspects and it's going to stretch us to the limit,' Ted replied immediately. 'And I'd be a lot happier going forward if we had something from Forensics to go on. It's a bit of a waiting game on that.

'Once Virgil has spoken to this Antoine we may know more. He seems to be the one most likely to have been in touch with Callum since the last meet-up, if anyone was.'

'But we might get a break and someone will phone in claiming to have seen something,' Jim said optimistically.

'It depends when it goes out, of course. Going into a weekend we might not get much feedback. And you know as well as I do there will be endless false trails to eliminate.'

'Stop being so bloody negative, Ted. It's not like you. We just need one single lead to set you off in the right direction and you'll be sorted. The public have helped us before; they may well come good again.'

He drained his mug and stood up. He seemed to have a heat-resistant throat, swallowing drinks that were far too hot for most people.

'Keep me posted, of course, at all times. I know you need bodies for taking phone calls but just keep an eye on the budget over the weekend, won't you?'

'I need to put Virgil on tomorrow, for sure. He's going to speak to this Antoine then because he's not been around all week. He's back tomorrow and we need to hear what he has to say for himself as soon as possible. If Callum was in touch with anyone, it would be him.'

'Right, well, that sounds fair enough. Have you got anything planned yourself this weekend?'

'Trev's competing in a karate tournament. I was hoping to go and watch, but I ought to keep an eye on things here.'

'Don't be daft,' Jim said firmly. 'That's why we got you a DI, so you don't always have to do everything yourself. Unless it's the other end of the country, you can surely take a couple of hours off at some point?'

It certainly sounded tempting. He needed to make time to talk to Jo to arrange weekend cover and see what new leads there were. He would dearly like to at least put in an appearance at the karate tournament to show his support for his partner. And it was only in Warrington. Not all that far away.

Trev was long-suffering and understanding of the demands of Ted's job. He was used to being stood up and always refused to meet Ted at a restaurant if they were going out. He said he preferred to wait at home so he was not on public display if he was once again left sitting there like Billy No Mates because Ted was tied up on a case.

'Happy to step in, boss,' Jo told him at once when Ted floated the idea past him. 'I love my family to bits, of course. But just occasionally, at the weekends, with all six of them and the missus under the same roof getting on one another's nerves, if we're not all going out somewhere different, it's nice to take a break.'

They sorted cover between them, Ted assuring him that as ever he was never more than a phone call away.

It was a frustrating wait for anything much to happen. Realistically, they weren't going to get any forensic results before the beginning of next week now. They were still waiting to hear if any of the killer's DNA had been found on the body, but that result would take time. For now, it was just a relentless slog of interviewing anyone known to have had a connection to the victim, then laboriously cross-checking what they all said, looking for any patterns to emerge.

Ted had promised to try to get home at a reasonable time so he could give Trev one more training session before the tournament. He had no doubt his partner was on peak form and was going to do well. He just hoped he could get to see at least some of it. He didn't want to say anything for fear of getting Trev's hopes up then having to let him down at the last minute.

'I was looking for the keys to Annie's place earlier,' Trev said as they ate supper together after another fast and furious training session. 'I thought I'd just have a quick look round to make sure everything was as it should be before the hand-over. And no doubt she'll want to go for one last look when I pick her up on Tuesday ready to sign the contract.'

'I probably picked them up and put them somewhere safe,' Ted replied evasively. 'I'll have a look in my pockets later. Are you sure you're still all right to meet her off the train, and to go with her to the solicitors, just in case I can't get away?'

'No worries at all. And I'm recording the news this evening so she can see you doing your bit at the press conference. You know how proud she gets.'

After they'd eaten they sat together on the sofa, buried under cats, feet up on the rests. Ted hated watching himself on television but Trev insisted when the evening news came on.

'You look so earnest. I wish I had information to give you because I would, seeing you looking into the camera like that. I hope it brings lots of results for you.'

He turned to give him a hug but Ted held up a hand, he eyes riveted to the screen as the next news item started.

' ... The prisoner has not yet been named but reports suggest she was on remand on a charge of assaulting a police officer. There are unconfirmed reports that she may herself have been a potential witness in a separate case and was due to appear in court for the prosecution.

'She had been taken from the prison to attend a routine medical appointment. Because she was categorised as a low risk prisoner, the journey was made by taxi, accompanied by two prison officers.

'A statement issued says that the taxi was brought to a halt for supposed roadworks on a quiet country road, which later proved not to be genuine. There the driver and the prison officers were immobilised without serious harm. The prisoner was then taken away in a waiting vehicle. Reports suggest that only one person was involved in the operation which Cheshire Police are describing as the work of a specialist.'

The report ended and gave way to the local weather forecast.

'Was that linked to something you're working on? A witness in one of your cases?'

'I don't know at the moment. It just looked interesting. It's not often we get prisoners sprung like that. Not round here, anyway.'

Ted tried to sound vague but his brain was working overtime. He was remembering his phone call to Harry and his evident interest in a witness and in Cheshire. The prisoner who had been taken was being held in a Cheshire prison.

The trouble was, knowing what he did about Mr Green, he couldn't be sure whether the news was good or bad.

He made an excuse of going to look for his mother's house keys and went out to the garage to make a phone call. The last number he had for Green was now out of service. Wherever he was now and whoever he was with, Ted was fairly sure it would be far away from Cheshire. He also knew that his mother's house would be empty and as clean and tidy as if no one had ever been there. Ted had long since stopped trying to work out how Green got in and out of secure premises without keys or leaving any sign to arouse suspicion.

'He's quite a lad, is Antoine,' Virgil reported back after his visit to see the last member of the football team to be interviewed so far. 'Spent most of his time calling me "bro" or "blud" but he clearly is a spoilt little rich kid. At least he stopped short of calling me "bredren". All that gang-speak is just an act. He's clearly wanted for nothing all his life. He's an only child, too. You should see his wheels. All paid for by his father.

'He's a bright lad, though. Intelligent, smart. This online trading he does is way beyond my comprehension and I didn't want to show my ignorance. But if we need to know more about it for any reason, I can ask Nat.'

Nathan Cowley had become friendly with Virgil when he met him on an earlier case. He was now going out with Jezza Vine. He'd been a financial trader in the past, before a catastrophic work error had seen him end up as homeless, living on the streets.

'No surprises but his version was exactly the same as the others. They all met up together at his place when Callum first got back from France. Antoine doesn't just have a bedroom, like most teenage lads. He has his own wing of the house, literally. An extension built on the side, with its own separate entrance, so he and his friends can come and go without disturbing his family.

'Antoine insisted, like the others all did, that they weren't planning to meet up again until they all got together to help Callum move his stuff up to Durham. Once that was done, Callum was going to buy them all a drink. By way of a farewell party, as they wouldn't be seeing one another for some time.'

Ted and Jo were both in. Steve still working on Callum's computer and was busy with that, but he broke off to hear Virgil's feedback. Ted voiced what everyone was thinking.

'Why weren't they planning on meeting before then? That was still a few weeks away. Surely, if they were as close as all that, they'd want to see as much of one another as possible before then?'

'I asked him that, boss, and he just said Callum had a lot of stuff to do before he went away so they wouldn't have time.'

'And what about continuing contact with the club?'

'According to Antoine, most of them still go to watch the occasional match and to show support. The club is holding a benefit match on the anniversary of Páraic's death. They want to raise funds to do something in his memory, something to help young team members. They'll all be going to that.'

Ted frowned.

'Isn't that this month? Didn't Páraic die in September? The fifteenth, wasn't it? And surely Callum wouldn't be going up to university until mid-October, at the earliest? Unless Durham has some strange term dates. Steve, can you check into that, please?

'In other words, they were all going to be seeing one another before Callum's move. Which means that every single one of them has knowingly lied to us, for some reason. If it was just one or two of them that could be an oversight. They may not regard being at the same match as a planned meeting. But all of them denying it? That means they've deliberately lied to us and we need to find out why.'

'You stole my thunder, boss,' Virgil told him, smiling. 'I was all set to present that as my trophy.'

'Good work, Virgil. Jo, we now need to interview every one of them again, separately, and as soon as possible, before they can get together and concoct more fairy stories. Can you sort that, please? I'd still like to nip out briefly this afternoon, but put me down to interview a couple of them before I do. It might be a good idea if someone different speaks to each of them this time to see if their story still holds. I'd quite like to talk to Nigel myself, if you can arrange that.'

A desk phone was ringing. Steve took the call, listened briefly, then put his hand over the mouthpiece and said, 'Sir, a possible sighting of Callum the night he was killed. I'll get all the details.'

Once the call had finished, he reported what he'd been told.

'That was a bus driver. He picked up someone who looked like the photo released of Callum, on the night in question.'

'What made him remember him in particular?'

Ted was looking for something which might suggest the caller was someone other than an attention seeker or simply a person trying to be helpful, with no real information to offer.

'He said he was so polite he stood out, sir.'

Ted gave a small laugh at that.

'Sad reflection of the times, that. I don't suppose he also remembers where he got off?'

'Luckily, he does. And again because the person in question thanked him and said goodbye as he was getting off. That was up near the junction of Marple Road and Bean Leach Road, the stop near the Spice Tower.'

'I know it, but I still think of it as the Wrights Arms. Right, so now you need to get on to the bus company and get hold of CCTV from that bus for the relevant timings. And let's hope they still have it. I doubt you'll get anywhere at a weekend but you never know your luck.

'Jo, let's add in to the next round of questioning of all the team members if they know anyone from up there that Callum might have gone to see. From memory, I can't think of any of them who live out that way, but I'll check through the list again.'

'I think there's only Antoine from out that side of town, boss, and he's further up, in Marple.'

'As long as the CCTV bears out that it was Callum, we've got a direction to go in, at least. Let's crack on with second interviews then, if nothing jumps out at us today, more of the same tomorrow, for whoever's on. We'll feed everything back on Monday morning.

'Jo, make sure PC Khan knows to ask the parents if they can think of anyone Callum would have gone to visit out in that direction.'

With the glimmer of a possible lead finally, Ted felt he could probably justify sloping away for a couple of hours to watch Trev compete. He knew it would mean a lot to his partner to have him there to support him, especially as it was totally unexpected.

The look on Trev's face when he saw Ted walk into the hall where the tournament was taking place was worth nicking off work for. Ted was lucky with the timings, too, as Trev's match was just coming up.

Mismatch would have been a better description. Ted suspected Trev would have outclassed the fighter he faced even without the boost of seeing him there unexpectedly. As it was, he wiped the mat with him.

They were always discreet in public, especially in case some of the juniors they taught self- defence to were in the audience. One of them, Flip, tried never to miss an opportunity to watch either of his heroes compete, and Ted had already spotted the young boy's mop of unruly hair among the watchers, sitting next to his foster mother.

When Trev had finished his match, he hurried over to Ted, grabbing a towel on the way to wipe his face, although he'd hardly had to break a sweat to win.

'You came!' he beamed delightedly. 'I wasn't expecting you. Does that mean you've caught the baddy?'

'Not yet, but we might have a decent lead, at last. So I thought I'd skive off and come and watch you. You were amazing. I was so proud of you.'

Trev's grin could hardly have got any wider.

'Oh god, what a pity we're on public display. Just make sure you're not late home tonight. I shall spend the rest of the day thinking of suitable ways to thank you for your support.'

# Chapter Eight

'Is this a good time to talk to you about stomach contents, Edwin?' Professor Nelson's bright and breezy voice asked Ted, without any preliminaries.

With a muted sigh, Ted pushed his plate of hot, buttered, wholemeal toast to one side. He'd somehow lost his appetite for it. The grisly side of post-mortem findings was an important part of his job, but not one he relished most of the time. Certainly not first thing on a Monday morning, before he'd even left for work.

'You don't want me to come down there and sniff anything do you?' he asked warily.

Bizzie Nelson gave a throaty chuckle.

'Not this time. I can spare you that ordeal and tell you that we found sedatives in young Callum's system. Enough to ensure that he was in all probability in a deep sleep and aware of very little at the time of his death. That, at least, is some consolation, and may perhaps be something which the parents would welcome being told.

'The drug in question is zopiclone, a nonbenzodiazepine hypnotic agent used to treat insomnia. The normal adult dose is 7.5mg and this young man had three times that in his system. He might, of course, have taken it himself for some reason. However, it's an interesting one for anyone to choose to give to someone else without their knowledge for a particular reason. Have you ever taken it?'

'Luckily, I've never had to resort to sleeping pills. I have sleepless nights, of course. It's inevitable in this job. But never enough to warrant taking tablets for. Is it a prescription-only drug?'

'Very much so. It's a controlled substance in several countries. The reason I say it would be an unusual choice is that it does have quite a bitter taste. It's not uncommonly prescribed for elderly patients, especially those suffering from dementia whose sleep patterns are often seriously disturbed. It was prescribed for both of my parents for that very reason.

'Back to the stomach contents. The young man had drunk the equivalent of two bottles of strong lager with blackcurrant, so I suppose that could well have masked the taste of the tablets.'

'Lager and black? Does anyone still drink that? Doesn't sound like much of a teenage drink to me. I'll have to ask one of the younger team members.'

'That's certainly not something I can help you with. I was never a beer drinker, even in my wildest days. I've always preferred a good wine or some decent Scotch to anything else.

'And I know you're going to ask me about further test results such as the DNA but I'm afraid I'm going to have to remind you again that such things take time. Occasionally, if we're very lucky, something can jump the queue, but not always.

'What I will say is there's a chance we might have the killer's DNA in the system somewhere. We found a minute trace of blood on the thumbprint, perhaps from an injury to the thumb itself. With luck, that will give us something although, of course, if the DNA's owner has not been tested before and isn't on record, it doesn't advance you all that much.

'Are you having any more luck from the crime scene?'

'Not really. I'll be catching up with Doug shortly when I go in but he's doing lots of muttering darkly about the inevitable lapse of time before his team went in.'

The Professor laughed again.

'That sounds like Doug all over. He's very good at his job,

isn't he? But he does like to moan. He can be a bit of an old woman in that respect. I shall leave you now and hope I haven't spoiled your breakfast.'

In fact it hadn't been as bad as Ted had feared. He'd successfully fought off the cats who were interested in the butter on his toast, now gone cold and limp. But it was better than nothing so he quickly smeared it with a bit of honey and ate it on the run as he went to get the car out.

It was a full briefing to start the week. PC Khan was there, as well as Doug, to give their input. DS Rakale and DC Eccles had come from South Manchester. They were ahead of time. Leona Rakale was certainly having a good effect on Charlie Eccles, who had not previously been known for good timekeeping.

Ted kicked off the briefing by introducing the two of them to any of those present who didn't know them. Then he reported his earlier conversation with the Professor and asked everyone for their thoughts.

'Lager and black? Isn't that a bit retro?' Jezza asked. 'I may be wrong but I can't think many teenagers would go into a pub these days and order one.'

'That's something we need to look into. With any luck, if it is unusual, someone in a pub might remember him going in there and ordering it. There's a pub at Bosden Farm, isn't there? That's a short walk from the bus stop. Jo, can we get that checked out in case that's where he was drinking. Get someone out there with Callum's photo. Ask if anyone remembers him or remembers anyone ordering lager and black on the night in question.'

'I will do, boss, but I think it's more of an eatery than a drinking pub,' Jo replied. 'Not sure it's somewhere anyone would go just for a couple of drinks, especially not the young crowd. It's not my personal type of place but that's the impression I get.'

'If he did go in just for a drink or two we might stand a

better chance of him having been noticed. Maurice, I want you to get on with cross-checking addresses we have for everyone connected to the case so far. Anyone at all who has any kind of connection to Callum. Do any of them live up that way? And that will include not just the football team ones but all the members of his lacrosse club.'

Maurice opened his mouth to protest but Ted cut him short.

'Yes, I know it's a lot of work but it's unfortunately something we need to do, unless we get a break from somewhere else in the meantime.

'PC Khan, can you ask the parents what Callum drank? I'm sure you know what you're doing, but if you could avoid mentioning the drink we're interested in. Just see what they say first, please. Can you also find out if he'd planned on going to the benefit match for Páraic on the fifteenth. I want all the team members asked about that, everyone, please.

'Also, PC Khan, and please excuse me if it sounds as if I'm telling you how to do your job. I just think it might be helpful to the parents to know that Callum wouldn't have known much at all of his last moments, from what the Professor told me.'

'I think so too, sir. I'll certainly do that. I think they're at the clutching at straws stage, so any crumb of comfort we can throw their way is bound to help.'

'Before we go through what the rest of the team have said to us, Steve, how did you get on with CCTV from the bus? Any luck yet?'

'No, sir, the person I needed to speak to wasn't available over the weekend, so I have to phone them back this morning. I'll get straight onto it when we've finished here.'

'Let me know as soon as possible, please. We need a positive ID on him or we could be wasting precious time looking in the wrong place. Again, PC Khan, please find out if the parents, or the brother, can shed any light on anyone he knew out that way. They've said he wasn't seeing anyone in particular but could there be someone out that way that we're not yet aware of?

'Doug, what news from the crime scene? And before you say anything, we appreciate the constraints you're under, but some good news would be welcome.'

Ted knew how to handle Doug by now. It was essential to divert him from the negative, the what his team couldn't do, onto something at which they'd succeeded. It worked.

'The weather wasn't kind to us before we could secure the scene, boss, but I can tell you one thing with confidence. Whoever tied the noose up in the tree was much heavier and had bigger feet than Callum did. In fact we didn't find any footprints which could have been Callum's at the site. So that fits with the Professor's findings that he was drugged. He was presumably carried there.

'What we did find were scrape marks in the soil and leaf mould. They're a match for residue we found on the heels of Callum's trainers. We also found faecal matter which is a match for his. The likely deduction from these findings is that Callum was carried to the foot of the tree where he was strangled before being hung. Even heavily sedated, his body would automatically have fought for air, so his legs would have been thrashing, resulting in the marks we found.'

There was silence for a moment while the team digested the mental image which Doug's words gave them all. Maurice was the first to verbalise what they were probably all thinking.

'Bloody hell. The poor lad.'

'Would he have been aware though? With that amount of sedative in his blood stream? Doug, can you answer that?'

'Almost certainly not, boss. The body will often twitch and react at the moment of death. You see it when animals are slaughtered or even put to sleep. But no, in all probability, mercifully, he would have been out of it.'

'Can you give us a shoe size from the prints you did find?'

'Not a snowball in hell's chance, boss, I'm afraid. The ground was too wet, even under the trees. The prints just didn't hold their form and we couldn't get reliable casts off any of them. All I can tell you is that they were quite deep, so it was someone heavy, and they were definitely bigger than Callum's trainers.'

Ted thanked him then asked for an update on the second interviews of the team members. There was nothing new to report. They were all resolutely sticking to identical stories about the last time they'd seen Callum and their plans of when to meet up with him next.

'I think we need as many of us as possible to attend this benefit match for Páraic on the fifteenth. I don't think we can yet rule out some sort of a link between the two cases. It would be interesting to see who goes to the match and if there is any significant interaction between any of them.

'Mike, after speaking to Nigel at the weekend, I agree with your summing up of him. With the right questioning, or the wrong, depending on your viewpoint, I think it would be possible to get him to say almost anything. He has a habit of offering information, looking for affirmation, then back-pedalling rapidly if he thinks he's said too much.

'I asked him if he knew the area near Roman Lakes where Callum was found. First he said he did. He said he goes mountain biking round there, with some of the others. Then when I deliberately left a silence for him to fill, he said he didn't know exactly where Callum had been found. He went on to say that when he said the others, he meant other lads he knows, not specifically the ones from the team. Naturally, he couldn't remember which ones or when.'

'Boss, do you think this is some weird thing where the rest of the team turned on Callum and killed him for some reason?' Jezza asked.

'Can I just cut in and answer that, boss?' Doug asked. When Ted nodded, he continued, 'From the CSI point of view that doesn't add up. There simply weren't enough footprints at the site to bear out a theory like that. So unless one of your team members is big and heavy and the rest of them just stood some way off watching, I'd say the forensic evidence rules that out.'

'Which means we're a bit back on the starting blocks for now, I'm afraid,' Ted said in conclusion. 'There isn't really any short-cut, just a lot of leg-work until we get a break. Thanks, everyone. I'll be in my office. Keep me posted of any developments.'

Ted hadn't long sat down at his desk to make a start on all the paperwork generated by a major enquiry when there was the familiar hesitant tap on his door.

'Come in, Steve,' he called out encouragingly.

He would be surprised if Steve had managed to track down the CCTV from the bus so quickly, so perhaps there was something else he'd found out. Steve hovered until Ted nodded at him to take a seat.

'Sir, I had an idea, but it's so completely daft I didn't want to say it during briefing.'

'Your ideas are usually very far from daft, Steve, and you know anyone is free to speak up.'

'Well, sir, if it was just the regular team ...'

Steve left it hanging. Ted understood. Charlie Eccles was not one to hold his tongue if he disagreed with something. He could produce a masterful sneer. Ted could easily see how the younger DC might be intimidated by him.

'I'm perfectly open to any suggestions right now, Steve. We've got nothing much to go on and your instincts are usually good. So let's hear it.'

'It's still the lack of any contact between any of them that's bothering me. They all seem to have been close and suddenly there's no communication at all, certainly not with Callum from what I can find so far. Of course, we've not had sight of laptops and phones from the others yet but I've gone through Callum's with a fine-tooth comb now and there just isn't anything. And I'm not buying that.

'There are several possibilities, of course. They have a regular meeting place, day and time, which they all know so they don't need to communicate. They're using cyber-cafes to access web-mail that we know nothing about. Or … and you'll see why I didn't want to say this in public, sir …'

Again the hesitation. This was clearly going to be something outside Steve's field of expertise, in which he was becoming increasingly confident.

Then he plunged on, 'What if they're doing it the old-fashioned way, sir? I don't mean letters, through the post. They could be traced. But I used to read old retro comics and adventure books when I was younger. Spies, that sort of stuff. What if they're using a drop somewhere? A cache, where they can leave one another written notes so nobody else knows they're in contact.'

Ted was trying to keep his expression neutral. It was starting to sound a bit Scooby-Doo to him. Steve sensed his scepticism and hurried on, 'These are tech-savvy young lads, sir. They know perfectly well how easy it is to trace emails and phone messages. They'll know about things like CCTV if they meet up in public places. So perhaps they have a cache. Maybe at their old sports ground, somewhere like that.'

Ted measured his words carefully. He was always sensitive about not discouraging any of his team, and not Steve in particular.

'Anything's a possibility, Steve. And I agree with you about the apparent lack of contact. I'm just not buying the idea of them never being in touch. I've no idea how we would begin to find out something like you suggested, though. I'll certainly keep it in mind, but let's for now concentrate on the material things we can check. Starting with that CCTV from the bus. Thanks for mentioning it, though.'

He hoped he hadn't been too discouraging as Steve left the office. He had no time to dwell on it as his mobile rang. Harry.

'Ted, you absolute belter. Thanks so much for putting me

in touch with our mutual friend. I see that he's made a start on the delivery he promised me. If it comes off, this could be the beginning of a very exciting chain of events. The fall of the first domino.

'Tell me, though, how far do you trust him?'

'About as far as I can throw him in judo. Which is to say, not very far at all. It's always worth keeping in mind that he works for the highest bidder. He admits that, freely. Sometimes it works for the greater good, but that's not his motivation. He takes jobs. Dirty jobs. And he's never short of work because of how good he is.'

'So was it him who ...?'

'I don't think we should be discussing anything like that, and certainly not on the phone,' Ted cut in quickly.

'Understood. Sorry, I got a bit carried away. D'you have an idea about what the delivery I'm expecting is?'

'Only in outline. I've not had time to look into the details. I'm tied up on a murder enquiry.'

'I've got a meeting with said friend ...'

'Don't tell me any details,' Ted cautioned.

'I wasn't going to. I just wondered if the word 'brioche' meant anything to you in this or any other context. Our mutual friend mentioned it, rather as if I should know what he meant by it.'

'Brioche? No, means nothing to me, except that sweet bread you get in France for breakfast sometimes. Keep me posted, though. I hope it all works out. Just remember, the less said the better. Especially when you're involved with our mutual friend.'

# Chapter Nine

When Steve left Ted's office, he made it his main priority to get hold of CCTV footage from the bus whose driver thought he'd recognised Callum. He was in luck. Not only was it still available, he had his hands on it by lunchtime and was able to report as much to the boss. Ted went in search of Jo to discuss their next move.

'Clearly, we need to get one of the family to ID Callum from the footage before we go chasing off on a possible wild goose chase. I'd quite like to make it the brother, and for someone to watch his reaction to it; how he handles it. How's his alibi checking out?'

'Rob's spoken to the lad he said he was with, who's confirmed it. He couldn't find anyone in the pub where they said they met up who remembered them but it was busy, so they may not have been noticed. They both said they just had a swift drink there together then went back to the other lad's house. There was no one else in at the time so there's no independent corroboration, unless we find something on CCTV somewhere. I'm getting his phone location checked, for one thing. You don't suspect him, though, do you?'

'Not really. I just want to check him out thoroughly before we rule him out. Can you go round to see him yourself, Jo? Take the footage on your phone to show him and watch carefully how he responds. You can make the excuse of not wanting to upset the parents with it if it's not his brother.'

'Will do, boss. I'll bell you as soon as I know anything.'

Before Jo left the office, Ted mentioned Steve's suggestion

about how the football team members might be communicating.

'You know, that's not as daft an idea as it might sound. Steve's a bright lad, when he finds the courage to speak up. I suspect he's a bit intimidated with having new officers around. And he could be right with his theory. My lot have been known to do stuff like that when they're trying to keep stuff from me for some reason. Of course, they forget their old dad is a copper who didn't come down with the last shower of rain so I often find their cache. In fact, it turned into a bit of a game between us. Which of them could come up with the best hiding place.'

'Out of interest, and in case we need to start thinking along those lines, what was the winning entry?'

'We have tubular steel curtain rails in the conservatory, with finials on the ends. George, the eldest, had put his note inside there.'

'Ingenious. So you think it's possible that Steve might have a workable theory?'

'I agree with him that it's more than strange that they weren't in touch all the time. The way the timings are, it's almost as if they'd decided something at their meet-up when Callum got back. Something they were going to do together that they didn't want anyone else to know about. And certainly it was something more than helping him to move to uni.

'Is it possible that something Callum said at that meeting turned the others against him? Of course we don't yet know how much the others were in contact with each other, without applying to see their phones and computers. Could they have turned on him, for some reason?'

'You heard what Doug said. There was no evidence at the murder scene that anyone had been there other than someone who was probably heavy with larger feet than Callum. Can you get someone on to checking height, weight and foot size of everyone? I don't suppose we have that information yet, and it might be relevant.'

By early afternoon, the enquiry was starting to swing into gear. The brother confirmed that it was Callum on the bus, getting off near to Bean Leach Road. Ted sent officers to talk to all the football team members again to check for anyone they knew living out in that direction who Callum might have been visiting. PC Khan phoned in to say the parents couldn't think of anyone.

Jo reported that Sean had seemed genuinely upset to see his brother in what were clearly his last hours. But his reaction had nothing of guilt about it.

Ted was just about to pick up his phone to call the Ice Queen to discuss a further press appeal. He wanted to release the footage from the bus to see if that might jog any other memories. Hopefully, by placing him in a certain area a few hours before his death, someone might just remember having seen him there. It was strange that the person he'd been visiting hadn't been in touch before now. If they were innocent, they would usually want to clear themselves of any suspicion early on. That left the possibilities that either they had not yet heard the news or they might have been involved in the killing.

His phone rang before he could make his call. It was the Super, summoning him, and the tone of her voice didn't auger well.

Kevin Turner was already there, standing in front of her desk, arms folded, brows drawn down in a frown. The Ice Queen herself looked furious, clattering delicate bone china as she prepared coffee. Ted had no idea what it was all about but he could tell it wasn't going to be good news.

'Sit down, gentlemen,' she ordered. 'Chief Inspector, I have already told Inspector Turner the bare details, so I'll now tell you. Quite by chance, the IT department have uncovered our mole.'

Ted didn't think she was deliberately pausing for effect as

she broke off to pour coffee. He noticed the slight tremor in her hands and realised she was in need of it. No doubt he soon would be too.

'There was a problem with Sergeant Wheeler's computer. IT were working on it. In the process, they discovered he was using it to access online gambling sites. It appears, from the sums of money involved, that he has quite a serious addiction.'

'Mickey Wheeler?' Ted asked in amazement. 'I had no idea.'

'Nor had anyone, it seems. And as a result of the amount of financial difficulty his habit had got him into, he was regularly selling any information which came his way to the highest bidder. It wasn't enough to clear his considerable debts, but it was at least small change to continue to fuel his playing. But I'm afraid there's much worse to come.'

Ted gazed from one to another or them, half hoping it was all some inappropriate joke gone too far. He was dreading what she was about to say next. Inevitably, given some of the recent cases he'd been working on, his mind when straight to child pornography.

'He had saved log-in details for a web mail account. In the circumstances, authority was sought and given to access it. Emails were found between Sergeant Wheeler and Superintendent Baker's daughter, Rosalie.'

'Well, that's understandable. He's her godfather. Unless there was anything inappropriate about them ...'

'It's the datelines which are inappropriate. They show, beyond a shadow of doubt, that he was in contact with Rosalie while she was missing. While there was an ongoing police investigation into her as a Missing Person. A costly and protracted operation which you yourself led for many years.'

Ted was speechless, trying to process what he'd just been told. No wonder the Super had felt in need of coffee. He reached for his own and took a swallow while he collected his thoughts.

'It goes without saying that all of this is confidential for the moment. Wheeler has been suspended with immediate effect while further investigations take place. He might just have got away with the gambling indiscretions. Possibly even the leaks, in view of his previously good record. A disciplinary, a warning. But it's hard to see how he could come back from withholding such information in a case like that.'

'How could he do that to Jim, though?' Ted was still having difficulty getting his head round it all. 'He knew what he was going through, all those years. We all did. He was supposed to be his friend. He was going to his house, going out together with him, the four of them, with the wives. How in god's name could he not just tell him she was alive and safe, to put him out of his misery?'

Kevin Turner was shaking his head, in between gulping his coffee.

'I'm having difficulty with that, too. Everybody in the nick at the time knew how much the Big Boss was suffering, with no news of Rosalie. I thought I knew Mickey. I've been out in a foursome with him and our two wives as well. He was always the life and soul of the party. Always put his hand in his pocket to stand a round when it was his turn. I'd no idea of what he was really like.'

'I'm afraid, Chief Inspector, that things are about to get even more difficult for you. Superintendent Baker knows nothing of this yet. Clearly someone needs to tell him, and as you are a close friend of his, I think it should be you.'

Ted had had a feeling she was about to say that. It made sense. He'd been friends with Jim a long time. Not as long as Mickey Wheeler. He dreaded to think what the news was going to do to the Big Boss, whoever broke it to him.

'And it goes without saying that you need to tell him in person. This is not something he should hear over the phone. It also needs to be done as soon as possible. We've outed the mole, at last, but you both know as well as I do that this place is a rumour mill. It won't be long before tongues wag about Wheeler's absence.'

Her dropping the sergeant's rank now when she referred to him was a strong measure of her anger and contempt at the whole thing. Ted instinctively knew it was going to be as nothing compared to how Jim Baker would react to the news. He voiced his feelings.

'Jim is going to go ape. He's going to want to kill Mickey.'

'Which is why I'm counting on you to break the news and to impress upon him that he must stay well out of Wheeler's way and let things run their proper course. There will be a rigorous internal enquiry, of course. Disciplinary proceedings. At this stage, I can't rule out the possibility of prosecution relating to withholding evidence. Please assure Superintendent Baker of that.

'So I would suggest you go and see him as soon as you can, if he's free. Are you at a point of the enquiry where you can delegate?'

'I was just coming to see you about releasing CCTV of Callum on a bus, to see if we can pin down more accurately where he was going.'

'Brief your DI and tell him to come and discuss it with me. That's what he's there for. It's imperative you break the news to Superintendent Baker in person as soon as possible.'

Ted went back to his own office before he took his phone out to call Jim. He had no idea what he was going to say, or how he was going to manage the situation. He was stunned himself by the revelations. He dreaded to think how Jim would react.

The Big Boss was at his desk for the afternoon, he discovered. He made what he hoped was a plausible excuse for going over in person to discuss developments in the Callum Mitchell case. If Jim was surprised that he didn't just brief him by phone or video link, he didn't show it. He sounded glad of an excuse to break off from paperwork and he looked pleased at the interruption when Ted got there.

Ted shook his head at the offer of coffee. This situation was going to be hard enough to handle without having to struggle through some of Jim's idea of what coffee should taste like.

'You've got a bit of a lead at least, then, have you?'

'A possible. But before we talk about that, there's something I need to tell you, Jim.'

He laid out the facts as clearly as he could, watching Jim's face darken in anger as he listened to the extent of the betrayal. When Ted had finished, the Big Boss sat for a moment, one large hand gripping his mug until his knuckles whitened. Then he leapt to his feet, sloshing hot black liquid all over his desk as he did so.

'I'll bloody kill him! The bastard! He knew? All those bloody years? He knew Rosie was alive and he never said a bloody thing? Wait till I get my bloody hands on him.'

Ted got quietly to his feet and stood between Jim and the door. The Big Boss towered over him and was twice as wide but Ted stood his ground. He would stop him if he had to. He just hoped it wouldn't come to that.

'You're not going near him, Jim. He'll be dealt with. If you lay a finger on him, you risk interfering with the process. And you could find yourself on a disciplinary. How would that help?'

'I don't bloody care!' Jim thundered. 'How could he do that to me? I thought he was my bloody friend. Why, Ted? Why?'

'Jim, sit down. You've had a shock. We all have. But sit down. You're not going anywhere.'

For a moment, Ted actually thought he might have to take his good friend on and he was dreading it. He'd do it if he had to, though. There was no way he was going to let him near Wheeler.

'Sit down, Jim,' he repeated firmly.

With a great sigh, which caught in the middle like a sob, the Big Boss meekly moved back to his chair and sank his bulk down onto it. He looked ready to cry. It wouldn't have been the first time he'd cried on Ted's shoulder.

Ted stayed with him long enough to feel satisfied that he was not going to do anything stupid. He listened to him ranting, trying to make sense of it all. When he judged him calm enough to leave, he drove back to his own office and picked up where he'd left off with the Mitchell case.

Jo and the Super had sorted out between them a new press release to go out with the CCTV from the bus together with a further appeal for sightings.

Maurice was still going through any names that had come up, looking for an address near to where Callum had got off the bus. So far nothing. Nor had questioning the parents or asking the same question of the other football team members shed any light on who he might have been visiting.

Ted was just getting his things together to head for home when his mobile rang. Jim Baker calling.

'Yes, Jim?' he asked in reply to the call. He didn't think their usual shared joke would be appropriate in the circumstances.

'Is that Ted?' a woman's voice he didn't immediately recognise asked. 'It's Bella here. I didn't know who else to call. I'm at the Infirmary. Manchester Royal. It's James. He collapsed at work this afternoon. A heart attack, they say. It's very serious, Ted. Could you come? Please? I've called Rosie, of course, but she's right up the other side of Windermere and she needs to sort out childcare and so on. It's going to be two hours at least and I'm afraid …

'Oh, Ted I'm so worried she might not get here in time. It's looking bad. Please can you come?'

'I'm on my way, Bella. I'll be there as soon as I can.'

# Chapter Ten

Ted paused only to stick his head round Jo's door to tell him the news and ask him to let everyone know, especially the Super. He promised to phone him as soon as there was anything further to report but said he had no idea when he'd be back.

He took his service vehicle. He thought he could justify to himself a quick blast from the blues and twos if he encountered heavy traffic. He was just anxious to get there as soon as he could.

It seemed to take forever to find a parking space, then he sprinted for the Accident and Emergency Department, waving his badge at the reception desk as he asked for any details.

'Are you a relative of Mr Baker?' the woman behind the desk asked him automatically.

'Detective Superintendent Baker,' Ted corrected her. 'He's my boss. Can you at least tell me where to find him, please?'

She consulted her computer screen. That, too, appeared to take far longer than it should have done. Ted was breathing hard, not just from his brief run, trying to control his impatience.

'Ah, yes, here it is. Mr Baker was taken up to our Acute Cardiac Centre on the first floor. If you want to go up there you can follow the signs ...'

But Ted was already on his way at a run, taking the stairs two at a time, unable to contemplate even a moment's delay for a lift to arrive.

There was a waiting area close to where he burst through

the doors. As soon as he did, Bella, who had been sitting anxiously in a chair, jumped to her feet and ran to meet him. She surprised him by rushing into his arms, sobbing on his shoulder. He held her awkwardly. He didn't know her that well but he imagined he was a case of any port in a storm.

'I'm so sorry, Ted,' she said when she'd regained some control. 'I'm just worried sick about James. They've taken him straight to theatre. He needs a heart bypass and something else I didn't understand. I only saw him very briefly and he looked dreadful. They told me his heart stopped completely in the ambulance and they only just got him back.'

Ted had been beating himself up all the way there. He was sure it was the news of Mickey Wheeler's betrayal which had brought on the heart attack. He'd gone over and over in his head how he'd delivered the news, constantly asking himself how he could have done it better. It couldn't have been unconnected.

'Come and sit down, Bella. I imagine we're in for a long wait if he's in theatre. Have you had something to drink? Do you want me to find you something?'

'Hot, sweet tea for shock?' she said with a wan smile. 'I suppose you're right. It certainly was a shock. He seemed absolutely fine when he left for work this morning. I have been nagging him to lose some weight and take a bit more exercise, but he kept insisting he was all right as he was. And he certainly seemed to be. He's not had any symptoms of anything. I know his work is stressful but ...'

'I'll go and get us a drink,' Ted said firmly, standing up. 'What would you like?'

'White coffee, please. No sugar.'

Ted didn't really want a drink, either. He just needed to buy himself some time while he decided how much it would be appropriate to tell Bella of his meeting with the Big Boss earlier on. He couldn't betray a confidence, but he would have to tell her something. He dreaded to think what her reaction would be when she learned that Rosie's behaviour towards her father had been even worse than she'd thought.

Jim had confided in Ted that Bella found it hard to forgive Rosie for what she'd put him through. Not a word, all the time she'd been missing. Not even a card to let him know she was at least alive. Jim, like any father, had simply been so thrilled when she finally reappeared that he was prepared to forgive and forget all that had happened. The sense of betrayal to hear that she had been in touch with her godfather and not him and that he'd not said a word must have cut deep. Ted wasn't sure how it would affect Bella and Rosie's relationship, when it all came out.

The coffee appeared to take a long time coming, too. It seemed the beans had to be ground first and everything prepared from scratch. It was a long way from the vending machine stuff Ted had been expecting. He took the opportunity to make some phone calls.

He called Jo first to tell him he was still waiting to hear about the Big Boss and to ask if there were any developments to report from his end.

'Maybe something and nothing. I sent Leona and Charlie to see Nigel Denby, this time. I thought it was probably best to keep Eccles working with someone experienced for now, knowing his history. Anyway, Nigel was doing his usual thing. When they asked him if he knew anyone who lived out Bean Leach way he said it might be Badger. Then he immediately did his back-pedalling trick and his version became he didn't know anyone called Badger and even if he did he was sure they didn't live there.

'He is very definitely the weakest link, boss. I've now got everyone asking all the others, including the parents and the brother, about a Badger. Nothing so far.

'So how's it going? What's the news on the Big Boss?'

'Bella's here, of course, Jim's fiancée, but Jim's in theatre and it could be some time. We're just waiting for his daughter to arrive. Apparently he arrested in the ambulance, so it's not sounding good at the moment. Are you ok with me staying on until I hear something, at least?'

'Yes, of course. Keep me posted. Oh, and I told the Super. She said the same thing. Stay until you hear something and let us all know.'

He made another quick call, to Trev, this time, warning him that he was likely to be late home.

'Oh, god, Ted, I'm so sorry to hear that. Are you all right? It must be a terrible shock for you. Do you want me to come round?'

'That's kind, thank you. But I'll be all right. Bella's here, and Rosie's on her way. I'll let you know as soon as I have any news, but it might be a long time yet. Just don't worry.'

Ted carried the cups carefully back to the Centre and handed one to Bella.

'They didn't seem to do just ordinary white coffee. It was all fancy *macchiato* and stuff so I got you a *cappuccino*. I hope that's all right?'

Again, she smiled slightly.

'Oh, James wouldn't approve of any of that fancy stuff. You know what he's like. He has to have that disgusting black brew he likes so much. Thank you, Ted.'

Ted took a sip of his hot chocolate. It was always Maurice Brown's go-to drink for circumstances like these, so it seemed appropriate.

They sat in companionable silence for a time, sipping their drinks. Ted was busily turning over in his mind what the reference to Badger might mean.

Bella appeared to be enjoying her drink. At least it was giving her something to focus on. Ted was certainly glad of the sweet comfort of his chocolate. She suddenly spoke up.

'We'll get a dog,' she said decidedly. 'James needs to take more exercise. I keep telling him. We'll get a retired greyhound. They need a lot of road walking, I believe. That would be good for him. It would mean he had to go out walking.'

'Does Jim like dogs, though? He likes his garden and flowers and things. Perhaps you could start by visiting parks and gardens together? Get him walking more that way. Or maybe try getting him dancing again. Perhaps something a bit easier than line dancing in cowboy boots, though.'

Jim's only attempt at line dancing with Bella had ended in a badly broken ankle. Ted understood what she was doing, with her talk of a dog to walk. She was painting herself a picture with Jim still in her future. Jim getting better from his current condition. But try as he might, Ted couldn't visualise Jim with a greyhound on a lead, walking it round the roads of Didsbury, carrying a poo bag in his spare hand.

Ted's mobile phone rang. Professor Nelson calling him.

'Would you excuse me, Bella, I need to take this.'

Ted stood to move away.

'Yes, of course, you know James would understand. Your work comes first. Always.'

Her words made Ted feel slightly guilty, although he knew they were not meant that way.

'Yes, Bizzie?'

'Are you out of the office? Only I emailed you and got no response.'

'Yes, sorry, I'm at MRI. Jim Baker's had a heart attack. He's in surgery now.'

'Oh, dear, I am sorry to hear that. Well, work things will wait ...'

'No, it's fine, honestly. I'd welcome some distraction, to be honest. The waiting is the worst part and they've warned us surgery might take some time. He arrested in the ambulance on the way here, and he's in theatre now.'

'Well, he's in the best possible place,' she said firmly. 'They have an excellent cardiac team there. It's rare indeed for pathologists to get a customer from them. Their success rate is very good.

'But back to your unfortunate young man. I mentioned the possibility of DNA from the thumbprint. We have successfully isolated it. Unfortunately, it's not a match for anyone currently on the database.

'I realise that of itself sounds disappointing, but it does at least mean that when you do get as far as having a suspect, they could now be matched to DNA found on the body. It would be hard to envisage a scenario they might put forward which would give an innocent explanation for that.'

Ted thanked her and went back to sit next to Bella. It seemed as if they had been waiting for hours. Ted had been surprised to see from his phone how little time had actually elapsed.

'How is the current case going?' Bella asked him.

He knew it was just something to say. Anything to pass the time. He gave her a broad outline. Then the doors burst open again and Jim's daughter hurried in. Rosalie, who always insisted on being called Rosie. Once a wayward teenager at constant war with her mother, Jim's ex-wife. Now a respectable married woman and young mother. She and her husband managed a small private hotel in the Lake District. It was where she'd been ever since her disappearance. She only got back in contact with her father once she heard he had finally thrown his two-timing wife out on her ear. And Ted now knew how she'd come by that information.

She barely acknowledged Bella but went straight to Ted, planting a brief kiss on his cheek and asking anxiously if there was any news.

'We might be in for a long wait,' he warned her. 'I can't imagine heart surgery that major is going to be all that quick. Do you want a drink?'

It was to be Ted's role for the next few hours. Fetching drinks, delivering platitudes. Making sure that Bella and Rosie were not rubbing each other up the wrong way.

Finally, swing doors at the far end of the corridor where they were sitting opened and a young woman came walking towards them. She was tall and slim, shaking long black hair free from under a scrub hat which she'd removed, then capturing it with a band into a high ponytail. She looked from one expectant face to the other.

'You're here for Mr Baker?' she asked.

She had an accent, although Ted wasn't sure what it was. Eastern European of some sort, he thought. Trev would have known instantly. Despite being tone deaf where music was concerned, he had an excellent ear for languages.

Rosie took a step forward, laying claim.

'I'm his daughter.'

Not to be outdone, Bella spoke up.

'And I'm his fiancée.'

'Well, I'm Ms Diachenko, Mr Baker's cardiac registrar. The consultant will be along to talk to you when he's free but he's been called straight to another emergency case.

'Mr Baker came through surgery reasonably well, after arresting a second time on the table. The next few hours will be critical but we are hopeful of him making a good recovery. He will need some time in hospital, however. At the moment he's on assisted breathing and is being constantly monitored.'

'Can we see him?' Rosie and Bella asked almost simultaneously, united in their anxiety for the man they both loved, in their own way.

'Not just at the moment, I'm afraid. But someone will come and tell you, as soon as it's possible.'

Bella was getting weepy again at the relief. Ted moved close enough to put a comforting arm around her, and to help her back to her seat. She clung onto his hand as she asked, 'He is going to be all right, Ted, isn't he?'

He didn't want to give her false hopes so he said, 'You know Jim. He's a stubborn old bugger.'

His words seemed to comfort her.

Ted turned to Rosie.

'I need to talk to you a minute, Rosie. Bella, are you all right waiting here for a bit? Just call my mobile if there's any more news, or if you need me.'

Ted held the door open then shepherded Rosie partway down the stairs where it would hopefully be quiet. She was looking anxiously at him.

'Is it about Daddy? Is he worse than we think? Do you know something the doctor hasn't told us?'

'I was with him earlier today. I had to give him some news which shocked him. There's a possibility it could have been a contributory factor. I haven't told Bella any of this yet and I don't want it to go any further. Do you understand me?'

She nodded warily. Ted was sounding at his most stern and policeman-like.

'Mickey Wheeler is in a lot of trouble. He's been suspended. The IT department had to get access to his computer and they found some of his emails.'

She stared at him, wide-eyed, her face draining of colour. She clearly knew exactly what Ted was talking about.

'Rosie, how could you? I tried to understand why you put him through what you did. I know it's hard. The longer you stay away, the harder it is to get back in touch. But how could you do this? To stay in contact with Mickey all the time and not let him at least tell your dad you were still alive.'

'Because I'm a selfish bitch! A silly, spoilt child.'

Her eyes were filling with tears as she spoke, streaking her cheeks with mascara.

'Because I expected him to choose me over my mother. To tell her to pack her bags and get out much sooner than he did. Then I'd come back. I was just waiting to hear the word from Uncle Mickey. Will he get into trouble because of me?'

'He's in very serious trouble. He will very likely lose his job and there's a chance it might be worse than that. He could go to prison. You only escaped a charge of wasting police time yourself because of who your dad is. And now your dad knows the extent of Mickey's betrayal … I'm not saying that's what caused his heart attack, but it certainly can't have helped. He was so angry when I told him I nearly had to physically restrain him. It must have put his blood pressure up dangerously high.'

Rosie was crying now, her head down, looking wretched.

'I'm so, so sorry, Ted. I never meant it to go as far as it did. Honestly I didn't.'

'Let's just hope you get a chance to put it right with your dad.'

It was gone midnight when they got the news that Big Jim's condition had stabilised and he was doing as well as could be expected. Bella and Rosie were allowed to see him briefly. Ted took the opportunity to head for home, reminding them both that he was only a phone call away.

Trev and the cats were snoozing in front of the television when Ted let himself in quietly. He leaned over the back of the sofa to kiss his partner, which woke him up.

'Hey, you, how's Jim?'

'Stable, they say, whatever that means.'

Ted sank wearily down next to him. The anxiety had taken it out of him.

'Are you hungry? D'you want me to make you something?'

Ted shook his head.

'I've been mainlining on hot chocolate, thanks, so I've no room for food. I'm not hungry now, really. You might be able to help me with a couple of things, though. Otherwise they'll keep me awake all night. You're good at cryptic clues. They may not mean anything, but they might be relevant to a couple of current cases.

'What does "*brioche*" mean to you?'

Trev stretched languidly.

'Mmmm, holidays under the French sunshine. A leisurely morning stroll to the *boulangerie* for the daily bread. Still-warm *brioche* smothered in unsalted butter and dripping in honey. Are you taking me on a holiday?'

'I should really. It's about time I treated you again. But anything else?'

'Well, you could say that *"qu'ils mangent de la brioche"* had a connection to the French Revolution. The loose translation is "let them eat cake", supposedly said by Marie Antoinette, although that's unlikely. It came to symbolise the artistocracy's total ignorance of the plight of peasants during famine so it's come to have a pro-revolutionary meaning.'

'And what about badger?'

'Britain's largest carnivore. A shy, nocturnal creature, persecuted in the belief it spreads bovine TB, a theory which is hotly disputed. How am I doing? Have I won a prize yet?'

'Not quite. What else about badgers?'

'Black and white, of course. So could they be a symbol of something. A sports team which wears black and white? You know I know probably less about football than you do but it's a quick Google search to find if any teams wear those colours and have that nickname.'

Ted stood up and took his partner by the arm.

'That will keep until tomorrow. Now you have won that prize and if you come with me, I'll be happy to deliver it in person.'

# Chapter Eleven

'First things first. The Big Boss is doing a bit better but he's not out of the woods yet, not by a long chalk,' Ted told his team members before he began the morning briefing.

Maurice Brown had known Jim Baker longer than any of them. It was he who asked, 'Should we send him something? Flowers, maybe? A card or something?'

'I don't think flowers are allowed on the unit he's on. A card, maybe, when he's a bit better. I don't think he's aware of very much at the moment. Nice thought, Maurice, thanks.

'Right, back to the case. I had time on my hands waiting for news yesterday so I was thinking about the mysterious Badger. I asked Trev if he had any ideas as he's good at the word association stuff and cryptic clues. He suggested it might be a nickname for someone from a sports team where they wear black and white. So, next question? What colour is the football team's strip? And the lacrosse team, come to that?'

Steve's fingers were flying over his keyboard as soon as the boss posed the question.

'Blue and gold, the football team, sir. I can't at the moment find a photo for the lacrosse one but I'll keep looking.'

'Good, thanks Steve. So not team colours, as far as we know for now. What else could Badger stand for?'

'Something to do with nature?' Jezza suggested. 'I think I've seen a badger as a logo for something like that. I'll look into it.'

'Thanks, Jezza. See if you can find if there's a local branch of whatever it is. They won't want to give you details of membership, no doubt, but see if they would at least confirm if they have any members in the right area. Then we could apply for the authority to look at their records for an exact address.

'What else? Could the name be connected in any way with Callum's work in France? What's French for badger?'

'*Blaireau,*' Jezza and Jo said simultaneously.

Jo laughed.

'My kids are bilingual English/Spanish and the older two are learning French. We often have discussions on the similarities between languages. But it's *tejón* in Spanish.'

'Boss, the lovely lot of fascist thugs I've been looking into. I wouldn't be surprised if some of them were into badger-baiting. They seem to be a right load of charmers. It could be a nickname for anyone with an interest in badgers and that could be for good reasons or otherwise,' Maurice put in.

'That's a very good point, Maurice. Rob, can you ask your Sally if there's much of a problem with that kind of thing on our patch. I suppose we still have badgers round here, do we? There may even be some up in those woods where Callum was found. Can you ask her that too, please, Rob.'

Rob's fiancée Sally was an RSPCA inspector who had worked with them before on cases.

'I've heard from the Professor that the killer's DNA doesn't match anything that's on record, so that's one possible lead down the drain. We're back to relying on legwork again. Has anyone turned up anything else at all of any use? How are we getting on with known contacts? Have we made a start on the lacrosse lot yet?'

'We're going to have to do phone calls rather than face-to-face for some of them, at least initially, boss,' Jo told him. 'There's so many to get through. Not just team members for both sports but club officials and so on. And families, bearing in mind what Jezza said about pushy parents. It's an extreme theory but I think we should keep it in mind.'

'All right, phone calls to start. But I want the others, the football team ones, seen in person each time. I just have a feeling they're giving us the run-around and they know more than they're saying. Which is why we need to see them in person and watch carefully for reactions.'

'On that subject, boss, can I just say again that Charlie and I agree with everything that's been said about Nigel. He's so eager to please it would be easy to get him to say anything, but I doubt if anything he said would be all that reliable,' Leona Rakale put in.

'But he did bring up the name Badger voluntarily, which was the first we'd heard of it. Although he went back on it afterwards, my feelings were that whoever it is, it's someone he knows, so there's a good chance the others know who it is, too. Even if they've all denied it so far.'

Steve clearly wanted to say something else but was looking ill at ease. Ted sensed he was uncomfortable in front of DC Eccles in particular. He had a go at feeding him the right line to get him started.

'Anything further from Callum's phone or laptop, Steve?'

'I'm still working on the laptop, sir, going through all the email history, and there's a lot of it. I'll print off anything relevant. Océane's still working on the phone. There were a lot of calls between Callum and Antoine all the time he was away, up until the fault developed.'

Ted was frowning, something niggling at the back of his brain.

'I still have a feeling the death of this lad Páraic is somehow connected. Callum was in Calais in September last year when it happened, presumably? So someone would have let him know, I imagine. Can you concentrate on that date and the days after it for now, please, Steve? And ask Océane to look at the phone around the same time for who he was talking to. I want to know when he found out about Páraic and who told him.

'If we're no further forward by the day of this benefit

match, we need to be on high alert there, looking for anything in case the two incidents are linked in some way. And I want as many of you as possible there, with your eyes peeled. Mike, can you sort rotas for the weekend to cover that.

'How are things going at the scene? Any update from Doug and his team? And what about foot size and weight of the various team members?'

'Doug called yesterday while you were out, boss,' Jo told him. 'He thinks they've done all they can there and it's not been much, unfortunately, because of the delay. And Mike is collating information on feet and weight.'

'Nearly done, boss, you'll have it very shortly.'

'Good, thank you. Because I don't need to remind you all, I'm sure, that we're a week into this case with precious little to show for it. I'm going to start getting jumped on for some results.'

It was likely to happen sooner rather than later, Ted knew. He'd spoken to both Kevin Turner and the Ice Queen first thing, to update them on Jim. The Super had told him that with Big Jim out of the frame, their own Chief Superintendent had declared his intention to take an overview on the case, where Ted would normally have been answerable to Jim.

Chief Superintendent Christopher Higginbotham was the Divisional Commander, the Ice Queen's immediate boss and in charge of everything which happened within the Division. Ted didn't usually have much contact with him on a daily basis but they generally got along when they did. Ted's clean-up rate was good and his team ran well. He would still have liked to have had something a bit more concrete to be offering up, a week into the case, for his meeting with him.

The Commander's office was at the opposite side of the building to Ted's, his door fiercely guarded by a PA. She approved of Ted, though, as he was unfailingly polite.

'Good morning, Chief Inspector. I'll just let the Chief Super know you're here. He is expecting you.'

She tapped at the door, put her head round then ushered Ted in as instructed, closing the door behind him. Ted went and stood in front of the Chief Super's desk. This would not be a cosy chat over coffee.

Higginbotham finished signing the pile of letters in front of him before he looked up.

'Ah, Ted, thanks for coming. How is Jim Baker doing?'

'I think the stock phrase is "as well as can be expected", sir. He's still heavily sedated, but when I spoke to Bella this morning, she said the medical team are pleased with his progress so far.'

'Good, good. This whole bad business with Sergeant Wheeler must have come as a considerable shock to him. Now, speaking of progress, do you have any to report on your murder case? As you can imagine, there's quite some focus on it after the initial mix-up of treating it as a suicide.'

'We're following up a number of leads, sir.'

'Ted, please,' there was a mild rebuke in his voice. 'That's the sort of bullshit we feed to the press. I want to hear from you what sort of a steer you've got on this.'

Ted went over everything they had to date. It didn't amount to a lot and it sounded even more lame when he had to trot it out to his Commander.

'So you definitely think there's a link to this earlier suicide, from the same club? Are you suggesting the Mitchell boy was in some way responsible for the younger lad's death and that this is a revenge killing?'

'I think a connection is likely, sir. Otherwise it's a big coincidence and I'm not keen on those. As for whether Callum was implicated in that death, from what we know of him to date, I'd say it was unlikely, but I'm not yet ruling anything out.'

'And you're gambling on that link by wanting all hands on deck to attend the match? That's a chunk of the budget potentially gone on watching a game of football if you're wrong, Ted. Are you sure you want to take that risk?'

'We may get there with the Badger angle before Saturday, sir, in which case we may be able to scale down the numbers needed at the match. I still think it's more likely than not that there is a connection between the two deaths and that the link centres round the club.'

'Well, you often have a good nose for these things so I'm happy to go with it for now. Keep me posted on it. And let me know how Jim's getting on. If you get to see him and he's communicating, give him my best wishes. It's likely Mickey Wheeler will be hung out to dry for what he did, at the very least. Although that's not much consolation to Jim.'

Ted wanted some time on his computer before he went any further with the Mitchell case. He hadn't heard any more from either Mr Green or Harry and he wanted to find out what was being said online about the prisoner who had been snatched. He'd already looked up details and discovered that a whistle-blower had come forward some time earlier claiming to be able to name names as high as the Cabinet in connection with historical allegations of child sexual abuse.

Details were sketchy but at some point the woman had allegedly assaulted a police officer who had been questioning her and had immediately been arrested and remanded in custody.

Trev mentioning the revolutionary connection with the word '*brioche*', which Harry said Green had used like a code word, had set Ted thinking. Any group with ideas of revolution would have a powerful weapon in holding a witness with potential powers to bring down a government. What Ted had no way of knowing was whether Green's role in springing her had been to enable her to testify, or to prevent her from doing so. The fact that he'd initially made contact with Harry was encouraging, but Ted knew from experience that with Mr Green, anything was possible.

Ted had asked for a further get-together at the end of the

day, desperately hoping for some scrap of progress. Despite the team's best efforts, there was still nothing concrete to show for their work. PC Khan had come over to join them, to give an update on her discussions with the parents.

'I asked them both at length about anyone known as Badger, sir. Sean came home at dinnertime, too, so I was able to ask him as well. None of them could think of anyone who might have that nickname. Callum wasn't particularly into wildlife or anything like that. They weren't aware of any sports team he might follow with that as a nickname either.'

'No Badger connection at Durham either, boss,' Jezza told him. 'I thought I'd check that out, as that's where Callum was going. I phoned to see if any of their football teams or lacrosse teams had that nickname, or even if any of them have a black and white strip. Big fat no all round.'

'All right, don't make the Badger angle too much of a high priority, in that case. Ask anyone you talk to if it means anything to them but no more than that for now. Let's see if tomorrow brings us anything more.'

Ted was getting a lift home from Mike Hallam as soon as they'd both finished clearing their desks for the day. He'd left Trev the car so he could go and collect Ted's mother Annie from the station. She'd come up from Wales to sign the final contract on her house. Trev would drive her home at the weekend and Ted had hoped to be going with them. That was looking like a total impossibility now, the way the case was going. He had yet to tell Trev that news.

Annie's train should have been in at ten to five and Trev was there waiting. It was more than half an hour late when it finally came rumbling to a halt alongside the platform. Trev looked along its length then spotted Ted's mother stepping out, glancing about anxiously to see if someone was still waiting for her.

Trev gave a delighted shout and raced along the platform to

greet her, smothering her in a big hug and nearly lifting her off her feet. He genuinely loved his mother-in-law who had been much more of a mother to him in the comparatively short time since he'd known her than his own, a cold and distant woman, had been in the fifteen years she'd been in his life.

'Ted has promised faithfully to try to get back early enough to eat with us, but nothing is ever guaranteed with his job,' Trev told her as he showed her into the house. 'I'll take your bags up for you then put the kettle on. Go on in and sit down. Oh, and meet Adam, the newest addition.'

He picked up a small kitten to show her. Annie was a big cat lover. But even Adam's breeder had described the kitten as an ugly little bugger. He'd come out all wrong, despite an impressive pedigree, but Trev loved him nonetheless.

'Oh, *bechod*!' Annie exclaimed, taking the funny little creature from him and cradling it in her arms, immediately rewarded with ecstatic purring. '*Wel, am hyll*. What a funny *twt* you are, Adam.'

'He's not ugly,' Trev protested. He was learning Welsh as rapidly as he picked up any other language. 'I think he's adorable.'

When the two of them were sitting cosily together on the sofa, drinking their tea, Annie said, 'It must be hard for you, with Teddy's job. Never knowing when you'll see him. Hard to make plans for anything, I imagine?'

'Impossible! Serves me right for marrying a policeman. It's a good job I love him to bits.'

'You do, don't you?' she smiled. 'Anyone can see that. And I know he adores you.'

'I know people think we're a strange match. And that I'm a self-seeking hedonist who'll finish up dumping him and breaking his heart. But I won't, you know. I promise you that, Annie. I may be many things but I'm not stupid. I've never met anyone who loves me like Ted does and that's a very powerful thing.'

'Tell me more about when you two first met.'

She loved listening to Trev talk about her son. He'd known him for longer than she had. She felt she'd got to know Ted much better from listening to his partner.

'I'd never met anyone like him before. He was my *sensei* at the judo club. My teacher. He's a brilliant teacher. And he was so funny. I could tell straight away he fancied the pants off me. His tongue was practically hanging out every time he looked at me or tried to say anything to me. But he was so serious, so professional.

'I'd always been a bit of a wanton child. Promiscuous, but not stupid. Ted knows all this. We have no secrets. He was different to anyone I'd ever met before. I had to make all the running. It was me who asked him out first. And even then he was so old-fashioned and correct. He actually courted me. Seriously. I'd never met anyone like him. He made me feel special. Makes. Still does.

'And he's an incredible lover.'

He saw her go pink and hugged her close, laughing.

'Sorry, I didn't mean to embarrass you. I don't just mean sex, although that's really good. No cause for complaint on that score. He's so attentive and considerate. He always puts me first, like giving up Firearms to be with me. First over everything. Except work. But I've learned to accept that. I know he always comes back to me, when he can. Always will. And speak of the devil, that's him now.'

They both heard the key in the door, then Ted came into the room, bending over the back of the sofa to kiss each in turn.

'Hey, you, are your ears burning? I was just embarrassing your mother telling her all about how we first met. But now you're back, you sit here and talk to Annie and I'll go and get the supper ready.'

# Chapter Twelve

'I was just going to bring you a cup of tea in bed, mam,' Ted told his mother as she came into the kitchen and he handed her a mug. 'Do you want something to eat? I'm making toast, if you want some.'

She was still in her dressing gown but looked wide awake. There was neither sight nor sound of Trev. He was seldom up and about before Ted left for work, unless he had somewhere other than his day job to be.

'Thanks, *bach*, for the tea. I'll wait for Trev before I have my breakfast.'

'I'm really sorry I can't come with you to the solicitor's today. I had intended to. It's just this latest case ...'

'Oh, don't worry about that, *bach*, I understand. Your job's important. Your dad would have been so proud to see how well you've done.'

'I'm not going to be able to come with you at the weekend either, and I was looking forward to it. I haven't told Trev yet and he's not going to be pleased. Goodness knows why he puts up with me. I'm always having to let him down at the last minute.'

'Because he loves you, Teddy,' she told him simply. 'We had a lovely talk yesterday and he was telling me all about why he loves you.'

'I can't imagine why he does, and I'd love to hear that sometime. But right now, I have to run. I hope it all goes well, mam, and I'm sorry again I can't be there. I'll do my best to get back in time to eat with you both tonight. I'd love to take you both out for a meal before you go back, but we'll just have to see how the week goes.'

Ted was relying on Mike Hallam for lifts again as Trev would need the car. He didn't dare bring his service vehicle home unless he had no alternative. There was no room for it in the garage with Trev's Triumph Bonneville bike in there and Ted didn't give much for its chances if he left it outside. Offerton had changed a lot since he'd first moved there as a small boy. Car crime in particular was high. The vehicle had good anti-theft devices but it wouldn't stop it being the target of an attempt, or even a random act of vandalism.

Mike was turning the car round as Ted came out of the house, still munching his toast. He licked the butter and honey off his fingers and brushed crumbs from his clothing before he got into the passenger seat.

'Thanks for this, Mike. I should be independently mobile again after today, except for the weekend.'

He made use of the journey time to phone Bella for an update on Jim.

'He's doing a bit better, I think, Ted. They seem pleased with his progress but he's not really very with it yet.'

'Tell him I was asking after him. Don't give him my love, it would only embarrass him. And please let me know when I can see him, even if it's only for five minutes.'

Ted desperately wished he had something more constructive to tell both the Ice Queen and the Chief Super over the next three days other than admitting each day that there were no new developments. He knew he was probably setting too much store by the upcoming football match. He couldn't shake off the idea that if the two deaths, those of Callum and Páraic, were linked, the match might give them some valuable insight into the case.

In the end, thinking of balancing his budget and not wasting too many personnel hours if they led to nothing, he decided he would go to the match himself, with Mike Hallam as he would need the lift. Jo said he was happy to go without logging the hours, if it helped. His three sons were all interested enough in sports to be happy to tag along. Besides which, they would be thrilled at the idea of being in on a case with their father, even if only to provide him with cover.

Mike had put Charlie Eccles on the rota to be there, together with Maurice Brown. Ted said he didn't want too many people hanging around looking like so many coppers. He thought they might find out more by keeping a slightly lower profile, which was why Jo being with his sons was the perfect solution. Just another dad with sports-mad boys watching a football match together.

The match on Saturday wasn't until after lunch but Ted still wanted to be in the office first thing. He had breakfast with his mother, promised faithfully to find time to visit her in Wales before much longer, then went outside to meet Mike for his lift in. He intended to spend the morning going over all the witness statements which had been taken so far, desperate to find anything at all he might have missed.

Ted and Mike arrived at the club's playing fields about half an hour before the start of the match. Ted wanted the chance to have a quiet word with the chairman of the club, who was organising the event. He didn't want to spread alarm by hinting at a connection between the two deaths, but he did want to identify as many people as possible who were involved in the club in any way.

Ted and Mike were there first, but Jo's car pulled up next to them moments later. He got out, with three boys, all unmistakably his sons, with the same looks.

'Boss, these are some of my brood. George, the eldest, this one's Carlos and the second youngest of all six is this one, Mateo. Boys, this is my boss, Mr Darling, and this is Sergeant Hallam. Right, here's some money to buy refreshments, you go off and do your own thing and be back at the car when the match ends. Got it?'

'Refreshments van. That's something else to add to our list,' Ted told the others, as the three boys went off happily with the money Jo had given them. 'Is there a regular catering van that goes to matches?'

'I highly doubt they have anything as grand as that most of the time. If there is food, and I heard there would be today, I imagine it's probably usually just some of the parents, or the club officials, doing something out of the back of a car. But maybe as this is a special day, they might have got a burger van or something to come.'

More cars were starting to pull into the car park now. Ted saw a familiar figure get out of one and start walking in his direction. He groaned.

'The local press,' he said. 'I don't want it known we're here mob-handed. Split up, mingle, keep your ears open and see what you can find out. And where's DC Eccles? He'd better not be late.'

Penny Hunter was on the timid side for a journalist. Nothing like as pushy as her predecessor had been. She still managed to write some good articles. People seemed willing to talk to her, probably because she was so quiet. Ted found the same thing himself.

'Hello, Chief Inspector,' she greeted him. 'I'm surprised to see you here. Are you involved in some sort of enquiry involving the club?'

'Hello, Penny. No, not really, just here to pay my respects,' Ted told her evasively.

'But your latest murder victim played for this club too, didn't he? The same as the suicide case we're here for today. Is there a link between the two?'

'No comment, Penny. Really. If I had anything I could tell you, I would, honestly.'

She was a lot less tenacious than Pocket Billiards had been. She seemed to accept Ted's words, where he wouldn't have done so, and went meekly on her way.

There was a man sitting next to a small, folding table at the entrance to the playing fields. People going through appeared to be paying him. Ted went across to speak to him. It was a damp and dismal day and the man was wearing a black waterproof jacket with a matching waxed hat, the brim of which kept dripping onto his paperwork.

Ted produced his warrant card and introduced himself.

'This is all perfectly legal, you know. We have permission to take donations in Páraic's memory, to get new kit for the younger team players.'

'It's fine, there's no worries. I'm just here to pay my respects,' Ted repeated his cover story as he put his badge away. 'Does the club have a chairman or someone like that I could talk to, please?'

The man turned and looked behind him towards the playing area. A large black estate car was parked closed to the pitch, its tailgate up. A man was busying himself getting things out.

'Des is over there, by the car. Des Clarke. He's our club chairman. I'm the treasurer. Bill Batley.'

Ted thanked him and walked over to the car. The open door was giving the man some cover from the light drizzle. He was busily changing his footwear and rummaging for a coat to put over the black and white striped football shirt he was wearing. Ted knew little about football but when the man turned, in response to his greeting, he could see that the badge on the shirt said Newcastle United.

'Mr Clarke? I'm Detective Chief Inspector Darling,' Ted again produced his warrant card. 'I'm the Senior Investigating Officer on the enquiry into the death of Callum Mitchell. It must be a doubly sad day for your club today, remembering two young former players.'

'A bad business. A very bad business,' the man agreed, pulling on his coat as he spoke. 'Are you saying there was some connection between the deaths?'

'No, not at all. We have no evidence to suggest that at the

moment. Simply a tragic coincidence. Can you tell me what the plan is for today?'

Clarke had pulled a black armband out of the pocket of his jacket and was fumbling to slide it on over the bulky sleeve.

'Allow me, Mr Clarke.'

Ted skilfully manoeuvred it into place for him.

'Thank you, Inspector.'

Ted was looking round the playing field. Quite a lot of people were arriving and taking their places already. He could see that there was a catering van over on the far side of the pitch. A St John Ambulance vehicle was just arriving and trundling its way slowly and carefully to find a prime site to park.

'Are you expecting a big turnout today? You seem to be set up for a decent crowd.'

'This is a great club. One big family. If anything happens to one of our members, we all rally round. Both Páraic and Callum were popular players. A lot of people will want to come and pay their respects. As for the plan, once most people are in place, I'm going to be saying a few words. Of course, it was all going to be about Páraic and our plans to do something in his memory, followed by a minute's silence. Now I'll speak about both of them and extend the silence to two minutes.

'After that, two of our teams will play matches against two different visiting clubs, which is why we should have a good turnout. The Under-17s and the Under-15s are playing, as both Callum and Páraic played for those teams.

'Now if you'll excuse me, Inspector, I need to go and make sure I have a working PA system so everyone can hear what I'm saying.'

Ted easily spotted the tall figure of Mike Hallam on the other side of the pitch and made his way over to him.

'Do you know much about football, Mike?'

'Probably no more than you do, boss. Try me.'

'I've just been speaking to the chairman. He was wearing a

Newcastle United shirt. Black and white stripes. I don't suppose, by any stroke of luck, they're known as the Badgers, are they?'

'Ask Maurice.'

'Is he into football?'

'I don't know. But he's a Geordie, first and foremost. Anyone from the Toon is bound to know that. Just like anyone from Stockport would know what colours County play in.'

Ted grinned at him guiltily and said, 'I bet you don't know that either. I think it's blue, but I've no idea what shade.'

'Ah, but I'm not from Stockport, boss. I know United wear red, but that's about the extent of my knowledge.'

'Have you seen Maurice around? And where's Charlie?'

'It's damp and chilly, boss. I'll bet you any money Maurice headed straight for the queue for a hot chocolate. And Charlie's over there, talking to people.'

Ted was just about to walk over in the direction of the refreshment van when Mike looked towards the entrance from the car park and said, 'Well, that all looks a bit stage-managed. Those are Callum's team-mates. That's ...'

Ted was looking in the same direction now and interrupted him.

'Don't tell me who's who. Let me see if I can work some of them out.'

Eleven young men were marching onto the playing area in twos, with one black youth in front of them. All wore black arm bands, their expressions solemn. They had on dark blue pre-match track suits. There was something military, almost menacing about the way they strode in. It reminded Ted of a film he'd watched with Trev. *Lord of the Flies*. Choirboys in their gowns, marching along a beach chanting the *Kyrie*. The spectacle was somehow sinister.

'Antoine in front, obviously. Team captain. Boss of the lot of them, both on the field and off. The other two black lads flanking him must be Jerome and Sammy, but I don't know which is which. And Nigel at the back, on the left. Am I right?'

'Spot on, boss. Nigel bringing up the rear like a puppy, so proud to be out with the big boys for a change. Watching what they all do and making sure he does exactly the same thing. Nigel. The weakest link.'

Mike was right about Maurice. Ted found him in the queue at the food outlet. He was at the back, so Ted stood next to him.

'Newcastle football team, Maurice. What's their nickname?'

'Magpies, boss. And the supporters are the Toon Army. Why?'

'I'm still looking for a Badger connection, and the chairman was wearing a Newcastle shirt. Black and white, of course.'

'Well, what about him, then?'

Maurice nodded towards the man in the catering vehicle, who was wearing a chef's skull cap in a big black and white check above his black tunic.

'Maybe they call him Badger, because of his hat,' Maurice suggested.

'Or maybe I'm just getting fixated on a Badger who has nothing to do with the case at all,' Ted sighed.

They each got a hot chocolate and a bacon barm. Trev would be away overnight so Ted wasn't planning to go home at any sort of a decent time. He thought he might as well eat something hot while he had the chance and they did smell good.

'Have you talked to anyone yet, Maurice? Found anything useful?'

'Talked to quite a few mams and dads. I've been saying I'm looking for a club for my lad, Felix, to join.'

Maurice was in a relationship with a former colleague, DC Megan Jennings, Felix's mother.

'Useful? I don't know. They all have nothing but praise for

the club so far. I asked, all innocent-like, about this Páraic having killed himself, and was it anything to do with how the club was run. No one seems to be aware of anything at the club which might have caused him to do it. So maybe we are looking in the wrong place and the club connection really is just a coincidence.'

They stood side by side at the edge of the pitch to watch as the chairman delivered his address. Callum's old team stood in a line, heads bowed, for the silence. Then the first of the matches began, with the older teams playing first.

'That complicates it even further,' Ted commented as the referee came onto the pitch. He was wearing a black strip with a white collar. 'There's another potential Badger. Did you ask anyone about a Badger?'

'Not yet, boss, I'll start doing that, if you like.'

Ted shook his head.

'I'm starting to think I'm focusing on something that has no significance. But give it a go. I'll go and talk to the treasurer again. He must know who everyone is. He might know. Then again, if it's a nickname the lads have for someone, he might not know it.'

The treasurer had abandoned his post now and was standing close to the pitch watching the match with apparent interest. Ted went and stood next to him. He wasn't interested in the game, nor knowledgeable enough to know how it was going.

'Is Badger here today?' Ted asked him conversationally.

'Badger? Who's that?' the treasurer replied, then his voice went up in volume as he said, 'Oh come on, ref. Did you not see that? Idiot.'

'Isn't one of the coaches known as Badger?'

Ted was fishing and hoped it didn't sound like it.

'News to me. Mind you, the kids often have nicknames for people that we don't know about. I believe one of the brainier, more literate ones started calling me Fagin behind my back, because I collect the money. But I've not heard of a Badger. Maybe it's one of the other clubs.'

Then he all but shouted, 'Watch him, ref! Little shit,' then he lowered his voice as he continued, 'Someone's going to get hurt if the dozy whatnot doesn't keep an eye out for fouls like that. Honestly, they should show some respect in a match like this, certainly.'

Ted tried to look as if he knew what was happening on the pitch. He didn't want to say anything which would reveal how little he really knew about the game. He was observant, though, and soon spotted one player from a visiting team whose tackles seemed to be on the aggressive side, provoking more criticism of the referee from the treasurer.

After one such hard tackle, one of the home team went down hard, clutching an ankle. Immediately a man in St John Ambulance uniform, together with two younger Brigade members, rushed onto the pitch to see to the fallen player.

'Good old Johnners,' the treasurer said. 'We don't often have them, unless it's a big tournament, but it looks like they may earn their keep today unless the ref grows a pair and sends that little shit off like he should have done the first time.'

Eventually the injured player was taken off in a carry chair, over to the ambulance where he was taken inside, presumably for further examination. A substitute player trotted onto the pitch.

Ted's attention was distracted by movement from Callum's old team. As the boy went down and the referee blew his whistle to halt play, one or two of them moved as if to go somewhere. Antoine put an arm out to stop them, leaning close to speak to them.

Clearly something significant had just happened. Ted wished he knew what it was.

# Chapter Thirteen

Ted's mobile rang as he was getting into Mike's car to go back to the station for a catch-up after the match. The display told him it was Harry calling so he answered it.

'It just so happens that I will shortly be on a train which passes through Stockport just before seven this evening. There's a scheduled stop there. I wondered if I should get off to let you know in person what I've been up to? Only our mutual friend said you might have a safe place I could spend the night.'

Ted's mind was working overtime. He didn't like to bring anything into his home which might present the slightest risk to Trev. They'd had problems before, related to the case Harry was working on and he didn't want the same, or worse, to happen again. On the other hand, he was itching to know more details. With Trev away, he thought the risk might be manageable. For once, he'd take his service vehicle home and pray the local criminal element didn't see it as a target.

'I may be a few moments late, but I'll be there,' he told Harry.

Once back at the office, Ted and the others took a few moments to catch up with any messages before getting together to discuss the afternoon's findings.

'There's a message from Rob, boss,' Jo told him. 'His Sally says there has been some trouble with badger baiting in the past, although less of it lately because their numbers are dwindling. And she said there used to be badgers out near Roman Lakes but again, not as many of them as there once were. She says that's because it got to be a popular spot for youths to go and hang out and do whatever it is they do. Usually involving drinking and probably drugs. Certainly bonfires, she said. They had to get Uniform officers to go up there a few times to move them on. Understandably, it had a detrimental effect on wildlife.'

'That's interesting. We need to know more about these goings-on. Jo, can you liaise with Inspector Turner, please, get some reports on the when and the whereabouts. There's a slim chance it could be connected with why the killer chose that particular spot for Callum.

'How did everyone get on this afternoon? Anything to report?'

'It was an expensive one for me,' Jo laughed ruefully. 'Carlos and Mateo liked what they saw of the club so much they want me to sign them up. Nothing but positive feedback from everyone I spoke to.'

'I found the same,' Maurice told them. 'It's a shame Felix is more into foxes than football. It sounds like it's a great club.'

'It might save time if we focus on any negative comments, in that case,' Ted told them. 'There must have been some, surely, on the law of averages? Did anyone have any theories about what happened to Páraic to make him take his own life, for instance?'

'I got talking to one of the dads who helps with the coaching from time to time, with the youngest players,' Charlie Eccles put it. 'He used to play a bit himself when he was younger. Once had a trial for County, so they call him Hatter to his face, although he said sometimes the kids call him the Mad Hatter if he gives them a hard time. While we were talking nicknames, I asked him about a Badger, but that meant nothing to him.'

Even Ted knew that Stockport County's nickname was The Hatters, a nod to Stockport's history of hat manufacturing.

'Anyway, he said Páraic was a really good player, talented,

dedicated. Then he got injured in a match. A bit like what happened on the pitch today. Nothing serious, but he was stretchered off by the Johnners. They were on duty as it was a big tournament day, lots of visiting clubs, loads of matches going on.

'Hatter was saying that the injury itself was something and nothing. Shouldn't have given him a problem for more than a week or three at the most. But it was like Páraic never really got over it. He became moody and withdrawn afterwards, not concentrating in training sessions. Went from star player to risking the subs' bench in a short time. And it wasn't all that long afterwards that he topped himself.'

Ted didn't like the expression, but he wasn't about to pull Charlie up on it in public. He'd done some good work. This was something interesting, new. A possible lead to follow up.

'Good work, Charlie. Talking of what happened on the pitch today, tell me what you all saw at the time of that injury.'

'Callum's old team weren't happy about that one bit,' Maurice spoke first. 'A couple of them looked like they were ready for a pitch invasion or something but that Antoine lad stopped them. He's certainly the boss of them all, still. They do what he tells them. Perhaps we should be looking at why he has such a hold on them.'

Ted nodded.

'Good point, Maurice. Exactly what I was thinking myself. So what exactly, or perhaps who, was it that upset them?'

'Dumb question, no doubt, because I know about as much as, or even less than the boss does about football,' Mike began, 'but would it always be the same referee for these matches? Could it be the lads were upset about his decisions? And might that be why Páraic was upset? He didn't feel he had the support, or the protection, of the match official when he should have done, maybe?'

'I doubt it would be the same one every time, but they

might stick to regular ones for the bigger matches,' Maurice suggested.

'Mike, add it to the list of things that need checking out, please. A full list of match officials they use. If remotely possibly, can we pin down when Páraic had that injury, or even ask someone, like the chairman, if he remembers. Then see who was likely to have been there that day.

'I'd also like all the team members spoken to again, this time about what happened today. See if they'll say what it was they were objecting to. Start by asking Antoine and Nigel. Separately, of course. Depending on what they say, we can see where to go next with that line of enquiry, if it looks like it has legs, that is.

'Right, get your notes written up before you knock off, please, but then we can call it a day. Well done, everyone. Some more ideas there, at least. Mike, I won't need a lift after all this evening, thanks. I have to pick someone up so I'll take my service vehicle.'

'Dodgy, boss,' Mike told him with a laugh. He also lived in Offerton. 'Are you sure it'll still have all its wheels on by morning? If not, phone me for a lift in.'

Ted was hoping Harry's train would be delayed as he was running slightly late as he left for the railway station and he didn't like to be late. He was in luck. Harry was just walking out of the station, carrying a holdall, as Ted got there.

'Hi again, Ted. Thanks for this, I appreciate it. Mr Green said you have something of a safe house I could perhaps use for the night.'

'It was my mother's but it's just been sold. My partner's away tonight, though, driving my mother back to Wales, so you can stay at our house. I should just warn you, we have cats.'

'I'm not much of an animal person, but I promise not to bother them if they don't bother me.'

'I'll have a word with them, but I'm afraid they don't

always listen. Now, shall we pick up a takeaway on the way back? If you want to tell me all about your meeting with Mr Green, I'm assuming you'd prefer not to do that in public. If so, what sort of food? We pass a decent Indian on the way back, if that suits you. My partner drinks wine but there may be some lager in the house. If not, there's an offy nearby we can stop at.'

'Indian is fine and a can or two would go down well. I must just say that your Mr Green is a very interesting character. And if you think Gayboy is an undesirable soubriquet, you should have heard what he called me.'

Ted laughed.

'I can well imagine. He doesn't do political correctness. And he's not my Mr Green. I've known him for a few years, been on a good few courses with him, but that's all. I've also done some one-on-one training with him, which is definitely not for the faint-hearted, I can tell you. An interesting character indeed, but not one I would ever claim to know much about. Except that he's the best there is at what he does.'

'Do you trust him?' Harry asked Ted the same question he'd asked him before. Ted's answer hadn't changed.

'Not remotely. He freely admits he works for the highest bidder and that might not always be to the common good. But he's a professional. Once he takes on a job, he always delivers. Always.'

'And sometimes it does work out for the common good?'

'Sometimes, but that's not his motivation, so it's not safe ever to assume he's working for altruistic reasons. Just hard cash. But you think he can be useful to you on this occasion?'

'The witness he has is dynamite, Ted. Pure gold. I've been up to talk to her on ...'

Ted immediately held a hand up.

'Don't tell me any of the details. It's always better that I know as little as possible. He must surely have told you that?'

'Sorry, yes, he did, you're absolutely right. I'm just excited by the potential of what we've got.'

'Here's the takeaway. Tell me what you want, I'll go in and order it. The offy is just higher up the road. See the sign? Get your drinks while I queue for the food.'

'Can I get you anything or will you have wine at the house?'

Ted shook his head firmly.

'Don't touch the stuff these days. Haven't done for a few years. It was starting to get the upper hand when I was in Firearms. You know what it can be like.'

'Oh, yes. I know, all right,' Harry told him as Ted parked by the kerb. 'My recent time in the Met was spent watching endless paedophile porn stuff. Try doing that all day and staying sober.'

When they arrived back at the house with their purchases, Ted pulled the vehicle up as close to the garage doors as he could get it. He just hoped it would be still in one piece the following morning, especially in case he got an early call-out for any reason.

He opened the door and led Harry straight through to the kitchen. Seven cats immediately came to check out the stranger. Adam, the kitten, was particularly intrigued by the visitor and at once started his trick of solemnly climbing up a trouser leg.

Harry detached him gently and lifted him up level with his face to scrutinise him.

'I thought you said you had cats, Ted. This looks more like a gremlin. What a funny little beggar it is.'

Ted carefully took the kitten from him and put him back on the floor.

'That's Adam. He's got the feline equivalent of royal genes in terms of his pedigree but he somehow came out all wrong. He must be a Friday afternoon design.'

'Speaking of royal blood and thinking of Mr Green ...' Harry began but Ted held up a hand to stop him.

'Don't even go there, Harry. Not even here, when it's just you and me. Part of the training Green delivers is to remember the need to know basis. If you don't know stuff, no one can ever force you to reveal it.

'Right, come through to the sitting room and I can lock this mob in here for now so you get some peace. I'll just go and sort out a bed for you. My mother's been staying since Tuesday but Trev will probably have stripped and remade the bed before they left this morning. I'll just check, though.'

'Seriously, Ted, anything will do. A blanket on the couch is enough. And unless your mother has fleas, I don't mind hot-bedding to save you the work.'

'It's fine, honestly. Make yourself at home. I'll just sort it out and I have a couple of phone calls to make, then we can eat in here. Put the telly on, if you like.'

Ted sprinted upstairs to sort out the sleeping arrangements. As he'd thought, Trev had already changed the bed but in his usual fashion, the washing hadn't even made it into the laundry basket. It was abandoned in an untidy heap alongside it. Ted phoned him while he was sorting things out.

'Did you get there safely?'

'Yes, no worries. Traffic was good. I'll see you sometime tomorrow but you know me, I doubt I'll be setting off early. How was your day?'

'Still going round in circles. I've got a friend staying tonight. The ex-Met officer I went down to London to meet that time. Remember? He just happened to be passing through Stockport so he asked to stay over. We've having a takeaway together.'

There was a pause, then Trev asked warily, 'Is there something funny going on, then? Only I remember what happened around the time you were involved in that case and I don't want anything like that happening again.'

'No, it's fine, don't worry. Just a couple of coppers enjoying a Madras and a few beers together. Well, Harry's drinking beer, I've got my ginger beer. Honestly, it's fine. See you tomorrow. Drive carefully.'

Next he called Bella to see how Jim was doing. Ted still hadn't been able to see him. He was too tied up on the case to get there for afternoon visiting and had been told that Jim was usually too tired by the evening to be up to visitors.

'He's improving slowly every day. But he's been asking after you, Ted,' Bella told him. 'Asking how your latest case is going.'

Ted laughed. That was so typical of Jim, worrying about work when he should have been resting and getting better.

'Tell him to keep his neb out. We're doing fine. I'll try to get in to see him early next week, tell him. And give him my best wishes.'

He went back downstairs to set the table in the sitting room and bring the food which had been keeping hot in the oven. He wanted to spare Harry the ordeal of eating in the kitchen with the cats. They were usually civilised but whenever there were strangers about they would almost always do something unsavoury involving litter trays while people were eating.

Ted enjoyed the company of other coppers and ex-coppers, even though he spent his days working alongside them. Trev was about as supportive a partner as he could have but only other officers truly understood what the job was like. He asked Harry to tell him about his potential witness.

'Honestly, Ted, she is dynamite. I spoke to her at length over a couple of days and her story never wavered. An excellent witness. I grilled her hard and she was solid the whole time. She says she was often hired as a waitress at occasions when there were children present for reasons we can both imagine. She was also expected to do more than hand round drinks, and it began when she was well under age. She gave names, dates, places, the works. Obviously, at the time, she had no idea who the people were. But as she got older and started watching the news on TV, she soon began to put names to faces.

'Ted, if we can pull this off it's the most reliable witness to these goings on who's ever come forward to date. And right now, she appears to be perfectly safe in the hands of our friend Green. It would be hard to get anywhere near where he's got her and even after just meeting him briefly, I wouldn't want to be the person charged with taking her away from him.

'I don't want to dump too much on you, and I don't want to give you details but remember I told you once I was surprised I hadn't yet finished up under a bus, digging into the stuff I have been doing? Well, this is pretty much guaranteed to see that I do. So promise me that if you hear of anything happening to me, you'll follow this up if I'm not in a position to.'

'It's all getting a bit heavy now,' Ted smiled. 'Let's hope it doesn't come to that. If you've had enough mains, I'll go and look in the fridge to see if there's a pudding of some sort. I don't know if you're an early riser or not but I'm going in to work in the morning so I'll need to get going early. I can drop you at the station on my way.'

'Fine by me. I don't sleep well anyway, especially not somewhere strange.'


Ted could hear from the running shower that Harry was up and about in good time as he was downstairs seeing to the cats and getting the kettle on. He was definitely not in the cats' good books for excluding them last night.

There was some bacon and tomatoes in the fridge, eggs in one of the cupboards. He was just getting everything out when his mobile rang.

'Morning, Ted. Kev here. Duty Inspector, for my sins. Now, I know how much you dislike coincidences so you are going to absolutely hate this news. We have another body for you. In exactly the same place as your last one was found. And – get this – found by the same poor dog-walking sod who found the last one.

'Scenes of Crime are on their way, the coroner's been informed and he's sending Professor Nelson, because this one is very definitely a murder, not suicide. Oh, and Ted? The early word from the scene is that you're going to need plenty of your little mint sweeties. It's apparently not very nice. Not nice at all.'

# Chapter Fourteen

'Harry?' Ted called up the stairs and heard the water being turned off. 'Got to go, I've got a shout. I can drop you at the station but then there's no time to offer you breakfast. Sorry, but you know how it goes.'

Harry came padding down the stairs in his bare feet, a towel wound round his waist.

'If you trust me not to turn your house over or burn it down, I could make myself a bite to eat and then call a taxi? If that's all right with you? I promise to behave.'

Ted hesitated for a second. He liked to keep his home life private. He wasn't keen on the idea of someone he didn't know well having the free run of the place while he was out. Then he silently told himself not to be unreasonable. Harry was ex-Force. He could surely trust him. He was just feeling more paranoid than usual after the disclosures about Mickey Wheeler.

'I was just sorting out the makings of a fry-up, if you could put things back in the fridge afterwards, away from marauding cats. Please don't let any of them sneak out of the front door when you go, because of the road. Just give the door a good slam and it will lock. We'll have to risk the alarm not being on for a few hours. Sorry to have to abandon you like this, but we've got another body.'

'Seriously, Ted, no worries. Thanks for putting me up. I'll leave things tidy, and I'll keep you posted. Don't forget, if anything should happen to me, I'm counting on you and Mr Green not to let things drop.'

The service vehicle still had all its wheels on, which was encouraging. Ted put his phone on hands-free and called Jo first as he backed out of the drive and headed off towards Marple.

'I was just about to call you, boss. George had a brainwave last night after the match ...'

'Can you tell me about it later, Jo? We've got a shout. Another body, in exactly the same place that Callum was found.'

Jo said something in Spanish which sounded like an oath.

'Early reports are that it's not nice, so let's excuse Mike. He can run things from the office. I'm on my way to the scene now. Can you join me and get Rob and Maurice there too for starters. I want to see the scene myself right at the beginning this time.'

The crime scene was a hive of activity already when Ted arrived. Access was down a rough track, now taped off, with officers from Uniform preventing access to anyone unauthorised. Ted parked his car behind Professor Nelson's big estate and signed in. It was wet and muddy underfoot and he was glad he'd thought to grab his walking boots and waterproof jacket before leaving home.

There was a second cordon round the area where the body had been found, now protected by a tent. A Crime Scene Investigator was standing fierce guard at the tape.

'Sorry, Doug's orders, but no one else is coming in for now, not even you,' he told Ted.

Doug had the authority to do that, as Crime Scene Manager, but Ted was desperate to get a look for himself. He felt he'd missed out on the chance with Callum to see exactly what had been going on. He didn't want the same thing happening this time.

'Can you get him for me, please? I need to speak to him.'

The CSI turned and called out, 'Doug! Chief Inspector's here and wants to see you.'

Doug ducked out from inside the tent and came over.

'Not even you, boss. Not yet. Not until we've sorted things a bit. It looks like there's been a platoon of soldiers through here already and I really don't want any more footprints to have to wade through. Not if you want us to give you something more to go on than we were able to last time.'

'I need to get a look at the body *in situ*, see what it can tell me,' Ted told him patiently, although he was champing at the bit to get on with his job.

'And you will, as soon as we can let you in. I've got some stepping plates down already but honestly, there are so many footprints in here it's going to be a hell of a job to sort it all out. None of them look very clear either, at first glance.

'Tell you what I can do, though. We're filming everything, of course. I'll get someone to take some close-ups of the body from all angles and come and show you that for now. It's not nice, though, I can tell you that for nothing.'

Ted had no choice but to stand and wait. He could see that Doug was right. The area beyond the tape was well trampled, as if by many feet. He could also see that over to the side of the tent, further back from it, were the last remaining embers of what had clearly been a bonfire. He thought again about the information from Sally, about this being a popular hang-out for youths, and wondered what had been going on. He still had no information on the identity of the body.

Eventually Doug himself came back out with his mobile in his hand.

'I took some film for you. Here you go. So far unidentified male, IC1, approximately mid-40s, we think. No ID on him, no mobile phone been found yet. The Professor is still working on him. She said she'll come and talk to you as soon as she can.

'Not a very nice one though. I'd get your sweets handy, if I was you.'

Ted had already started on the Fisherman's Friend lozenges he kept for such occasions. Doug held the phone screen towards him and pressed play.

A man's naked body was spread-eagled on the ground, face down, each wrist and ankle tethered to a wooden post driven into the ground. What looked like a gag was knotted at the back of the head. There was blood on the body from a number of what appeared to be relatively superficial slash wounds to the back. More blood was pooled between his outstretched legs.

Ted was heartily relieved he hadn't had time for a morning fry-up when he saw what looked like a metal rod or pole protruding from between the white, fleshy buttocks.

He looked up at Doug who nodded as he said, 'That's right. The Professor is saying it looks likely from her initial findings that the cause of death was impaling. To make matters worse, she thinks that metal rod might have first been heated in the bonfire over there. But clearly, she'll tell you more when she's done more of an examination.

'She's not yet had the body turned so we haven't had much of a look at the face yet but we will keep you posted. And I honestly will let you in soon as possible. It's just there's so much potential evidence this time we need to preserve as much of the scene as we can.'

Doug turned and went back to the tent, carefully stepping on the plates so as not to add to the confusion. Jo had just arrived and made his way over to where Ted was waiting, trying to be patient.

'What we got, boss? Are we not allowed in yet?'

Ted explained the situation.

'Shit! Poor bastard. What a way to go, eh? Any ID?'

'Nothing so far. Another strange coincidence; it was the same man, out walking his dog, who found this one as the last one.'

Again, Jo resorted to Spanish for what was probably an expletive. He knew the boss wasn't keen on strong language but he clearly felt the situation called for it.

'Are we sure that really is a coincidence? The dog walker's not just some sicko who kills them and then calls it in, playing the innocent, so he's got the chance to be right here, where the action is? Watching everyone running round like headless chickens because he's been too clever for us?'

'It's a possibility, for sure. Although from what Doug is saying there's been more than one person at work here. It wouldn't be the first time something like that had happened, although it's usually arsonists who like to come back to the scene. When Rob arrives, put him on to questioning the dog walker. You and Maurice have a mooch around and see if there's anyone living or working nearby who might have seen something.

'I'm particularly interested in any reports of groups of youths hanging out down here lighting fires. Can you phone Mike and get him to liaise with Kevin again about that. Any recent reports. I'll hang on here for now in the hopes of getting a look at the scene for myself. Doug's saying it looks like there's been quite a group of people over the ground, which would fit with the idea of a bunch of youths.'

'Will do, boss,' Jo told him and went on his way.

It wasn't long before Doug was back, armed with a full set of cover-alls which he handed to Ted.

'Everything on, please, mask included. Then follow me, doing a Good King Wenceslas.'

Ted was used to Doug's slightly strange sense of humour. He put on the gear then followed Doug who walked in front singing part of the Christmas carol to himself.

'Mark my footsteps, good my page. Tread thou in them boldly.'

'Ah, Chief Inspector, good morning to you,' Professor Bizzie Nelson greeted Ted, being formal in public. 'We thought you might like to take a look at our unfortunate victim before we move him. We're just getting ready to turn him over, to see what else the body can tell us.'

'Have we got close-ups of the knots he's tied with, please? And can we cut the ropes so the knots are intact? They may be significant.'

'All in hand,' Doug told him. 'We thought of that just in case there was a connection to your other lad, as they both ended their days here.'

'What can you tell me so far, Professor? Just from the body. I know I'll need to wait for the full PM, but anything at all you can give me for now would be a useful start.'

'On initial examination, the various blade wounds you can see appear to be superficial. I can't immediately see anything which would of itself have been a mortal wound. You're observant enough to notice, of course, that the unfortunate victim has been impaled rectally. Again, I can't at this moment tell you the length of the steel rod that's been used but from the amount of blood, I would say it's quite long and that it's touched one or more major organs on its passage, which is likely to be the cause of death.

'That's just on preliminary observation, of course. An entirely different picture may emerge once we turn him over, which we are just about to do.'

She had one of her mortuary assistants with her to help. He was busy spreading a sheet to turn the body on to, to preserve every available trace of evidence and to avoid contamination from the soil around. Every care was taken to remove the bindings leaving the knots intact. Then the Professor and her assistant carefully and expertly transferred the body onto its back to the waiting sheet. They could see now that the gag was inserted inside the victim's mouth, leaving much of the face clear.

Ted craned his neck for a closer look at the face, his brows drawn down in a frown.

'He looks vaguely familiar. I can't place him, but I've a feeling I've seen the face before, quite recently. Can you give me a very approximate height and weight estimate, Professor, and I'll get my team to start checking Missing Persons, see if we can find out who he is.'

Professor Nelson gave him the details which he relayed to Jo over the phone.

'The first thing you can observe is that there are no visible injuries to his front. That all of the damage done to him was inflicted with him lying face down,' she continued in her usual matter-of-fact tone. 'Any theories about that, Chief Inspector?'

'It's the most vulnerable position you can put anyone in. For a man, possibly the stuff of nightmares,' he replied. 'Pinned down like that, unable to defend himself, left him open to man's deepest, darkest fear. Which is precisely what's happened to him.'

'I really can't tell you very much more for now until the post-mortem and I can't at the moment tell you when it will be, before you ask. But certainly not today.'

'And again, not wishing to press you, but based on what you can see here, do you think he was alive when the rod was inserted?'

'Sadly, I think that is a strong possibility, judging by the rictus of his face and the degree to which his eyes are bulging. That would indicate to me extreme pain which I would not expect from what appear to be superficial wounds to his back.'

Ted sucked hard on his lozenge. He could have done with another but it would be impossible to get one out of his pocket, hampered as he was by the suit over his own clothes and his hands in gloves. He tried to think of something to take his mind off what he was seeing and hearing. At least Trev would be back home later that day. That was something to look forward to.

'And those wounds on his back are definitely all superficial? Nothing there life-threatening at first sight? And were they inflicted before or after he died?'

'Ante-mortem, most definitely, all of them, because of the bleeding. Given the presence of a fire nearby I can't yet rule out the possibility that the rod was heated up in it. You'll notice a distinct burn there on the back of one leg.'

'So first they stripped, gagged and tortured him with a series of wounds which presumably would have hurt?'

She nodded in confirmation, so Ted went on, 'Showing him what they were capable of, but not up to that point doing anything life-threatening. Until the rod appeared.'

He was looking at the position of the body, gauging its relationship to where the fire had been burning. If the man had been conscious, he would clearly have been able to see what was going on at the fire. It must have been terrifying for him, imagining what might be going to happen to him.

'Can you tell how long he would have remained conscious? Or alive, Professor?'

'It would be pointless to speculate further. I'm intending to leave the gag in place for now, until we get him back to the mortuary. The more evidence we can preserve for you, the better chance we have of giving you something to find out who has done this. There's an outside chance he may have vomited with the shock and aspirated, which would have speeded up his death.'

Ted had seen about all he needed or wanted to of the body. He asked Doug if he could look at any more of the scene. In particular, he wanted to have a look at the area where the fire had been.

'Same rule as before, boss. Grandmother's footsteps. What's the time, Mr Wolf? Whatever you want to call it. Only step where I step so we don't add any more prints to the jumble we have already.'

'Any ideas about how many people we're talking about here, Doug? Is it a lot or could it be a few trampling about to make it look like a lot?'

'I'm flattered at your opinion of my brilliance. Absolutely impossible to tell at the moment. I don't want to sound pessimistic but I don't think we're going to be able to answer that for you for a few days. Ideally, once this fire has safely gone right out, I'd like another tent over the area so we can preserve what we can. There's just one or two hot-spots still and I don't want to risk igniting a tent. The killers probably brought some sort of accelerant with them to get it going and keep it burning. Maybe even a blowtorch. We'll test the ash for any traces.'

They'd reached the fire and now stood in quiet contemplation of the scene. Doug seemed to be reading Ted's thoughts.

'From where he was pinned down and tied, he would almost certainly have been able to see what someone was doing here. Especially when they turned to walk towards him with what was presumably by then a glowing metal rod in their hands.'

'Right, Doug. You know what they say about doing the impossible today but miracles taking longer? On this one, I want the miracles today, please. Or the nearest to them you can do. It is the Sabbath, after all, if you set store by such things.'

Ted carefully retraced his steps to go in search of Jo. He was talking to Rob O'Connell who had just finished interviewing the unfortunate man who had found the second body.

'Boss, I've just asked Uniform to take him and his little dog home, and suggested they should get him some medical attention. He's in a right old state. It was the first time he's been back through these woods since he found Callum's body. He didn't want to come here again but apparently it's the dog's favourite walk, so he did today.

'When the dog ran off again, he thought it was just reacting to the scent of all the people who've been working on the crime scene. But when it refused to come back, he went in search of it and saw the body. He managed to grab the dog and make it back down here to the track before he threw up, which was something. I gather it's not a pretty sight?'

'Not at all. I think you did the right thing. Do you think he's genuine? Just the unfortunate witness he claims to be?'

'I'm fairly certain, boss. He's small, thin and frail with evident arthritis in his hands, and he's in his eighties. Even if he'd somehow managed to drug Callum, I'm finding it really hard to imagine how he could have strung him up in a tree by himself. I've not seen today's victim of course.'

'I can confirm that he's in his forties, quite big and well-built and tied down at all four corners with ropes lashed to wooden anchors in the ground. So it certainly doesn't seem likely a small, elderly man could have done all that on his own. Plus according to what Doug's found so far from the scene, we're looking for a number of suspects. He can't yet tell me how many, but several, certainly. So the next thing we need to look for is how did they all get here, and how did their victim?

'And of course, we need to know who our victim is. I've got an inkling I may have seen him before, fairly recently, but I can't for the moment put my finger on where. So let's find out.'

# Chapter Fifteen

They'd done about all they could at the scene for now so Ted called a halt and suggested they regroup at the station. With any luck, Mike Hallam might have something to report from Missing Persons, a possible match for who their victim might be.

'So far no one corresponding to the approximate height, weight and age, boss. I'm still searching. Have we got any idea of the time of death?'

'The Professor was being her usual guarded self. All she would say so far was some time last night. She'll probably have a better idea for us once she's got him back to the mortuary.'

'So that means he died on the fifteenth. The anniversary of Páraic's death. Is that significant, boss?' Rob O'Connell asked. 'Does that make it more likely that all three deaths are connected in some way?'

'Without getting ahead of ourselves, I think we have to accept the strong possibility of a connection. The same date Páraic died, the same place that Callum did. One coincidence too many, I think.

'Any signs of where vehicles might have been parked? Hopefully not the same spot we all chose or we might not find any traces. Early indications suggest there may have been a few people involved so I imagine we're looking for more than one car. Or perhaps even something like a minibus with several seats. Or maybe motorbikes, or mountain bikes. In other words, anything.'

'Bloody hell,' Maurice muttered. 'That sounds a bit sick. Bringing them in by the bus-load either to kill him or to watch him die?'

'So it could be one of the football teams?' Jo suggested, voicing what they were all thinking.

'It could be,' Ted conceded, 'but we don't want to go off on the wrong assumption.'

'Uniform are still searching the scene, boss,' Rob told him. 'There wasn't really a lot of point in me hanging around while they did it. It sounds as if there's been enough feet trampling all over everywhere without any of us adding to it.'

'And that, of course, might be the intention. Once we get feedback from the Investigators it may turn out there were fewer than we thought and they were busily trying to create the impression of lots of people involved. We need to get lucky with an ID next.'

'If he only died last night, there's a chance he won't have been reported missing yet. Especially if it's someone who lived alone,' Mike pointed out.

'I've still got this niggling feeling I've seen his face before, but I can't think where.'

'Someone from the match yesterday, boss?' Jo asked him. 'Someone you spoke to?'

Ted shook his head.

'No one I spoke to or I would have remembered him better. Just a face in a crowd, perhaps. I've got a reasonable memory for faces. I just can't put this one into context at the moment.'

'Speaking of the match,' Jo went on, 'let me tell you what young George dug up for us about Badgers. The St John Ambulance has a junior group, seven to ten-year-olds, when they're too young to join as a cadet. They're called Badgers.'

'Shit!' Ted said loudly, surprising them all. He didn't often use such language in front of them. 'That's where I've seen him before. The victim. I can't swear to it but I think he might have been the St John officer who ran onto the pitch with the two cadets when that lad was injured.'

'You mean our victim was under all our noses yesterday afternoon? Bloody hell, boss, when the press get wind of this we're in deep shit.'

Maurice voiced exactly what Ted's first thought had been. His second was how he was going to explain to the Chief Superintendent that with a DCI, a DI, a DS and a DC at the match no one had spotted anything untoward going on and the day had ended with another murder.

'So it could have been the football team who did it. Callum's team. They were all there. And they reacted to the incident on the pitch. It might not have been the ref they had a problem with so much as the first-aider.'

'We're getting ahead of ourselves again. First thing we need to do is find the name of that St John officer. Mike, you've got the list of club officials. Have a ring round and see if anyone knows his name and address. And while you're at it, see if you can find details of the lad who was injured and what happened to him. Did the ambulance need to take him for treatment? I can't say I saw what happened afterwards.'

'The match wasn't holding my attention so I did notice. When it was finishing up, Antoine and the others were having something of a discussion, then Nigel went over to the ambulance. The injured lad was just coming out. He seemed to be okay. Nigel appeared to stop and talk to the first aider for a bit.'

'Nigel? That's interesting. Once we get a definite ID on our victim, we need to talk to all the team members yet again. I think a bit more formally this time. Bring some of them in. Check alibis. Especially if the victim does turn out to be the first aider. There's clearly a good chance they know him, if it's the same one who covers a few of the matches. Another thing to check, please, Mike.'

'On it, boss.'

Ted went back to his office to tackle paperwork. He was still kicking himself that he hadn't remembered sooner where he'd seen the victim before. It didn't help a great deal but he felt he should have done.

He found a moment to phone Bella for the latest on Jim. He was doing better, she told him. Asking after Ted but insisting he quite understood if he couldn't find the time to visit. That made Ted feel even guiltier.

He'd also had a call from Trev saying he hoped to be home from Wales mid-afternoon and asking Ted when he'd be back and what he wanted to do about food.

'I don't know yet about timings. And anything that's going, food-wise,' Ted told him in reply. 'I've had a couple of sandwiches just now but that's about it. I got called out early and I was rather relieved I hadn't had breakfast before I saw the body.'

'And has your friend from the Met gone? I won't find him in the house when I get back, will I?'

'No, he's left, you're quite safe. I hope you're not talking while you drive?'

'No, officer,' Trev laughed. 'I've stopped to pick up a cup of tea and a sandwich to keep me going. I hope you're not home too late. I missed you. Laters. Love you.'

It was mid-afternoon when Ted got another call from Kevin Turner.

'Might not be relevant to you and your body at all, Ted, but we've just had a call about a possible missing person. An elderly lady was found wandering in the road in her nightie and bare feet saying she couldn't find her son. He hadn't come home to look after her.

'One of the neighbours found her and took her in then called us. Apparently the poor old dear has dementia. Her son lives with her and takes care of her. He works nights because she usually sleeps through. The neighbours hinted that he probably gives her pills at night to make sure she does sleep. But he hasn't come home today so she got worried, and probably hungry by now, I imagine. She somehow managed to let herself out of the house to go looking for him.'

'Any details of who the son is or where he works?'

'Hold your horses, just coming to that. His name's Derek Waldren and he's an ambulance driver. Lives up Shearwater Road.'

Ted let out a low groan.

'I'm sensing this is not good news, Ted.'

'It just means I've been slow on the uptake all along. If it's who I think it is, he was at the football match we were at yesterday. And Shearwater Road is right near our last sighting of Callum on the night he was killed, of course.'

'Well, unless your bloke at the match was walking round with a T-shirt saying "I'm about to be murdered" I don't see what you could possibly have done to prevent it,' Kevin told him. 'All the same, I bet you're glad it's not Pocket Billiards on the local paper when news of this leaks out.'

'It's going to be bad enough explaining it to the Chief Super. Have you got someone round at the house in Shearwater?'

Kevin sighed theatrically.

'No, I have second sight, that's how I know all this. I've got two officers there now, trying to see to the old lady and find out what they can from the neighbours. They'll also see if they can contact someone to ask at his work if the son ever turned up for his night shift last night, if he was meant to. Presumably if he did, that rules him out as your victim?'

'Yes, ours was killed sometime last night in all probability. Sorry, Kev, I'm being dozier than usual on this one, it seems. Can you see if your officers can find a photo of the missing son for us? Then we can perhaps get an ID on our body at least. And why are you still on duty? I thought you were on the overnight shift?'

'I was but Colin called in sick just as I was about to knock off. Poor bugger is genuine, too. He's got gastroenteritis or something. He was throwing up while he was trying to talk to me.'

'Were there any reports last night of youths hanging around those woods again, where the bodies were found? Especially any talk of bonfires down there? Did you send anyone out there?'

'Are you having a bloody laugh, Ted? Have you really forgotten what Uniform life is like? I didn't have enough bodies to send to live, ongoing crime, never mind some kids scaring off the bunnies and the badgers in the woods.'

'Funny you should mention badgers. It might possibly have been our victim's nickname and I think it's a name that's going to come back to haunt me a few times in this enquiry. And I suspect we might both have a bit of explaining to do to the top brass tomorrow over this.

'When do you finally get off?'

'Soon, or at least I bloody hope so or I'll be fit for nothing. I've called in the cavalry. I'll let you know if I hear anything further, and I'll make sure that whoever does finally relieve me is kept in the loop. But if I don't get some kip soon, you might be arresting me for assaulting someone.'

Kevin must have managed to get home at some point as it was the replacement Duty Inspector who called Ted just as Mike was telling him that if he wanted a lift back home, he needed to think about making a move. Ted had already filled Mike, Jo and Maurice in on all the detail he had so far.

'We've just got confirmation from the ambulance service that Derek Waldren wasn't on the rota for last night. He mostly works weekdays because he volunteers with the St John at the weekend,' the Inspector told him.

'The attending officers are just back and they've got a photo for you, from the house. One of them will bring it up now. They've been there ages trying to fix up a safe place for the mother, the poor old duck. She's completely away with the pixies. Doesn't know which way is up, just that she has a son somewhere and he should have been home from work by now to make her a cup of tea.'

'Thanks, Irene. I have a horrible feeling that she's seen the last of her son but I'll know better when I see the photo. I only saw him fleetingly at the football match yesterday but I'm pretty sure our body is the same man. From what you've told me, I don't suppose the mother would be able to identify the body?'

'Not remotely likely, I'm afraid. She couldn't tell the officers her own name but she knew all about her son and the fact that he should have been home ages ago. Funny old thing, the human mind, isn't it?'

There was a knock on Ted's door so he thanked her again and rang off, calling out a 'Come in.'

'Sir, this is the photo from the house where the old lady's son is missing,' a PC from Uniform told him, holding out a framed photograph of a man in Ambulance Service uniform. 'The neighbours confirmed that this is the missing man, Derek Waldren.'

Ted thanked her as he took the photo and looked at it. He was pretty certain that this was the face of both his victim and of the St John officer he'd seen at the match the day before. He would need to track down someone to officially identify the body at the mortuary before they could be certain. At least they now had a possible starting point.

He followed the PC out of his office to go and talk to Jo and Mike. Maurice was just putting his coat on ready to go home.

'News, boss? Do you want me to stay?'

'No, you might as well knock off now, Maurice, and we'll start back fresh in the morning. It's a possible ID but still unconfirmed. It's looking likely that it was our St John man, though.

'Oh, Maurice, I keep meaning to ask you. None of my business really, but what about Steve, now you and Megan are expecting twins? Will he move in with Océane? If he needs a place, tell him to talk to Bill Baxter. I've been trying to persuade the stubborn old bugger he needs some company.'

'Bill? Steve's terrified of him. Steve's terrified of almost everyone,' Maurice laughed. 'I'll be sorry to see him move on. He's such a good lad, is Steve. But we are going to need the room, that's for sure. Thanks for the suggestion.'

'And tell Steve I'll happily go with him to talk to Bill, if he's too scared to go on his own. I just think it would be good for both of them.'

'Cheers, Ted, you're not a bad boss,' Maurice told him with a grin.

He slipped into informality with no one within earshot. He'd known the boss long enough, since Ted had first joined the team as a DS, brand new to CID and still finding his feet.

Jo and Mike were both getting ready to leave when Ted went into the office they shared, holding the photograph of Derek Waldren, which he showed them.

'I'm fairly certain this is the face of our victim, and I'm pretty sure it's also the man I saw at the match yesterday. What do you think?'

'You're the one who's best at face recognition, boss,' Mike told him. 'He looks vaguely familiar but I couldn't say where I'd seen him, and I wouldn't swear that I had.'

'Same as Mike,' Jo put in. 'But if it is the same man, then there's our Badger connection right there, probably. And if it is him and Nigel might have been one of the last people who talked to him, certainly at the match, then that young lad has got some serious explaining to do.'

Ted got Mike to drop him on the main road so he could walk the short distance back to his house, carrying his coat and boots, still muddy from the woods earlier on. The weather was set to not too clever mode for the day, it seemed, but he felt the need of a breath of fresh air and a bit of a leg stretch before he got home. Work took its toll on him, especially on a day like today, and he didn't like to take it home with him.

He let himself in, dumped his briefcase and carried his wet coat and boots through to the kitchen to see to them. He was rewarded by a rib-cracking hug from Trev, as if they'd been apart far longer than one night.

'How's everything? How's the case? How's Jim getting on? And did you miss me?'

Ted smiled.

'Crap. Going nowhere. Doing better. And of course. Don't I always? I still haven't found time to go and see Jim, though. We've got another body and if it's who I think it is, this case just got even more complicated than I thought it was. How's mam? Pleased to be back home in Wales?'

Trev turned back to his cooking. Whatever he was making was giving off an inviting aroma.

'It's all a bit final, isn't it? Now her house is sold. I mean, I knew she probably wasn't going to come back to live. But now she doesn't even have the possibility to reconsider, without a base here.

'She's happy as a pig in muck there, though. Speaking Welsh all the time, back with lots of childhood friends. It's better for her, I'm sure, but I'm going to miss her.'

'As soon as we wind up this case, we'll go down and visit her. Promise.'

'I thought you were going to take me to France to eat *brioche* in the sunshine?'

'We can do both, if you play your cards right. I just need to make some headway on this case.'

Trev laughed and turned back to him, folding him in another hug.

'Then it will be the next case. And the one after that. And the one after that. Why did I have to fall madly in love with a policeman, of all things?'

Now he was kissing Ted, reaching behind him to turn the heat off under the pan he was using.

'I think supper might keep a bit, don't you?'

# Chapter Sixteen

Ted started Monday morning with a team briefing as usual, but he was having difficulty concentrating on it. He'd been summoned to a ten o'clock meeting with the Ice Queen and Kevin Turner in the presence of the Chief Super. His mind kept going over whether or not he'd missed spotting something at the match which could have prevented the death.

'Mike, can you sort out someone who can formally identify the body, please. Probably from where he worked if he had no relatives other than his mother. Then we can move on from there. I'm still waiting to hear from the Professor when she can do the post-mortem. I'd quite like to be there myself for that. Rob, you're with me on it, please.

'Jo, can you sort out another round of chats with Antoine and the rest of the team. All separate, all recorded, but not under caution at this stage. I especially want Nigel brought in and kept away from the others for as long as possible. I don't want anyone coaching him in what to say or not to say before he's been interviewed. Maurice, have you spoken to him yet?

When Maurice shook his head, Ted went on, 'Then I want you on it. You and Jezza.'

'Good cop, bad cop, boss?' Jezza asked with a grin, knowing how much Ted disliked the mere suggestion.

Ted knew his stern look was totally wasted on Jezza but he tried one anyway.

'Jezza, you're good at picking up on small details. Maurice, you can do your Daddy Hen impression, win him over, make him feel comfortable. Jezza, you be ready to leap in and pick up on any inconsistencies at all in what he says. Ask him particularly about him having mentioned Badger and there being someone in the area he was speaking about who might possibly have had that nickname.

'It goes without saying that I don't want any of them at this stage to know the possible ID of the latest victim, nor any other details. I just want you all to get their individual version of the incident on the pitch and what any of them can tell you about anyone who was there at the time. Don't focus on the first aider, of course. Ask about everyone, the referee in particular.

'Antoine is clearly still the boss of them all, but who's his second? Who's the next most dominant one on the team?'

'It always used to be Callum. Now it's more usually Jerome Brooks,' Charlie Eccles put in. 'I got that from talking to some of the parents at the match on Saturday. They'd all seen the old team's showy entrance so I was asking them a bit about them as if I didn't know who they were. And about the hierarchy in that team. They all mentioned Callum. Said they'd been shocked to hear he'd committed suicide, then even more gobsmacked when they found out it had been a murder.'

Ted had noticed that Eccles seemed to be doing well on this case and he was pleased to see it.

'Right, well, let's have Jerome in as well and make it a bit more formal. Charlie, can you handle that?'

DC Eccles looked pleased to be given the chance. He'd made a mess of a witness interview when Ted had worked with him before. Ted had arranged some training for him and wanted to give him a chance to show what he could do as a result.

'Obviously, things could change dramatically once we start to get some forensic results, either from the site or from the body. I doubt we'll get anything at all from Doug until tomorrow at the earliest. So for now, let's work with what we know or can piece together. Derek Waldren was probably at the match on Saturday, subject to formal identification. If it was him, he spoke to Nigel, at least, out of all the team members. At some point he went, or was taken, to the woods up beyond Roman Lakes where he met an unpleasant death.

'We need to find out more about the significance of those woods. Did our football team lot go there regularly? Either together or individually. Is it some sort of a hang-out they used? I'd really like to know who any other youngsters are who hang round there and what they get up to. There may be more than one group that does, so that knowledge could be useful to us.'

When he'd wound up the briefing, he went to have a quick word with Jo.

'I've got a meeting coming up with the Super and the Chief and I've no idea how long I'll be tied up, so can you take charge while I'm gone? Apart from anything else, I imagine we're going to have to talk damage limitation when the press get hold of the latest developments.'

'Just as well the mole is out of harm's way now, eh? It doesn't bear thinking about what sort of damage could be done with someone on the inside leaking further info. And thank god we've no longer got Pocket Billiards to contend with. That young lass who's taken over doesn't seem to be quite such a thorn in the flesh as he was.'

'I have a feeling that might be like summoning up the devil, Jo. As soon as you say his name, he might just appear. If he does, it's your fault so it will be down to you to go and wine and dine him.'

Ted went to find Kevin before his next meeting. Kev was still looking tired and more than a bit frazzled. Ted knew the recent staffing level reductions were causing him no end of worries. As were the constantly flying rumours of further changes to come in restructuring the running of the station and the division.

'D'you know what, Ted? If the Chief Super starts on about why didn't I send someone round to the woods, I've half a mind to go to the press myself and tell them what staffing levels were like that night and what we were tied up doing.'

Ted could see that he was already wound up, before their meeting had even started. He opened his mouth to say something but Kev cut in, 'I won't, of course. But I might just tell him a few home truths and ask him how he expects me to police the patch with not enough bodies to send out on routine patrols, never mind anything else.'

He was rummaging in a drawer as he spoke, looked for his antacids. His ulcers had been mostly under control with the tablets he was on but Ted could see the way he was rubbing his stomach and guessed that the stress he was under wasn't helping.

'We're all under the cosh, Kev. The Super knows that and so does the Chief. Don't go getting yourself in a state. It won't do your ulcers any good and I don't want to have to wade in between you and the Chief if it comes to that.'

He was prevented from further comment by his mobile phone ringing. He looked at the screen in disbelief. Pocket Billiards.

'Alastair!' he said with forced joviality. 'I thought you'd moved on to pastures new in Liverpool?'

'My old mate Fred from the Evening News asked me to give you a call. He knows you and I got along like a house on fire. He doesn't seem to be getting the info he used to get and Penny, bless her … well, she's not quite got the ruthless streak.'

Ted made a face at Kevin Turner, indicating his phone.

'He won't be getting the tip-offs now, that's right. Your mole has been outed.'

'We thought as much. Which is why Fred asked me to ring you, remind you of our special relationship. Two murders in as many weeks in exactly the same place. There must be something you can give me on that, Ted? For old time's sake?'

'There'll be a press release going out shortly, Alastair. Tell

Fred he'll get a copy. Have to go now, places to be, cases to solve.'

At least listening to the one-sided conversation had put a bit of a smile back on Kev's face, for the time being. He and Ted were united in their dislike and mistrust of the former local reporter.

'I'm going to put Jo on point duty,' Ted muttered darkly when he'd ended the call. 'I told him he would summon up the devil if he mentioned Pocket Billiards by name and he did. Interesting how much they're floundering though, without Mickey tipping them off.'

The meeting was happening in a small room on the ground floor rather than up in the Chief Super's office. Ted and Kev found the Ice Queen already in there, fussing about with glasses and water jugs. She was clearly anticipating a long session.

'How is Superintendent Baker now?' she asked Ted as they stood about waiting for the Chief Super to arrive. He was running late.

'Bella says they're hoping to be able to send him home tomorrow, if they're happy with his latest tests and whatever. I've still not managed to get to see him. I thought it would be easier once he's home, without the restriction of hospital visiting times.'

'You must make the time, if for any reason he has to stay in longer. We can't have him thinking we've all forgotten about him.'

She was attempting to make small-talk. She had many excellent skills. It was not one of them. She was saved from further awkwardness by the door bursting open and the Chief Super hurrying in, carrying a sheaf of papers.

'Good morning, everyone, sorry to have kept you waiting. I had the ACC on the phone just as I was getting ready to come down, wanting to hear of any progress. So I hope you have some to report, Ted?'

He looked expectantly at Ted who desperately wished he had. He outlined what they did have to date, as succinctly and dispassionately as he could. The Chief Super had brought his own notes with him and was going through them as Ted spoke.

'We're clearly going to have to put out a fairly detailed press release on this latest killing in the hopes of stopping the papers going off on trails of speculation. It's the exact same spot, for each killing? Not just a coincidence of being in the same woods?'

'Exactly the same place, sir,' Ted told him.

'And there have been previous reports of incidents in those woods? Youths making fires? When was the last such report?'

Ted hesitated, desperately not wanting to drop Kevin in it but aware that it looked bad, on paper, at least.

'Saturday night, sir,' Kev put in, then his tone sounded defensive as he continued, 'and before you ask, no, I didn't despatch a unit. I was Duty Inspector but I didn't have anyone to send. And d'you know why, sir? Every available officer was tied up doing stuff which was more social welfare issues than policing.'

He was going red in the face now, clearly winding himself up, but wanting to make his feelings heard. Ted tried a low, 'Kev,' of warning, but it did no good.

'We had a couple of high risk MissPers to track down, not to mention some people who'd given up waiting hours for emergency medical attention at A&E so had just wandered off. They all needed to be found, brought back and seen to. We were stretched to the limit. We had no routine patrols at all going on. The Great Train Robbery could have been going down at Edgeley Station and I wouldn't have had a single spare officer to send there.'

He left enough of a pause to make his feelings clearly known before adding, 'Sir,' to keep it the right side of insolence.

'Kevin, Kevin, I hear you,' the Chief Super told him, his

manner pacifying. 'I really do. If I had extra officers to give you, they would be yours for the taking. I'm not here to apportion blame. This is all about damage limitation. I need to know all the facts, exactly what happened, then I'm in a better position to know what we say to the press.'

Kevin was still flushed, breathing hard. The Ice Queen looked concerned and wordlessly passed him a glass of water. He looked as if he was on the point of telling her what he thought about water as the answer to anything. Then he got a grip of himself and took a swallow of it.

'What we need to decide now is whether it will help or hinder your enquiry, Ted, if the degree of the link between the two cases were to come out at this stage. In other words, do we make a pre-emptive strike and tell the press we are considering the two deaths to be one single investigation? Or do we fall back on the old "police are keeping an open mind about the possibility of a link" line, which we love to feed to the wolf pack?

'Ted, it's your case. What are your thoughts?'

'I think it's too soon to say anything very much, sir. I'd prefer to wait for the formal ID. We're going on the assumption that it's Derek Waldren but we could be making a serious error of judgement if it turns out not to be. Although I think the chances of that being the case are slim. I would just prefer to wait until it's definitely been confirmed.'

'I agree. Debra?'

'I would certainly err on the side of caution until we're sure.'

'Kevin?'

He looked surprised to be asked. He clearly thought he'd blown things with his uncharacteristic outburst.

'I agree, sir. Keeping our heads below the parapet for now sounds like a good idea to me.'

'Right, then that's what we'll do. Debra, can you please liaise with the Press Office to produce something bland for now. Ted, please keep me in the loop at all times of any new developments. Forewarned is forearmed. Kevin, let's you and I go and have a chat in my office and see if there's not something, at least, we can work on together to ease the burden a bit.'

He rose and left the room, Kevin trailing in his wake and not looking too happy about it.

'I know it's early days, Ted, but what are your initial thoughts on this? What do you see as the common denominator between Callum and this man Derek Waldren which might have got them both killed?'

'Honestly? At this stage, I've no idea. I'd feel a lot more optimistic of an early result if I had.'

It was late afternoon before they were able to find anyone to identify the latest victim for them. Ted got a call from the mortuary to say a work colleague had confirmed that the body was that of Derek Waldren, ambulance driver and St John volunteer. The man who had been at the match on Saturday. Ted was also told that Professor Nelson would be carrying out the post-mortem on the body the following morning, first thing. He groaned to himself, knowing what Bizzie meant by first thing. It was a time when most people were still in bed, even coppers used to early rising.

He let Rob O'Connell know to be there in good time, then asked Steve to find out if Derek Waldren had had any involvement with the junior section of the St John Ambulance which might have earned him the nickname of Badger.

'Boss, while you're here, there's something else that might be significant,' Jezza told him. 'Océane has been working on Callum's phone and I asked her to concentrate on a year ago, at the time Páraic died, like you said. There were quite a few calls between him and Antoine just after the death. Then no phone contact between them for a week, until calls resumed again.

'I got back to the people who'd known Callum in Calais

who told me he'd had a visitor from England at about that time. From the description they gave me, it was Antoine.'

'So was his visit pre-planned and the dates just a coincidence? Or was Páraic's death of sufficient importance for him to make a special trip out to France to see Callum and discuss it with him? Jezza, make sure that whoever talks to Antoine knows about this and knows to ask those questions.

'Jo, we need to dig a bit deeper into the story behind Páraic's death. There has to be a link between all three that we haven't yet picked up on. And yes, I know what you're going to say. We haven't enough available personnel. If someone can dig out any relevant files, I can go over some of them myself, whenever I get a moment.

'And think yourself lucky I'm not sending you back to Uniform. Just after you mentioned Pocket Billiards by name, I got a phone call from him so I'm blaming you for summoning him up.'


Ted was just getting his things together at the end of the day when his desk phone rang. As soon as he heard that the call was from Manchester Royal Infirmary, his heart started thudding. Jim Baker! Had he left it too late to see his old friend again?

'Inspector Darling? I'm sorry to bother you. It's Manchester Royal here. We have a patient who's asking for you. A Mr Grenville, Philip Grenville.'

Philip. One of Ted's former partners. The man he had unceremoniously dumped when he'd first met Trev.

'Mr Grenville is asking if you could come in to see him. We were trying to get hold of some next of kin but he says there's no one. Only you.'

'I'm not really ...' Ted started to say.

The woman interrupted him.

'Mr Grenville gave me permission to give you the facts. We were trying to contact next of kin because Mr Grenville really needs someone to be with him. He said it would mean a lot to him if you could come.'

'You mean he's dying?' Ted asked her bluntly.

'We don't expect him to last the night. Can I tell him you'll come?'

Ted sighed inwardly. It was not really what he needed. But Philip had meant something to him once and he'd taken their split badly.

'Tell him I'm on my way,' he told her, and noted the directions she gave him to find the right ward.

He made a quick call to Trev.

'I've no idea what time I'll be back tonight, if at all. I have to be somewhere.'

'That sounds very mysterious. Are you all right?'

'I will be. I'll be back when I can, but don't wait up for me. And I've got a post-mortem early doors tomorrow. I'll see you when I see you.'

# Chapter Seventeen

Ted went to put his head round Kev's door before he left for the Infirmary. He wanted to see how he'd got on with the Chief Super. He imagined Kev would have liked to go for a drink with him at the end of the day and he would have gone with him, gladly. He was closer to Kev than he was to Philip, after all these years. But the news that his former partner was dying and had asked for him had stirred up old feelings of guilt at their abrupt break-up. Ted had finished with him as soon as he'd met Trev. He didn't even know if Trev was available or indeed gay. He just didn't think it fair to stay with Philip if he could feel as attracted to Trev as he had been.

'How did you get on with the Chief?'

'He made all the right sort of noises but at the end of the day it amounted to bugger all. I still haven't got anything like the number of officers I need but I'm just supposed to manage somehow. Have you time for a drink or are you just off somewhere?'

'I just got a call from Manchester Royal.'

Seeing Kev's expression change, he hurried to reassure him.

'Not Big Jim. He's doing well enough to be discharged tomorrow, hopefully. This is someone I used to know, way back. An ex-partner. They phoned me to say he's asking for me and they don't think he'll last the night.'

'Shit, that's tough. So you're still in touch with him? Trev doesn't mind?'

'No, that's the strange thing. I've only seen him once since we split up, years ago. When I needed some legal help. He's with CPS. But he took it badly, me dumping him, and he made it clear he didn't want any further contact after that one time. If he's asking for me, it sounds as if he has no one else, which is sad. I can't really not go, so I'm sorry I can't come with you tonight. Tomorrow, eh?'

'You're a decent bloke, Ted. Most people wouldn't give the time of day to an ex, even if they were dying. Hope it's not too tough on you.'

Ted found the right ward at the Infirmary easily enough and approached the first nurse he saw to identify himself and ask about Philip.

'Oh, you're Philip's "Darling", are you? Lovely name. He talks about you a lot. I'm glad you've managed to come at last. He said you were always busy at work.'

Ted frowned.

'He does know we're not still together, does he? Haven't been for more than ten years now.'

'Oh, that is a shame,' she said. 'No, I don't think he does know really. He gets very confused, with the medication he's on. He is very poorly and he's on a lot of it. I'll take you to him. We have him in a side ward, where it's quiet.'

'Can you tell me what's wrong with him? I understand he gave his permission for someone to discuss his details with me.'

'He has a number of very serious issues, but the current principle concern is the pneumonia. Given his condition, his system is simply too weak to fight it. That and the cirrhosis of the liver.'

'His condition?' Ted queried.

'I'll take you to see him. Let him tell you what he wants to. Then if you have any more questions, come and find me. They have warned you that the prognosis is very poor, haven't they?'

Philip had always been thin, all the time Ted had known him. The figure in the bed which confronted him was emaciated. Hollow cheeks, yellow skin like parchment, stretched taut over bones which seemed to stand out. He appeared to have drips and tubes protruding from everywhere, and there was an oxygen pipe under his nose. Ted knew Philip had always drunk more than he should. It seemed, from the look of him, that his drinking had become far worse since he'd been with him, and even since he'd seen him last.

'Is he asleep or unconscious?'

'Sleeping,' the nurse told him. 'He spends a lot of time asleep. It's probably better that way. Here's a chair, if you want to sit with him. I know it would mean a lot to him to see you here, when he next wakes up.'

'And will he? Wake up?'

She gave him a sad smile and lowered her voice.

'We often find that people who've asked for someone who means a lot to them will hang on until that person gets here. But often not for very long afterwards. I'll leave you to it now, but if you have any concerns, just press that red call button and someone will come, as soon as they can.'

Ted sat down quietly, his eyes never leaving the figure in the bed. He couldn't believe it was the same man he'd dined out with. Gone to the cinema with, or for walks round Roman Lakes. Slept with. He put one hand gently on the bed, almost but not quite touching Philip's. After a few moments, Philip's eyelids fluttered then finally opened, revealing eyes where the whites were as yellow as the surrounding skin.

'Ted! My Darling. You came. I knew you would.'

The voice was weak and Ted could hear Philip's chest crackling and wheezing with the effort to force out the few words.

'Hello, Phil. Yes, I came. Don't try to talk, though. Save your breath.'

There was a noise between a rasp and a gurgle. Ted realised his former partner was trying to laugh.

'Save it for what, my Darling? They must have told you

I'm dying. I assume that's why you came. It's sweet of you to have done so. Thank you. I had no one else to call.'

He paused for a moment, taking ragged breaths. It had clearly cost him an enormous effort to try to speak at all. He lifted the hand nearest to Ted and took hold of his, his touch cold and clammy. Ted gently squeezed his hand back in acknowledgement.

'Have they told you all this is AIDs-related? That and the demon drink, of course. It shouldn't happen, these days, I know. I went a little bit off the rails after we parted and I wasn't at all careful. Too many one night stands with beautiful young things, trying to recreate the love of my life.

'But don't worry, it was after we separated. You were never at any risk. I should have sought help earlier, but I was in denial. I left it far too late for any of the wonderful modern drugs to work their magic.

'So here I am. Close to the end. But I finally have you back with me, where you belong. All I ask of you now is to stay there and hold my hand, until the end. Please, my Darling.'

It was not until gone two in the morning that Philip finally took his last breath and the hand holding onto Ted's weakened its hold and fell away. Ted stood up, stiff from sitting in the same position for hours on end, his bladder reminding him it needed attention. He bent over the bed and gently kissed Philip on the forehead. Then he went to find someone to tell them that he'd gone.

As he drove back from Manchester through the seemingly still sleeping streets of Stockport, Ted wondered if the Uniform night shift were having a quieter time of it. It had bothered him to see Kev nearly losing it in the meeting the previous day. He understood the pressures he was under and wished he could have gone for that drink with him. He promised himself he'd make time for it. He also needed to find the time to go and see Jim.

He let himself quietly into the house, desperate to get in the shower to get rid of the stink of hospital which seemed to insinuate itself into every pore. The thought that in just a few short hours he would be back in another hospital, watching a fairly gruesome post-mortem on a murder victim, hardly filled him with pleasant anticipation.

He looked in on his sleeping partner to assess his chances of finding a spare bit of the bed to slide into. Zero, he reckoned. Trev was fast asleep, dead to the world, long limbs spread everywhere. Any square inch he wasn't occupying was taken by sleeping cats. Only young Adam woke, yawning widely, showing a pink tongue and needle-sharp teeth.

As he didn't have much time to sleep before he needed to get up again and would doubtless have trouble dropping off, Ted decided to snatch what shut-eye he could in the spare room. He wasn't sure he would sleep but he set the alarm on his mobile phone just in case.

He must have dozed off at some point, although it didn't feel like it, because he was jolted awake by his mobile alarm. He felt scratchy, irritable, from the lack of sleep. He took another quick shower to wake himself up fully before dressing and heading for the post-mortem.

He paused to leave a note for Trev, apologising for his absence and warning him that he might once again be late home. He didn't really want to go into the reasons why in a note. It would be hard to find the right words. He'd explain everything when they finally caught up.

Rob arrived at the hospital only minutes after him, still ahead of the appointed hour. The whole team knew that Ted was a stickler for punctuality and were always careful to be on time.

Ted was already getting his Fisherman's Friends out of his pocket in anticipation of a grim time ahead of them. He offered one to Rob who shook his head.

'No thanks boss, I've got something a bit milder.'

They made their way down to Professor Nelson's autopsy suite and donned coveralls. The Professor was already there and preparing to start. Her welcome was, as ever, bright and breezy, despite the early morning hour.

'There were no personal possessions at all found at the scene, I understand, so there's nothing to clerk in. I was informed at the scene that he was just there in his birthday suit, much as you see him now, with no signs of his clothes or anything else.

'Because of the lack of an initial ID on the victim, the samples at the scene were put in for rapid DNA testing. It wasn't quite as rapid as usual on a Sunday but I did get the results late yesterday.'

She seemed to be stringing it out for effect. Ted found himself getting impatient. It wasn't like him. He crunched his lozenge to curb his irritation.

'You'd already left the office and your mobile was switched off so I thought it would keep until now. I hope that was all right.

'We couldn't get any identification that way as our victim appears not to have a criminal record of any kind. Certainly his identity couldn't be established from his DNA. But we did find out something really rather remarkable on a cross-check with recent samples.'

Ted wanted to swear. He wanted to shake her. Or punch the wall. It completely out of character for him. He put it down to sleep deprivation.

'This victim's DNA is an exact match from that recovered from Callum Mitchell's throat, via the blood traces there. In other words, it is almost certain that this man is the person who killed Callum Mitchell.'

'Blimey, I didn't see that coming,' Rob said in surprise, voicing precisely what Ted was thinking. 'I thought it would be the same person who killed both of them.' Then he went on, 'So if Badger killed Callum, then why did he do so? And who the heck killed Badger?'

'Presumably Badger is a nickname for Derek Waldren?' Bizzie Nelson asked them. 'I can't tell you gentlemen who killed him, but I will do my best to tell you everything I can about how they did it. I understand from Doug that there's a strong possibility that several people were involved. I would have to say that accords with my initial observations of the slash wounds to the back, but I'll be able to tell you more about that as I progress.'

She began her examination methodically, as ever, everything she noted being recorded for later transcription. She kept up a monologue for the tape, occasionally making an aside to Ted and Rob.

'We didn't find anything in the bloods to indicate that he was drugged or sedated.'

'So you mean he was awake and fully alert while that,' Ted nodded towards the metal rod which was still protruding, 'was done to him?'

'Unfortunately, yes. I think that is borne out also by the amount of chafing to his wrists and ankles, where he was bound. Look, you can see here. Friction marks. As if he was struggling quite violently against his restraints.'

'I think I'd struggle if someone staked me out like that, before I even knew what was going to happen to me,' Rob put in.

'It is true that this is a very vulnerable position in which to restrain anyone. Especially you gentlemen, it seems to me. It immediately conjures up all sorts of imagined future horrors, I expect.'

She continued to work away swiftly and professionally. The body was on its back, allowing her access to the major internal organs, several of which were removed, weighed and carefully checked for damage. Once that was done, she asked her assistant's help to turn the body, which they did deftly. The rod made a metallic twang against the stainless steel table as it was moved.

'Now we come to the business end of things, if you'll excuse the expression. I first want to take a closer look at these flesh wounds. Then I'll need to deal with removing the rod and I suspect that might be the moment, gentlemen, when you will choose to look away now.

'Speaking of the rod, I think I mentioned at the scene that this burn mark, here, on the back of the right thigh, rather suggests to me that the rod, having been heated, may have been dropped onto the leg, rather than held there. Had it been held, I would have expected the burn to be deep and uniform, rather like branding cattle. This is neither. It would certainly have hurt but it could potentially have inflicted a far more painful wound.

'I'll take measurements of the thickness of the burn which will expand on my theory, and I'll include that in my written report, which you will have as soon as possible.'

'And the ropes which tied him? Anything unusual about the knots?' Ted asked.

It was not really the normal area of expertise of a Home Office pathologist, but Ted knew Bizzie Nelson had had the sort of outdoorsy background and upbringing that may well have seen her sailing boats in her childhood.

'Certainly not the same as those in Callum's case. I hear the noose was tied to the tree with a round turn and two half hitches. These were nothing distinctive like that but they've gone off to the lab for further examination and analysis.

'I thought at the scene, and I think even more so now, under better lighting, that these superficial wounds were made by more than one person. You see this one, here? On the back of the rib area? This was definitely made by someone right-handed. Look closely here. You can see where the slash began and ended.

'Now look at this one, here on the buttock. Note the direction of the cut. This was made by someone left-handed.

It's quite easy to see the difference.'

'Could it have been one person using different hands, Professor? To give the impression that there was more than one person involved?'

'That's an intelligent question, Sergeant O'Connell. On the balance of probabilities, however, I would say no. Genuinely ambidextrous people are comparatively rare. I believe my predecessor was one. Unless someone spent a lot of time honing their knife skills with either hand, I would expect to see evidence that they were not using their dominant hand to inflict the injury. Something of a wobble, perhaps. But these are clean cuts, with no signs of difficulty.

'Now as to the blade, I would say something relatively simple. Perhaps a Stanley knife. It would appear that these were inflicted to cause some degree of pain but above all fear of what was to come. None are serious wounds at all. I count twelve in total, all of them flesh wounds.

'Which brings us to what I am about to do, and that is to withdraw the rod. I can then confirm my initial findings, from opening the front, of how far it penetrated and what major organs were damaged. This was undoubtedly the instrument which caused the death.

'I'll also be able to tell you at that point if the theory about it having been heated first can be substantiated or not. Death was certainly due to internal trauma and blood loss as a result of its use. I can only hope that the sheer shock might have caused the unfortunate victim to slip into unconsciousness fairly early on. The alternative truly doesn't bear thinking about.'

# Chapter Eighteen

'Rob, you go on in and I'll be there shortly. I just need to call somewhere first,' Ted told him after the post-mortem finished. 'Can you ask Jo to arrange a full briefing for everyone, including Doug and PC Khan, for last thing today. We'll have a quick catch-up as soon as I get back in.'

What he didn't tell Rob was that he was heading in search of something to eat. His stomach thought his throat was cut. Or as his dad would have said, he could have eaten a meat and potato pie on a barm. He realised he hadn't eaten since some time around midday the day before. He seldom risked breakfast before a post-mortem and he'd missed a meal last night, being at the Infirmary.

He knew a good place for bacon rolls and he hoped a couple of those and some tea might improve his mood. He couldn't do much about the lack of sleep but at least some food might make him less tetchy.

He felt slightly more human when he got back to the station and called the team together for the update from the post-mortem.

'So we know that Badger killed Callum, but where does that lead us? And there's a strong likelihood that the second crime was committed by more than one person. Professor Nelson found twelve cuts on his back, all superficial. Any theories?'

'That makes the football team members likely suspects then, surely?' Mike Hallam said.

'Eleven players on a football team. Twelve if you count the

reserve, Nigel. But that's not the only body to have twelve members,' Jezza put in. 'It could be a jury. A kangaroo court. Twelve people who somehow knew that Badger was Callum's killer so they decided to have their own trial, sentence him to death and execute him.'

'Does the way he was impaled make it likely that he was involved in the sexual abuse of boys?' Jo suggested. 'Or that someone thought he was?'

Leona Rakale spoke up. 'Boss, we know Callum was drugged with zopiclone and Badger's neighbours mentioned something about his mother being on sleeping pills so he could go out to work at night. Could that have been the source?'

'Excellent point, Leona. Jo, I need a thorough search of Derek Waldren's house. Find out what tablets his mother was on. We also need to find his clothes. There was nothing at the site, so where are they? His phone, too. Find out his mobile number from his work then let's see if we can trace it. Where it is now and where it's been since he left his house. Particularly where did he go after the match.

'We need a full profile of him, at work and outside. I'm assuming he has a clean record if he's in the St John and working with young people at events, but let's check him. He's not on the database so he has no convictions but has he ever been spoken to for any reason, about anything?'

'I'll organise for us to speak to the various club officials and someone from St John, just in case there's ever been a whisper of anything there, boss,' Jo told him.

'Good, thank you. Abuse is a likely reason behind it all but we need to think of other possible motives in case we're not on the right track. Why did Callum go to Waldren's house in the first place, if he did go there first? And was he killed to stop him revealing something he knew?'

'And how did the others know it was Badger who killed Callum when we hadn't worked it out yet?' Maurice Brown said.

'Nigel was the one we saw talking to Badger at the match, but I can't see him managing a killing like this on his own. Was it his job to lure him somewhere so the others could grab him and do the deed?' Charlie suggested.

'Hopefully by later today, Doug might have news from the site for us. At least be able to give us a better idea of how many people were involved there.'

'Boss, do you want me to sort door-to-door in Shearwater Road? If Callum went there willingly and was drugged at the house, Badger must have had to get him out and into his car when he was unconscious, so someone might have seen something,' Mike Hallam suggested.

Jezza came in quickly on that one.

'That's easy to explain, I bet. If Badger lived with his mother and she was elderly and had dementia, there's a chance he might sometimes have taken her out in a wheelchair or the ambulance chair. I know she was found walking in the road so she obviously could walk, but perhaps sometimes it was just easier to plonk her in a chair, strap her in and have control of her that way. If he was wheeling someone out of the house and anyone did see anything, but not too closely, they would surely assume he was taking his mother somewhere.'

'Good point, Jezza, and your reward for making it is to take charge of the house-to-house to find out if anyone did see something,' Ted told her.

Jezza rolled her eyes in an exaggerated fashion, although she was secretly pleased to be given the responsibility.

'Make sure all your notes are up to date for this evening, please, everyone. I want to be in a position to know exactly what's going on and what direction we're going in by then. I'll need to let the Super and the Chief know where we're up to.'

Ted went back to his office. He had his usual pile of paperwork to clear before he could think of anything else. He took a few minutes to call Bella, though, for an update on Jim.

'As long as this morning's tests don't throw up any nasty

last-minute surprises, I can pick him up at midday.'

'Is he likely to be too tired for a quick visit this evening, if I get chance?'

'You know James, he'll be delighted to see you. He's been hoping to for some time now, but of course he understands about work, in the middle of a case. Just promise me you won't let him start talking about the job and worrying about getting back there. The doctors have warned him that he has a long road to recovery ahead of him.'

Ted's next call was to Kevin.

'I probably can't do this evening, Kev, sorry. But what about a swift half in The Grapes at dinnertime? We could get a sandwich together and talk a bit. I know it's not the same but...'

'I know how it is,' Kev finished for him. 'Yes, that would be good. You're on. How did it go with your ex last night?'

'He died,' Ted said shortly. 'I'll tell you in the pub, if you're interested.'

He didn't. He skilfully steered the conversation away from it and onto how things were going with Kev's staffing crisis. He didn't really want to talk about Philip. As far as he was concerned, it was chapter closed. For some reason, he didn't particularly want to talk about it even with Trev. He simply sent him a quick text to say he would be calling on Jim after work so wasn't sure what time he would be back. He told Trev to go ahead and eat if he was hungry. He'd have something at whatever time he got in.

He was building his hopes on some helpful news from the crime scene via Doug at the end of the day meeting, but he was in for a disappointment.

'Don't shoot the messenger, boss, but the news is not good. We've found next to nothing, and we're not likely to. From what we did find, there's no way there's going to be any convenient DNA or clear footprints to help you. The reason being what we did find. Traces of white fibres, similar to those of a CSI suit but polypropylene. The sort of thing you can buy in any DIY store or online for protection when you're painting and decorating, things like that.

'Going back to the footprints. The reason they seem to be so blurred is that microscopic traces found indicate that shoe coverings were worn. And the total lack of fingerprints also indicates gloves being used. So whoever we're dealing with and however many of them there were, they were well equipped, and this whole thing was clearly well planned.'

'And you still can't give us any idea of how many people were involved?' Ted asked him.

'I would if I could but I can't. More than one, is all I can say. Four, six, eight. Take an educated guess. We can't. We're still working there but I honestly think there's not much more the scene can tell us. I'm thinking of winding up at the end of play tomorrow, unless we get a sudden miraculous breakthrough.

'Of course if it was an old TV western, the Native American tracker could just look at the ground and tell you everything. Unfortunately, I don't have those skills. We have tried lifting a couple of casts from footprints, more in hope than anticipation, just in case we can take even a best guess at different people, from size or weight. But everything is blurred by the overshoes. Sorry, boss. I wish I had better news for you.'

'Thanks, Doug. I know you and your team will have given it your best shot. So, we can't count on a forensic breakthrough. It just means more legwork, more talking to people. Anything new from the team members? It's probably time now we started checking out in detail any alibis they have for after the match on Saturday. Anyone picked up on anything yet on that score?'

'I asked Jerome while I was talking to him, boss. He was quite chatty so I dropped the question in as a logical continuation of talking about the match,' Charlie responded. 'According to him, they all spent the whole evening together at

Antoine's place and they all crashed there for the night.

'They picked up food and drink from a supermarket then went back there. Antoine's got a hi-tech home cinema set-up in his part of the house. They watched films, did some gaming, that sort of stuff. They'd arranged to be together to sink a few beers for Callum, he told me.'

'Excellent, Charlie. If they went to a supermarket there might well be CCTV of them, so let's start by checking that out and see if we can pinpoint them at any particular time. Ask them all individually for their movements from the end of the match through to the following morning. And now you can tell them whose death is being investigated and watch for their reactions.

'PC Khan, can you now mention Derek Waldren by name to Callum's parents and his brother. See if that means anything to any of them. Ask if he ever had an injury that meant he needed to be treated by the St John people, or if he might have encountered any of them anywhere other than through the club.'

'Maurice and Jezza, what did you make of Nigel?'

'He'd tell you black was white if he thought that's what you wanted to hear,' Maurice spoke first.

'I second that, boss. He also sounds as if he's lying even when he's probably telling the truth. I think he's highly unreliable. He would certainly crack and talk but I don't know if we could ever be sure that what he was telling us would be of any use to us.'

'What does he do for a living?'

'He works for a contract cleaning firm who do the hospital. He works the night shift usually, but occasionally swaps shifts round to cover holidays.'

'And is he still saying he doesn't know anyone called Badger? Is it possible their paths could have crossed at the hospital at some point, for instance?'

'You know the size of that place, boss. It's like a small

town. It is possible but they've got more than five thousand staff apparently, so it's conceivable they never met there. And yes, he still says he doesn't know a Badger. He's not sure why he mentioned one, it was just a nickname that popped into his head for some reason but he doesn't know why.'

'Mike, can you pull together everything we know about each of the team members, please, including their jobs. It might come in useful.

'I also don't want to lose sight of that knot from Callum's killing. Do any of them have any connection to Scouts, Guides, sailing, anything which might mean they would know about knots? And the same for Derek Waldren. Did he do first aid cover for other youth organisations? Or maybe deliver training to any of them perhaps.

'Right, thank you everyone. That'll do for today. We'll start in fresh again tomorrow.'

'Boss, these white suits,' Charlie put in before anyone could make a move. 'Jerome is a painter and decorator. He works for his dad's firm, and they're sub-contractors for Antoine's dad's property development business.'

Ted looked at him appraisingly. This was a different Charlie to the one he'd first met. Leona Rakale was clearly having a good effect on her small team.

'Charlie, you get the gold star today. Right, everyone, extend it a bit and find out occupations of family as well as the lads themselves.'

'Boss, two things,' Jezza put in. 'Decorators might well have a van which would be large enough to transport a number of people at a time. And if there was something going on with Badger towards team members and Callum was killed because, perhaps, he was about to say something, should we also be looking closely at the fathers? Including Mr Mitchell? They might have decided to do away with Badger if they knew he'd been messing about with their sons.'

'That's another excellent point, Jezza, and one which opens

up a whole new line of enquiry.'

'Sir?' Steve said hesitantly.

Ted nodded at him encouragingly, pleased he had at least spoken up with more than his own team members present.

'If Nigel works for the cleaners at the hospital, might he perhaps have access to the incinerators there? The ones for burning clinical waste? So could that possibly be where Badger's clothes ended up? Maybe his mobile, too. If it was the team who were involved.'

'Steve's got a good point there, boss,' Doug put in. 'And if he's right, I doubt you'll ever find any white suits or shoe covers. That's where they could very well have landed up.'

'What about the murder weapon? Anything useful there?' Jo asked.

'It was a rebar,' Rob said before Ted could speak. 'Or a least a part of one.'

'What's a rebar?' Ted asked him. 'I didn't think to ask what sort of rod it was.'

'A reinforcing bar, boss, you use them for strengthening concrete. Sally's dad's a builder, helped us a lot with our house so I learned a few words from him.'

Ted went back to his office to collect his things, annoyed with himself for the slip-up. He should have asked about the rod at the post-mortem. Big Jim would have jumped all over him for a lapse like that, and rightly so. He was more determined now to find time to visit him, if only briefly.

Jo came and stuck his head round the door to tell him he was going home.

'What about our little Steve then, eh? The lad has some brilliant ideas and it's great that he's finding the confidence to voice them. With the amount of interviews we have to get through, I was thinking of using him, too, and maybe letting him have a crack at Nigel. What d'you think?'

'Excellent idea. Give him chance to show us what he can do. And he certainly won't intimidate Nigel so he might get more out of him than anyone else has so far.'

Bella opened the front door of Jim's house in Didsbury. She was more or less a permanent fixture there now. Rosalie had gone back up to the Lakes because of her small son but was keeping in contact and had promised to try to visit whenever she could.

'Hello, Ted, it's lovely to see you. James will be pleased. Go on through. He's in the conservatory. Would you like a drink of something? A cup of tea, perhaps?'

He thanked her but declined. He wasn't planning on staying long. He didn't want to tire Jim out, and he needed to get back to explain his absence the previous night to Trev in person, rather than in a text message or a phone call.

Jim was sitting in a chair looking out at his garden. For a man who had nearly died just over a week ago, he looked in reasonable shape.

'Nice to see you, Ted. Pull up a chair and tell me where you're at with the case.'

Ted laughed as he sat down.

'Not a chance. I'm under orders from Bella not to tire you out or talk shop. How are you feeling, anyway?'

'Like someone cracked my chest open with a pneumatic drill,' he growled. 'But bloody glad to be still alive. And I'll tell you what, Ted. All that crap about your life flashing before your eyes is true. It's made me realise I need to put my affairs in order. Sort things out. Make an honest woman of Bella so she'll be all right after I'm gone.

'And I'll tell you another thing for nothing. You should bloody well marry your Trevor. He won't get your pension if you don't, as things stand. Never mind what stupid old farts like me think about same sex marriage. It's clear to anyone you love each other, so bloody well put a ring on his finger and make an honest man of him. I'll even come to the wedding.'

There was an awkward pause while Ted studied his feet.

Then he looked at Jim.

'Actually, we're already married, Jim. We did it a while ago. We weren't going to bother, but it was the police pension thing that swung it. We just sloped off to Wales with my mam and Trev's sister and had a quiet civil ceremony. I'm sorry I didn't tell you. I just didn't want to offend your beliefs and I knew you'd have a hard time accepting the idea.'

Jim looked hurt for a moment, then he stuck out a big hand, beaming broadly. Ted shook it.

'Well, bloody good for you. Congratulations. About time, too. I don't profess to understand it, but if Bella and me manage to stay together and to be as close as you two are, that will do for me. And I hope you'll agree to be my best man, even if I didn't get to be yours.'

# Chapter Nineteen

'Hey, you. You're home in time to eat. That's great. It won't be long, but now I know you're back in time for us to eat together, I can hurry it up a bit, if you like?'

Ted crossed the kitchen to plant a kiss on Trev's cheek. His partner was attempting to tidy up after his cooking, rinsing things under a running tap, making a bad job of loading the dishwasher. Ted knew he should have been pleased he was at least making an effort. Somehow it annoyed him more than it should have.

Trev abandoned his task and turned to look at him appraisingly. The kiss had lacked its customary warmth.

'Are you all right? You look knackered. What time did you get back last night? And where did you get to?'

Ted almost made the old Monty Python joke about not expecting the Spanish Inquisition. He couldn't even summon up the effort to do that.

'I'm fine, don't fuss. I'll just get changed before we eat.'

He didn't feel like talking. Not even to Trev. No doubt he was just tired after a bad night and from feeling disheartened by the case. The last thing he wanted to do was to talk about Philip, to anyone. But he owed Trev some sort of an explanation for his absence.

Trev was setting the table when Ted came back downstairs. Trev was the cats' idol, the one they worshipped unreservedly, although they were usually welcoming of Ted. For some reason the funny little kitten Adam was besotted with Ted. As soon as he saw him return, he trotted up to him, meowing for his attention. Ted smiled as he picked him up. Perhaps a bit of kitten cuddling was just what he needed to put him in a better humour.

'So what happened to you last night? Another shout? Not another body, I hope.'

'I was with Philip,' Ted told him, tickling Adam's stomach as he lay on his back in his arms.

'Philip?' Trev asked in surprise. 'I didn't know you were still in touch with him.'

'I wasn't. The Infirmary called me. They were trying to trace his next of kin but he gave them my name.'

'That sounds serious. Is he all right?'

'He died,' Ted said shortly, now gently rocking the kitten who was purring loudly in delight.

'God, Ted, I'm sorry. Did you get there in time to see him?'

'I was with him when he died. That's why I was so late back.'

'What time did you get home? Your side of the bed looked like it hadn't been slept in.'

'It hadn't. I got back about three, I suppose. I looked in on you but there was no room for me, what with you and the cats hogging the bed. I got a couple of hours in the spare room before I had to go to the post-mortem.'

'Ted, I'm really sorry. Honestly. You'd had a really rough night. You should have woken me up. You know what I'm like.'

Ted shrugged dismissively.

'It's fine.'

'Are you sure you're all right?'

'I will be if you stop fussing.' Then he added a, 'Please,' to soften it and went on, 'I think me and Adam will just have a walk round the garden together. I could do with a bit of fresh air, if there's time before it's ready?'

Trev watched him go out, his face concerned. He didn't

like it when Ted started shutting down like that. He was never good at talking about his feelings, not even to his therapist. When he let things bottle up too much, the outcome was never good. He could do with taking him away somewhere, even if only for an afternoon out. Riding, perhaps, now Ted had discovered he was not bad at it and quite enjoyed it. But Trev knew the chances of that happening in the middle of a case were somewhere between zero and bugger all.

Through the window he could see Ted wandering about, still holding the little cat like a baby in his arms, to Adam's evident delight. Perhaps he just needed a bit of time. Trev set the table then tapped on the window to get his attention, making eating motions to let him know food was ready.

Ted put Adam down carefully when he came back in, washed his hands then sat down at the table. They began the meal in silence. Eventually Trev broke it.

'How is Jim now? I bet he's pleased to be back home.'

'I think it gave him a bit of a wake-up call. He's going to marry Bella, put all his affairs in order. He told me I should do the same, so I had to tell him we were already married.'

There was another silence while they both ate. Trev was desperate to try to get things back to the usual ease between them.

'Bernard phoned me. The gym's back in service so self-defence and judo are both on again for tomorrow night. I know you're up to your eyes at the moment, but might you be able to get there for a bit of judo, if nothing else?'

'I very much doubt it. I want to try to get up to Roman Lakes at some point tomorrow, but it's likely to be later on. There's so much to get through at work.'

'Because it was where you used to go with Philip?' Trev asked him.

His tone was completely neutral, but it proved to be like a spark to tinder. Ted dropped his knife and fork with a noisy clatter which startled the cats and Trev in equal measure.

'It's the current case,' he said, more sharply than he intended. 'It's a double murder scene. It has nothing to do with Philip. Forget Philip. He's dead.'

He stood up abruptly, shoving his chair back so a couple of the cats had to leap out of the way. His voice softened slightly as he went on, 'Look, sorry, I'm just not very good company this evening. I didn't mean to snap. I think I'll go out for a bit. Go for a drive. Maybe walk a bit, until I'm in a better mood. I've no idea what time I'll be back. Don't wait up.'

'Ted ...' Trev started to say.

But Ted was gone.

Trev heard him pick up the car keys, pause to put on outdoor shoes, grab a coat. Then the front door closed, with more of a bang than usual, and he was left alone with the cats.

Ted didn't really know where he was going or why. He just felt he needed to be by himself for a bit. There was enough light left for him to go for a bit of a poke about at Roman Lakes, to see if anything jumped out at him.

Trev had unwittingly touched a bit of a raw nerve. It was true that the location held a lot of memories for Ted. It was where he'd gone fishing, many times, with his dad. Philip had not been much of a walker, not like Ted. But they had enjoyed many a gentle stroll around there when they had been seeing one another. It was a long time ago, but the memories were still there.

It was also where he'd taken his mother when she'd come back into his life after such a long absence. Where they'd finally opened up to one another about things which had happened in their lives while they'd been apart.

But now it was the scene of two murders. Ones he was not getting much nearer to solving for the time being. It was coming up for three weeks since the first one, that of Callum Mitchell. If there was no real progress soon, there would need to be a twenty-eight day review and there was an outside chance Ted would be taken off the case. Jim Baker would have stuck with him, loyally. But now the Chief Super was in overall charge, he might take a different view.

Ted parked the car and got out to walk. Walking should help clear his mind and hopefully improve his mood. Then he could go home and grovel suitably to Trev. He'd behaved badly towards his partner and he wasn't proud of himself.

He skirted the water for now, more interested in what he could see in the woods where the murders had taken place, now the Crime Scene Investigators had finished with the site. As he was walking along the track, he saw an older couple coming towards him, the woman with her mobile phone out, taking photos.

Ted nodded to them as they drew level.

'Evening,' the man greeted him. 'Nice enough for a walk now, isn't it?'

'At least it's not raining,' Ted agreed. 'I used to come here fishing with my dad when I was little. It always seemed to be raining.'

'You don't see so many youngsters fishing these days. It seems a bit too quiet for the young ones of today.'

'Do young people come up here for anything these days?'

The woman answered him. The man was looking at him rather suspiciously.

'We're not often up here late on but I've heard there's been trouble with teens in the woods of a night. Lighting fires, making a noise, that sort of thing.'

'Are you a journalist?' the man asked him. 'Snooping round because of the murders? Hoping to get a scoop or something?'

'No, I'm a police officer,' Ted assured him, reaching for his warrant card. He always had it with him. When he changed clothes, he automatically transferred it to the pocket of what he was wearing.

'I'm involved in the investigation. I was just trying to find out who comes up here at night time.'

'Not us, for sure,' the man told him. 'These days you never know who you might run into.'

'And what do they do up here?'

'Probably nothing worse than we got up to in my day,' the man said with a laugh. 'The wife and I did some of our courting up here. Just the kids these days make more noise because they all have their mobile phones for playing music. Or what they call music. Just sounds like noise to me.'

'And how do they come up here?'

'They don't walk, that's for sure, idle beggars. We always used to walk up, or at best, come on our bikes. But these days it seems like they all have cars.'

'Sorry to hold you up with all these questions, but it's very useful to me. Whereabouts would they park, to get into the woods?'

The man waved an arm as he explained to Ted. The place he was describing was the opposite direction to the way he'd arrived at the crime scene. He thanked them and went on his way. He'd like to go and have a scout round, to see if it gave him any new ideas. He knew he should at least text Trev with an apology but he couldn't bring himself to do it yet. He thought he'd just find the nearest pub after he'd looked in the woods. Maybe have a quick drink and see what local information he could glean.

On his way back to his car he walked along the edge of the water, remembering so many trips there with his dad. Ted had grown up idolising his father and hating his mother, thinking she'd walked out on him and broken off all contact. It was only much later he'd found out the truth and felt bitterly disappointed by his father's deception.

He stood looking out across the water, the sun starting to disappear now, casting a reddish glow in the sky. He spoke aloud.

'Why, Dad? Why did you never tell me the truth? Why didn't you let me keep in touch with mam? At least let me know that it wasn't my fault she left.'

None of it was helping his current mood. He realised he probably shouldn't have come. Too many memories stirred up which should have stayed buried. Time to have a ginger beer then to head for home.

Only it turned out not to be a ginger beer sort of a pub, when Ted walked in. It was quiet, hardly anyone in there, and so dimly lit Ted thought at first there must have been a problem with the electricity. He probably couldn't have picked a more depressing-looking watering hole if he'd tried. He should have turned and walked out. Instead, he went up to the bar, putting his hands against it and leaning his weight on his arms. There was a young man sitting there on a stool. Ted nodded in greeting as he waited for the man behind the bar to finish stacking mixers and serve him.

'What'll it be?'

'Snakebite,' Ted said, without pausing to think. 'Large one.'

He knew he shouldn't. He'd gone so long without. But it's what he felt like and he reasoned to himself that one wouldn't hurt. He wouldn't drink more because he had the car and he wasn't stupid enough to drink when driving.

He stood looking at the tall glass for a long moment after he'd paid the man who then went back to refilling shelves ready for an evening rush which would probably never happen.

Finally, he got a grip of himself and turned to look at the man on the stool next to him. He put him in his early-twenties, about.

'I ordered this but I really shouldn't,' he told him. 'Would you like it? I've not touched it.'

The young man was looking at him suspiciously.

'Are you trying to pick me up, mate? Only you're wasting your time. I'm not a queer and this isn't that sort of pub. You'd be better off going up Canal Street, if that's your game.'

Then he made an error. A serious error. He slid off his stool and went to shove Ted in the centre of the chest. Ted's reaction was entirely instinctive. With a deft movement he blocked the arm heading his way, turned it and locked it up the younger man's back, pinning him against the bar. At the same time he pulled out his warrant card and held it up towards the barman as he saw him grab his phone.

His voice was calm and polite as he said, 'Before you call the police, they're already here.'

Then, to the man he had hold of, 'You took that the wrong way, mate. I was genuinely offering you a free drink, not trying to pick you up. That's not my style. Never has been. You could have just refused politely, without getting personal.

'And here's a little tip for you. Make sure you know who you're about to take a swing at, so you don't finish up getting yourself seriously hurt one of these days. Now, before I let go of you, are we good?'

'Sorry, mate, I was just messing. I thought you were a knob jockey or something. No offence, mate.'

'None at all taken. And, as it happens, I am gay, but you are seriously not my type. So please, just drink the drink to save me from myself. Okay?'

'Okay, mate, whatever you say. Sorry.'

Ted suspected the younger man's hand would be shaking too much, once he let go of him, for him to manage to lift the glass. He also knew he was in absolutely no danger of a repeat performance. The barman was still hovering, unsure what to do.

Ted let go of the arm lock and stepped back.

'Right, then, gents, I'll wish you both a good evening,' and he walked back out into the fresh air.

He'd scared himself. Seriously. Not only by how close he'd come to falling off the wagon, but by how much he'd been spoiling for a fight. He needed to talk to someone. Not Trev. Trev was too close. He'd only fuss and worry. And suggest

179

more counselling. Only another copper could truly understand what it could be like sometimes, in the job. He could have gone to see Kev and been made welcome. But he was not far from where Bill lived. Bill would understand. He'd go there.

He realised how hungry he was, having swerved his evening meal, and he decided to pick up a takeaway. There was a Chinese nearby that wasn't bad. He got spare ribs for Bill, knowing he wasn't adventurous, and a Chinese for himself. Then he drove round to Bill's, parked the car nearby and rang the bell. He held the bags up in front of himself, like an offering, when Bill came to open the door.

Bill's greeting was not exactly suffused with warmth. He could be prickly in his own home.

'What d'you want, Ted? Haven't you got a home to go to?'

'I just need the company of another copper for a bit. I brought food.'

'It better not be bloody Chinese muck. Come in. Go on through to the kitchen. I haven't eaten yet, as it happens. And I'm not a bloody copper any more, remember?'

Bill's parrot Father Jack started shouting as soon as he heard someone come in.

'Feck! Arse! Drink!'

'Hello, Jack, pleased to see you again, too.'

'Did you bring beer?'

'Sorry, I forgot.'

'I've got some somewhere, but I've nowt to offer you. Only corporation pop.'

Despite his grumpy exterior, Bill was a good listener. He understood what the job could be like. He would have flatly denied it but Ted suspected he was glad of a bit of company. He'd lived alone since his wife had died, apart from Father Jack, and Ted was certain he must feel lonely sometimes, despite his protestations.

They ate and talked and it was just what Ted needed. Bill had taken him under his wing when he'd first taken up his post at Stockport. He was someone who wouldn't mince his words, and he certainly didn't.

'You're a bloody selfish sod sometimes, Ted. You live with a bloke who loves you and you come round here whingeing that he fusses over you too much. Don't you think I'd love to still have an other half who fussed over me?'

'Sorry, Bill, you're right. I've just had a bit of a bellyful these last couple of days. I so nearly drank that bloody snakebite. D'you want me to piss off now?'

'Stop here a bit longer. I'll put the kettle on. Your Trev doesn't deserve you inflicting yourself on him in a mood like you're in.'

Ted had rather lost track of the time and was shocked by what his phone was showing when it rang. Maurice Brown calling him. That surprised him; he thought it might have been Trev.

'Ted, you'd bloody well better not be on top of Kinder again. My feet have only just recovered from coming and fetching you down the last time. I've had your Trev on asking where you are and what's going on. He said he didn't want to ring you direct because you nearly bit his head off earlier. What're you playing at?'

'Sorry, Maurice. Sorry you got dragged into it. I'm just having a bad day so I took myself off to calm down a bit. I'll text him now. Thanks. And I owe you a pint.'

'Bloody right you do. At least one. I'm not a marriage guidance counsellor, you know.'

Maurice was another one who'd known Ted long enough not to mince words talking to him when they weren't at work.

Ted tapped out a careful text and sent it off to Trev.

'So sorry. Lost track of time. Not good company so thought I'd give you some space. Will see you tomorrow and explain. Ted xx'

Then he asked Bill, 'Sorry to be a total pain in the arse,

Bill, but can I crash on your sofa tonight? Just to let the dust settle at home?'

'I'll find you a pillow and a blanket. And you better not snore. I don't want Jack kept awake all night.'

# Chapter Twenty

Ted ran into the Ice Queen as he parked at the station the following morning after leaving Bill's house. He was thankful he always kept a full change of clothing, shoes and a wash-kit and razor in his car, just in case he ever needed them. He hadn't been home, but he was presentable for work. At least he didn't look as if he'd spent the night on Bill's far from comfortable sofa listening to Father Jack grumbling to himself from time to time.

She eyed him critically then said, 'You're cutting it very fine, Ted. I do hope you haven't forgotten you have a meeting at Central Park this morning?'

'No, ma'am,' Ted lied swiftly and shamelessly. 'I've just come to collect my service vehicle, then I'm on my way.'

She gave him the sort of look which told him plainly that, as the mother of two teenage boys, she could tell perfectly well when she wasn't being told the truth. Especially when he used the formality unnecessarily, as there was no one other than the two of them on the car park.

Ted excused himself and sprinted for the entrance to grab the keys to his car. If he got his foot down and gave the odd flash of the blues, he could still just about make it on time. He had totally forgotten about it, with all that had been going on. He phoned Jo as he ran.

'I completely forgot I have a meeting of Pen-pushers Anonymous at HQ, Jo. Can you take charge until I get back? God knows when that will be.'

'No worries at all, boss. We've got this one. You go and

have fun counting paper clips or whatever else it is you high-powered types get up to on these occasions.'

His words were too close to the truth to be funny. Ted had indeed been stuck in meetings where the topics had included such banal things as risk assessments on stationery. It was no wonder crime detection rates were down in many areas, with fewer officers patrolling and senior ranks often tied up with such mundane matters.

Inevitably, because he was running late, every single traffic light was against him. Every pedestrian crossing had someone waiting to use it. None of it was improving his mood, but he finally made it by the skin of his teeth. It worried him that he'd forgotten about the meeting and might have missed it altogether if he'd not encountered the Super. Perhaps he'd blotted it out subconsciously.

The meeting was about the last thing he needed. He would have preferred to be on the ground, working on the case. But his promotion to Chief Inspector meant his job was increasingly about the paperwork and management and less about hands-on crime detection.

To make matters worse, at such gatherings he was seeing more and more of the new breed of senior officer. Young, intelligent, ambitious, graduate entry, fast-tracked – even faster than he had been - but with little to no experience in the front line of policing. Ted doubted if most of them had ever had to face down a drunk armed with a broken bottle during a Saturday night pub brawl.

He tried not to be an old Luddite fighting progress. But there were times when he had to bite his tongue on such occasions at some of the things which were said. He knew he was far from being the only one. The older generation of senior officers, including his own Assistant Chief Constable (Crime), Russell Evans, who would be chairing the meeting, had come up the hard way, starting on the beat. Some even had the scars to prove it, like their Chief Constable, Jon Woodrow.

Ted didn't much care for the modern informality, either. In some nicks everyone was on first name terms from the most senior rank down. It wasn't Ted's style. He was only just into his forties but he was starting to feel old-fashioned, something of an anachronism with the new regime.

There was a bit of general socialising over coffee and biscuits to begin the day. The ACC, Russell Evans, made a beeline for Ted. They generally got on well.

'How's the latest case, Ted? Sounds like a strange one. Your second victim killed your first victim, I hear. Any further forward?'

'Rather too many suspects at the moment, sir. No forensics. And not enough officers to get through interviewing them all. It's a bit of a pared down team for a Major Incident.'

Ted knew he was preaching to the converted, but he always tried.

Russell Evans sighed. 'We're all feeling the squeeze, Ted, all of us. And knowing you, you'll be champing at the bit to get back there rather than being here with the number-crunchers. I'll try and keep it as short and sweet as I can, but you know how some of them love bumping their gums. You've got a good DI in Jo Rodriguez though, I hear?'

'Yes, sir, very good. We'd be lost without him.'

'Well, then, let's get the boring bits out of the way and balance the books for you so you can keep him a bit longer.'

Despite the ACC trying to keep things moving, the meeting dragged on until lunchtime, when sandwiches appeared and people were expected to stay and make small talk. Ted was ready to climb the walls but trying not to show it. He wondered what some of the other DCIs did all day if they could happily be away from their patch for so long, seemingly without remorse.

As soon as he could decently escape, he made a run for his car, once again on the phone to Jo.

'Jo, I finally got let out of school. I'm on my way. Can we

have a catch-up as soon as I get back, please, you and I?'

'Right, boss,' Jo began as the two of them sat down together in Jo's office. 'We've got a bit of a chicken and egg situation going on here. Agreed?'

Ted nodded so Jo continued.

'We now know Badger killed Callum. We suspect that's why he was killed himself. What we don't know so far is why he did it. So we've been focusing on finding out everything we can about Badger. Squeaky clean at work, and with the St John. Nothing but positive things to say about him. Likewise from the neighbours. A few of them said his mother could be very difficult and they admired him for having her with him and not in a home.

'Doping her for the night seems to have been the only way he could manage to work and to look after her. I'm not sure when or how he got chance for much sleep when he worked nights and his mother would have been awake during the days when he needed to sleep.

'The night-time pills were given in full agreement with the family doctor, who prescribed them. And yes, they were zopiclone, the drug used to knock Callum out. The search of Badger's house also found bottled lager and blackcurrant cordial, so there's pretty strong circumstantial evidence that that's where Callum was drugged, although we don't yet know why he went there.

'I imagine that, with that and the post-mortem findings, we can at least close the case of Callum's murder and put it down to Derek Waldren. Do you want the parents informing of that? It gives them closure of sorts, although I'm not sure how helpful that is when something like this happens. I'm quite happy to go and do that, with PC Khan.'

Ted nodded again. Jo was so on the ball he was starting to feel redundant.

'Okay, so the most likely motive for killing Callum was

that he knew, or suspected something about this man, Derek Waldren, alias Badger, and was about to reveal it. Unless he was intending to blackmail him about it. Badger laptop's been recovered from the house so I gave it to Steve for him to get it to give up its secrets. It made the poor lad blush a bit.'

'Child porn?' Ted asked, but Jo shook his head.

'Not really. It seems Badger got his jollies by watching young lads masturbate. It's surprisingly easy to find videos of it online and let's face it, as you and I both know, no doubt, it's something young lads do. Just not usually in front of a camera, but it seems that some do that, too.'

'So you're thinking he might have been encouraging lads from the football teams to do that? Maybe filming them?'

'I think that might be making five out of two and two. Me being a good Catholic boy and knowing what that upbringing can be like, I've had the team digging into Páraic's background and sure enough, he was Catholic. Catholic schools, both primary and High School, churchgoing family, so he would most likely have gone to confession. Same High School as Nigel Denby.

'Quick lesson here for you on Catholic doctrine, if you're not familiar. The Catholic Church maintains that masturbation is an intrinsically and gravely disordered action. Some older priests still drum that message home. So of course, as a good Catholic boy, I've never indulged, myself.'

Jo gave Ted a wink as he said it. His tone was always ironic when he spoke about his Catholicism, although Ted knew that he and his family were regular church-goers.

'I'm wondering if somehow Badger was, if not encouraging the lads to pleasure themselves, as my church would call it, at least telling them it was perfectly fine and healthy to do so. Then if young Páraic were to confess his sins and was told something entirely different by his parish priest ...' Jo left the suggestion in suspension.

'Surely that wouldn't be enough to drive him to kill

himself, though? If he did tell his priest, what would his penance be likely to be?'

'I can only speculate, of course, never having trodden that sinful path. Seriously though, you need to understand the whole Catholic guilt-tripping thing. It can be very powerful. Especially for a lad who might be getting the same stuff rammed down his throat at school and at home as well.'

'All right, that's a possibility. But if Badger was doing something like that, why have none of the lads ever reported it? Surely someone would have said something?'

'Ted, seriously?' Jo was informal with just the two of them there. 'Have you forgotten what it was like to be a young lad raging with hormones? A grown-up tells you it's perfectly normal and absolutely fine for you to have a J Arthur any time you feel like it. And the bloke's a paramedic too, so he clearly knows what he's talking about. It's an absolute gift. Why would you tell anyone else? Except perhaps your closest mates and who would they then tell?'

'All right, point taken. But supposing he went beyond talking about it to Páraic? Might that have been a stronger motive for his suicide?'

'It might well. It would also give the football team, if that's who it was, grounds to suspect Badger of being implicated in the death. And that could, in turn, lead to them exacting revenge. Whichever way you look at it, the football lads must remain our strongest suspects, right?'

'I agree. There's a very probable motive there. We've already talked about the means, with the materials associated with the building trade. So that leaves us with opportunity. How's that looking? How are you getting on with checking out their alibis?'

'This is where it starts to get interesting. And for this, you need to watch some CCTV.'

Jo found the right place on his computer. Before he started the footage running, he explained, 'So far all the lads who've been spoken to have said exactly the same thing. After the match, they all went together to a supermarket to buy beer, pizzas, crisps, that sort of thing. From there they went back to Antoine's place. Watched films, played games, crashed the night. They all effectively alibi one another.'

The tape started at the entrance to the supermarket. The youths were still wearing the track suits they'd had on at the match but had removed their black arm bands. They erupted, seemingly making a lot of noise, into the store, although the tape had no sound. They had a couple of trolleys and were clowning around with them, taking turns to ride on them, racing one another.

Jo pointed out the different faces to Ted. He'd seen them at the match but didn't have names to put to each of them. Antoine, Jerome, Jordan, Wayne, Will, Sammy, Terry, Marvin, Alan, Gary.

As the first camera lost them, the footage cut to another one which showed them selecting things from the shelves, dumping them into the trolleys. Sometimes they'd deliberately pick up something inappropriate and wrestle about putting it back.

'They're doing a lot to draw attention to themselves,' Ted commented. 'A perfect way to set up an independent alibi?'

'Good detecting,' Jo laughed. 'Anything else?'

'Where's Nigel?'

'Good question. According to him, and to the others we've spoken to, they were together all the time. He went with them to the supermarket. Unfortunately for our Nigel, the tapes seem to show different. We've not spotted him at all in any of the tapes we've had. Do you want to see for yourself?'

'I'll take your word for it, Jo. In view of your earlier assurances, I've no reason to doubt that your eyesight is good,' Ted told him with a smile.

Jo laughed loudly at the reference, then became serious again.

'The only problem is, I'm really struggling to see Nigel in

the role of a killer. Certainly by himself. Especially for something like Badger's killing. It's clearly not something one person could do by themselves, even if the crime scene didn't suggest others were involved. They've all said that Nigel was with them, so what plausible reasons are there for him not to show up on the tapes?'

'He didn't go in at the same time as the others, perhaps? Have you checked the tapes for earlier? Or later? Is there another entrance? Did he have to make a trip to the lav and had to stay there longer than he intended? Or he ran into someone he knew on the car park and stayed outside talking to them?'

'We're still checking, but so far we haven't found him on any tapes. But, as the old saying goes, absence of evidence is not evidence of absence. We can't prove he wasn't there.'

'Very good work, Jo, thanks. I'm glad something useful's come out of today so far, apart from me now knowing the ins and outs of a duck's arse about the latest risk assessment regulations. I'll go and let the Super know we're closing the case on Callum's murder, at least. As long as she and the Chief don't see any objection to that, and I don't see why they would.'

Ted and the Super were summoned to the Chief Super's office but left standing in front of his desk. He listened while the Ice Queen summed up what Ted had already told her.

'You have the evidence to show categorically that this man Waldren killed the boy?'

'Yes, sir. Traces of his blood were found on Callum Mitchell's throat, where the thumb mark indicating he'd been strangled was found. Professor Nelson pointed out to me at the post-mortem that the skin around Waldren's thumbnail had been bitten down to the quick leaving a crevice which would clearly bleed from time to time. Had Waldren been still alive I believe we would have crossed the evidence threshold to charge him with the murder.'

'Very well, we'll close the file on that one, at least. Have the parents been informed?'

'DI Rodriguez will do that shortly, sir, now I have your confirmation to close the file.'

'Debra, you and I will need to discuss how much information we release to the press, in light of this.'

'Sir, can I just say that I would suggest it's the minimum amount possible,' Ted put in. 'If word gets out too soon that Waldren killed Callum Mitchell, I would be worried that we'll get far less assistance from the public about his own killing than we would otherwise. There'll be no sympathy for a man who was the killer of a young lad like Callum, with his whole future ahead of him. Nobody's going to shed a tear for him and I doubt anyone would come forward with information which might lead us to the arrest of his killer.'

'Point taken, Ted, we'll certainly bear that in mind. Thank you. That will be all for now.'


Ted had promised Maurice his pint after work, knowing that Trev would be going off to judo. He hadn't heard anything from him and had decided he would wait until he saw him afterwards to try to put things right between them.

'So, come on then, if you weren't up Kinder last night, where were you and what were you up to?' Maurice asked him when Ted put the low-alcohol lager in front of him. He was still getting used to Maurice easing off the drink. His relationship with Megan Jennings was clearly doing wonders for him, as was anticipating being a father to another set of twins.

'I finished up round at Bill's, as it happens, and just rather lost track of time. Don't look at me like that, Maurice, that's the truth. I wasn't in a very good mood. I'd had a rough couple of days. I behaved like a dick, though. Sorry you got dragged into it. I'll sort it out with Trev tonight when he gets back from judo.

'So, what about young Steve? Have you talked to him yet about moving out? I laid the ground with Bill last night. I told him Steve was having to move out and he needed someone to keep an eye on him. Bill pretends otherwise but he's great at taking people under his wing. He did with me.'

'I just don't really know how to bring it up with Steve. We both like having him there. It's just that we need the room. But I feel mean, sounding like I'm chucking him out on his ear.'

'D'you want me to have a word with Steve? I could tell him I'm worried that Bill is lonely on his own and he could do with someone to keep him company.'

Maurice shook his head with a smile.

'You can be a right devious sod when you want to be, Ted.'

When Ted got back to the house, he half expected the oven to be on a low light with something simmering away inside, as was usually the case on a judo night. Instead it was switched off and there was a note on the kitchen table.

'Going out on the piss after judo. Don't wait up. Assuming you bother to come home at all.'

Not signed. Certainly no kiss at the end.

Adam the kitten had climbed most of the way up Ted's leg so he gently detached him and lifted him higher, rewarded by loud purring and a little head butting the underside of his chin.

'Houston, we have a problem,' Ted told him, his tone glum. 'I think it's going to take more than a red rose to get me out of this fine mess, Stanley.'

# Chapter Twenty-one

Ted put Adam down gently on the nearest chair then went to rummage in the fridge to see what he could find to eat. He wondered if he should perhaps make enough for two, in case Trev changed his mind and came home earlier and hungry.

There wasn't a huge choice. He was just sorting out some sausages, eggs, tomatoes for a bit of a fry-up when his mobile rang. The screen told him it was Siobhan, Trev's sister. She'd always been happy with her school nickname, Shewee, which everyone used. But her new boyfriend, Henry, didn't approve of it so she now insisted on her proper name.

'Hello, Siobhan.'

'Ted, why are you being horrible to my brother?' she demanded without preamble. 'He's very upset with you.'

Ted sighed to himself. All he needed right now was unsolicited marriage guidance from a teenager.

'I'm not intentionally being horrible to him. I've just had a bit of a rough week.'

'Are you getting divorced?'

'No, of course not,' Ted hastened to reassure her, then he went on, worried by her words, 'unless Trev's said something to you?'

'Just that he's really pissed off with you shutting him out all the time. You'd better sort it out, Ted. You two are supposed to be the grown-ups and I'm having to tell you what to do.'

She rang off abruptly, leaving Ted feeling bemused. He hadn't quite realised how bad things had got. He turned back to his supper preparations when his phone rang again.

'Hello, mam,' he said, wondering if there was anyone Trev hadn't told about their current difficulties.

'Are you all right, Teddy, *bach*? Only Trev seems a bit worried about you.'

'I'm fine, mam. *Fydd popeth yn iawn*. Just a hard case, and I've been neglecting Trev a bit. I'll sort it out with him tonight, promise. Then I'll try and book a weekend off for us to come and visit you soon.'

'Well, if you're sure, *bach*. Don't forget you can always phone and talk to your mam if you need to. It's what I'm here for. *Hwyl nawr 'te*, Teddy *bach*.'

*'Hwyl, mam. Diolch.'*

He surprised himself how the Welsh words still sometimes came back to him, even after all these years, when he talked to his mother.

Once again, he was just about to start cooking when his mobile rang. Someone else Trev had been talking to their current problems? Perhaps this would be Willow. Or even Trev's French friend, Laurence, whom Ted had never met. And was it just his imagination or was senior cat, Queen, glaring at him reproachfully from her customary place on the kitchen table?

This time there was no caller ID to tell him who the call was from so he answered guardedly.

'What news of your sunburned friend from down south, Gayboy?'

No preamble. Mr Green. As politically incorrect as ever.

'Have you not heard from him?'

The familiar tut of annoyance.

'Wake up, Gayboy. Would I be asking you if I had? The number I had is out of service.'

'Sorry. Bad day. Leave it with me, I'll try to find a different contact number for you asap.'

'I need to remind him this delivery has a sell-by date and

it's rapidly approaching.'

His words sent a chill through Ted's veins. He didn't dare think of the implications of that remark for the witness Green had sprung. He fervently hoped she would not be sold on to the highest bidder, if Harry couldn't arrange to collect as promised. And he was worried to hear that Harry was out of contact.

He pushed the makings of his supper to one side and tried the number he had for Harry, just on the off chance it had been a temporary fault when Green had attempted to call him. It was indeed out of service so he phoned Steve.

'Steve, I'm sorry to bother you when you've knocked off, but I need your help.'

'No worries, sir, happy to help. What can I do for you?'

'You remember that ex-Met officer you put me in touch with? Harry? I need to contact him urgently and the only phone number I have for him is dead. I think you found him on Twitter? You know I'm useless at social media and this needs to be kept under the radar. Could you see if you can make contact with him somehow? Did you have an email for him?'

Steve started to speak but Ted interrupted him.

'The main thing is, I don't want you to put yourself at any kind of risk at all. We don't want a repeat performance of what happened last time. So I only want you to do this if you can assure me you can do it safely.'

'Sir, I'm with Océane at the moment. If it's all right to bring her in on this, she'll be able to help me make sure I can do it all without it being easily monitored.'

'I'm even sorrier to be gatecrashing on your off-duty time then, if you're together. But yes, she has the clearance. I just need to get a message to him asking him to contact me urgently about a delivery, please. And seriously, Steve, don't either of you put yourself at any risk doing it. I owe you both a drink some time.'

'Sir, can I just ask, does that mean you think there's some sort of a paedophile ring connection with our current case?'

'Steve, we're both off duty. You're doing me a favour. You don't have to call me sir all the time. And no. Or at least I hope not. This is just a few loose ends to tidy up from before. Thanks, Steve, I really appreciate this. Just be careful.'

He didn't expect to hear anything from Harry soon so he took the chance to cook himself something. He'd brought home copies of all the witness statements taken to date from the football team members about their whereabouts on the night Derek Waldren was murdered. He wanted to go through them all in detail to look for inconsistencies. It would give him something to occupy himself until Trev got home. He'd no idea what time that would be but he was determined to stay up to apologise, grovel, do whatever it would take to put things right. He hated being at odds with him.

It was nearly midnight when he heard a car pull up outside. He went to the window and saw Trev get out of the rear passenger side and make his way up the drive, not entirely steady on his feet. At least he never took the bike if he was planning on going drinking. It had been safely locked up in the garage when Ted got home. Trev would have walked down to the dojo and got a lift back from whoever he'd been out with afterwards.

Ted hurried to open the door with a smile of welcome. Trev's face was like thunder.

'Hi, did you have a good time?'

He leaned towards his partner to try to plant a kiss on his cheek but Trev ignored him and strode past, heading for the kitchen.

'Look, I really am sorry about last night,' Ted said as he followed him. 'I behaved like a total prick and I shouldn't have done. I'm sorry I worried you. I should have let you know where I was.'

Trev ran himself a glass of water and drained it in one, moving towards the door.

'I'm going to bed. You can sleep in the spare room.'

'Trev, please, don't be like that,' Ted tried to put a hand on his arm but Trev shook it off roughly. 'I know I'm in the wrong here and I am really sorry. I don't know how many times I can say it before you believe me. Of course I'll sleep in the spare room, if that's what you really want. But can we talk about this sensibly? Tomorrow, when I get back from work?'

Trev's blue eyes were sparking with anger as he replied, 'It's one of my karate nights. It always has been, since we first met. So no, we can't talk about it tomorrow and at the moment, I can't tell you when I will feel like talking to you about it.'

He turned on his heel, nearly losing his balance as he did so and started climbing the stairs. Most of the cats had already gone up. Queen followed at his heels. Only young Adam stayed behind, looking adoringly up at Ted, who sighed heavily.

'I don't know what else I can say or do, Adam. I seem to make it worse every time I open my mouth. So, do you want to come and join me in the spare room tonight, or are you going up with the others?'

Ted's phone rang again before the kitten could give his opinion. Another Unknown Caller. He hoped it wasn't Green hassling him again before he had any news for him.

The voice which greeted him sounded breathless.

'Ted? Harry. You wanted me?'

'Are you all right? Our mutual friend is getting worried about the delivery he's trying to make. He asked me to remind you it has a sell by date.'

'That sounds ominous. But I've had to make arrangements for safe delivery and there was a setback. My flat was visited. Nothing taken, just very thoroughly turned over so I got the message and moved out. I had my mobile phone with me, thankfully, but I've junked the old one and this is just a burner. I think I'm in a position now to contact our mutual friend about delivery arrangements. I'll keep in touch. I'll let you know when I have a safe messaging number to give you.'

'Take care, Harry,' Ted told him, but the call had ended.

He picked Adam up gently.

'Well, come on, young man. It looks like it's thee and me for the spare room tonight.'


Ted wasn't quite sure whether it was worth leaving another note before he went to work, or what he could possibly write in it that wouldn't make things worse. He decided it was worth a shot.

'Sorry again. I know I'm impossible. Really hope we can talk soon. Ted x'

He was going to leave Jo to conduct the morning briefing as he had his finger on the pulse. Ted would just sit quietly and listen. He and Jo got together briefly first to talk tactics.

'Despite lack of forensics and seemingly tight alibis, I don't see how we can discount the football team as suspects, boss. Unless we're overlooking something blindly bloody obvious, I'd go so far as to say at this stage they're our only suspects. Most of the lacrosse team are in the clear with solid alibis. There's just another couple to check.'

'We shouldn't overlook someone in Páraic's background, though. His family must have been devastated when he took his own life. If they got wind of Badger possibly being behind it, maybe they would take the law into their own hands.'

'I've got Rob onto that. Páraic's from a big family, lots of brothers, cousins, uncles. If for any reason they did know or even suspect, there would be enough of them to account for all the footprints at the crime scene. Oh, and get this. One of Páraic's older brothers is a cage fighter. A pretty good one, too, making quite a name for himself.'

Ted frowned. 'I can see a cage fighter wanting to beat the crap out of someone he thought might have been responsible for his kid brother killing himself. But the kind of sadistic streak behind what happened to Badger doesn't quite sit right with me for that sort of person. Too cold-blooded.'

'Nor me, but I think in a case like this it's better no stone left unturned, eh?'

'What's still baffling me for the moment is why Callum went to see Badger. If he had something on him, why didn't he just go to the police? He must have realised he was potentially putting himself in danger.'

'My theory? I think Callum was a fair-minded lad. His choice of future career suggests that. I think it's just possible he wanted to give Badger a chance to give himself up. If the others were all planning to turn him in, perhaps Callum wanted him to have the opportunity to do the decent thing himself first. He was training for law, of course, so he probably realised it could well work in Badger's favour if he did give himself up and confessed everything. If what Badger was doing really was confined to telling lads it was fine to have a bit of hand relief, and it never went further than that, he wasn't facing the possibility of a custodial sentence, surely?'

'There's got to be more to it than we're seeing at the moment, Jo. The way he was killed, the way the rod was inserted. That could be sending out a message about what the killers thought they were dealing with. Actual sexual abuse of young boys. Which of course, he might well have been doing and we've just not found the evidence for it.

'One more thing I think we should keep in mind. Steve's theory of a paper drop or something similar for them to have kept in contact. I know it sounds a bit Boys' Own but they must have had some way of being in touch because they're far too smart to rely on any electronic means, knowing how easily they can be traced. We need to pinpoint where their phones were for when Badger was killed. They could be using burners, of course, I suppose.'

'We haven't got enough bodies to interview everyone we need to, boss. I can't see how we're going to find time to look for bits of paper which may not exist,' Jo began then, seeing Ted get that stubborn look he knew well, he went on, 'but we can at least ask each of the lads how they would communicate with one another if for any reason they didn't have access to phones or email.'

'Don't forget that by end of play today, tomorrow at the latest, I need some sort of spreadsheet of all the details of all the team members, including Nigel, and Páraic, plus their families and extended families. We've got a possible motive, of sorts. Now we need to find which of them had the means and the opportunity to kill Badger.'

Ted wanted to catch Steve before the briefing started, to thank him for his help the previous evening.

'I'll buy you that drink at dinner time, Steve,' he told him. 'There's something I wanted to talk to you about anyway.'

He saw Steve's immediate look of concern and went on, 'Don't worry, it's nothing bad. Just something else you might be able to help out with.'

Jo handled the team briefing skilfully, as ever. The only chink in the cover story any of them had come up with so far was all of them saying Nigel was with them at the supermarket but the CCTV footage telling a different story. They would have to speak to all of them yet again, to keep probing until they got a satisfactory explanation. It was going to be labour intensive but neither Jo nor Ted could see any short-cuts.

As soon as the briefing finished, Ted had to go down to see the Ice Queen to discuss the budget. He saw there were three mugs ready for coffee so he waited before sitting down. Sure enough, the Chief Super joined them.

'I'm hoping you can tell me there's a bit of progress, Ted,' he said, sitting down and gratefully accepting the coffee. 'This enquiry has run up a lot of hours already, as you know, without much to show for it so far. So make my day. Tell me we're going to get a breakthrough soon.'

'If we're right in our theories so far, we might well already know who our killers are but have absolutely no evidence to prove it, sir. It looks as if our best – in fact our only – hope is if we can crack one of the team into changing their story.

'With that in mind, I wanted to talk to you both about the possibility of bringing in an expert. I know it will push the budget up, but in the long run it might save us valuable hours. I was thinking of the psychologist we've used before on a couple of cases. Anthony Hopkins. His speciality is younger people. We think, from what we've seen so far, that Nigel is the most likely one to crack and tell us something useful. But I'm not an expert and we could waste valuable hours going after him if we're wrong about it.

'I'd like to bring Hopkins in to go over some of the interview tapes to tell us which of the team members would be the best to lean on, in the hopes of getting the breakthrough we need.'

'Well, I know that you don't readily accept help from shrinks,' the Chief Super replied. 'So if you're asking, then I think it's something we should do, if Debra is in agreement?'

'I'm certainly in favour. We know Hopkins' track record is excellent. He secured a relatively easy conviction for us in the Morgane Edwards case so I'd be quite happy to use him again.'

'That's settled, then, Ted. You call up the cavalry, I'll happily sign off on the costs.'


Over a drink in The Grapes at lunchtime – a Gunner for Ted, half of shandy for Steve - Ted mentioned the idea of Steve approaching Bill Baxter about lodgings. He even offered to go with him to mediate if Steve was worried.

He was surprised at Steve's enthusiasm when he mentioned the bird, Father Jack.

'He has a parrot? I actually really like birds. That wouldn't be a problem for me.'

'Parrot might not be the right word. He's one of those white ones with yellow feathers on his head.'

'A sulphur crested cockatoo? That sounds great. They're really good talkers. I always wanted a pet of some sort, preferably a bird, when I was little.'

Ted knew Steve's early life had not been an easy one. It looked like one of Ted's little schemes might be about to come off beneficially for two people he cared a lot about. That just left his own private life to sort out.

On a whim, he decided to finish at a decent time and go to the karate club. Trev wasn't expecting him to be there. It might hopefully be a nice surprise for him. A sign of how much Ted was trying to sort things out between them.

Trev was certainly surprised to see him. His greeting was still frosty but at least he spoke. As usual, they were paired off for *kumite* together after the warm-up.

Trev's attacking moves were ferocious. He was clearly still seething. Ted was technically superior, though he didn't have Trev's long reach. Theoretically, he could have blocked anything Trev threw at him. His reflexes were lightning-fast. But he was tired and he'd not had as much martial arts time of late as he would have liked.

Trev threw a roundhouse punch towards his face and Ted raised both arms to protect himself and deflect it. For a split second it left the opposite side of his face exposed to danger and Trev exploited it ruthlessly. His foot shot up in a side kick which connected, hard, with the left side of Ted's face.

Ted's head exploded with pain, tears started to his eyes. He wasn't sure if the crack he'd heard was made by Trev's foot or his cheekbone. Their *sensei* was there in an instant, intervening to stop them both and assess the injury.

'A&E, Ted,' he said firmly after a swift examination.

'I'm fine, it's nothing, just a bruise.'

'You know the rules. Head injury. A&E. And don't come back here until you have a medical certificate to say you're fit to. Trev, you drive him there.'

'Yes, *sensei*,' Ted said meekly, allowing himself to be led out by a now worried Trev who was apologising as much as Ted had previously been trying to do to him.

# Chapter Twenty-two

It was worth the time waiting in A&E. It was worth the pain. The throbbing, constant pain. The gradually increasing puffiness which was pushing his lower eyelid up, compromising his vision. It was worth it all because Trev was sitting beside him, his hand on Ted's, his blue eyes, warm again now, anxiously scanning his face. Constantly repeating how sorry he was for hurting him. Asking over and over if he was sure he was feeling all right. Was he dizzy? Feeling sick? Blurred vision? Did he want anything? A hot drink? But then no, he'd better not. Not before he'd been seen.

His fussing would normally have driven Ted to distraction. He was just so pleased that Trev was talking to him again he didn't mind what he was saying. He was aware he was probably sitting there with a soppy grin on his face, probably somewhat lop-sided because it hurt to stretch his left cheek. He didn't care.

It had certainly been worth the calculated risk of leaving the side of his face deliberately unguarded for the split second it had taken Trev to see and exploit it. Best of all, Trev seemed to be blissfully unaware that Ted had let himself be hurt. Desperate measures and all that, he told himself.

Trev had been shamelessly trying to get Ted bumped up the queue. He chatted up anyone who came near, exploiting his good looks and twinkling eyes. He kept explaining that Ted was a police officer, injured in the line of duty, working on an important case, possibly with a serious head injury, so needed to be seen urgently.

Ted wasn't sure if it had had any effect but someone did come to find him sooner than he'd feared. He was led away to a cubicle and told to wait again.

Eventually, after what felt like hours more, plus a trip to X-ray, he came back out. He found Trev hovering anxiously, waiting to greet him with a gentle hug.

'What did they say? Are you all right? Is it serious?'

'It's fine, nothing to worry about. I have a hairline fracture of the cheekbone which probably won't need any treatment at all. I'll most likely have an eye like a prize fighter by tomorrow, but apart from watching out for any signs of concussion and taking the odd painkiller, there's nothing to be done. It will heal in its own good time. You'll have to drive home though, if you don't mind. I haven't got very good vision on that side because of the swelling and the doctor said I'd perhaps better not drive for twenty-four hours just in case of delayed concussion.'

Trev draped a gentle arm around his shoulder and steered him towards the exit.

'Oh, god, Ted, I am so sorry. I feel awful about this. I mean, I was really angry with you. Literally fighting mad. But I certainly didn't intend to hurt you. Not enough to put you in A&E, for sure. I just can't understand how you let that kick past. It's not like you at all. Your reflexes are usually much better than that. A lot faster than mine most of the time.'

'I was tired. Not concentrating as well as I should,' Ted said evasively, putting his hand up to touch the swelling around his eye. Avoiding looking at Trev.

Trev stopped dead in his tracks. He slowly pivoted Ted round until they were facing one another.

'Ted Darling. You devious little detective. You did it deliberately, didn't you? You let your guard down so I'd hurt you and have to speak to you again.'

His voice was warm as he said it, though, his eyes sparkling with their familiar fun.

'You just wait until I get you home. I can see I'm going to have to deal severely with you.'

Ted tried to smile but it hurt too much now the swelling was increasing.

'I was getting desperate,' he admitted. 'I thought it was worth the risk to get you to speak to me again.'

Now Trev was laughing, back to his old self.

'You're always saying you love me beyond reason and this certainly proves it. Let's get back home. Are you starving? We're probably just about in time to grab a takeaway if you like? I was meant to be going out for a meal, remember, and I was still sulking too much to have left you anything to eat.'

'I'd better phone Mike and tell him I'll need a lift to work in the morning. Before it gets a bit late to be calling him.'

Ted took his phone out of his pocket to make the call. Trev laughed again.

'Typical Ted. Always the policeman. Always thinking about work. Here I am, proposing a romantic making-up session and all you can think about is how you're going to get to the nick tomorrow.'

'Ouch,' Mike said emphatically when he saw Ted's face as he opened the car door to get into the passenger side the following morning. 'That looks painful.'

'A moment's lack of concentration at martial arts training last night,' Ted told him dismissively. 'The moral of that story being don't attempt *kumite* with Trev when you're tired and not paying attention.'

Mike was still looking at him intently, his expression suspicious. He'd had experience of domestic violence in the past and Ted could see what was going through his mind.

'Really, Mike, a karate kick I should have seen coming a mile off but didn't. Nothing serious. I'm not supposed to drive for twenty-four hours in case of concussion, that's all. And to be honest, I'm struggling to see properly out of this eye anyway. So thanks for picking me up.'

Things were now completely back to normal between him and Trev. Ted had finally sat down to talk to him properly as they ate. He'd done his best to explain why seeing Philip as he was at the end, and sitting with him while he died, had stirred up feelings of guilt, although he knew it was irrational. He'd also admitted that the case being based around Roman Lakes hadn't helped. It had dredged up things about his father he'd not fully acknowledged before, not even to himself.

This time he told Trev everything, hid nothing. Trev listened in attentive silence while he recounted ordering a snakebite in the pub and so nearly getting himself into a fight over it.

Ted finished up by promising that he would try his best in future to talk more and not to bottle things up like he usually did. He realised himself how close he'd come to getting into serious trouble, drinking and pub brawling. He wasn't going to let that happen. This week had given him a wake-up call. It had also made him determined to find time to take Trev on a special holiday to thank him for putting up with him.

Ted had to explain his injury a few times during the next day at work. Bill spotted it the minute he walked through the door. Ted stopped to speak to him before he went upstairs.

'Oh dear, Trev finally caught up with you and didn't approve of you staying out all night then?' he asked.

'I wouldn't have blamed him if he had thumped me, but this was karate training last night. I wasn't concentrating.'

Bill was looking at him shrewdly. He was retired now, a civilian. He still sported a uniform, of sorts, which he claimed made him look like a parking attendant. But he'd been an excellent copper in his day, with a bravery decoration. Above all, he'd been a good sergeant. A shrewd judge of character, good at keeping young officers on the straight and narrow. In other words, he could spot a mile off when he was being spun a yarn.

'And he believed that load of old bull, did he?'

Ted grinned, as far as the pain would allow.

'No more than you did. But at least he's talking to me again now. And I talked to young Steve. He needs to move out of Maurice's and at the moment, he's got nowhere to go. Oh, and he loves birds. He always wanted a parrot like Jack.'

'Cockatoo,' Bill corrected him testily. 'All right, I'll talk to him. But I still don't know why you think I need a lodger.'

'Because you're a grumpy old bugger, even worse than Jack, and it would do you good to have someone to keep an eye on,' Ted told him cheerfully before heading for the stairs.

Inevitably there were more inquisitive looks at the start of morning briefing. Some of the team were too diplomatic to comment on the boss's shiner. For those who did he merely mentioned the karate session and left it at that. Jezza in particular looked suspicious. She was a kickboxer herself and she knew the boss's capabilities. But even she realised when it was best to keep her mouth shut.

Once again Ted was happy to let Jo lead the briefing after they'd had a quick discussion on how to proceed with the case.

'I got lucky with the psychologist,' Ted told him. 'He's free on Monday. So by end of play today I need the spreadsheet. Fully up to date, with all the football team members and anyone else we should be considering as a possible suspect. I want to spend the weekend going through it, but I thought I might work from home. I'm not keen on driving until I can see a bit better and I don't want to have to rely on lifts.'

'Why don't you just take the weekend off? You look like you need it. I know you like to keep hold of the reins but someone else could do that job.'

Ted made a rueful face.

'It's not that I doubt your ability, Jo. I honestly don't. I'm just a control freak. I need to keep my hand in. But I will work from home. Just make sure whoever's on duty knows they can call me at any time if I'm needed.

'I'd like to have Nigel brought in again on Monday for another interview. When the psychologist is here as I'd like him to see something of how Nigel performs under questioning, through the two-way. I know Nigel works nights and these are voluntary interviews, so can you ask someone to find out a convenient time for him to come in? Maybe late morning, if that suits? Make it sound informal, but I really want the psych to have a look at him and to tell us if we're wasting our time going after him in case he's a fantasist.

'In the meantime, I want to listen to all the recordings of him being interviewed to date. Just to get a feel for him. Not that I'm anything like the expert Hopkins is.

'Also I'd like someone to dig a bit more deeply into Callum's brother, Sean, and his alibi for the night Badger was killed. Let's just suppose for a moment that he knew or even suspected who had killed his brother and decided to take action. Who are his friends? Does he know anyone who would have helped him with something like this? We keep being told they weren't all that close, but he might still have wanted justice for his brother. The same goes for Callum's father.

'How did it go with the family, telling them who killed Callum? Did they appear surprised? Did the name mean anything to them, do you think?'

'PC Khan and I discussed it at length after we'd told them. She's very good. Very observant. We both agreed that unless either of the parents is an Oscar-winning actor, the name meant nothing to them and they had no idea why Badger might have killed Callum. They didn't know they knew each other, although clearly they knew there were sometimes first aiders present at the matches. And yes, Callum had had a minor injury once and had to be helped off the pitch and examined.'

'So it's possible Badger had trotted out his "it's perfectly normal and it won't make you go blind" speech to Callum, so he knew what he was like. Right, once I've finished with briefings and meetings, I'll make a start on listening to those recordings to date, and going over the notes. I know you're all over it. There's a remote possibility my fresh eyes, or at least one and a half of them, might pick up on something we've not yet thought of. At least it will make me feel I'm doing something useful. And I want to be well up to speed for when I talk to the psychologist.

'Speaking of PC Khan, I think the budget's about at an end to keep an FLO with the family after today. Especially now the file is officially closed on the case. Let's have a catch-up at the end of the day and bring her in on it. Can you make it five o'clock, please? I'm determined to get away at a halfway decent time this evening.'

'Can't say I blame you. I bet that hurts.'

'I wish I could say "you should see the other bloke" but there's not a mark on him.'


Once the briefing had finished and Ted went back to his own office, an incoming phone call told him Jim Baker was calling him.

'How are you doing, Jim? Making progress?'

'I'm calling to ask if you and Trev can come to lunch on Sunday.'

Ted hesitated.

'I was rather planning on a working weekend, Jim. I'm calling in that psychologist again on this one, the same one we've used before, and I wanted to make sure I'm fully up to speed before I see him on Monday.'

'Let me put it another way, Chief Inspector. I am ordering you, as your senior officer, to come to lunch on Sunday and to bring young Trevor with you. Look on it as crime prevention. Bella is driving me mad with her fussing and I might possibly finish up doing something drastic if you don't come and rescue me. You and I can have a good catch-up and Bella can talk wedding outfits with Trev. She's really taken with him.'

'You can't actually order me to do anything, Jim. You're on sick leave, remember? But all right, you've twisted my arm. As long as you remember I'm under strict orders from Bella not to allow you to talk shop. I'll need to check with Trev that he's got nothing on. If you don't hear to the contrary, we'll be there. Look on it as my contribution to community policing.'

Ted was just going downstairs to update the Ice Queen on the progress, or lack of it, on the case, when he ran into the Chief Super going up.

'Good grief, Ted, what the hell happened to you?'

'Martial arts training, sir.'

'I thought you were supposed to be good at that stuff? Ex-SFO?'

'I was fighting someone who was better than me.'

'And you're sure that's all it was? I'd hate to think I had senior officers who were brawling.'

'Definitely not brawling, sir. Controlled karate, only I lost concentration for a fraction of a second at the wrong moment.'

'And is there any progress to report on the case?'

'Psychologist is coming in on Monday, sir. I'm going to get him to observe the one we think might be the easiest to crack and hoping he can advise on how best to proceed with interviewing him and the rest of them.'

'Keep me posted. I want some good news on this one soon, Ted.'

He said the second half of the sentence as he continued on his way, taking the steps two at a time.

Ted risked putting his head round Kevin Turner's door next. Sooner or later he'd run into him. He might as well get the remarks out of the way first. As it was, Kev was so busy ranting about the latest strain on his officers he barely commented on Ted's battered face.

'It gets bloody worse, Ted. We've now got people phoning in because their favourite takeaway is closed for no apparent reason and we're supposed to advise them what to do. And then they wonder why they have difficulty getting through and we haven't enough officers to send out on real crimes. Anyway, what happened to you? Is the other bloke worse off?'

'Surely you must have felt like banging your head against a wall in this job a few times?'

The Ice Queen was at least tactful. She could hardly miss the state Ted was in. His eye, now half-closed, and the area round it had turned a few interesting colours already. All she did was to enquire whether he was fit to be at work and to put coffee in front of him.

'I'm assuming we'll be standing PC Khan down now? I've asked for her to come in for debriefing this afternoon, on that assumption. There's no chance of keeping her on a bit longer to help with interviewing witnesses, perhaps? She's proved herself to be a good, observant officer who would be a useful addition.'

'Unfortunately, she's already spoken for. Another bereaved family in another town is in need of her services. I appreciate there are a lot of witnesses and potential suspects to be interviewed. Liaise with Inspector Turner for some help from Uniform.'

Ted thought it wise not to predict what Kev's likely response to that would be.


Even the informal voluntary interviews were recorded by phone for later checking, and it was those recordings Ted wanted to listen to. He was particularly keen to hear the one of Steve talking to Nigel. Steve hadn't done a lot of interviewing as he could be tongue-tied and awkward, despite the training he'd had as well as sitting in with other more experienced officers. Jo putting him with Nigel was a good idea. If Nigel would open up to anyone, it could well be to Steve.

Ted listened to it a couple of times then went over and over Steve's meticulous notes of the interview. He hadn't been wrong. He buzzed Jo and asked him to come.

'Steve did a very good job with Nigel, I'm impressed,' he began, when his DI joined him.

'I haven't had the time to go through it in detail. I've just scanned the notes and listened to a bit of a recording, but I think he did very well, too.'

'I've been going over that one in particular in detail because I wanted to hear how Steve got on. And I agree. He did a good job. He just perhaps lacks the experience to pick up on detail yet. Because that interview was very significant. Listen.'

He found the right place and pressed play.

'You mentioned Badger to my colleagues, Nigel. Who is he?'

'I don't know. It's just a name that popped into my mind. I must have heard it somewhere, but I don't know where. I don't think it's anything significant. Maybe it was in a film I saw. Someone had that nickname. I don't actually know anyone called Badger.'

'Now listen to this, later on.'

'After the player was injured and was taken off by the first aiders, you went over to the ambulance, Nigel. Why was that?'

'I just wanted to ask Derek how Jamie was. That was the name of the lad who got hurt.'

'Do any of the first aiders have nicknames?'

'I don't know. I don't know any of them personally, by name or by nickname. We mostly just call them the Johnners. It's not always the same people at the matches. I just wanted to find out if Jamie was okay.'

Ted switched it off and looked expectantly at Jo who was saying something in Spanish. Ted could have a rough guess at what it might be.

'I should have picked up on that sooner, boss. You spotted it with one eye closed, literally. He doesn't know any of them. Yet he called him Derek. Before Steve had even mentioned he name.'

'Precisely. So it's even more important that we have young Nigel back in. This time I'd like you to question him yourself and have Jezza with you. She's brilliant on details. And the psych and I will be watching. Let's find out what else young Nigel knows and is trying not to tell us.'

# Chapter Twenty-three

'You're home at a decent time. Does that mean you've made some progress? And how are you feeling now? I've just put supper in the oven, but I need a quick shower next. I've been tinkering about with a real old-fashioned oil-spitting monster of a bike in between the hi-tech stuff today.'

Trev was busy seeing to the cats, who were swarming and purring round his legs at the sight of food. All except young Adam. As soon as he saw Ted come in, he left the bowls and the feeding frenzy and started his solemn ascent of his trouser leg. Ted smiled as he picked him up.

'That kitty has a serious case of hero worship,' Trev laughed.

'He slept with me when you wouldn't. He's a funny little thing.'

Trev lifted him from Ted's arms and plonked him back on the floor next to the nearest available food dish. Then he gave Ted a kiss on his good cheek and pointed to a paper bag in the middle of the kitchen table.

'I went to the health food shop today to get you some things to try to heal that up a bit faster. There's some arnica cream to put on it. That's magic stuff for bruising.'

He started pulling the contents of the bag out and putting them on the table.

'The young lady in the shop was ever so helpful. She suggested these homeopathic pills as well for an extra boost. They're arnica, too. She said take three at a time but if it's very painful you can go up to four.'

Ted looked at him sceptically.

'You do realise they're probably just little sugar pills?'

'It's worth a try though, surely? They can't hurt.'

Trev was still pulling things out of the bag. A magician releasing doves.

'And I got you a load of different teas to try. Herbal. Anti-inflammatory ones. This one's marjoram. That's very good for something, but I can't remember what. And turmeric, look. That's an excellent anti-inflammatory. Try them, Ted, they might help. Anyway, I'll grab a quick shower. Are you coming?'

'No, I'll just get changed in a minute but first I'm going to try some of this stuff. Thank you, it's very kind. I'm not planning to go into work this weekend. I've brought a load of notes home that I need to go through. But we could perhaps go out for a walk tomorrow afternoon somewhere. Lyme Park, maybe? Or Kinder?'

'Kinder!' Trev said enthusiastically. It was their special place.

'And we're invited to Jim's on Sunday for lunch. Bella's into wedding planning so I'm sure she'd love to talk to you about it while Jim and I talk shop.'

'Fabulous! That sounds like the perfect weekend. I'll just go and get that shower. I'll put the cream on your face for you once my hands are clean. Try some of the pills and the teas.'

Trev went sprinting up the stairs, clearly pleased with himself as he was singing loudly and tunelessly as he went.

Ted took the lid off the container of pills, shook three of them into his hand, then stepped carefully over the cats, went to the sink and turned on the cold tap. Adam immediately looked up to see what he was doing. Ted dropped the pills down the plughole and let the water wash them away.

'Don't you say a word, young man,' he told Adam sternly.

He boiled up the kettle, dunked one of the marjoram tea bags briefly in the hot water then replaced it with one of his green tea bags. He wouldn't hurt Trev's feelings for the world but he wasn't a great believer in any of that stuff. Too much of a cynical copper, he told himself.

'First question, Bella, and almost as important as what you're wearing for the big day. Where is Jim taking you on honeymoon?' Trev asked.

Bella smiled fondly towards Big Jim as she replied, 'Well, we thought of a quiet little cottage in the Lakes, perhaps. James has to take things easy for a while, of course.'

'Nonsense! Not remotely romantic enough. Insist on Venice. Or Florence. Or even Paris. You can always go by train so it's restful. Now, why don't I come and help you in the kitchen so we can bitch about our miserly menfolk while they talk shop?'

'Just remember, James, you're supposed to be avoiding all stress. Perhaps you should talk about something else?'

'Yes, dear,' Big Jim told her with a sly wink at Ted.

The two of them went through to the conservatory and sat down.

'Are you sure that was karate? It looks bloody sore.'

'Quite sure. And it's better than it was. Trev's bought me a load of magic potions from the health food shop to help it. I think they saw him and his credit card coming. Homeopathic pills and the like'

'That stuff? Isn't it a load of rubbish?'

'I'm sure it's very helpful for some people. I just don't think it's right for cranky old coppers like us two.'

'Well, I bloody hope he doesn't persuade Bella to try it out on me. I'm already dangerously close to the edge with all her fussing.'

'What an ungrateful pair of bastards we are, eh, Jim? I got told off by Bill when I was complaining about Trev's fussing. He reminded me how much he would love still to have his missus with him, making all the fuss she wanted to.

'Now, am I really allowed to tell you about the case, or will Bella ban me from having pudding if I do?'

Jim listened to all he had to say, interjecting from time to time, questioning, suggesting. Ted appreciated his input. They had always worked well together.

When Bella called them to the table, Jim added a final word.

'Just don't let Chris Higginbotham stick his neb in. He's a good copper. At least he came up the proper way. But he knows bugger all about detective work, so don't let him forget that.'

The psychologist arrived promptly on Monday morning. Ted met him in reception and showed him up to his office. He was leaving Jo to get on with the morning briefing while he talked to Anthony Hopkins about what he was hoping to get from his presence. Hopkins always qualified his name by saying he pronounced the H in Anthony, unlike the actor.

While Ted made green tea for both of them, Hopkins asked him, 'Would it be tactless of me to ask about the interesting facial pop art?'

Ted smiled. It was getting less painful to do so. The swelling to his eye had gone down but the cheekbone was still puffy. The bruising was now a colourful palette of blues, purples and yellows. Trev had likened it to an Andy Warhol.

'Martial arts are better engaged in when you're not preoccupied with a case. Which is where you can hopefully shed some light on things for me.'

'I think I've explained before, Ted, it's not, unfortunately, as easy as me just looking at someone and telling you if he's your killer or not. I would need to spend some time talking to them before I could make any balanced sort of judgement. So what is it you hope I can do for you?

Ted set out succinctly all that they knew so far and what had been surmised about Badger.

'Ah, yes, now I can make an educated guess for you there, based on my previous experience in various cases. He was a paramedic, you say? And a first aider at various youth football matches, who had a penchant for watching young boys masturbate? I have come across something similar, so I would conjecture that the initial conversation might go something like 'you risk serious groin strain if you don't masturbate effectively and frequently, so if you like I can show you/help you/watch you/let you watch me' - delete where not applicable.'

'As easy as that?'

'Oh, even a seasoned police officer such as yourself may be surprised at some of the things I've heard in my time of working with disturbed young people, which have proved sufficient to start things rolling.

'What sort of age group are we talking about with these football players?'

'Well, Nigel and the others we're currently talking to, and Callum, the youth who was murdered, are all around nineteen now. They haven't played for the team for two years or more. But most of them were involved with the club from quite young, and several of them have stayed in touch.

'Nigel's coming in later this morning and I've got my DI and a very sharp DC going to talk to him. It appears clear that he did know the second victim, Derek Waldren, although he's got a habit of backtracking on everything he says. You're the expert, not me, but my theory is he's a people-pleaser. He feeds off body language, seeks approval, and says whatever he feels will bring it.

'He's being interviewed purely as a witness at the moment, not a suspect. We haven't a scrap of forensic evidence against anyone to back up our conjecture. No eye witnesses, either. Which is why if we stand any chance of charging anyone for this, we're going to need a confession. Or a cast iron witness statement from someone who's not going to retract immediately they've said it. A credible witness who would stand up to robust cross-examination in court. And I don't think that's Nigel.

'I'd like us to watch and listen to what Nigel has to say for himself this time. He's already been spoken to on several occasions by different officers. I'll have a wire direct to my DI, Jo Rodriguez, so if there's anything in particular you'd like him to ask, we can pass it on. And if you'd like and you have time, I could buy you a meal at our local before you go on your way, to discuss your views. There's a private room we can use there.'

'That all sounds fine to me, Ted. Especially the lunch.'

Jo let them know when he and Jezza were ready to start. Ted and Anthony took their seats in the room next door from where they could see and hear everything which was going on, without being seen themselves.

'Thanks for coming in again, Nigel. We really appreciate your continued cooperation. I'm DI Rodriguez, and I think you've met DC Vine before. Let me just reiterate that you're here on an entirely voluntary basis, as a potential witness. You're not under arrest, so no caution is necessary, nor is legal representation, and you are free to leave at any time. DC Vine will be recording what is said on her phone but purely to aid with note-taking. Do you understand all that and are you happy to proceed on that basis?'

'Yes, that's fine. I'm happy to help, especially when it comes to Callum's death,' Nigel replied. His face was eager. He was making eye contact with Jo, his expression earnest.

'Thank you, Nigel. I know it's a bit of a pain for you to keep coming in, with working nights, but we really do appreciate your help.

'Now, just to recap. I think you know by now that we have evidence to show that the person who killed Callum Mitchell was Derek Waldren, who was himself killed on the evening of the benefit match for Páraic. You were at that match, with the rest of the former team members. You were all on the youth team at the same time as Callum. Is that right?'

Nigel barely had time to confirm it before Jezza started questioning him.

'Nigel, did you know Derek Waldren?'

'No, not really. I may have seen him around at the matches if he was a Johnner.'

'And yet when you spoke to my colleague, DC Ellis,' Jezza made an elaborate show of looking at her notes, 'you referred to him as Derek when you said you'd gone across to the ambulance to see how the injured boy, Jamie, was. Yet DC Ellis hadn't mentioned his name by that point.'

Nigel frowned as he said, 'I don't think I did. I don't think I'd heard his name. Not that I remember.'

Jezza looked at him long enough to make him start to shift uncomfortably in his seat.

'I can play you the tape of the interview, if you'd like me to?'

'No, no, that's fine, if you say so, I must have said it. So I suppose I must have heard his name at some point, maybe subconsciously, and just trotted it out.'

'Who's Badger, Nigel?'

'I don't know. It's just a name I got from somewhere. Maybe in a film I watched?'

'Did you ever need first aid when you were playing, Nigel? I suppose most players get injured at some time. Were you ever treated by someone from St John?'

A slight hesitation before Nigel replied, 'I did have the odd injury, yes. I was taken off in a tournament one time, treated in an ambulance, but I didn't need to go to hospital or anything.'

'Who treated you? Was it Derek?' Jezza, this time.

'No. I don't think so. I don't know. Whoever it was didn't tell me their name.'

'That's unusual, surely?' Jezza again. 'I've had first aid

treatment a few times and it's usually the first thing they say to you. "Hello, my name's Derek, can you tell me your name?" It's a good way to check for head injuries, for one thing.'

'I honestly don't remember.' Nigel was starting to sound confused.

'She's really rather good, your DC Vine, isn't she?' the psychologist said to Ted on the other side of the glass. 'I should be quite terrified of being questioned by her. And, to use a technical term, your young Nigel appears to be lying through his teeth.'

'Let me refresh your memory for you,' Jezza told him, looking through her notes again. 'You're possibly not aware but all injuries at matches and even during training sessions have to be logged and the forms kept for future examination. The club you used to play for keeps an accident book, with everything recorded in it for easy access.

'I've found one injury recorded here for you. It's about four years ago, when you were playing for the Under-16s. Do you remember that?'

Nigel was looking from her to Jo and back now, licking his lips nervously. A beaker of water had been provided for him and he took a swallow from it.

'Not specifically.'

'When first aiders attend for the matches, they also have to keep a detailed log of any injuries, of course. We checked theirs against this one and the first aider who attended to you on that day was Derek Waldren. But you say you don't remember the incident? Or the name of the first aider?'

'No, not really. I think I was concussed.'

'It says in the notes you suffered a groin strain,' Jezza told him. 'That must have been one heck of a groin strain if it managed to give you concussion as well.'

Anthony Hopkins exchanged a look with Ted and chuckled to himself.

'Was the first aider someone you'd seen before at the

matches?' Jo asked him.

'I honestly don't remember. He was just the paramedic who treated me. I didn't take all that much notice.'

Jezza pounced immediately.

'Paramedic?'

Nigel looked at her, his expression puzzled.

'Why did you call him a paramedic?'

'Well, isn't that what he was?'

'Derek Waldren was a paramedic, yes. But most first aiders are not paramedics. They're first aiders. So why did you choose that word?'

'I … I got confused. It thought it meant the same thing.'

'You work at the hospital don't you, Nigel?' Jo put in.

'Yes, but only with the cleaning contractors. Nothing medical. I don't know all the right terms. I might have got that wrong.'

'What does your job involve?' Jo continued. 'Do you have anything to do with disposing of clinical waste, for example?'

'I'm sure you don't need me to point out to you, Ted, that that question touched a nerve with our young friend. Your observation of body language is probably even better than mine, in your line of work, but I thought I'd just flag it up,' the psychologist said, in the next room.

'I … sometimes, yes, but not exclusively. I mostly use the big cleaning machines, doing the floors.'

'Going back to that injury, Nigel,' Jezza picked up the threads as if there'd been no change in the line of questioning. 'A groin strain. You were taken off the pitch to the ambulance and seen by a male paramedic or first aider who was unknown to you. What did his examination and treatment consist of? Don't feel embarrassed about discussing it. I have a younger brother.'

'Well, he asked me where the pain was ...'

'Just so we can picture the scene, Nigel,' Jo cut in. 'You

were in the back of the ambulance at this time. Was anyone else there? Or was it just you and the first aider?'

'No, it was just me and him. He asked me to describe where the pain was and what it felt like.'

'Without introducing himself to you first?' Jezza asked.

'He … er … he might have said his name and I just didn't register it.'

'And you were alone with him in the ambulance?' Jezza again. 'Were you comfortable with that? It was quite an intimate place for an injury, but you were alone with a man you say you didn't know. Did he close the ambulance door?'

'Well, he was a first aider, not just some random bloke. In uniform. The door was closed, yes.'

'Go on, Nigel. Tell us what happened next,' Jo said encouragingly.

'I told him how the accident happened and what the pain was like and he said it was most likely to be a groin strain.'

'Did he examine you physically?' Jezza asked. 'Did he touch you at all?'

Nigel was looking distinctly uncomfortable, moving about in his chair and looking from one to another of them.

'He needed to. Of course he did. To make a proper diagnosis. But he asked me first if it was all right if he did.'

'And you were still all right with this?' Jezza persisted. 'You were fifteen, alone in an ambulance with a man you didn't know, about to touch you in an intimate place, and you were quite comfortable with the whole thing?'

'Might I suggest you ask them to change the subject at this point, Ted? I'll explain why later.'

'Jo, can you move on from there, please?'

'Tell us about the evening after the benefit match, please, Nigel,' Jo cut in. 'You say you were at the supermarket with the rest of your old team mates. But you don't show up anywhere on any of the CCTV from in store. Can you suggest why that should be?'

'I don't know. I was there. Perhaps I was behind the others?'

'What were you doing there?' Jezza asked him. She'd picked up her cue from Jo that it was time to change the subject, without needing to be told.

'Buying stuff. Shopping,' Nigel told her, happier now he felt himself on safer ground.

'Anything else?

Nigel hesitated for a fraction of a second. He seemed unsure, unprepared for the question. He broke eye contact while he fished for an answer.

'Just mucking about a bit. You know, messing.'

'In what particular way?' she insisted.

'Making a bit of noise. Fooling about, like.'

'And you're absolutely certain you were there while all this was going on, Nigel?' Jo put in. 'Only as we've said, you don't show up anywhere on any of the tapes.'

Nigel's smile had an air of triumph about it as he replied, 'Like you said, I'm here voluntarily to help you. If you don't think I was in the supermarket with the others, isn't it for you to prove that I wasn't not for me to prove that I was?'

# Chapter Twenty-four

Monday lunchtimes in the The Grapes tended to be quiet so Ted had asked the landlord, Dave, if he could use the back room for his meal with the psychologist. That way they could discuss the case without being overheard. It was certainly a more convivial setting than Ted's cramped office. It was where Ted had proposed to Trev, down on one knee, and Trev had finally accepted after many years of refusing.

Dave was happy to oblige. The officers from the station were good customers. Ted's team in particular he approved of as they were well-behaved, never causing him any trouble.

Both Ted and Anthony chose the hotpot, a house speciality. They waited, chatting inconsequentially, until Dave had brought it through with their drinks. Both were quiet for a moment while they took their first taste.

Hopkins nodded his approval.

'This is very good. Excellent suggestion, Ted. Thank you. Now, shall I begin by saying why I asked for the change of subject when I did?'

Ted's mouth was full so he merely nodded in his turn.

'I agree entirely with your judgement of Nigel as a people pleaser. It was clear that he was feeding the answers he thought were anticipated which may or may not have been true. I felt that if your officers continued to press at that moment, it could well have been counter-productive.

'His parting shot was rather different, though, didn't you find? Shortly before he asked to terminate the interview to give him chance to get to bed for a few hours before his night shift.

Saying the onus of proof was on you and not him. That seemed completely different, to me. Almost as if he'd been coached to say that.'

Anthony attacked his plate of food once more so Ted finished his mouthful to respond.

'That's how it seemed to me, too. From what I've heard of Nigel so far, whatever his involvement in any of this is, he's not the brains behind it. I would put him as a follower, rather than a leader. Which would probably explain why he was more often than not on the subs' bench rather than the team. Did anything else strike you about him? Or about the case in general, from the notes I sent you? It's no secret that we're struggling a bit with this one, with absolutely no forensic evidence to date, so all theories are welcome.'

'Do you read much, Ted? Or watch classic black and white films?' Hopkins replied with questions of his own.

'Ah,' Ted told him, taking a drink of his Gunner. 'Now, I think I might just be able to stun you with my incredible psychic powers. I'm not a great reader, but my partner is a real film buff. Do I win a prize if I tell you the film and book I believe you're thinking of is *Lord of the Flies*?'

The psychologist laughed.

'Well, that is really impressive. That's exactly the one I was going to mention. Do you read tea-leaves as well?'

'I was at the benefit match Nigel and the others attended. They made something of a dramatic entrance at the start. It reminded me of that scene in the film where the choirboys come marching up the beach singing. The earlier, black and white film. Choirboys, right? They should symbolise innocence. For me, that was one of the most chilling scenes in the film. Full of latent menace.'

'You're very perceptive. Not many people get that message from that scene.'

'So is Nigel like Simon in the film? Is he likely to be our next victim?'

'I'm afraid I don't have your psychic powers, Ted. I would just advise caution in how you deal with him, though. There's a weakness there. A vulnerability. Lean on him too hard at the wrong moment and you might very well find that he breaks. But not necessarily in the way you're hoping for. Not enough to advance your case in any way.

'And remember, the message of the book is about descent into primitive savagery. If you try too hard to break Nigel, you might possibly be putting his life at risk. The pack may well turn on the weakest member to save themselves. That's the rule of nature and we are all savages under the skin. In something like this, it's every man for himself.'

Once they'd finished their meal and their discussion of the interview, Ted and Hopkins left the pub together.

'My car's just round the corner, in fact,' the psychologist told him. 'I spotted a parking space so I grabbed it, in case parking was an issue at your station. I think I had a problem the last time I came here. I'll send you my full written report as soon as I'm able to get my notes typed up, and good luck with the case.'

They shook hands then Hopkins went on his way. Ted was just about to go back to the station when his finely-tuned senses told him he was being watched from behind. He pivoted swiftly on his feet, sensing trouble, anticipating danger.

'Ted, it's me. Mickey. I need to talk to you.'

Ted would barely have recognised disgraced Sergeant Mickey Wheeler if he hadn't identified himself. He'd lost weight since Ted had seen him last. His cheeks were hollow and unshaven. He looked as if he'd barely slept in days. Or if he had done so, it was in the clothes he was wearing. He certainly didn't smell particularly fragrant.

'I can't talk to you, Mickey. You know that.'

'Please, Ted. I'm going crazy here. I need to know how Jim is and no one will tell me. No one will give me the time of day.'

'Can you blame them, after what you did? And stay away from Jim. You're the last person he wants to hear from.'

'Just give me five minutes, Ted. Please.'

Ted hesitated. He knew he shouldn't get involved. Mickey Wheeler was being treated as a pariah because he effectively was one. Everyone in the nick now knew he'd concealed the knowledge that the Big Boss's daughter was alive and well all the years she was supposedly missing. No decent copper was going to forget or forgive that in a hurry.

'Five minutes. One drink. Then you're on your bike.'

He asked Dave if they could go through to the back again, once they'd bought their drinks. He didn't want to run the risk of them being seen together. Ted opted for a simple ginger beer to save time. Mickey asked for a Scotch and looked like a man in dire need of one. His hands were shaking badly so Ted carried it through to the back for him.

'How is Jim? I heard he'd had a heart attack but no more than that. I tried phoning him, after I was suspended. Bella answered, but she just screamed at me that I'd nearly killed him, then hung up on me. The hospital wouldn't tell me anything because I'm not a relative.'

'He very nearly died. His heart stopped twice. He's had a bypass and he should make a full recovery. No thanks to you, though. What were you thinking of, Mickey? You knew he was going out of his mind all the time Rosie was missing. Why didn't you just tell him?'

To Ted's horror, Wheeler was openly crying now, tears running down his face, his voice thick when he tried to speak.

'Because I'm a total piece of shit, Ted. I can't deny it. I was up to all sorts of crap, trying to fund the gambling habit. When Rosie contacted me, I got scared that if I said anything I might bring something down on my head. I don't know, Internal Affairs snooping through my computer and phone or something. Now they're going to hang me out to dry. They're talking of sticking me with a Misconduct in Public Office charge. I could go to prison, Ted. For a long time. You know what they do to coppers inside.'

'I'm not bloody surprised that's what they're talking about,' Ted snapped. 'It's no more than you deserve for what you did to Jim.'

He was struggling to find any sympathy for Wheeler. He understood about powerful addictions like gambling. He'd seen what drink dependency had done to his father. But his loyalty was always to Jim and he could never forgive Mickey for what he'd put him through. Especially as Wheeler was supposed to be one of Jim's closest friends, as well as being Rosie's godfather.

'Apart from anything else, it was your job, as a copper, to step forward and say what you knew. You were here at the time, for god's sake, Mickey. You saw the hours we were all putting in trying to find her. You must have known what it did to the budget, never mind to Jim. If we hadn't wasted all those hours needlessly, does it not occur to you that we might have had the resources to find some of the other MissPers who didn't have a happy ending?

'And all that stuff you fed to the press for a few quid. You must realise how much trouble that caused us. I got my arse well and truly kicked by the Chief one time because of something you'd flogged to Pocket Billiards.'

Wheeler wiped his cheeks with a not so clean hand.

'You can't make me feel any worse than I do now. Can you please just tell Jim how very sorry I am? At least do that for me, Ted.'

Ted drained his glass and stood up.

'No. I'm not telling anyone we had this conversation. You know you could have compromised me already. It's likely I'll be called as a witness at your trial because I was leading the search for Rosie for some of the time. Now, you've had your drink and your five minutes, so get out of here and don't contact me again. And if you've got any sense, you'll keep as far away from the nick, and from Big Jim, as you possibly can.'

Mickey knocked back the rest of his drink and rose.

'Ted, look, this is really awkward, but the missus has kicked me out. I've got nowhere to go and no cash. Could you...'

'Forget it, Mickey.'

Ted's tone was harsh as he spoke. He was beyond angry at the betrayal of Jim. And there was no way he was being suckered into giving money to a gambling addict.

'You're getting nothing more from me. Go home and sort it out with Jean while you still can. I'm sorry about the gambling. I can't begin to imagine what that kind of an addiction is like to live with. But what you did to Jim? None of us can ever forgive you for that, Mickey. You've made your bed. You'll have to lie in it. And I mean it - don't contact me again.'

Ted was in such a bad mood after the encounter he had to make time to walk briskly twice round the block before he went back to the office. Otherwise he felt himself in grave danger of doing the brawling the Chief Super had suspected him of with the next person who crossed his path. He tried to remember what he'd learned on the Anger Management course he'd once been forced to attend. Whatever it was certainly wasn't helping him much at the moment.

Once he got back to the station, he went to find Jo and asked Jezza to join them, to feed back what information he'd had so far from the psychologist.

'That was good work, Jezza, the way you found the right form to show it was Derek Waldren who treated Nigel for that injury,' he told her before they began.

'Did I buggery, boss,' Jezza grinned shamelessly. 'I found a form with Nigel's details on it but honestly, the signature could have been a drunken spider on speed. Obviously, I'm going to check it out, show it to Waldren's employers to see if they can identify it. But I hadn't had time to do that before we spoke to Nigel so I decided to wing it. He wasn't to know that, though.'

Ted tried the stern look again, although he knew he was wasting his time. He was glad he'd walked his anger off, though. He didn't like anything like that which could come back to bite them when a file was being put together for the CPS.

'See that you do, please, and try to play it by the book in future.

'Jo, if Nigel wasn't at the supermarket with the others, clearly we need to find out where he was at that time, and where he was for the rest of the evening. What are they all saying so far?'

'We're busy checking and cross-checking, boss. So far they all stick to the same story and they all alibi one another. They were all at the supermarket together. They don't know why there's no film of Nigel but he was there with them. Then they were together all evening and all night at Antoine's place. We're checking phone locations at the moment to see if they confirm that.'

'Does Nigel have a car? How does he say he got to the supermarket?'

'He has a scooter. He says he went there with one of the others. They had three cars between them. Some of them are saying they can't remember accurately who went in which car here and back, but I suppose that's fair enough.'

'Traffic cameras? I don't suppose any of them obligingly got a speeding ticket either on the way there or back?'

'Rob's on that, boss. Nothing so far.'

'And anything resembling any of their cars heading up towards Roman Lakes later in the evening?'

Jo shook his head, then added, 'But then again, like we've said before, they could have had access to a van. Supposing Nigel wasn't at the supermarket because it was his job to pick up their victim and get him out to Roman Lakes, but the others went there in the van.'

'So if Nigel picked Badger up, because we know Badger left his own car at home, did he do it on his scooter? We might get lucky with traffic cam footage of them somewhere between his house and where he was killed. Derek was a good bit bigger than Nigel. It should be easy enough to spot them if they went past any cameras. Shall I look into that, boss?' Jezza offered.

'Did I not make myself clear enough, DC Vine? You are doing nothing else until you sort out the question of that signature. If we find ourselves needing that as a pivotal piece of evidence and you've deliberately led a witness to incriminate himself on the basis of a falsehood, we could be in serious trouble.'

Jezza opened her mouth to protest but seeing the look Ted was giving her, even she decided it was not the right moment.

'On it now, boss,' she said, gathering her notes and heading back to her own desk.

Jo chuckled to himself as she went out and shut the door.

'She's a sharp one, is Jezza. It's a wonder she doesn't cut herself. Sorry, boss, I should have checked up on the signature when she mentioned it to me.'

'She needs an eye keeping on her. She's good, but she'll go out on a limb if she's not supervised. Right, I need to go and update the Super on what value for money we got from the psych, since it was a fair chunk of the budget. Can you get everyone together for end of play and we'll see where we're up to and where to go next. We need a good go at kicking some ideas around. There must be somehow we can make more headway than we've done to date on this.'

'You still think it's the old team who were behind Badger's killing? Have we got any realistic chance of proving that without any forensic evidence? Especially as at the moment they're all giving each other an alibi and sticking to it.'

'They're our most likely suspects to date, for sure. And don't forget, the more of them who were involved, the mor likely it is that one of them will start to crack and show us the holes in their alibis. We'll just have to keep questioning them separately and see if we can open up an element of doubt in one of their stories.'

He said more or less the same thing to the Super in their catch-up later in the day, hoping it sounded convincing. He was acutely aware that what they had so far amounted to a big fat zero in real terms, not a position he liked to be in so far into a case.

'As you can imagine, the Chief Super keeps asking me for a progress report, Ted. I appreciate you're doing everything you can. You always do. Realistically, how optimistic are you of a result?'

It was a question Ted knew she would ask him. It was one he couldn't really answer, but he gave it his best shot.

'We could, of course, be looking in completely the wrong direction by focusing on Callum's football team mates. We've ruled out almost all of the lacrosse players now. But the footballers are the most likely by far to date. We're looking at Callum's and Páraic's family too. Realistically, at this stage, we have no other probable suspects, short of an unexpected breakthrough.'

Ted hesitated. It already sounded lame and now he was going to take a big risk in broaching another subject with her. He simply thought it might be a good idea to be proactive.

'I spoke to Mickey Wheeler today,' he began.

'Really?' she sounded surprised. 'I'm sure you don't need me to tell you how ill-advised that was.'

'He was lying in wait for me, outside The Grapes when I came out with Hopkins. He looks dreadful.'

'Not half as bad as Jim Baker after he heard the news, I imagine.'

'Agreed. I didn't discuss his case with him, of course. He told me they're going for Misconduct. He just wanted to know about Jim'

'How is he?'

'Doing better. Planning his wedding. It's just this whole thing with Mickey got me thinking. Why didn't any of us notice what was going on? Should we be doing more? It was right under our noses the whole time. We're all supposed to be police officers, yet none of us noticed anything.'

'Addiction is, mercifully, not something I know a great deal about. What I do know, from courses I've attended, is that addicts are extremely adept at concealing their problems, even from the people closest to them.'

'And what would be the alternative? Frequent, periodic sweeps of everyone's computer, to see what they were getting up to? You know there aren't the resources available for that. We'll just have to learn what lessons from it that we can and move on.'

Ted knew she was right. It just didn't sit well with him. But for the moment, he had more important things to worry about. What he needed was a good brainstorming session with the team. Between them, they'd find a way forward.

'So the word from the psych is not to push Nigel too hard or it may be counter-productive. He also thinks he's been coached by whoever is the brains behind the team,' he summed up to his team when they all got together.

'Antoine,' several voices said in unison.

'And they all say they were together, at his place, on the night in question? How are we doing with phone searches? Do they back up what they're saying?'

'So far it looks like the phones were stationary at that location the whole evening.'

'Can we check incoming and outgoing calls? For all of them. They could at least help us pinpoint timings a bit better.'

'Negative, boss,' Jo told him. 'A few of the lads have said in interview that they have a rule when they're having one of their film and gaming nights. No one is allowed to make or receive any calls for any reason the whole evening. Sammy told us that there's a bowl in Antoine's lounge and they all have to put their phones in it. Anyone who breaks the rule has to buy all the food and drink for the next evening session.'

Ted looked round at the team members before he spoke again.

'They really have got an answer for everything, haven't they? Too much so? This all smacks of careful planning, anticipating anything we might ask and having an answer ready. If we have to go softly, softly with Nigel, on expert advice, we need to start probing more into whoever is the next weakest link. So who would that be?'

Again, a chorus of voices, of those who had interviewed him, answered his question.

'Terry Russell.'

'Right, let's have him in again and I'd like a go at questioning him. Maurice, you and me on this one. See what we can get out of him together.'

# Chapter Twenty-five

'Thank you for coming in, Terry. I'm Detective Chief Inspector Darling, this is my colleague Detective Constable Brown. I'm the Senior Investigating Officer on both the killing of Callum Mitchell and of Derek Waldren.'

Ted had wanted to have a crack at some of the potential suspects himself. Not something many SIOs would do. It wasn't that he didn't trust his team. He knew they were good. Well up to the task. He was simply feeling too detached from the case and needed to get more hands-on.

Some DCIs were more than happy to sit back and take the glory when their team had done all the legwork. They preferred the admin side of the job. The endless meetings and courses, seemingly for the sake of it. Ted wasn't like that. There were times when he wished he'd stayed a DI.

He'd chosen Maurice to sit in with him for this interview because he could effectively look silent and menacing. But he could just as easily switch into Daddy Hen mode if necessary, should anyone they were interviewing start to crack and need some support.

'Once again, this is a purely voluntary interview. You're free to leave at any time, but we really appreciate your cooperation in coming in.'

'No problems at all. I'm happy to help. Callum was my friend, and a good one.'

'And Derek Waldren? Did you know him at all?'

'No, I don't think so. I mean, I know he was with the St John's Ambulance, so I might have seen him at matches and things. But I wouldn't say I knew him at all. Not by name or anything.'

'What about by a nickname? Did you or any of the other players have nicknames for the first aiders?'

'I've only heard them called the Johnners. All of them. So if there was one on duty and we needed to talk about them, you'd probably just say the Johnner, you know.'

Ted made a show of going through his notes. Terry was watching him carefully.

'I see you were in the Scouts when you were younger, Terry.'

'Yeah, I quite like that sort of outdoors stuff. We went on some camps and that. We went with the football team once, too, to North Wales.'

'Tell me about that. Who went on it? When and where was this?

'Must be more than two years now, because it was when we were all still playing. Under-17s. We went and the Under-15s. The club's always been like a big family so there were some parents, too. Des, the chairman, and his wife went. And Antoine's parents as well. They sponsor some of the teams, through his dad's business. We were all staying at an Outward Bound sort of place. Near Snowdon. Like a youth hostel. But they didn't stay with us, they went to a posh hotel.

'Jerome's parents came as well. His mum helped out with the cooking. She's a brilliant cook. His dad has a van, for his decorating business, so it was great for chucking all our kit in. Sleeping bags, rucksacks and stuff. The players went in a couple of minibuses the club hired, so there wasn't a lot of room for all the stuff.

'I don't remember all of the parents who went. But Porridge was there, with his mum and dad and a couple of his brothers, I think.'

'Porridge?' Ted asked him.

'You know, the Irish lad who killed himself. Páraic. Some

of the others teased him a bit about his name. With his accent it sounded a bit like Porridge when he said it so the nickname stuck a bit.'

'Did he mind? Some people get a bit sensitive about their names. Making fun of them, even if it's not meant in a hurtful way, can sometimes feel like bullying.'

Ted was speaking from bitter experience as a boy at school with the name Darling to live with.

'No, he didn't mind. If he had, he'd have got his brothers onto us. They're all well hard and one of them's a cage fighter.'

'What happened about first aid provision for something like that? It must be a bit of a nightmare to organise. Are any of the parents trained first aiders? I'm imagining you were doing things other than playing football, so there must have been a lot of Health and Safety hoops to jump through.'

'I'm not sure about stuff like that. The centre had its own staff and they supervised us for a lot of the time. Yeah, we did some great stuff. Rock climbing, canoeing, abseiling. All that sort of thing. I'd already done some of it with the Scouts.'

'Did you do any first aid courses as part of your time with the Scouts?'

'Yes, we had to do it to get some of the badges.'

'And who taught those courses?'

For the first time, Terry looked slightly hesitant.

'I don't really remember, to be honest. Someone from the Red Cross or something like that, you know.'

'So it could have been someone from the St John perhaps?'

'Well, it could have been. I didn't really take much notice of who was teaching it. I was busy trying to learn stuff so could pass the tests and get my badges.'

It was Maurice's turn to shuffle papers and ask questions.

'You don't remember if Derek Waldren ever taught you on any of the courses? Because we're getting the lists of all the courses he was involved with, where they were and on what dates. So knowing what age you would have been when you were in the Scouts, we should be able to confirm whether or not it was him who taught the courses you were on.'

Terry looked anxiously from one to another as he replied.

'I never said it wasn't him. I just said I couldn't remember who it was.'

'I see,' Ted said levelly.

His team all knew that when he used that particular tone it meant he was not convinced by what he was being told. Again, he left enough of a pause to start to put some pressure on Terry. If those who had already spoken to him were correct in saying he was the next weakest link after Nigel, he wanted to make him feel uncomfortable. It could help to lower his guard.

'Turning back to the evening after the benefit match, Terry. The one for young Páraic. You say that first of all you went to the supermarket to get food and drink for the evening. And that all of you were there. Can you remind me again who that would have been, please?'

Terry gave an exaggerated sigh then reeled off the names.

'Me, Antoine, Jerome, Jordan, Wayne, Will, Sammy, Marvin, Alan, Gary. And Nigel.'

'We have CCTV footage of you at the supermarket, doing your shopping. Yet Nigel doesn't seem to appear anywhere. Can you give me an explanation for that?'

Terry shrugged.

'Not really. He was there with us. Perhaps he went to the bogs?'

'I see,' Ted said again. 'Tell me about the rest of the evening, Terry. What happened after you left the supermarket?'

'We all piled back in the cars and went back to Antoine's place.'

'Whose car did you travel in, Terry?' Maurice Brown asked him.

'Just the nearest one. Different going and coming back. I

think I was with Will and Jordan going to Antoine's.'

'My colleagues tell me that you have a rule for these evenings that you're not allowed to use your phones. Does that mean you switch them off?' Ted asked him.

'No, we have to leave them on. Then it's more tempting to want to answer them. But the first person who does, or who even looks at their phone, has to buy the food and drink the next time.'

'So who bought it on this occasion?'

Again, Terry looked from one to the other at Ted's question. He clearly hadn't been expecting it. He laughed nervously.

'Well, it wasn't me. I haven't got that kind of money so I'm always careful not to break the rule.'

'It's not important if you can't remember,' Ted told him reassuringly. 'We know, from the cameras, what time you were there so we can check the till rolls, if someone paid by card.'

'I think Antoine paid with his card.'

'Really?' Ted feigned surprise. 'The team captain is a rule breaker?'

'No, he wasn't the one, but he sometimes paid with his card and whoever it was paid him back in cash. Saved him going to the cash-point, I suppose.'

'I see,' Ted said again, this time making it clear he didn't believe a word of it. 'Tell me what happened when you all got back to Antoine's place, please. In your own words.'

'We were starving, so we went to the kitchen to cook stuff first off. Antoine has a small kitchen in his part of the house but it's not big enough for us all so we went to his parents' side and used theirs. They were away for the weekend.'

'Do you happen to know where they were?' Ted asked, making a show of noting the details.

'Er, I'm not sure,' Terry was watching Ted's pen scribbling away. 'They've got a cottage somewhere. The Lake District maybe, I think. Somewhere like that.'

'So you were all in the larger kitchen, cooking together. Anything else?'

'We did a load of selfies. You know, because we were going to be putting our phones away for the rest of the evening. So we took some team photos first. D'you want to see?'

He fished out his phone and expertly pulled up the shots. Ted had noticed that he was starting to drop 'you know' into his speech quite frequently now. It was something of a regional idiom but he'd done a recent course on statement analysis which had highlighted that it was also a form of affirmation. When an interviewee was trying to give credibility to something they knew to be false, they would often use the phrase, or offer up more details than had been asked for. Just as Terry seemed to be doing in drawing attention to the photos when he'd not been asked to produce his phone.

'It was a bit of a squash getting us all in a shot so I broke mine up into our old football positions. The defenders, with Marvin, the goalie, and then the forwards, and the midfielders, look. Good job Antoine's mum didn't see the mess her kitchen was in. Look at all those pizza wrappers and stuff all over her work-surface. She'd have gone mad. We did clean it all up before they got back, though.'

He was laying it on with a trowel now, Ted noticed. Placing himself, creating an alibi. There was a dateline on the photos he was happily showing them, with enough of the surroundings visible for identification of the location. It could have been pure coincidence but one shot even included the timer display on the impressive built-in cooker behind the players.

'I can't see Nigel in any of your photos, Terry. Yet again, he seems to be missing. But you say he was with you all evening.'

'Oh well, that's because these are team photos. And Nige was reserve, you know. He only ever played with the team if someone got injured.'

'Despite that, you included him in your activities? He hung around with you?'

'Yeah, Nige is all right, really. Just not a good enough player for the first team, except in emergencies. But we all like him well enough, so we let him tag long. Like a team mascot, you could say.'

'And whose car did Nigel travel in, from the supermarket to Antoine's place?' Ted asked him.

'I've no idea. He wasn't in the same one as me, that much I do remember. We swap about all the time when we're out like this. Look, I'm not being funny or anything but is it all right if I go now? Only I need to get to work. I'm going in a bit later because I'm working late tonight. We've got a big stock-take to do.'

'No problem at all, Terry. Thanks very much for coming in. You've been most helpful. What work do you do?'

'I work in a big sports shop. Sports and outdoor pursuits, that sort of thing. Sales assistant. Well, trainee manager, really.'

'Sounds like a job which is ideally suited to you, with your football background and Scouting. I bet if I gave you a piece of rope you could still tie a round turn and two half hitches, couldn't you?'

Terry laughed.

'I can still tie all the knots, I think, but I'm not sure if I can remember all the right names for them.'

They saw him out. Then, as they made their way upstairs together, Ted asked Maurice, 'What did you make of that lot, then?'

'Load of old bollocks, boss.'

'Pretty much sums up my thoughts. Let's get a drink and talk through it. I think we need to get the full team together again as soon as possible. We may need to go in a totally different direction.'

Ted put his head round Jo's door to ask for a meeting. Jo

promised to let him know as soon as he could pull everyone in. From there Ted led the way to his office, Maurice following, and put the kettle on.

'So you think we're looking at the wrong generation?' Maurice asked him. 'All this time we've been concentrating on the lads, and now this talk of the parents being involved, especially in that camp thing. Does that present the possibility that some of the dads were involved in killing Badger?'

'It's something we certainly need to look into. Especially as Páraic and his family were there. Maybe they worked out afterwards that something which happened on that trip led to him killing himself, which is why they decided to go after Derek Waldren.

'I'm also wondering if we have the wrong Badger. If the person with that nickname is someone else entirely. Someone we've not yet unearthed. Remember I asked you about the Newcastle shirt, because it was Des Clarke, the chairman, who was wearing it?'

'Aye, but they're the Magpies, like I told you.'

'Yes, but that would be too obvious, surely? And whoever s behind this is certainly not stupid. We're going to have to start digging deeper and further afield. We might have been a bit blinkered, up to now.'

'But Derek Waldren was the one who was killed. Nigel first mentioned the name Badger in relation to who Callum might have been going to visit and Waldren did live up where Callum was last seen alive.'

'We'll see what anyone else can put in. Give me a shout when everyone's back and let's regroup.'

I think we may need to be looking at the parents as well as the team players, in light of what Terry told us today,' Ted began, once the whole team was assembled. 'If members of Páraic's family were at this camp in North Wales, is it possible that something happened to him there? Or that with hindsight, after his death, his family members realised that might have been the start of his problems? And did they, and perhaps some of the other parents, decide to take the law into their own hands to deal with the person they thought was accountable?

'We need to start by finding out exactly who went on this camp. There may be no connection. But something happened to Páraic at some point to make him want to take his own life, and there's a strong probability that it was his death which precipitated the other two.

'Jo, as the team's representative of the Church of Rome, I have a question for you. Although I'm pretty certain I know what your answer is going to be, before I even ask it. If you went to see Páraic's priest, would he tell you if Páraic had ever said anything that might be relevant to this case?'

Jo shook his head emphatically.

'Not a hope in hell, boss. Most Catholic priests are adamant they would rather go to prison than betray the secrets of the confessional. It goes against everything they believe in.'

'That's ridiculous,' Jezza scoffed. 'How are we ever supposed to catch the perverts who do the stuff we deal with if all they have to do is trot round to their priest, tell them everything and come out with a clear conscience.'

'All right, DC Vine, it's neither the time nor the place for this debate.'

Ted always reverted to rank when he was trying to make a point as strongly as he could. Sometimes it worked.

'We have more important things to do. Jo, give it your very best shot, please. Anything at all you can get might help us.

'Another thing. Terry was very keen to show Maurice and me his team photos on his phone, taken on the night Derek Waldren was murdered. Before we even asked about phones. It was as if he was setting up an alibi for himself and the rest of them. We now know from the phones that they remained in one place that whole evening and night, which fits with the story they're all telling. But Nigel wasn't in any of the photos Terry showed us. Anyone else have the same?'

Almost all heads nodded and there were murmurs of assent.

'Most of them have done the same thing,' Mike Hallam put in. 'They're all freely showing the photos on their phones, so it does look like a concerted effort to establish alibis. For everyone except Nigel, that is.'

'So why are they effectively hanging Nigel out to dry?' Ted asked. 'It would seem to be physically impossible for him to have acted alone in killing Derek Waldren. As far as we know so far, he didn't have access to a car and we've not found any traffic cam footage of a scooter with two people on who could have been him and Waldren.

'But let's just suppose for a moment that Nigel was involved. That he was the bait to draw Waldren out for someone else to kill him. Could that someone else have been some of the parents, rather than the players themselves? They've all got seemingly water-tight alibis and although there's no footage of Nigel, if they all insist he was with them the whole time, we'd struggle to prove beyond reasonable doubt that he wasn't.

'This is why we need to start looking at parents and families at this stage, I think. Nigel says that Antoine's parents were away. Where were they and can they prove where they were? The same goes for Páraic's family. And the club officials, including Des Clarke, the chairman, and the treasurer, Bill Batley.

'Jezza, tell us about the door-to-door near where Derek Waldren lived. Did you find out anything of any further use to us?'

'Absolutely no sightings of anyone going to the house the night he was killed. And nothing the night Callum went there and was later murdered. The near neighbours seem to keep to themselves a bit, but all the ones we talked to spoke highly of Badger.'

'Just for the moment, let's call him Waldren. I'm starting to doubt who Badger really is in all this, so let's use real names rather than nicknames to avoid confusion.'

'Okay, so they spoke highly of Waldren and the way he looked after his mother. They said he spent all his available time with her and when he had to work days or to go away, rather than put her into respite care, he paid live-in carers to look after her.'

'So he did go away sometimes?' Ted asked.

'Sir,' Steve put in, with his customary hesitancy.

He was, as usual, listening and following whilst using his computer at the same time. Ted never objected because he knew it was always work-related and Steve would often be finding things they were talking about.

'I thought I'd look on the club's website to see if there were any photos of the trip to Wales, in case it saved a bit of time. There's a whole album labelled Snowdonia, from the right sort of dates. Lots of photos. I've been scrolling through them. It looks like they had some sort of a prize-giving ceremony at the end of the camp, and there's a photo of everyone present, with the awards they won.

'Sir, Derek Waldren is standing at one end of the back row. He was there with them, on that trip to Wales.'

# Chapter Twenty-six

Ted almost swore out loud. Something he tried not to do in front of the team. He knew coppers who swore like troopers the whole time. His dad had been strict on swearing. He'd always told Ted to think of something more constructive to say. He was struggling to do so. But he could always rely on Maurice.

'Bloody hell! The little bastards have been lying to us all along. Pissing us about. They all knew Badger. Or at least they must all have known who Derek Waldren was. If they'd spent a week away at camp with him, how can they not have known?'

For once, Ted didn't pull him up on the language. He agreed with him. He simply said levelly, 'This means we're going to have to start back at the beginning and interview all of the team members again. Show them the photo and ask for their explanations.'

Steve was already printing the photo off and handing it round to the team members.

'They're doubtless going to fall back on the not knowing his name excuse, just that he was there as a first aider. Look at his group photo, all of you. And thanks for finding it, Steve. There's not that many people in it. They must have known. We'll speak to the team members, then start on the parents and other relatives who were there.'

'Boss, we need to talk to all the Under-15s from that photo as well,' Jezza pointed out. 'This was two years or more ago and look at the size of some of them back then. They're going to be even bigger by now. They're all around sixteen, seventeen now and we all know teenagers that age can be big.

And they were Páraic's team mates. They would have more of a motive than anyone if they thought Derek Waldren was the cause of his suicide. And it looks like they'd have the brawn to do it, too. Especially if they're even bigger than they were back then.

'But it's going to take us ages to get through all this lot. I'm not trying to be negative here but ...'

'I know, Jezza, it's a lot of legwork. We'll just have to get stuck in. I'll do some, and I'll talk to Inspector Turner about some help from Uniform, whenever he has anyone to spare. I'll also ask the Super once more about drafting in some more help. With so many to get through, you'll have to go singly, so make sure you record everything.'

'Boss, just a suggestion, but when I was talking to my bredren Antoine, he dropped into the conversation a few times that his dad's a bit of a big shot locally. Rotary, I think. Something like that. I just wondered if, diplomatically speaking, while you're going to be doing some interviews anyway, you should be the one to take him,' Virgil suggested. His tone was deliberately ironic when he called Antoine his bredren.

'All right, I'm happy with that. Mike, can you and Leona set up the next round of interviews. I'd like to see Antoine's father at his house, if at all possible. It would give me a chance to get a feel for the lie of the land. I want to see if the team could have gone out again after they'd eaten without attracting attention from the neighbours.

'Yet another thing we need to consider at this point is tha perhaps not all of Callum's team mates were involved in killing Waldren. Suppose it was just a few of them, perhaps even working with someone else. And that those staying behind a the house were there to alibi them.'

'Security cameras, boss,' Charlie Eccles put in. 'If the father is a property developer with a big posh house, there's a good chance there'll be cameras there. If he knows the lads ar innocent, he should bend over backwards to make them available to prove they were there all the time.'

'Good point, Charlie. Mike, can you ask about that when you phone to make an appointment. What's the father's name?'

'Martin,' Virgil told him. 'Louis Martin. The family roots are in Martinique, Antoine told me, a few generations back, so it was originally the French pronunciation but they Anglicized it. He was quite talkative.'

'Did he tell you anything of a bit more use to us than that?'

'One thing he didn't tell me, which I've since found out, was that he was twice suspended from school for fighting. Nothing serious enough to get him into any real bother, but it seems he's always had a bit of a low flashpoint. On the pitch, too. He was sent off more than once for losing it.'

'Interesting. So he's the brainy one, but also the hothead?' Ted asked him.

'Definitely brainy. That was apparently half the problem. School-work was too easy for him so he got frustrated. A bit of a rebel by nature. Could get very wound up if he disagreed with a ref on the pitch when he was playing.'

'Good work, Virgil. Where did you get all this from?'

'I flashed my irresistible smile at some of the neighbours, together with my badge, and they were only too happy to talk. Gossip, would be a better term. It's fairly quiet and suburban up there. I think having a detective around asking questions could well be the most fun they've had in ages.'

'Realistically, how many people would it take to overpower someone the size of Derek Waldren and do what was done to him?' Leona Rakale asked.

All eyes looked expectantly towards Ted. With his specialist Firearms Officer training, he could usually answer such questions better than anyone.

'It's more about technique than strength or numbers for something like this. If you had even one person trained in restraint procedures, that would make a big difference. There's always an outside possibility that one of them was armed with something, as a warning. We know they had a Stanley knife to inflict the injuries, for instance. It's surprisingly easy to get someone to do what you want them to if you're holding a gun or you have a knife to their throat.

'And don't forget, if we're right and it was team members or their families who killed Derek Waldren, he might have had no reason to fear them or to struggle until it was too late.'

'Oh, come on, boss, isn't that a bit far-fetched?' Jezza asked him. 'They told him "take all your kit off and lie down here spread-eagled while we tie you up and nothing is going to happen to you"? Even with a knife at his throat, surely he would struggle. And shout.'

'There's another possibility we have to consider,' Ted replied. 'We don't know if Waldren went voluntarily, with someone he knew and wasn't afraid of, to the place where he was killed. And we don't yet know who that someone was. It could have been one person. Someone he knew and trusted. Possibly Nigel, for example.

'As yet, we don't know the nature of the relationship he may have had with that person. We're all grown-ups here, so I'm sure I don't have to spell out for you a possibility. That Waldren would not have been afraid of being stripped, gagged and tied up. That that might well have been what he went to those woods for, with whoever it was. But once he was helpless, naked, gagged and immobilised, things suddenly went from what he was expecting to what actually happened, when more people appeared on the scene.'

He paused to let that sink in. It was again Maurice who spoke first.

'Kinky sex, you mean? A bit of S&M? Is that what this is all about? So you mean Waldren was interested in a bit more than wan ...'

He stopped himself just in time before finishing the word. The boss had ignored his swearing so far but even Mauric reckoned he'd be pushing his luck unless he rephrased what he'd been about to say.

'It wasn't just watching lads masturbate that turned him on? He actually enjoyed a bit of pain?'

'This is all purely speculation. I'm just trying to find a scenario which might help us to explain why he went voluntarily back to the place where he killed Callum. Obviously he knew the significance of the location, so why would be go back there with someone?'

'Sir,' Steve began hesitantly. His ideas were invariably good. He just lacked the courage to speak up.

'Go ahead, Steve. Any and all theories are welcome on this.'

'Well, I interviewed Nigel once. He seems a sensitive sort. He seemed to be genuinely moved talking about Callum's death. We know he's a bit on the edge of the group. He's certainly not the brightest of them, for one thing. Tolerated rather than liked, perhaps. That comment you noted about him being like a mascot.'

Ted kept his expression encouraging. He saw Charlie Eccles start to fidget impatiently in his seat as it appeared that Steve was going all round the houses before advancing his theory. Ted knew instinctively that it would be worth waiting for so he threw Charlie a look which he hoped would keep him quiet long enough for Steve to finish.

'Nigel's mum is a single parent. He doesn't have a father figure in his life. Never has had. This is only a theory of course ...' he hesitated.

It looked as if Eccles could contain himself no longer. Just as he opened his mouth to speak, Ted cut in with words of encouragement.

'Go ahead, Steve. Your ideas are always sound. Even if it's not the right theory, it will be one worth considering.'

'Supposing Nigel did know Waldren? Knew him well? Suppose he was his father figure? The person he turned to when he needed an older man's advice? We know Nigel went to speak to Waldren at the ambulance just after the incident on the pitch. If it was his job to get Waldren out to the site, perhaps he told him how much the day had upset him. That he wanted to go and pay his respects at the place where Callum was killed, and asked Derek Waldren to go with him. That wouldn't arouse any suspicions, surely?'

Steve ground to an abrupt halt, looking round anxiously in case his idea was stupid. Surprisingly, it was Charlie Eccles who spoke first and his words were complimentary.

'Sounds like a reasonable theory, that.'

'It is only a theory at this stage,' Ted cautioned, 'but it is a plausible one. It gives us an idea of how someone could have got Waldren out to the scene. We still have a long way to go, but it's an excellent start. Well done Steve. Now I need to go and update the Super. Before you say anything, Jo, yes, I will ask about extra bodies, again. Let me know when I can go and talk to Louis Martin.

'We'll catch up again end of play and hope we have something a bit more to go on by then.'

Ted decided to make a bit of a joke of his visit to Kevin Turner to ask for extra bodies. He had an idea what the response was going to be and he didn't want to upset Kevin further. His recent uncharacteristic meltdown had been worrying.

He tapped lightly on his door but merely put an arm through the gap, waving the clean white handkerchief Trev always ironed and put in the pocket of his work suit for him.

'Piss off, Ted. Whatever you want, you can't have it,' Kevin called out, but at least his tone was good-humoured.

Ted went in, pocketing his handkerchief, and sat down opposite him.

'Seriously, though, can you lend me any bodies at all? I've now got about thirty possible suspects I need to interview some not for the first time, so I'd be grateful for anyone.'

'As long as no more takeaways run out of food, and provided the local scallies all play nicely and don't give us any trouble, I'll see what I can do for you.'

'Thanks, Kev, I appreciate it. How are you doing?'

'Are you really asking or just making polite conversation because you want something?'

'Really asking, of course. We're supposed to be mates, aren't we?'

'Well, as mates, and strictly between us, I'm weighing up my options and wondering whether to cut my losses. I never thought I'd be saying this. I'm like you. Career copper. All I ever wanted to do. But now? I'm really starting to think working in a DIY store would be preferable. And I don't even like bloody DIY.'

Ted was shocked and didn't bother hiding the fact.

'You've surely not done enough years for your pension yet, have you? And you're not serious?'

Kevin sighed as he replied, 'Some days I am serious. When we get it right and get the convictions, do we get any thanks for it? Do we buggery. But when we can't respond to a crime because we're overstretched and swamped with timewasters we get hung out to dry in public. And some days I just want to walk out into the sunset and not come back.'

'Well, I'm just going to talk to Her Frostiness to see if she can put a few more bodies my way, in which case I won't need to rob any of yours. I can't tonight, but when next I get to finish at a decent time, we could do a drink together and I'll drive you home. Pour you back into the arms of your loving and long-suffering wife.'

At least that made Kev laugh.

'I have no idea why she puts up with me. How's Jim, by the way? And have you heard? Mickey's been formally charged with Misconduct. And he's facing a disciplinary. They're going to eat him up and spit out the very small pieces which remain.'

'Not surprised at all. Addict or not, he pretty much deserves it. Jim's doing a lot better, which means that he's going stir-crazy. He phoned me earlier. Wants me and Trev to visit again at the weekend if we get chance. He says if he has to look at one more possible wedding venue or frock he won't be responsible for his actions. And of course Trev loves all that sort of stuff. He can occupy Bella while Jim and I talk shop.'

When Ted went into the Ice Queen's office nearby, he caught her clearly getting ready to leave. He asked her if she had five minutes.

'Five but no more,' she told him. 'The Chief Super and I are just on our way up to Central Park. A meeting for Divisional Commanders and Assistants. Perhaps they may finally be going to tell us what further divisional reorganisation awaits us.'

'Any chance of any more bodies?' Ted asked hopefully. 'Only with a new development, we're now facing the prospect of around thirty more interviews before we can get a clear picture of a possible suspect or suspects.'

He filled her in on all the new detail and its possible implications.

'I agree that it is a highly complex case. I promise you that I will do my best to find you even one or two extra bodies. Who's left minding the shop for DS Rakale? If things are quiet there, could they come and lend a hand, whilst staying on call? And is there anything else we can do to make progress? A televised appeal for information, perhaps? An appeal for witnesses?'

'The problem with that is that now we've had to go public with saying it was Waldren who killed Callum, I wonder how sympathetic the public would be to helping find the killer of the bad man?'

She was gathering her things together again and preparing to leave.

'Well, start with DC Winter, isn't it, at South Manchester

Bring him in. And I promise to see what else I can do.'

Ted was hoping he wouldn't be too late getting away. It was his night for self-defence and judo. He'd warned Trev he would be unlikely to make it in time for the juniors but that he would try his best to get there for judo. Now that things were back to normal between them and Ted's face was looking much better, though was still painful, it would do no harm to remind Trev that he seldom let his guard down without good reason. It could make for a lively evening, which was what he needed.

It was late afternoon when Jo came to find him, just before the planned end of day get-together.

'I'm just back from seeing Páraic's parish priest, Father Hughes. John,' Jo told him. 'This probably sounds daft but would it be all right if I fed back to you here in private, rather than go over it with the full team? I know you're never going to understand my beliefs, and I try not to let them interfere with work. But it's how I was brought up. It would just feel wrong to me to talk about it in public. Does that sound completely stupid, Ted?'

'I don't agree with what you believe in, Jo, that's no secret. But I respect your right to hold those beliefs. Right up until the minute it does start to interfere with work. At that point, you and I might need to have a long and serious talk about conflicting interests.'

'Fair enough. So, Father Hughes. Younger than I anticipated, for some reason. Quite progressive. Not sufficiently so to even consider betraying the secrets of the confessional, as I predicted. But he did try very hard to meet me halfway. Which is why I would feel bad about discussing it except on a need to know basis.

'He did a lot of "hypothetically speaking" and "if ever that were to arise". But I honestly believe he was coming as close as he was comfortable with to speaking about Páraic directly.

He said he does follow and preach the doctrine of Rome on masturbation. Sometimes young lads talk to him about it, inevitably. He tries his best to explain to them that the church decrees that it's wrong, a sin, but that it is something that happens.

'Basically, setting aside all his dressing up, it would seem that Páraic had spoken to him about masturbation. He'd mentioned an older man who had told him it was perfectly natural so Páraic, as a good Catholic boy like myself, had wanted guidance from his parish priest.

'He said that as far as he could make out from what he'd been told, it had gone no further than talking. No touching, no watching, nothing like that. He assured me that had there been anything of that sort, he would have found a way to tell me whilst keeping his conscience clear.

'I asked him outright if he had any idea what would have led Páraic to kill himself. Of course the family asked him that too, immediately after it happened. Again, he said he would tell me if he knew and if he thought it would be helpful. I was inclined to believe him. As far as he was aware, there was nothing more than an adult talking to boys about masturbation.

'There's something else which occurs to me at this point. Coming back to what we've said before. The way Waldren was killed. That metal rod up his jacksy. To me that says someone thinks he did a lot worse than talk about masturbation. That tells me whoever did that to him thought he'd been sodomising lads.

'So is that true and if so, which boys? And more to the point, who would have known that?'

# Chapter Twenty-seven

'Thank you for agreeing to see me, Mr Martin. I appreciate you're probably a busy man and it's good of you to accommodate me at relatively short notice.'

'Come in. Chief Inspector, did you say? We'll go through to the kitchen. I was just about to make coffee. Just a little word of caution first, though. You're wasting your time buttering me up. I'm immune to that.'

'Oh, I'm not doing that at all, sir,' Ted told him evenly as they arrived in the kitchen. He recognised it from the team photos he'd seen, which had clearly been the intention. 'I'm equally polite to everyone. I'm a great believer in equality.'

'Please call me Louis. And what should I call you?'

'Chief Inspector is absolutely fine, sir. And I think I'll stick with Mr Martin for now, if that's all right with you?'

Martin's eyes narrowed and his earlier smile disappeared in an instant. As did the initial show of bonhomie.

'Is this a formal interview, then? In which case I would like to call my solicitor.'

'No, nothing like that at all, Mr Martin. If it had been formal, it would have been at the station and you would have been advised in advance of your right to legal representation. We're simply trying to talk to everyone who knew the deceased man, Derek Waldren.'

'I wouldn't say I knew him, as such. Not by name, although I heard that he was a first aider. Coffee? How do you take it? Espresso?'

He was gesturing towards some sort of contraption which

looked to Ted as if it wouldn't be out of place on the flight deck of the Star Ship Enterprise. Again, he recognised it as having been in shot on some of the team photos.

'I'm a bit of a coffee wimp, I'm afraid, so something white and sweet would be more to my taste, please.'

'A cappuccino then,' Martin said, with barely concealed scorn. He spent a moment fiddling about with capsules and levers and in no time presented Ted with something hot and frothy.

'Are you all right here in the kitchen?' Martin asked, although he was already hitching himself onto a stool next to the central island in the spacious room.

Ted suspected he was making a point. Martin was a tall and imposing figure. It was easy enough for him to take a seat on the high stool without it looking awkward. For Ted, being much smaller, it was not quite so simple. He covered the moment by taking out the print-out Steve had found of the Snowdonia trip, which he slid across the island's surface to put in front of Martin.

'This is Derek Waldren, Mr Martin,' he said, tapping the photo to indicate him. 'This photo was taken at the club's camp in Snowdonia, a couple of years ago. Mr Waldren was a first aider who sometimes covered matches, so he was presumably there in that capacity. And that's you in the centre of the row in front of him, isn't it? With your wife, I presume, and the club chairman, Des Clarke. Can you confirm that?'

Martin's glance at the photo was brief and disinterested before he pushed it away.

'Yes, I was there with Marie-Claire. We didn't stay at the camp with the others, though. My wife is an interior designer. You can probably tell by the house. Not at all the camping type. More into expensive boutique hotels than chalets or tents. We stayed at the nearest decent hotel we could find. Not that it was up to her usual standard. But that meant we didn't mix socially with the rest of them much of the time.

'So is this bloke Walden the one who killed Callum?'

'Waldren. Derek Waldren,' Ted corrected him. 'And we're not in a position to confirm that. All we have said is that following the death of Derek Waldren, we're not looking for anyone else in connection with the death of Callum Mitchell.

'So do you remember Derek Waldren being at the camp? Did you have any kind of contact with him during that time?'

Martin pulled the photo back towards himself and looked at it more closely.

'I saw him there, of course, now I look at him again. I don't remember having any sort of contact with him. He was just there in the background, from what I remember.'

'I see. Thank you. And going back to the weekend of the benefit match for Páraic. I understand that you sponsor some of the teams. Were you there for that match?'

'Yes, I sponsor the Under-17s and the Under-15s as they're the teams Antoine used to captain. I couldn't be there for the match that weekend though. I had business meetings up in the Lake District. We have a cottage there. It's pretty much obligatory in my line of work to have a cottage somewhere fashionable. The Cotswolds, Cornwall. The Lakes is much handier for us, though.

'My wife and I drove up on the Friday evening and spent a quiet night in. I had business lunches on both the Saturday and the Sunday and we came home on Sunday evening, quite late on. I'd had a drink or two at lunchtime so I needed some time before I drove back. I'm completely law-abiding.'

'And have you any way to show the journeys you made? Did you perhaps have your satnav switched on?'

'Whatever for? I make that journey so often I could do it with my eyes closed. I bet the Jeep could drive itself there.'

'You didn't perhaps have it on to check for roadworks or anything like that?'

'Are you asking me to provide an alibi for myself? Does that mean I'm under suspicion of something?'

'Not at all, sir. As I said, this is an informal interview. I'm just trying to get an idea of where everyone was.'

'Well, I didn't have it switched on. If I had encountered any roadworks, I might have switched it on to find a different route. But there weren't any. Presumably you can check on that. If necessary, I can give you the contact details of the clients I had lunch with on both days. Although clearly I'd prefer not to involve them unless it was absolutely necessary.'

'Thank you, Mr Martin. So while you and your wife were away for the weekend, Antoine had the run of the house and had his friends round?'

'Well, clearly, as I wasn't here, I can't say what Antoine was doing. But that's what he told me he had planned and I have no reason to doubt him. My son doesn't lie.'

'I noticed as I came in that you have security cameras at the front. A good idea, I imagine, with a nice house like this. Do you have any covering the back of the house, and is there any rear access? Would you have any footage from the evening in question?'

To his surprise, Martin laughed.

'You'll ruin my reputation if this gets out but they're not currently working. I keep meaning to get them fixed but despite employing people who can do that sort of stuff, they're always tied up on the properties we're developing for sale. My own home comes a poor second.

'And yes, there are some at the rear and theoretically, it is accessible, although not easily. There are open fields behind. There are horses there at the moment. Sometimes there are cows. Marie-Claire doesn't like that. We get too many flies when the cows are there.'

'I see, sir. Turning back to the football club, was there ever any trouble there that you were aware of?'

'Trouble? What kind of trouble?'

'Anything, really. Did Antoine ever mention anything like bullying, perhaps? Inappropriate behaviour?'

Again, Martin laughed.

'Oh come on, Chief Inspector. It's a sports club for young lads. We were both that age once. Isn't there always something going on? Someone says or does something and one of them runs crying to teacher saying they're being picked on.'

'Except that sometimes it really is bullying, don't you find?' Ted asked mildly.

'Antoine and his friends weren't bullies. Quite the reverse, in fact. They always let that half-witted lad Nigel hang about with them.'

'Would you call him half-witted? I've interviewed him myself and he seemed bright enough.'

'Well, he's not quite in the same league as most of the others. Rubbish player, too. Not really good enough even for the subs' bench. But he was always dedicated, I'll give him that. Always turned up to training sessions and matches, in all weathers.

'I don't mean to sound like a massive snob or anything but Antoine has been making a good living for himself for a while now with the online currency trading he does. I think Nigel cleans hospital corridors. So to me, that doesn't make him the sharpest knife in the drawer.'

'And as far as you're aware, there's been no talk of anything inappropriate going on at the club? I'm not talking so much about the boys here as between them and any adults.'

'Kiddy-fiddling, you mean? Is that what you think was going on? For god's sake, Chief Inspector, Antoine was a member of that club for years. Do you seriously think I'd have let him keep going there if there was the slightest suggestion of anything like that?'

'It was just a routine question. And one final one, Mr Martin, then I'll let you get on. Did you and your family ever go to Roman Lakes at all?'

'A couple of times, when Antoine was small and wanted to go everywhere on his bike. Apart from his football, we're not really an outdoorsy sort of family at all. Despite a cottage in the Lakes. Especially Marie-Claire. She thinks she's been hiking if she has to walk across a car park from the Jeep to a restaurant.'

'Thank you very much for your time, Mr Martin. You've been very helpful and I really appreciate it.'

Ted had left his service vehicle outside the property, on the road. Before he got in it to drive off, he went for a walk around the quiet close in which Martin's house was situated. The area reeked of money. Big houses, big cars, often several of them on the driveways, even at a time of day when many people might be out at work.

He'd checked aerial maps of the area so knew roughly where he needed to walk to see the rear of the property from the fields behind. If the former team members had wanted to go out quietly the evening of Waldren's death, he wanted to assess how easy it would have been for them to do so by using the back way.

It was certainly possible, from what his exploration showed him. If they had left that way, if indeed any or all of them were involved at all, a short walk across the field would have taken them to a lane where they could have had one or more vehicles parked and waiting.

He'd need to get his team onto checking any traffic camera footage from that area. With all of the young men giving each other alibis, he would need something solid to show any kind of valid reason to make any or all of them official suspects.

Ted had arranged to do a few interviews during the day, which would keep him out of the office for a chunk of it. It was so rare for that to happen it felt a bit like wagging off school. Not that he'd ever done that. He'd not enjoyed his school-days having been the object of bullying and worse. But he'd been smart enough to know that to follow his chosen career path, he needed good grades to get to university so he'd always worked hard.

It was good to be away from his desk for a change, although he was on call to return if necessary. He was in generally good spirits after his evening's judo session with Trev. His martial arts were always good for him, when he could find the time.

He'd timed his day so that he could call on Jim Baker for the half-hour or so it would take to have a drink and a sandwich. He wanted to talk over the case with him again, if Bella would allow it. Pick his brains for anything he might have missed himself.

First, he was on his way to talk to the club chairman, Des Clarke. He was an accountant with premises in Cheadle, which wasn't too far out of his way to go on to Jim's house in Didsbury afterwards.

Ted was punctual, as ever. The receptionist asked him to go straight through, indicating Clarke's office. The man rose to greet him with a handshake.

'Hello, again, Inspector. When I saw you last, at the match, I never for a moment imagined there would be another death for you to investigate, connected to our club. Please take a seat. Can I get a drink for you?'

'No, thank you, Mr Clarke, I've not long had one with Louis Martin. Thanks for making time for me. This is just an informal witness interview, at this stage. We're talking to everyone who may have had contact with Derek Waldren on the day of his death.'

Clarke frowned as he replied, 'Louis wasn't there that day, as I remember. He's a great supporter of the club, but I think he was away on business for the benefit match day.'

'That's right, so he told me. What can you tell me about Derek Waldren, Mr Clarke? Did you know him?'

'I think know is too strong a word. I know who he was, of

course. He was often at matches.'

Ted produced the photo again and put it in front of the other man.

'Not just at matches, it seems.'

Clarke picked the photo up and looked at it closely.

'D'you know, I'd honestly forgotten he was there at that camp. So is it true, the rumours we've heard? That Derek Waldren murdered Callum? Any idea why he would do that?'

'All I can say is that following the death of Mr Waldren we are no longer looking for anyone else in connection with Callum's death,' Ted trotted out the official line once more. 'So please can you tell me what you know about him?'

'Not a lot really. He was an excellent first aider. I think he worked as a paramedic for the Ambulance Service. I seem to remember that's why he came along to camp with us.'

'Were there ever any problems with him?'

'Problems? Not that I remember. Like I said, he was an excellent first aider. And of course he had all his police checks and stuff like that, for his St John's work, so we were lucky to have him. Has there been some talk about him?'

'Are you aware of any? As Mr Waldren is dead and I'm investigating his murder, it would be helpful if you could tell me anything you heard, even if it amounts to little more than gossip. It could be helpful to our enquiries.'

'All I can tell you is that our club has had very few problems, although I appreciate you may find that hard to believe with three deaths now associated with it. If there had been the slightest whiff of anything dodgy going on, I and the other officials would have dealt with it immediately. But there honestly hasn't been, not in all the years I've been chairman.'

'Thank you. One more thing. Can I ask where you were on the evening after the match, please?'

'Well, I certainly wasn't killing Derek Waldren, which imagine is your reason for asking. Once the match was finished and everyone had gone home, I went for a curry with Bi

Batley, the treasurer and Phil Booth, the coach for the Under-17s and Under-15s. It's an after-match tradition we have. The three of us have a curry and a few beers at one of our houses while our wives have a girls' night in at another house.'

'So on the night Derek Waldren was killed, you, Bill Batley and Phil Booth were together in whose house?'

'It was at mine. The ladies went to Bill's house.'

'Until what time?'

'Quite a late one. My wife came back in a taxi about one o'clock, I think it was. She went straight to bed. The lads and I stayed on drinking for a good hour after that, I'd say. They must have left at about two or half past.'

'So just about all of your potential suspects have solid alibis for the night Waldren was killed?' Jim Baker asked Ted when he called round after talking to Clarke.

'They have alibis but it's usually from someone who could also be a potential suspect,' Ted told him. 'In other words, we're a bit going round in circles really.'

'Not too much shop talk now, you two,' Bella told them firmly, coming in with a tray. There was tea for Ted and a plate of sandwiches to share. Ted noticed the wholemeal bread and abundant salad with the cheese and guessed that Bella was taking strict charge of Jim's diet. He also noticed Big Jim's coffee looked and smelled much weaker than he usually took it.

'Are you sure you dare eat Bella's sandwiches, Ted? You're not afraid she's laced them with deadly nightshade or something?' Jim teased him.

Ted had briefly been suspicious of Jim's intended the first time he'd met her as she'd matched the profile of a killer he was tracking at the time.

Ted shot him a mock glare as he said, 'I think I preferred you when you were in intensive care.'

It was good to see his boss looking so much better. He

hoped it wouldn't be long before he was back holding the reins. Although Ted's relationship with the Ice Queen had mellowed considerably, Jim was his friend as well as his boss which usually made it easier to work with him.

'So what's your strategy now?' Jim asked him, talking around a large bite of his sandwich.

'Just keep chipping away at them, until someone finally changes their story and leaves someone else out on a limb without an alibi.'

Ted's next call on the way back to the office to confront the paperwork ready for yet another management meeting was to see the club coach, Phil Booth. He managed a car saleroom on the edge of Stockport. When Ted arrived, a young man busily polishing an already gleaming car pointed out Booth's office. The coach saw him coming and came to the door to meet him.

Ted introduced himself and showed his badge as Booth invited him into the office and they sat down at opposite sides of a desk. Ted went through his usual spiel and produced the photo.

'I'm principally here making enquiries into the death of Derek Waldren,' he began, indicating Waldren's position on the photo.

'That was a weird business, for sure,' Booth replied. 'Are the rumours true? Is he really the one who killed Callum?'

Yet again, Ted repeated the official line about no longer looking for anyone in connection with Callum's killing, then asked, 'Did you know Derek Waldren at all?'

'Badger? Yes, reasonably well. I had a drink with him few times, especially at camp. He was a good bloke. That's why I was so stunned to hear he probably killed Callum. mean, he had practically no life of his own, between looking after his mother and doing all the first aid stuff he did for the Johnners and various youth groups. I don't know how he found the time to sleep.'

'Badger?' Ted queried.

'It's what some of the lads called him. It was to do with him being involved with the Junior Johnners. They're called the Badgers.'

'I asked around at the match and no one seemed to know him as Badger. Not even your treasurer.'

'Oh, that's quite likely. I'm much closer to the lads than the club officials are so I hear more of that sort of stuff from them. It was when Antoine was playing the nickname started, I think. It was probably Antoine who picked it. He was always calling people by nicknames, and not always complimentary ones at that.'

# Chapter Twenty-eight

'How did the players get on with Badger? Did they have much contact with him?' Ted went on.

'They all seemed to get on great. As well as the first aid stuff, he used to do talks with them. Things to help with their training. The importance of warm-up exercises, how to deal with minor injuries themselves. You know, things like muscle strain, that sort of thing.'

'Anything more than that?'

Booth looked at him, puzzled.

'I'm not sure what you mean.'

'Well, I'm a martial artist myself. Football has never been my thing although I played some, reluctantly, at school. But some of the common football injuries are a bit intimate, aren't they? Groin strain? That type of thing?'

Booth's expression had turned to one of incredulity.

'Are you suggesting Badger was into kiddy-fiddling, Badger? I know there isn't any particular type but he never struck me as being that way inclined at all. I know we used to speculate that he was completely asexual, you know? He was never with anyone, not a woman or a man. He never seemed to have the time, for one thing. But there was never any kind of talk, not even rumour, about him behaving inappropriately with any of the lads. Believe me, I would have heard if there had been. Then not only would he have been out of any association with the club but I'd have frogmarched him down to the nick myself and had him arrested.'

'With respect, Mr Booth, if a player was taken off the pitch by the first aiders and examined in the ambulance, for instance, would you have known what was said or done?'

'All those lads trust me. They have to, for us to train well together. If there was anything going on, I'd have known about it. I'd have seen a change in their performance, for one thing.'

'Didn't Páraic's performance drop off? And wasn't that after a minor injury? No one yet seems to know the real reason for his suicide. Is it possible that something had happened which no one knew about?'

'I suppose anything is theoretically possible,' Booth said reluctantly. 'I'd still be bloody surprised at anything like that involving Badger, of all people. I mean, the Johnners and the Ambulance Service must have vetted him up to the eyeballs for that sort of work, surely?'

'Of course. As far as you know, did any of the players ever see Badger outside the club circle? Did any of them go for a drink with him, perhaps?'

'They're under age to go out drinking.'

'They could, of course, go to a pub with an adult and have soft drinks. So is it something they might perhaps have done?'

'I'm really gobsmacked by all this. I honestly am. It's like you're talking about people I don't know. These lads are all dedicated players. You said you do martial arts. So I bet you don't go out drinking much, if you take it seriously. The players don't either. And believe me, I would notice if they were doing that, because then their performance really would drop off.'

'Like I said, they might perhaps have gone for a soft drink with him from time to time?'

'I suppose they might,' he sounded hesitant now.

'Thank you. I won't keep you any longer, Mr Booth, you've been very helpful.'

Ted's mind was churning as he drove back to the station. Antoine and the others had been lying to them on so many points he was starting to wonder if anything they'd told them was true.

The main office was deserted when he got back. Only Jo was holding the fort in his own office, the door open so he could see what was going on. Ted went in for a catch-up.

'Caught our little friends out in another big fat lie,' Ted told him. 'According to the coach, Phil Booth, a lot of the lads used to call Derek Waldren Badger and it was possibly Antoine who coined the nickname for him.'

'Little toerags. Everyone's out interviewing, including Graham Winters. He's on board now. I briefed him before he started. Oh, except Steve, who asked if he could go and take a look round the crime scene by himself. He was being very mysterious. He just said he had an idea he wanted to check out and promised not to be long.'

'Steve actually asked to go off piste?' Ted asked in surprise. 'That's not like him.'

'It's since he moved in with Bill a couple of days ago. That was inspirational on your part. He's suddenly coming out of his shell, with Bill to guide him. Oh, and early news on the latest round of interviews so far. They're all gradually changing their stories. Now it's become "Nigel was with us at some point but we can't remember if he was there all the time or if he left at some time." In other words, Nigel is quickly turning out to be the only one of them who doesn't appear to have a solid alibi.'

'There's no way Nigel could have killed Badger on his own, though. I'm not even convinced, from what I've seen of him, that he would have been at the scene while it was happening. I could be wrong on that, of course. I'll talk to Anthony Hopkins again about his impressions of him.

'For now, I have to pay the price for playing truant all day and catch up on the paperwork. Let me know when everyone's back in. I'm especially interested to see if Steve turns anything up.'

Steve was the last of the team back in at the end of the day. He arrived flushed and breathing hard as if he'd been running, but his expression was triumphant. He was clutching an evidence bag with a piece of paper and a bottle in it.

'So sorry I'm late. It took longer than I thought,' he panted, scuttling to his desk.

Jo was in charge, Ted standing in the background.

'Go on then, Steve, you've clearly found something, so let's hear about it.'

'Well, you know I keep saying I think the team members must have had a way of contacting one another without using phones or internet? They're just too clever to leave any kind of an electronic trail, and there were gaps in Callum's phone history and emails when I was sure he must have been talking to someone.'

Charlie Eccles was already sighing and shifting in his seat, sensing another long explanation. Steve saw the gesture but for once, he ploughed on.

'I know it sounds stupid,' he said directly to Charlie, with an unaccustomed defiant lift of the chin. 'But as it turned out, it wasn't stupid. I found this.'

He held up the clear plastic bag in a gesture of triumph.

'It's a handwritten note. Not signed. But it is dated. The day Callum died. He must have left it there sometime earlier in the day. Before he went to see Badger. It just says "I'm going to give him a chance to give himself up before we do it for him. I know it's not what we agreed but I think we owe him that".'

There was a brief moment of silence, then Maurice spoke first.

'Bloody hell, Steve, lad. Good work. Where was it?'

'A bit further into the woods from where Callum was. There's a tree where some of the roots stick out a bit above the ground. There's a hollow there with a big stone. The note was in an old beer bottle behind the stone.'

Jo was shaking his head.

'I have to give it to you, Steve. I didn't think you were right with this one. But you were, and you followed your instincts. Good work. We'll need to get the note tested now for fingerprints, and for a cross-match on the handwriting to see if it was Callum who wrote it. You did remember gloves before you handled it, didn't you?'

'Of course I did,' Steve said indignantly.

Ted and Jo exchanged a grin. This was a different Steve to the one they were used to seeing.

'Get it sent off asap then, Steve, and let's see what it can tell us. I don't understand why none of the lads picked the note up, though. They must have realised we might find it at any time.'

'I think it's probably because they had no way of knowing whether the crime scene was being watched after Callum died. They couldn't be seen going there because I think they've all told us so far they didn't know the place where both Callum and Badger were killed. If one of them went up there rooting round and was seen, that would take some explaining, wouldn't it?'

'Very good work, Steve. I think you have a point there. Who did you interview today?' Ted asked him.

'I had Nigel again. I asked him about Derek Waldren being at camp. He said he was, but he'd forgotten. He's still sticking to the same story as before. He didn't know him other than to see him at the matches, and he admitted they'd been at the same camp. He only went over to the ambulance at the match to ask how the injured player was. And he's adamant that he was with the rest of the team from the moment they left the match to the following morning when he went home after breakfast. He even obligingly told me what he'd had for breakfast.'

'He has a tendency to do that,' Ted put in. 'So does Terry. They're both affirming, adding extra detail to make it sound more believable. In fact, it does the exact opposite.'

'Boss, perhaps before we start on a round-up of what everyone found out, you could give us the highlights of your interviews?' Jo suggested.

'I had a look round at Antoine's place. As you'd expect, it was easy to identify where the photos they were all so keen on showing us were taken. The security cameras are apparently not working, and that may well be genuine.

'It would be easy for any of them to have left the back way, over the fence, across a field and into a waiting vehicle. We need full details of what they all drive, if we don't have that already, and that needs checking against traffic camera footage from the area at the back of the house and beyond, wherever there are any cameras.

'Antoine's father was interesting. He's quite powerfully built. Strong character. Arrogant. Sure of himself. He's the boss of the company now but he looks as if he's worked hard, physically, to get there. I get the impression he can handle himself. He says he away was in the Lake District for the weekend and had business lunches both days.

'His cottage is in Cartmel, so that's under two hours to get back here. Especially if he got his foot down. He drives a big black Jeep with a personalised number plate. He made a point of telling me he's careful not to drive too soon after drinking. He could still have had plenty of time to get back here and help dealing with Badger. I doubt he'd be stupid enough to get himself clocked for serious speeding on the way, but it's worth checking to see if he was picked up anywhere on camera. Mike, can you liaise with Traffic, please, just in case?'

'Will do, boss. But would Antoine's father have had a motive for killing Badger? If anything had happened to Antoine, why didn't he just go round and thump him one, or cop him?'

'That's the million dollar question. As Jo's pointed out, the method of killing suggests strongly that someone thought

Badger had been sexually abusing someone. So far, unless anyone has heard different, we've not found anything to suggest that.

'But that reminds me. Someone needs to check out the PM report on Páraic to see if there was any suggestion of sexual abuse. I don't recall any mention of it anywhere, but please check.

'The most interesting development came from talking to the coach, Phil Booth. As soon as I mentioned Derek Waldren's name he called him Badger. What's more, he said he thinks it was Antoine who coined the name in the first place and that it's what all of Antoine's team members used to call him.

'I asked him why none of the other officials seemed to know the name but he did. He said it was probably because he was closer to the players, which makes sense. He also had nothing but praise for Waldren. He'd never heard anything against him, and again, that sounded genuine.'

'Yet another thing the little bastards have been lying to us about,' Maurice muttered.

'And speaking of lying,' Jo put in, 'where are we at with the alibi situation? Mike, you said that was starting to break apart?'

'That's the info I have to date, but I've not caught up with everyone yet. So let's go round, see what everyone found out. I spoke to Will. Will Walker. I'd not encountered him before. Pleasant lad. Polite. I went over his initial interviews with him and pressed him. To start with, he'd been adamant that the whole team had been together all evening. He did the same trick of showing me his photos. I asked him why Nigel wasn't there. Usual excuse. He was a sub, the photos were team members, blah, blah, blah. The more I pressed, the more vague he became. He couldn't actually remember if Nigel had been there all evening or not. He might have been, or he could have left at some point and no one noticed.'

'Maurice?' Jo prompted.

'Exactly the same from Jerome. Yes, they were definitely together all evening, but then by the time I'd asked him a few different questions, we got to "well I thought he was, but I wouldn't be prepared to swear to it".'

'And the same thing from Jordan Kennedy,' Rob said. 'Started out giving Nigel a solid alibi which quickly evaporated the more I questioned him.

'Wayne Edwards was the same, too. Almost word for word,' Leona Rakale nodded in agreement.

'Sam Jackson was a bit more inventive,' Charlie Eccles spoke next. 'He made a big show of trying to find the photos on his phone which he assured me would prove that Nigel had been with them. There were none there, so then he started with the, "well, I was sure he was there but now I can't swear to it" version. It seems fishy to me that suddenly they're all changing their stories. Is Nigel the sacrificial lamb?'

'As the boss and I were saying earlier, there's no way Nigel could have carried out this killing on his own,' Jo replied. 'If he was involved, he must have had help. And on that score, it's time for me to talk about my visit to the Shaugnessy clan, Páraic's family.

'It was the two older boys who were at camp, Ciaran, the cage fighter, and Donal. I managed to catch them at the same time as the father, Paddy. They're all working on the same building site in Manchester at the moment. They have different trades, bricklaying, carpentry, plasterer. I spoke to them separately, of course.

'The father really couldn't offer any explanation as to why Páraic took his own life. He said he'd become a bit quiet, more withdrawn than usual, but he put it down to a phase he was going through.

'As for the night Badger was killed, Ciaran was at a fight in Manchester, with a big crowd. The whole family was there with him, and I've got footage of it coming from a mate of theirs who was filming the whole thing. That might well show us if all of the family really were there all the time. There may, of course, not be enough footage of the crowd for us to be sure one way or the other.

'Physically, Ciaran and Donal look like possibles. Not just the cage fighting but the way those lads were rushing about that site carrying all sorts of heavy stuff was impressive. I could see the two of them being more than a match for Badger. But if Ciaran was fighting in full view of a large crowd, it can't have been him. I suppose there's a possibility that Donal or his dad, or both, might have slipped away. There might even have been other friends or relatives there, and if they believed Badger was responsible for Páraic's death, there's your motive, right there.'

'We could do with narrowing down the number of suspects, not expanding them,' Ted said drily.

'Graham, what about you?' Jo asked him. 'Who did you speak to?'

'I spoke to Terry Russell and it was exactly like everyone else has been saying. Rock solid, word perfect on his script to begin with. The more questions I asked, the more he couldn't be sure if he'd seen Nigel the whole evening or not. Nor does he remember if he was there for breakfast. I asked him what they had for breakfast, in case it was an important detail for corroboration, but he said he only had coffee, from a fancy machine, as he put it. He doesn't do breakfast, apparently, so he didn't take much notice of what anyone else was having. He did say someone was frying bacon and making a bit of a mess, so they had some cleaning up to do afterwards.'

'Yet more embellishment to make it sound credible,' Ted put in. 'They're still lying, but it's not getting us very far for now.'

Virgil reported the same thing from Marvin.

'Marvin Gray, poor lad. His parents clearly had a sense of humour when it came to naming him. His version was th same. Almost word for word. They've clearly all got together, apart from Nigel, and rehearsed exactly how they're changing their original statements.

'I also spoke to Gary Roper. Exactly the same version, almost word for word.'

'Another possibly significant link, but again the same story,' Jezza said. 'I spoke to Alan Barnes at work. He works for Phil Booth, the trainer, at his car saleroom. Supposedly a trainee manager but more of a general dogs' body, from what I saw. He seems to spend a lot of his time valeting cars and brewing up. He said the police were also going in to talk to his boss later on.'

'That was me,' Ted told her. 'I saw Booth this afternoon and I saw a young lad cleaning cars while I was there. It's strange that Booth didn't mention he had one of the team working for him. I should have recognised him. I did think he looked familiar, but no more than that.'

'We've also made a start on the younger team,' Mike Hallam said. 'Luckily, there's some solid alibis there which already check out, so we're not going to have another eleven to add to the list. Two joined up. One's in the Navy, currently in training, the other's in the Army, and they both check out. One is staying with family in Australia, another's doing voluntary work in Africa. In fact there's only a couple of them still to track down and check alibis for. So that's something. And we've caught up with all the lacrosse players now, too. All with solid alibis, all checked out.'

'Next step, boss?' Jo asked him.

'It's time we hauled Nigel in for a formal interview under caution, I think, with his alibi now in serious doubt. Mike, can you get hold of him and arrange that for tomorrow morning. Tell him he might want to get a solicitor, so we better not make it too early, to give him time to find one. If not, offer to get a duty one for him, please. Let's do it by the book, and let's tread carefully with him, bearing in mind what the psych said about him. Jo, I'd like you on that, and Steve, you sit in. The three of us will meet up first thing to discuss how the interview needs to go.

'Right, everyone, good work. Fresh start tomorrow, but we might finally be seeing daylight at the end of the tunnel. Or least someone might have cut the ribbon to declare the tunnel open.'

Ted was just getting his things together in his office when Maurice put his head round the door.

'I just wanted to say thanks, Ted, for sorting Steve out. He and Bill seem like a pair of happy pigs in shit together, so I'd say you played a blinder there.'

Ted smiled. He'd hoped it would work out and it seemed to be doing. He was going for a drink with Kev after work, as Trev would be at karate, and he'd asked Bill to join them, as he often did. He was surprised when Bill refused, saying that Steve was getting them a takeaway so he didn't want to be late. Father Jack, the swearing cockatoo, had taken an instant liking to Steve, apparently, which meant he was all right, as far as Bill was concerned.

'The downside, though,' Maurice continued, 'is that now we've got the spare room back, Megan's pestering me to start decorating it for the new babies.'

'How is Megan?'

'Fit as a lop. She's doing fine.'

'Do you know the gender yet?'

Maurice beamed with pride as he said, 'Two little lads. Imagine that. We were thinking of calling one of them Ted.'

'Oh, don't do that to the poor bugger,' Ted said with feeling. 'He'll spend his school-days being called Teddy Bear, Little Ted, Paddington, Pooh – shall I go on?'

Maurice laughed and asked, 'All right, so do you have middle name?'

'No, just Ted. That was my dad's choice. My mam wanted to called me Owain, after Owain Glyndŵr.'

'Owain. I like that. I'll ask Megan.'

Ted's mobile pinged at that moment with an incoming message so Maurice left him to it. Ted opened it and read the screen.

'The eagle has landed. H.'

# Chapter Twenty-nine

Ted made a quick call to Kevin Turner to tell him he was running slightly late for their drink but would meet him in The Grapes in about ten minutes.

'I'll give you fifteen. If you're not there, I'm coming to arrest you for wasting police time,' Kev told him cheerfully. He did seem to be in a slightly better mood than he had been.

Ted sat back down at his computer and began searching for rolling news feeds which might mention something related to the message from Harry. He took it to mean that Harry had now received delivery of the witness Mr Green had sprung from custody.

Eventually he found a live item with a news reporter doing a piece to camera in a well-known central London location.

'… known only as BRIOCHE. The group's name believed to be a reference to the French revolution. The people behind it are understood to have revolutionary tendencies, with a stated aim of bringing down the Government. spokesperson for the Metropolitan Police would say only that they are aware of the group's existence and that it has come to the attention of their Counter-Terrorism Unit.

'Little is known of the identity of the alleged witness other than that it's a woman, known only as Witness X, believed to be a person who was being held in a Cheshire prison. The person was unlawfully taken from custody on a routine medical visit in what the police described at the time as a professional operation.

'The statement from BRIOCHE claims that the woman was

a witness at a number of events at which highly-placed members of the Government were in attendance while children were being abused. It is thought that she has named at least one senior member of the Cabinet in her allegations.'

Ted muted the sound on his computer as his mobile rang. An unknown number. He answered guardedly.

'You've heard the news, Gayboy? Delivery made.'

'I'm just watching it online now. Explosive stuff.'

'I'm going to tell you something now. If it goes any further, I will know, and I will find you. You know the rest.'

Ted did know. And he believed him. Mr Green was not someone you messed with.

'I'm retiring. This was my last job. I got back in touch with my family. I haven't seen them for years, but I've always supported them. I've discovered I have a grandson. One of my daughters has a little boy. Robbie. I've never met him, of course. It's time I did.

'I did this last job at a cut-price rate. That tin-pot bunch of pretend revolutionaries could never afford my prices. But it's time we finally wound up the bunch of bastards behind this kind of stuff. All of them. And now I know I have a grandson, it matters to me.'

Ted was staggered by what he was hearing. It was probably the longest speech he'd ever heard from Green, unless he was delivering instructions at a training session. It showed a side to his character he had never imagined was there.

'So this was my swansong and I'm hanging up my holsters, if they let me. If ever you need me, you can still leave a message via the usual means. Goodbye, Gayboy. And make sure you remember the importance of family.'

The call ended before Ted could say anything. He just sat for a moment in stunned silence. Then he gathered his things to put in his car and went to find Kevin in the pub.

Kev was already halfway through his first pint. He produced a pair of handcuffs from his coat pocket and dangled them towards Ted as he joined him at the table, carrying his Gunner.

'Made it by the skin of your teeth,' Kev told him. 'I was just coming for you.'

They spent a companionable hour or so together. At least Kev had stopped talking about jacking it in and going to work in a shop. He wasn't on a bender this time, either, although Ted still wouldn't let him drive home, just in case.

Ted was thoughtful after Green's call. It had surprised him. But it had also reminded him of how much his own family life with Trev meant to him and how much he'd been neglecting him of late. He stopped to buy him some red roses and a bottle of wine for when he got home.

Trev had left their supper in the oven on a low light. It smelled inviting and Ted was hungry. But as soon as he heard the motorbike pull into the drive, he went to wait, with the front door open, for Trev to put it away and come in. He greeted him with the roses, a hug and a kiss.

'Wow, this is nice. What have you done?' Trev laughed.

'Not told you often enough how important you are to me. How I couldn't get through my job without you. Will the supper be burned to a frazzle if we don't eat it straight away?'

'I'm suddenly not all that interested in supper,' Trev laughed again, as he started up the stairs two at a time, Ted right on his heels.


'Nigel, I'm Detective Inspector Rodriguez, and you already know Detective Constable Ellis,' Jo kicked off the interview with Nigel the following morning, with Steve sitting beside him.

He'd explained carefully, with the tape running, that this was a formal interview under caution concerning the death of Derek Waldren.

'You've been advised of your right to have legal representation, which you have declined. Are you sure you' happy to proceed without a solicitor present, Nigel?'

'I don't need a solicitor. I haven't done anything wrong,' Nigel replied calmly. 'I've cooperated with you all along. I've given you my alibi for when Derek was killed. I wasn't there and you can't prove I was.'

He sounded sure of himself, smiling from Jo to Steve and back again. Untouchable, as far as he was concerned.

'We'll come to the question of your alibi in a moment, Nigel. First of all, though, Derek isn't what you would usually call Mr Waldren, is it? Wasn't he known to you and to the rest of the team members as Badger?'

'Never heard that.'

'And yet your coach, Phil Booth, told us that the name Badger was coined for him by Antoine Martin, and that it was widely used by all the team members. And you yourself were the first person to mention the nickname Badger to us.'

'I didn't. You say I did but you can't prove that. Anyway, does it matter? If some people called him Derek and some called him Badger? Is that important?'

He was starting to sound defensive now. Ted was watching from the other side of the glass. He, Jo and Steve had spent some time going over the line the questioning was going to take. Ted had also decided that he would put a tail on Nigel once he left the station. Rob and Jezza were on standby to follow him. They were almost certain he would immediately run in search of some of the others once he was told how they were all starting to withdraw their alibi for him.

'Of itself, it may well be of no importance. The problem with us is that once someone tells us something that's not true – like you claiming not to know the nickname Badger – it means we start looking at everything else you say to us with a different eye.'

'Well, I just knew him the Johnner until you told me his name was Derek. And everything else I've told you is true.'

'Everything else? So you concede that the part about Badger isn't true?'

Jo was quick to pounce on the slip. If Nigel had had a solicitor present, they would never have allowed him to reply to most of the questions. They would certainly have prevented him from tying himself in knots as he was in danger of doing.

Steve took over at that point, at a barely perceptible signal from Jo. He had a piece of paper in an evidence bag on the table in front of him. It wasn't the original of the note he'd found, which had gone off to the lab. But interviewees tended to react more warily to anything in an evidence bag than to an obvious photocopy. It could have advantages.

'Nigel, do you recognise the handwriting on this note?'

Nigel's reaction was revealing. His body language changed immediately. Now he was tense, on his guard. He made a show of glancing disinterestedly at the note Steve pushed toward him. But the hand he reached out to shove it back again was noticeably trembling.

'No idea who wrote that.'

'That's not what I asked you, Nigel,' Steve continued persistently. 'I asked you if you recognised the handwriting. It's not quite the same question. Can you look at it again more closely, please?'

Ted smiled to himself in the next room. Steve was doing a grand job.

Grudgingly, Nigel pulled the note back, being careful not to lift it up and draw attention to how much he was shaking. He scanned it, then shook his head.

'No, I don't recognise the handwriting.'

'Do you know what this note is about, Nigel? Who is the 'he' it refers to?'

'I don't know anything about it. So how would I know what it refers to?'

'Did you and your friends from the team ever have occasion to write to one another? To send letters? Or perhaps to leave notes for each other? In a special place? Like a cache?'

Nigel was clearly rattled now. He licked his lips, moved nervously in his seat, his eyes darting from side to side. He took a moment before he answered.

'Of course not. My generation, we don't write stuff much. It's all texts or email or social media.'

Jo took over seamlessly once more.

'Tell us again about the Saturday night after the match, Nigel. The night that Derek Waldren was killed. Where were you?'

'I've told you. Several times. After the match, we all went to the supermarket to get stuff to eat and drink.'

'Whose turn was it to pay?'

'I can't remember whose turn it was, but Antoine paid at the till with his card.'

'Can you explain why you don't appear in any of the CCTV footage at the store, which clearly shows the rest of the team?'

'No, I can't explain that. I was there. Then we all went back to Antoine's place to cook the pizzas and stuff before we watched films.'

'Again, how is it that you don't appear in any of the photos taken at that time?'

'They were team photos. I wasn't on the team. I was reserve. I only went on if someone was injured. But I was there. The others will all confirm that.'

'But this is where we have a problem, Nigel,' Jo told him pleasantly. 'You see, none of them can actually confirm that. They all say they think you were there. But they couldn't swear to it. Antoine says he thinks he remembers you at the start of the evening, but he couldn't say if you stayed there the whole time.'

'Jerome said exactly the same thing,' Steve put in.

He and Jo had spent a few moments rehearsing this part.

They wanted to draw the moment out. It was more likely to get a reaction if they did.

'And Jordan.'

'Wayne said he can't really say at what point he saw you.'

Nigel was visibly sweating now, constantly licking his lips. He'd been provided with some water from which he took a large swallow, spilling some of it because of the tremor in his hand.

'But that's not right. That's not what we ...' he broke off abruptly, uncertainly.

'That's not what you decided between you that your cover story was going to be? Well, I have news for you, Nigel. The others are rapidly back-pedalling on their stories. At the moment, it's starting to look like you're the only one who doesn't have an alibi for the time in question.

'At this point, Nigel, I must remind you again that you aren't obliged to say anything but that anything you do say may be given in evidence. Think about that very carefully, Nigel. I propose we take a five-minute break now to let you reflect. You should also reconsider your decision to have legal representation for the rest of this interview.'

Jo and Steve rose and went next door to talk to Ted. They'd agreed between them beforehand that if they reached the critical point, they would regroup and decide how to proceed.

'We've not got anything at all to ask for a remand in custody, boss,' Jo said. 'If we carry on, he's likely to crack, but without any forensics at all, even if he admits his involvement, where can we go from there? We've nothing to arrest anyone else on, even if he gives us some names.

'Is it worth letting him go at this point? Telling him to go and sort out a solicitor for himself and come back tomorrow? Then Rob and Jezza can tail him and see who he runs to first. That might possibly give us an indication of who else is involved. They can't all have been there, surely? I'm leaning more and more to the theory of maybe four or five of them, with Nigel as the bait, and the rest back at the house to provide the alibi.'

'But which ones?' Ted asked. 'That's what we need to know. I agree. Let's let him sweat another five minutes then let him run and see where he goes first. I bet it's straight round to Antoine's. Get Rob and Jezza on standby and make sure they keep in contact with you the whole time, Jo. And keep me posted, please.'

'I spy with my little eye.'

Rob spoke as he and Jezza were sitting in a service vehicle near to Nigel's house in Heaviley. He'd gone straight home as soon as he left the station, parked his scooter outside the house and disappeared inside. They hadn't seen hide nor hair of him for more than an hour.

'Maybe he's just gone to bed to get some kip before his night shift?' Jezza suggested.

'If he has he's either innocent or he's a very cool customer. After a grilling from Jo and discovering his so-called friends have all chucked him overboard without a lifebelt, I would have thought sleep was the last thing on his mind.'

'So how's things going between you and Nat? Isn't it about time you were shacking up together?'

'Oh, look, ideal opportunity to avoid inappropriately intrusive questions from a work colleague. Here comes Nigel, emerging into the daylight.'

Jezza's tone was ironic. She didn't mind the question. The team members were close. She just wasn't ready to tell the others yet that her boyfriend Nathan had, in fact, moved in with her and her kid brother Tommy a couple of weeks ago.

Rob started the car and followed as Nigel, on his scooter, headed out of the side road onto the A6, turning south. Jezza relayed their position over the radio to Jo.

'It's a bit early for him to be going to work, surely?' Rob

commented. 'Unless he's changed shifts.'

'Well, he's not turning in to the hospital,' Jezza replied as Nigel ignored the entrance to Stepping Hill and carried on.

'Who lives out this way?'

'He could be going this way to go up towards Marple to see Antoine, possibly.'

Then, a few minutes later, Jezza relayed a position update.

'He's heading for the Post Office. He's got an A4 brown envelope in his hand.'

When Nigel emerged again, without the envelope, he got back on his scooter, Rob carefully tailing him, and went next to Hazel Grove station, where he parked and went inside.

Rob and Jezza followed. Nigel went straight to the platform for Manchester-bound trains. Jezza stood a short distance away, using her phone to look up real-time train arrivals and departures. Rob stayed back, though had his eyes firmly on Nigel the whole time. Nigel was standing a short way away patiently waiting, seemingly unconcerned and unaware that he was being watched. There weren't many commuters about at that time of day, just a handful apparently waiting for the Manchester train.

Jezza was still using the radio for contact with Rob and with Jo back at the police station.

'Next train through, any minute now, is a non-stopper, but there's a Manchester train due shortly after that. The stone train goes through first.'

'Stone train?' Rob and Jo both queried at almost the same time.

Jezza was a walking encyclopaedia thanks to her brother Tommy's obsession with making his own set of Trivial Pursuit questions.

'It comes down from the quarries at Peak Forest with stone for cement production. Runs straight through a few times a day, most days. The next stopper is the Manchester train. Don't the Shaugnessys live up in Manchester? Perhaps he's going to see them. He might have opted for the train thinking we could be keeping an eye out for his scooter. If you want to board if he does, Rob, I'll get the car.'

'You learn something new every day with you around, Jezza,' Rob laughed. 'That might come in handy for a pub quiz one of these days. I can see this famous stone train coming now.'

The next thing Jezza heard was Rob's shout of, 'Jesus Christ!'

She didn't hear his follow-up of, 'Fuck, no!' which was drowned out by a high-pitched metallic screaming, so loud it was painful to the ears, which seemed to go on endlessly.

The brakes of the big heavy train were screeching in protest as the driver applied them. There was a banging sound as the laden wagons jolted and bumped about with the desperate attempt to stop the forty-mile-an-hour progress of the locomotive.

One hundred yards. Two hundred yards. The train was still howling along, still making its loud and laboured commentary. Three hundred yards.

A railway employee had come running out of the ticket office at the first sounds. She had her mouth open in silent horror as the train powered on past. She was frozen to the spot, seemingly incapable of knowing what to do.

Jezza went into professional mode, approaching the woman with her warrant card in hand, taking charge of the situation. She knew Rob would already be calling it in. So too, no doubt, would the train driver. Her priority now was to calm the woman down and get her to move the few shocked commuters on the platform to a safe place and to keep them there until they could all be spoken to.

The train had run on another hundred yards or so before it finally came to a noisy, juddering halt, more than four hundred yards from where Nigel had jumped into its path. Of him, there was no sign, for which Jezza felt a profound sense of relief.

Rob had come hurrying up the platform to find her, scanning his colleague's face in concern.

'Are you all right? Shit, that was awful. I'd no idea he was going to do that. He seemed so calm. Just waiting. Should I have done something? Could I have stopped him?'

Rob was white in the face, visibly shocked. As the senior of the two of them, he was clearly feeling the burden of responsibility. Jezza took charge, as only she could.

'Rob, stop talking crap and flapping like a budgie. You couldn't have known. Neither of us could. Neither of us did Nobody saw that coming. If Jo and the boss had thought he was a suicide risk, do you honestly think they would just have let him go like that?

'The question is, did he jump because he was guilty. O because he was innocent and he knew he had no way o proving it.'

# Chapter Thirty

Ted stopped at the front desk to talk to Bill once he'd been to see the Ice Queen to keep her up to date after they let Nigel go. He wished he had more to report but at least it was a start.

'Will he talk eventually, do you think?' she'd asked him.

'I doubt it. We've told him he needs a solicitor and no lawyer worth his salt would let him say anything to incriminate himself. The best we're likely to get from him is an admission that it was his job to get Badger to the woods but that he had no idea what the others had planned for him there. And that's with a solicitor allowing him to take a huge risk as we could probably move on a conspiracy to murder charge.

'It's not an ideal situation to be in at any time, and certainly not going into the weekend.'

'It's not been the easiest of cases, with the lack of any forensics. But I know you and your team will be doing everything you can to bring it to a conclusion.'

Her vote of confidence surprised him but it was encouraging. He went in search of Bill.

'I don't know what you're sprinkling on young Steve's cornflakes in the mornings, Bill, but it's certainly having an effect on him. He's a changed man.'

'He's a good lad, is Steve. Jack approves of him, and that says a lot. He just lacks confidence. I've been telling him about how you were when you first started.'

Ted laughed.

'That better not be true. I'll never live it down. I know I was a pain in the backside.'

He was interrupted by his mobile phone. Rob calling him.

'Boss, Nigel jumped. Right in front of the stone train.'

Jo was just coming down the stairs to find Ted, his face grim.

'Are you and Jezza both all right?' Ted's first concern, as ever, was for his team members. 'Sit tight, Jo and I are on our way now.'

'You heard then?' Jo asked him as they headed for the car. 'The shit's going to hit the fan with this one, I imagine.'

'I didn't detect anything in his behaviour to suggest he might have suicide in mind. Did you? He seemed slightly agitated at learning his alibi was turning to worms, but no more than that.'

'I'd have to agree with that, and I was in the room with him. A bit rattled, as you'd expect, but nothing more.

'Jezza reported he stopped to post something on the way to the station. We need to get hold of whatever it was, in case it's relevant in some way. Mike's on it already. He's sending someone round to the Post Office to see if we can track it down. I have a horrible feeling we'll have missed the collection, though. Plus I imagine they get a fair few brown envelopes through their hands, so without knowing who it was addressed to, we may be out of luck.'

'You're thinking it might have been his suicide note?' Ted asked him.

'I'm hoping it was. And I'm hoping it might give us some of the answers we badly need. Because with Nigel out of the picture now, I'm struggling to see how we go forward from here, realistically speaking.'

Officers from Uniform had arrived at the railway station shortly before Ted and Jo got there and were already taping off the area, turning people away. Access to the station would be strictly controlled and the area treated as a potential crime scene until a full investigation had taken place. The Transport Police would be handling it, but there would also be a presence from the rail network and safety investigators. Ted and Jo signed themselves in and went to find Rob and Jezza.

Rob looked the more shaken of the two. Jezza seemed more in control. Rob launched straight into profuse apologies when he saw Jo and the boss.

'Sorry, boss, I had no inkling what was on his mind ...'

'It's neither the time nor the place for that, Rob,' Ted told him levelly. 'There'll be CCTV camera which will show exactly what happened. You'll both be questioned by the Transport Police. Make sure you cooperate fully, and make sure your notes are up to date. If there's anywhere to get a coffee, you could do worse than do that while you wait.'

'There's a little coffee shop on this platform,' Jezza told him. 'If they're still serving after this.'

'Can you get me a coffee, please, I'll be right there,' Rob told her.

Jezza and Jo withdrew tactfully, guessing Rob had more he wanted to say to Ted.

'I wasn't near enough to him, boss. By the time I realised what he was going to do, it was too late to do anything to stop him.'

Ted laid a hand on his arm and spoke quietly.

'Seriously, Rob, there is absolutely no point in beating yourself up. There'll be a full-scale enquiry into what happened here, and then probably one of the whole case to date. It's standard procedure. There'll be no scapegoating, just fact-finding. And if there is blame, I'm where the buck stops. Remember that. Now, let's go and get that coffee. We could be in for a long wait.'

Ted wasn't wrong about the timings. There was a lot of hanging about. Once the Transport Police arrived in force, Ted introduced himself to their senior officer and explained his presence.

'So was he your guilty party, and was that why he jumped?

It would wrap it up nicely for everyone concerned if it was as simple as that,' the officer responded.

'Sadly, it leaves us with a big hole as we hadn't finished with him. We'll need access to the CCTV asap, please. We're going to be under pressure over letting him leave if he was a suicide risk. He showed no sign of it at all while we were interviewing him, and my officers say he was just standing waiting, quite calmly, right up until the stone train came. Then he just ran and jumped.'

'I always feel sorry for the driver in cases like this. Terrible experience for them. Some of them never get over it.'

Ted's mobile interrupted them. He looked at the screen and said, 'Sorry, I have to take this. My boss.'

'What is the situation there?' the Ice Queen asked him. 'This was definitely the young man who was interviewed earlier on?'

'Yes, ma'am,' Ted replied, deciding he'd better keep it formal. 'DS O'Connell and DC Vine followed him to the station. He appeared to be waiting calmly for a train.'

'Well, he was clearly waiting for one, but not for the motives anticipated. The Chief Super wants you and me to meet with him as soon as possible. When can you leave the scene? And are our two officers all right?'

At least she showed concern for the officers under her command.

'Realistically, there's not a lot I can do here for now. I just wanted to check on Rob and Jezza and touch base with the Transport Police. I could leave now.'

'We'll meet in half an hour.'

Ted went to find Jo.

'I've been summoned. The Ice Queen and the Chief Super want me. Can you stay here with Rob and Jezza, to make sure they're all right? Let me have the car, and you get a lift back with them.'

Ted knew it was inevitable. There would be endless high

level meetings to find out what had gone wrong. What could or should have been done differently. It was the part of his job he disliked the most, but it went with his role as SIO on the case.

'So are we going to get a conviction of any sort at the end of this?' was the first thing the Chief Super asked him. 'That would off-set what's just happened very nicely if we could.'

'I wish I could say with any certainty, sir,' Ted told him candidly. 'We were hoping that Nigel would either confess or run straight to one of the others which might have lead us somewhere.'

The Chief Super was shaking his head.

'This is a PR nightmare. Especially if we have nothing to show for it at the end other than another dead body. Ted, put a full, detailed report together as soon as possible. The ACC wants to see the three of us at Central Park first thing on Monday morning, to see how we're going to emerge from this in the best possible light. We'll try and keep a bit of a lid on it until then.'

Ted had warned Trev not to expect to see much of him over the weekend while he worked on the report. He was feeling at a low ebb but trying not to show it in front of the team. He'd called slightly more of the team in for Saturday than would usually have been the case. He needed everyone's notes collated and prepared ready for his Monday morning meeting.

He was at his own desk on Saturday, going over all the case notes. He looked up at a knock on his door followed by Steve coming in. He was holding some papers, a computer printout by the look of it.

'Have you got something, Steve? Only we could really do with a new lead.'

'The letter Nigel posted, sir. He sent it to me, for some reason. Here at the station. As soon as I realised what it was, I handled it with gloves on and bagged it, but I made you a photocopy.'

He put the papers on the desk in front of Ted who nodded at him to sit down, then started to read.

*'I want you to know what really happened. About Callum, and Badger, and Páraic. Badger was a good bloke. He was all right. He was my friend. I could talk to him about anything. He was a bit weird. He had a thing about fapping. He was always talking about it. All the time.'*

Ted looked at Steve over the top of his reading glasses.

'Fapping?' he queried.

'Masturbating, sir,' Steve managed to say it without going pink. 'It's what young people call it these days.'

*'He never did anything to anyone before all this kicked off. Never touched any of us. Nothing like that. But he was always talking about it. Saying it was ok, healthy, even. It was great to have an adult you could talk to about stuff like that. I've never had a dad to talk to.*

*'Páraic used to talk to me, too. We were at the same school, but he was younger. But we knew one another through the club. He went to confession and stuff but I never did any of that. He told me he'd been getting grief from Father Hughes about fapping. He was the sort who really believed you had to confess to stuff like that. But he was worried because when he did it, he said he was thinking about a lad in his class, not a girl or anything, so he was scared he was gay. I think that's the reason he killed himself. He didn't know how his family would react, or his church or anything. His brothers are all really blokey, especially the cage fighter. Páraic was really sensitive but he tried not to show it. He hated being called Porridge.*

*Antoine started that. He could be cruel. As soon as he knew you didn't like something, he did it all the time. He called me Niggle and I hated that. But it was best just to keep quiet or it made him worse. Even if Páraic had told his brothers and they'd gone and sorted Antoine out, he could have made things difficult at the club for Páraic so he just kept his mouth shut.*

*'When Páraic killed himself, we all got together to talk about it. I didn't mention the gay thing. I didn't want the others to know. They were all convinced Badger must have done something to him. Something more than just talking. We went up the woods. We often went there. Badger sometimes came with us. Just hanging out round a fire, the odd beer, nothing more. Callum was in France so we didn't want to do anything until he was back. Antoine didn't want to wait, so he went out to talk to him. Antoine had a lot of respect for Callum. He was the only one he listened to. Callum persuaded him not to do anything until he came back from France. Then we decided that after the match for Páraic we'd all go to the police and say that Badger had been doing inappropriate stuff and talking about fapping all the time and that might have upset Páraic enough, with the religious stuff, to make him kill himself.*

*'Only when Callum got back from France he must have decided to give Badger a chance to turn himself in and gone round there to talk to him. He would never have thought Badger would turn nasty or anything. None of us had ever seen that side to him and we knew him well. But he must have been shitting himself. If he got in trouble with the police after doing stuff like that with young lads I suppose he could have lost his job and been chucked out of the Johnners and everything. And that was mental because he'd never*

done anything wrong. Never did anything to any of us. But he must have figured that even if he said it was just talking it would look bad for him. So he must just have panicked and killed Callum. When you showed me the note I guessed he'd left that just in case anything went wrong. But none of us went near the place after he was found dead.

'We got together and decided Badger had to pay for it this time. Because we all guessed what had happened and we knew it must have been Badger who killed Callum. But there was never any talk us of killing him. None of us agreed to that. Antoine said we should grab him and put the fear of god up him to make sure he went and told the police what he did, to Callum and all the rest of it.

'I asked Badger at the match if he would go up to the woods with me so I could pay my last respects to Callum because I didn't want to go on my own. He had no way of knowing we knew what he'd done so he agreed easily enough. Marvin lent me his car and I met Badger near the pub. We drove up to the woods and sat talking in the car for ages, like we often did. Then the others came. Antoine, Jerome, Marvin and Donal, Páraic's brother. They came in Donal's car. They went out the back way from Antoine's and he picked them up. The others all stayed at the house to alibi all of us. Antoine had got Donal involved, telling him about Badger talking about fapping all the time. Donal knew his family would alibi him and say he was at the cage fight the whole time.

'Antoine's a real nutter. He's into violent films and games and stuff. He even gets hold of snuff movies. He watches a lot of crime stuff, too, all the CSI things, so he knows a lot about forensic evidence. They were all suited up, with masks and shoe covers, the whole works, but they told me to stay in the car because I wasn't. Antoine stuck a bag over Badger's head before they dragged him out of the car so he didn't struggle all that much.

'They were gone ages. I know they lit a fire because I could see it through the trees and smell the smoke. I was crapping myself. I nearly drove off but I was afraid of what Antoine would do to me if I did. Then they all came back out of the trees and they were laughing, like really high, and saying it was all sorted. They put all the suits and stuff with Badger's things in a bag and I took it into the hospital afterwards and shoved it in the clinical waste incinerator.

'Donal went straight off back to Manchester, the rest of them got in Marvin's car. He drove, I sat in the back. They were high as kites, but they didn't say what had actually happened until we all got back to Antoine's house. The rest of us were really shocked when they admitted what they'd done. Marvin said he'd tried to stop Antoine from finishing it off like he did but he couldn't. Antoine was like he didn't give a shit. I said we ought to go to the police, it would be better if we turned ourselves in but Antoine just laughed. He said there was no way they could prove anything against us so as long as we all stuck to the same story and gave each other an alibi we'd get away with it. He said if I did try to squeal on them, I'd still be charged with murder like the rest of them because I was the one who'd got Badger to go there in the first place.

'I thought it was going to be all right. For a time. Everyone was sticking to the plan. Then they all started changing their stories and I knew what they were doing. They were going to let me take the rap for the rest of them. And I knew they were right. There *was no evidence against any of them and if I was the only one without an alibi, the police were going to keep coming after me until they managed to pin it on me. And I didn't do anything. I didn't know they were going to kill him. Honestly.*

*'I thought they were my friends. I thought they were starting to accept me. They let me hang out with them more and more. I thought they liked me. They were just setting me up.'*

It ended abruptly. There was no signature or date.

'You clearly made a connection with him, Steve, if he chose you to share this with. Well done. It looks like it was the betrayal by the others he couldn't handle, rather than any real sense of guilt.'

'When people you thought were your friends treat you like that, it can cut very deep,' Steve replied.

From his tone, Ted knew he was speaking from bitter experience. He didn't really know all that much about Steve and his background. He was pleased it was working out for him with Bill. They'd be good for one another.

'Get everyone together can you, please, and we'll go through this with them. Say ten minutes?'

After he'd circulated copies of the letter to everyone and they'd discussed the implications, it was a long day of paperwork ahead for Ted. His was always exemplary but it was even more important now that everything was in order.

'You look worn out. Hard day?' Trev asked him when he finally got home.

'You know I told you our main suspect killed himself yesterday? I'll have all sorts of people all over the paperwork on this case now so I've got to make sure everything's in order. I've got a meeting with the ACC on Monday.'

'Everything's all right, though? You're not going to get any grief over it all?'

'There'll be an enquiry. Another force will come in with their team and go all over our case files like a rash. It's standard. But it will be fine. Just a bit of a pain. You know Jim always said I should be called Teflon. Nothing sticks. I'll have to make sure every bit of paperwork is in order for them to go over. Once that's all done and dusted, I'll take some time off and we can go away somewhere. You can choose where.'

'We could go to Wales! See Annie.'

'I was thinking of somewhere for just the two of us. A bit of us time. France, maybe.'

'We can do France another time. After a case like this and everything else that's gone on, you'd probably like to see Jack again.'

DS Jack Gregson had been Ted's friend when he'd first joined CID at Stockport. Jack had had to leave because of ill health, but Ted still kept in touch when he could.

'I could drop you off at Jack's for a day and Annie and I could go off for a jolly round the country lanes. Do some shopping. Find the odd little tea shop or two. It would be wonderful. And we could have the nights together. A nice little country hotel somewhere.'

The Monday morning meeting at Central Park was in the ACC's office. Ted travelled up with the Chief Super, sitting in the front next to his driver while the Ice Queen was in the back with Higginbotham. She was still being surprisingly supportive. He was still muttering darkly about the lack of a result.

The ACC was much more pragmatic when Ted had finished his summing up. He understood the nature of Ted's job much better. He read through the copy of Nigel's letter then said, 'Well, we're stuffed and there's nothing we can do about With him out of the picture and no forensics, I don't see how you can go any further, Ted. But I know it's not for want of trying.

'There'll have to be an enquiry, of course. You know tⱼ Nothing we can do about it. And it needs to be another forceᵢ keep it squeaky clean. It should be nothing but a formality let's get it done and put behind us.

'Ted, I know it's a choker when you don't get a result. happened to me, too. Thankfully only once in my career, buₗ still sticks in my throat when I think about it. So let's drav line and move on as soon as we can.'

As everyone rose to end the meeting, the ACC asked ʰ to stay a few more moments as the Chief Super and the Queen went back to the car.

'Anyone else in your position, I'd tell them to spend next few days double-checking all their files, to make s nothing was missed. I know you. Yours will be bob on alrea The enquiry will take a time to sort out and get started, so w don't you take a few days off while you're waiting to h when it will begin?'

Ted was already feeling prickly, defensive.

'Am I being suspended, sir?'

'Don't be so bloody daft, man. Of course you're not. ℎ this is the one that got away. Your first one. And I know h that feels. So take your Trev off somewhere nice for a ʄ days, come back, get the enquiry done and dusted. Then it ⱴ be business as usual. And you'll get the next one, like ⱴ always have done.'

**The End**